SEASON
for
SCANDAL

THERESA
ROMAIN

ZEBRA BOOKS
KENSINGTON PUBLISHING CORP.

http://www.kensingtonbooks.com

ZEBRA BOOKS are published by

Kensington Publishing Corp.
119 West 40th Street
New York, NY 10018

All Kensington titles, imprints and distributed lines are available at special quantity discounts for bulk purchases for sales promotion, premiums, fund-raising, educational or institutional use.

Special book excerpts or customized printings can also be created to fit specific needs. For details, write or phone the office of the Kensington Special Sales Manager. Attn.: Special Sales Department. Kensington Publishing Corp., 119 West 40th Street, New York, NY 10018. Phone: 1-800-221-2647.

Zebra and the Z logo Reg. U.S. Pat. & TM Off.

ISBN-13: 978-1-4201-3243-4
ISBN-10: 1-4201-3243-1
First Printing: October 2013

eISBN-13: 978-1-4201-3244-1
eISBN-10: 1-4201-3244-X
First Electronic Edition: October 2013

10 9 8 7 6 5 4 3 2 1

Printed in the United States of America

Chapter 1

Concerning Cousins, Husbands, and the Correct Number of Aces

October 18, 1819
London

Jane Tindall could have changed her life, if only Lord Sheringbrook hadn't played the fifth ace.

Tonight she ignored the viscount's ballroom in favor of his cramped, smoky card room. For hours, she counted every card turned, waiting for the perfect hand of *vingt-et-un*.

At half one, her chance came at last: all the aces had been played, and Sheringbrook dealt himself a nine. He could have nineteen at best, then. Jane's twenty would win.

Yet somehow Sheringbrook had managed to produce that perfectly timed ace. It mocked Jane from its bed of green baize; such a small and flimsy rectangle on which to pin her hopes, then puncture them.

"We tie at twenty, madam," Sheringbrook said. His voice was low and smooth, almost regretful. "And so you lose again. My, my. You wagered a great deal that time."

Indeed she had. A ruinously great deal.

Yet she *knew* that had been the fifth ace. Of domestic gifts, she had none, but she possessed a mind like an abacus.

"You are very silent, madam. Something on your mind?" Below his dark demi-mask, his thin mouth curved, taunting her.

Guests came to Sheringbrook's card tables masked, the anonymity often inspiring them to leave behind greater sums. But Jane had easily recognized her host's treacle-sleek voice, the sharp widow's peak on his high forehead. She even recognized the three other men with whom she'd been playing—by type, if not by name: a cit, a drunkard, and a rake.

The only thing she had not recognized was that Sheringbrook was talented enough to cheat without her seeing how he did it.

Her mind reeled; the musty, acrid scent of tobacco smoke stung her eyes and nose. For an instant she toyed with accusing the viscount openly. *Yes*, she could say. *I was wondering, did you hide the extra ace in your coat sleeve, or was it in your pantaloons? There must be plenty of room to spare in there, you pitiful excuse for a man.*

If she were a man, she could call him out. As a woman, her revenge must be indirect.

Her fingers traced the edges of her cards, borrowed jewels catching the dim light. Languidly, she flipped the cards facedown and returned them to the pile.

"No, indeed," she said in a bored voice. "Congratulations on a hand most . . . creatively played."

If there was anything Jane could do better than count cards, it was act a part, and no cheat could take this talent from her. She was deep in debt, but salvation would come only from pretending her loss scarcely lightened her purse.

"How do you wish to pay your debt?" pressed Sheringbrook. He ran a finger up Jane's arm, snagging the edge of her ruched cap sleeve.

No one imagined a respectable virgin would find her way into this makeshift hell. On the other side of the doorway, the fringes of society wound blithely through a country dance, but in the privacy of the card room, the atmosphere was coarse and desperate.

That was exactly why Jane had come here.

She drew herself up to her full height in her chair, knowing that she must look insignificant to the four hulking men with whom she played. Small enough to take advantage of; small enough to dismiss.

That was their mistake. She was the only woman in the card room, and therefore, she was as powerful as they thought her powerless.

Jane covered Sheringbrook's hand with her own, drawing it off her arm. "Must our play come to an end so soon? I've not yet had my fill of this evening's pleasures, no matter their price."

She summoned the wispy impressions of a decade of house parties and a dozen bawdy novels, and she used them to become beautiful. Noble. Seductive. The tip of her tongue moistened her lower lip, which she had painted with rouge until it was as full and red as the ripest of forbidden fruits. She twined a fingertip in a heavy curl, drawing it over her shoulder, and trailed her fingers down her rather meager bosom to the low bodice of her inky-blue gown. She acted as if the simple motion would slay them.

And they became slain. As simply as that. All four men shifted in their chairs as if their pantaloons had grown too tight.

Four half-drunk men, one of whom she now knew to be a cheat. This had, perhaps, been her riskiest gamble of the night, but she was counting on the crowd in the card room to keep her safe. Her companions might say whatever filthy things they liked, but they couldn't touch her. And as long as the cards remained on the table, she had a chance at the truth.

The rake spoke first. "Has the game grown too rich for your blood?" Above the curve of his own demi-mask, hawkish brows lifted. "I could give you private instruction to improve your skill."

"I like this type of game," Jane murmured. "I am used to deep play, after all. Deep and frequent." Again the tongue peeping between her lips, promising a taste. The rake groaned.

She let her sly smile grow. "Shall we have another hand, then?"

"Damme," slurred the drunkard, "you can have my hand wherever you like it, madam." Hands unsteady after hours of imbibing brandy of decreasing quality, he fumbled the notes and coins before him. Too much of a fool to know the worth of what he lost, or to hold fast to his winnings. Too foolish to know that money was more than amusement: it was power, and escape.

"If she has your hand, I'll take hers," the rake spoke up. "What d'you say, madam? Can you take me in hand?" He sniggered at his own wit.

This was the time to check the cards: now, while they were all distracted. "I confess, our dealer's hands are the ones that fascinate me." She looked her host up and down deliberately.

Sheringbrook cleared his throat. "Shall we unmask?" His voice cracked like a schoolboy's on the final word, hands lifting to fuss with the fastening of his mask.

Now. Jane feigned a tremor, reaching for the deck and knocking the cards into an untidy heap. With her thumbnail, she flipped a section of the deck faceup.

One ace . . . two . . . if she could turn them all, she'd have proof of Sheringbrook's dishonesty.

"So careless," she said. "I beg your pardon. Now they've turned every which way." She gave a blithe laugh and extended her hand again, turning the remainder of the cards in one swift movement. Before she had time to spread them over the table, the viscount's hand closed about her wrist.

"Don't trouble yourself, madam." His smile had gone a bit twitchy at the edge. "We'll start with a fresh deck, if you care to play again."

With a snap to a nearby footman in rumpled livery, the viscount had the table cleared. It was all over in less than ten seconds; not enough time to think of a strategy. Jane could only watch as the evidence she needed was carried away on a salver.

Nothing was left behind but a stretch of empty green baize and a false debt that she could never repay.

The cards now gone, Sheringbrook's smile returned in force, and he turned his attention back to Jane. "Do show us your face, madam. Such a delectable foe deserves our full attention."

Around the table, the four men unmasked, their expressions ranging from uninterested to hungry to—was that a trace of suspicion on the viscount's features?

Jane had no choice but to follow suit. With a careless hand, she flicked her mask up atop her head. As she recognized none but her host, she felt sure they would have no notion who she was.

Except the movement of her mask set her jeweled earbobs swinging. Sheringbrook narrowed his eyes. "Those are the Xavier jewels," he said. "Pigeon's blood rubies. Famous. Can you be . . . ?"

"I've never known Xavier to give the family jewels to a hussy before," said the cit.

The rake snorted. "Xavier? Before he was married, he never gave the family jewels to anyone *but* a hussy." This feeble joke was greeted with much more amusement than it deserved.

Jane felt the threads of her disguise unraveling. *Damnation.* She had borrowed her cousin's jewels to create her character, not unmake it. They were simply for effect, to give the impression of startling wealth that would convince these men to loosen their purse strings. She had never expected the gems to be recognized.

Damned Xavier, with his damned famous jewels. It was horribly fitting that he should be invoked at this table, since he was the reason she sat here. Since he thought she could not be trusted, especially with money.

She squelched the dreadful, sick feeling that he had been perfectly correct. There was nothing for it now but to brazen through.

"Lord Xavier is my husband," she said, mentally apologizing to her friend Louisa, Lady Xavier. Better to be thought a powerful countess than a doxy. Fortunately,

Louisa had mixed little in these dubious circles of society since her recent marriage, and the fringes of the *ton* were not likely to recognize Jane's falsehood.

Sheringbrook looked doubtful, though. "I've seen the earl recently. He mentioned his wife, but I had the idea she was a dark lady."

Jane blessed her nondescript coloring: eyes the color of dying grass, hair the color of sand. She could be described as blond or brunette, with eyes brown or green or hazel.

"As you see." She smiled with deadly force. "Should you doubt me, I can tell you that his lordship has a rather horrible-looking scar on the inside of his right thigh."

Her words were quite true, as she was the one who had given her cousin that scar a decade before. It was his fault for insisting that she learn how to fence, then being unprepared when she proved an excellent student.

The four men exchanged glances, shrugs. She had disposed of their doubts, at least well enough to continue the play. As Sheringbrook slid Jane a fresh deck to cut, she held on to the mien of a countess. Until she climbed out of her sudden, startling debt, it was much safer to be someone besides insignificant Jane Tindall.

A gloved hand touched her shoulder, jostling her arm as she separated the cards. "Jane?"

Jane closed her eyes.

She knew few enough people who would run in Sheringbrook's questionable circles. It was the worst sort of luck that one of her acquaintances should attend this ball, then enter the card room. Worse than worst that she should have lifted her mask only a moment before.

The hand gripped her shoulder more tightly. "Jane. How surprised I am to find you here."

Jane bit the inside of her cheek to keep herself from exclaiming. She *knew* that voice, with just a hint of the rough southern coast in its patterns.

Kirkpatrick.

She tipped her face up; as always, her insides gave a longing squirm when she saw him. Six feet of lifelong dreams: dark-haired, blue-eyed, kind and good-humored.

Except right now, he looked quite the opposite of good-humored. Edmund Ware, Baron Kirkpatrick, was one of her cousin Xavier's oldest friends—which he apparently thought gave him the right to glare at her with a dark, foreboding expression. Rather like Byron, if Byron were protective instead of lusty.

She was in trouble, and not only from her opponents.

Trying to salvage the moment, she replied with lofty unconcern. "I'm surprised to find you here, too, Kirkpatrick. Do you intend to play *vingt-et-un* with us? I would rather expect you to be squiring an assortment of young ladies about the ballroom."

"One young lady will do. Come with me, Jane." His grip on her shoulder turned into a tug.

Sheringbrook broke in. "Jane, you say? A . . . maiden?" His look of revulsion would have been comical in another time and place.

"She said Lord Xavier was her husband," slurred the drunkard. "You ain't Lord Xavier. So why d'you call her by her Christian name?"

Jane willed her face not to turn a sickly color.

Without a pause, Kirkpatrick answered, "You might have heard wrong. The room is rather loud, is it not? Lord Xavier is this lady's *cousin*, not her *husband*. The mistake is understandable."

That was rather clever of him. Jane turned a brilliant smile upon her companions.

But they refused to be dazzled this time. A man might mishear a single word, but they had also used the word *wife*, and there was no explaining that away. Jane had lied, and they knew it.

If only Kirkpatrick had blundered in half an hour later, Jane would have had time to lessen her loss, even turn it into a gain. As it stood now, she was ten thousand pounds in debt, though it might as well have been one hundred thousand. Or one million. Or the whole English treasury. She simply could not repay it.

"I think we have finished our play," said Sheringbrook. His large hand covered his winnings, a pile of coin and bills and slips of paper. "Perhaps you'll settle with me, Miss . . . Jane."

Jane raised haughty eyebrows, flicking through options in her head. She would have to leave them with her vowels tonight. And then . . .

She would have to tell her cousin Xavier what she had done. He would pay the debt, but he would box her up forever. She had proven him right; she could not be trusted. Like a lapdog, she would be leashed and admonished, and she would have no money and never travel away or be anyone else besides poor and plain Jane.

"Of course I will pay," she said in a voice with no life left. "I will only require a day to gather the money. Excuse me, gentlemen."

She rose from the table, nerveless hands grasping its edge, stiff arms levering up the dead weight of her body into a stand.

Sheringbrook reached up, crooked a finger into the hem of Jane's sleeve again. His hand contracted around the fabric. "I believe not. You've deceived us, madam, and now you'll have to pay. There can be no debt of honor without honor."

Jane stared at the hand on her arm. He dared speak to her of honor; he, who had cheated.

Somehow she managed to beam at the viscount, as if she could imagine no greater pleasure than to have him ruin her sleeve along with her life. "My lord, I promise you I will cover all my debts. Lord Kirkpatrick can vouch for my reliability."

The viscount settled back in his chair, raking appraising eyes over Jane's form. "I'm not interested in your promise. I will accept your jewels as surety for your payment. Better yet, as the payment itself."

A chill bead of sweat slid between her shoulder blades. "Impossible. They are worth far more than what I've lost."

Sheringbrook shrugged. "Then I cannot allow you to leave this room, madam. Which is acceptable to me. I can think of numerous ways for you to work off your debt."

Jane lifted her chin, as much to keep the sick from rising into her throat as to convince him of her confidence. Impossible to leave behind her cousin's gems; no other way she would be allowed to escape. The other men at the card table were watching her with interest, as if they wanted a piece of the pie when it was served out. She could not look for help from that quarter.

The femininity that had seemed her advantage a few minutes ago was now her weakness. It was *infuriating.* A man would never have been treated so, especially not a nobleman. Nor even a noblewoman, for that matter. Not the real Lady Xavier.

It was hell to be Jane Tindall. Especially tonight.

A touch at her elbow: Kirkpatrick stood next to her,

bracing her arm as her thoughts whirled uselessly. His support was not unwelcome, though it did her no good.

"Permit me to pay, my dear." His eyes were fixed deep on hers, sending some message.

"Why should you . . ." she began in a low voice, shaking her head. The room was distant and muddy around her, but Kirkpatrick's blue eyes were clear.

"As your betrothed, it is only right," he continued. "Your debts will be mine, and therefore my money is yours."

He reached past Jane to slip his card onto the table before Sheringbrook. "My man of business will take care of Miss Tindall's debts. You may call upon him at your leisure."

A nobleman, playing the most important card of the game. How easy it was for him.

Kirkpatrick turned to her. "Shall we go, darling?"

Darling, he called her, as she had always wanted; yet it was only an act. Her insides squirmed again, but it felt like illness this time rather than desire.

Jane could not speak as he drew her fingers into the crook of his arm. With a curt nod to the bemused *vingt-et-un* players, he helped her to rise and led her to the door.

Away from her fortune. Her future.

Since there was nowhere for her to go, anywhere was better than here.

Chapter 2

Concerning Unexpectedly Large Numbers

Edmund gritted his teeth. The corridor was no place to admonish a woman, even one who deserved it as much as Jane Tindall. Yet he had to listen at two doors before he found a side room free from the grunts and squeals of illicit lovers.

He motioned his *betrothed* through the doorway and booted it closed behind them. A single lamp lit the room, and even before his eyes had adjusted to the dimness, Jane's voice was beating at his ears.

"I suppose you fancy yourself my savior, Kirkpatrick?"

Well, yes. "Nothing of the sort," he lied. "I tried to be of service; that's all."

"'*Of service*'? You've ruined me, Kirkpatrick. You interrupted my game at the worst of all possible times."

That was rich. "If you were ruined, it was certainly none of my doing. And considering the way your companions were looking at you, you were about to become more ruined than you could possibly imagine."

She drew herself up to her full height, which was not very impressive. "I assure you, I had the situation under control. I am more than capable of turning a loss into a gain."

"I know you are."

This evidently surprised her; she opened and closed her mouth before choking out a reply. "You know." She tilted her head. "You know?"

"Yes. I've known Xavier—and you—long enough to be aware of your uncommon talent at *vingt-et-un*. Do you remember which cards have been played?"

"Yes. I've always been able to." She was looking at him with a sort of astounded curiosity. Rather as though he had a horn on his head.

Or a devil chasing him.

He shook off the thought. With a lady in distress, and a debt to be dealt with, his own troubles could wait. They had already waited for twenty years.

"That's a great gift, but it doesn't matter here." Edmund considered how best to frame the bad news. "You'd better sit."

His eyes were adjusting to the light now, and he saw that they were in a small parlor. A harp graced a corner, its strings loose from disuse. The pianoforte's lid was up, showing missing keys. Bawdy drawings hung on the walls, and a pile of pillows and silks had been flung near a mahogany settee upholstered in dark figured fabric.

Wonderful. They were in a music room turned harem.

The only place to sit, unless he wanted to play the sultan and loll around on pillows, was on the settee. He guided Jane to it, then sat next to her. She began fumbling with the clasp of her intricate ruby necklace.

"Allow me," he said. She frowned at him, but turned to present him with the back of her neck.

"As I was saying," Edmund repeated, his fingers tracing metal loops over warm skin, "there was no way that situation was going to end well. Sheringbrook cheats."

Jane's reply was unintelligible, except for the word *damn*. Then she twisted to face him. "Everyone knows this?"

"It can't be proven. But yes, that's my strong suspicion. How many aces were in play?"

She glowered. "Five. Plus however many more he had stuffed in his smallclothes."

"There you have it. No doubt his smalls are made with many pockets so he can lay hands on any card that might be needed." He smiled, hoping to coax a matching response from Jane, but she just looked bleak.

"I'm truly sorry, Jane." Edmund realized his hand was still resting at the curve of her neck, poised to undo the complex clasp of her necklace. "Why are we taking off your jewelry?"

"Because I cannot be trusted with it." Jane batted his hand away, and after a few seconds of fumbling, she had the clasp open. She tugged the heavy piece from about her neck and held it out. "Will you take it? As my *betrothed*?"

He ignored both the necklace and the sarcasm. "In most circumstances, and with most other women, I would apologize for presuming upon our acquaintance. But I think the occasion warranted any falsehood that would save you from—well."

"Speak plainly, Kirkpatrick." Jane gripped the

rubies in a white-knuckled fist. "You think they meant to hurt me."

"If you declined to pay, yes. Or if you continued playing. I'm sorry for my ruse, but at least it got you away from the table. Sheringbrook's a nasty character. No doubt you realized as much as soon as he played that fifth ace."

"I'm a nasty character, too. Unfortunately, I'm also deeply in debt, which considerably decreases my fearsomeness."

"Not at all." It was a reflex, to agree with a lady, and it took Edmund a moment to realize that he had just informed a respectable maiden that she was fearsome.

Fortunately, Jane only nodded her agreement. "I can't think what to do about the money I owe. Piracy? Blackmail? Theft?" She gnawed on her lower lip. "Blackmail would be the easiest."

His heart thudded. "No," Edmund said, more harshly than he'd intended.

Jane lifted her eyebrows, but before she could question him, he turned the subject. "Why were you here tonight, and without a chaperone? Your cousin is not in attendance; nor is your mother."

"Oh. That." She sagged against the settee. Her dark dress blended with the deep color of the upholstery, her face a pale oval above. "No, I've been visiting Xavier and Louisa for a few weeks. And today I got some dreadful news."

So did I. "I'm sorry to hear that," said Edmund over a still-pounding heart.

"You might know that Xavier meant to create a trust for me, to fall under my control when I turned twenty-one. He's been laying money aside for years, but hadn't completed the legalities. Well, my birthday has passed, but today he told me he didn't think me dependable enough to be given control of money, even through trustees. So it's to be a dowry instead."

She gave a harsh little laugh. "Xavier, lecturing anyone on dependability. Can you credit it? But he won't let anything tarnish his shining reputation, precious and newfound as it is."

Edmund struggled to follow; her words seemed to jumble on their way from his ears to his brain. Lately he had suffered from insomnia, and the days felt far too long. Only obligation had brought him to the ball tonight; a promise to Lady Sheringbrook that he would attend. The mother of a card cheat. Her own son let her down, but Edmund would not. Not even today.

He pressed at his temples, willing himself to remain focused upon Jane's problem. "No trust; only a dowry. I see. So you thought to come and win a bundle at cards."

She shrugged. "I knew I could win. As long as I looked wealthy and played only with strangers, people would allow me to gamble with them. I've done it before."

"You've done it—" Edmund's head shot up. "No. Please tell me you are jesting."

"Well, not *here*. I haven't played here before. But yes, I've slipped out before and gambled. That's how I raised the stake for tonight."

She folded herself up against the scrolled arm of the settee. He hoped it was a trick of the light, or of his bleary eyes, that made Jane look afraid. Because Jane Tindall had never been afraid of anything, as long as Edmund had known her.

This was worrisome. "How much did you lose?"

She set her jaw.

"How much, Jane? As your *betrothed*, I have a right to know."

To her credit, she looked him in the eye. "Ten thousand pounds. As much as my dowry."

Edmund's arms went numb. Ten thousand pounds, and he had promised to pay her debt.

When Xavier had laid aside Jane's dowry, the sum had probably seemed significant to him, but hardly ruinous. He took in well over that in a single year—and spent much of it, too. Edmund's barony was not so wealthy. Cornwall was a windswept land of tin miners and tenacious farmers, and Edmund shepherded his resources carefully to keep his London household and support those he'd left behind.

He had never worried before about running shy of money. But to raise ten thousand pounds, he would have to have his man of business scrape together every bit of ready cash, then sell shares in the funds. It would be a severe blow, and not only to himself. But not to pay a debt of honor was unthinkable.

Unless . . .

"I shall have to confess my sins to Xavier," Jane was saying, "and he'll lock me in a cage. If he sells tickets to view the mad girl, I might be able to pay you back in fifty years or so."

Mad. Yes . . . Edmund was getting a mad idea. So mad that it seemed absolutely perfect. The answer to his needs, and hers, all at once.

No. He couldn't. He had known Jane since she sported short frocks and skinned knees. She was far too small and brassy to be the shield he needed.

But whom else could he find so quickly? The matter of marriage had become urgent when that letter was put into his hand: he needed an heir, *soon*, to protect his succession and provide for the remnants of his family. Because he had no notion how much longer he would be able to do so himself.

And then there was Jane's debt. Likely no one else would take her without a dowry. Yet she deserved better than to be cheated—literally—out of her chance to marry. If she even wanted to marry. If she could be persuaded.

Yes—now that he considered the possibility, Jane would be a good partner. She wasn't exactly a beauty, but with wide eyes and mobile features, she was as interesting to look at as to talk to. And she was sensible, too, with the exception of this evening's card-play.

A marriage of convenience between old friends. Why not? The boundaries would be clear: mutual regard, but no love. Certainly no love.

Even so, it was far more than he deserved.

Jane was talking again. Of course she was. "You'd better tell Sheringbrook to call upon Xavier instead. As my closest male relative, he owns me for now. There's no reason you should pay my debt."

Edmund turned his head, giving her his profile. It was a trick he'd developed years ago, when he realized his peripheral vision was uncommonly good. He could watch her reaction without her thinking he saw her at all.

"What if there *were* a reason?" He held himself motionless.

Jane also froze. "What do you mean, Kirkpatrick?"

He waited for more of a response, but that was all she said. No other reaction; not even a flurry of blinking. He'd forgotten what a good actress she was, able to control every nuance of gesture.

He let his posture relax. Leaned against the settee and

laid an arm along its back, brushing the bare skin of Jane's neck.

That got a reaction. She scrambled forward, slipping from the upholstered seat and sliding onto the floor. Edmund had no choice but to rise, extending a hand to help her up.

As she stood, her breath came quick and shallow. "What do you mean, Kirkpatrick?" Her voice was low and a little shaky.

With her hand still clasped in his, he sank to one knee.

Her eyes flew open wide. "No. Not that. No, no. Please."

She tugged at his arm, as though she could drag him to his feet. But changing his stance wouldn't change her debt. It wouldn't alter the letter he had received. His need for a wife. An heir.

"Jane. Would you do me the honor of becoming my wife?"

She was tugging more frantically now, trying to free her hand. "Don't say it, Kirkpatrick. Don't. I know you don't want it. You don't have to do this to me."

Startled, Edmund released her hand, and she stumbled backward a step.

You don't have to do this to me, she said. What did that mean? *You don't have to do this*, he would understand. Even *You don't have to do this* for *me*. But *to me*? That sounded as though he had wounded her, just by asking.

He rose to his feet. A familiar, gnawing pain had awoken below his breastbone. He dragged in a deep breath, then another, until the pain ebbed.

"Jane. Please consider it. It would solve your difficulty, and—and I would be very good to you."

A small smile trembled. "You're good to everyone, Kirkpatrick."

"Well. Ah." He didn't know what to say to that.

"Why should you marry me? How would it benefit you?" She turned her fine-boned face away, dignified as a swan. The lamplight gilded her cheek, hid her features from him.

That was Jane in a single gesture, wasn't it? Not regal, but able to make herself seem so. Able to hold secrets. Able—he hoped—to live with them, too. With attics full. A mind full.

Yes. Come to think of it, a woman who could play cards with such coolness was well suited to a lifelong gamble.

Edmund decided to give her as much of the truth as possible. "I planned to marry eventually. And I admire you, Jane."

She turned slowly to face him. "You admire me. Is it because of my beauty or charm? My feminine accomplishments? What, pray tell me, do you admire about me?"

She was mocking him now. As far as he knew, she could not paint or sing or play. She was not fashionably tall or elegant.

Yet he had not lied. To say he loved her would be a lie. But there was a great deal to admire about her.

He cleaved close to the truth again. "You are determined. And ingenious."

Jane's pointed jaw fell open, then closed with a click of teeth. "Thank you, Kirkpatrick."

The gnawing pain was back again; it made him catch his breath, hurry her along. "May I speak to your cousin tomorrow?"

He'd overstepped; he could see that at once. Her deep eyes went hard with suspicion. "Will you meet my terms?"

"How dreadful are they?"

"You will have to settle my dowry on Sheringbrook to pay my debt."

Edmund nodded. "I realize that. I assume you plan never to play cards with him again?"

"What would be the point? I play to win. I will also require pin money in the amount of two hundred pounds per annum."

"Why the rapaciousness?"

"You just said I was ingenious. I'm only trying to take care of myself."

She blinked, and Edmund wondered if her hazel eyes hid tears she was ashamed of. She had hoped to gamble her way into independence tonight, and she had failed. He could not fault her for gambling on his own agreement now. And considering he could tell her nothing of his past in exchange for her hand, a few hundred pounds was a small price to pay.

"Very well," he agreed. "You shall have your exorbitant pin money."

"I want a maid of my own, and . . . six new gowns?" She bit her lip as though she thought she'd been too extravagant, and Edmund's heart squeezed. She was only eight years younger than he, yet devastatingly hopeful.

"All new gowns," he said. "And you shall choose them yourself."

For the first time since he had knelt before her, she managed a smile. "A horse of my own?"

"A mare. And you shall choose her, too."

"Jewels?" Her smile grew, and relief bled through him, sweetly cool as ice on a fever. If she would be content with these trappings of the tonnish life, he had indeed chosen well.

"Rubies, if you like. You seem to have a taste for

them." He indicated the priceless necklace, discarded on the seat of the settee. "Enough, now, Jane. If you've an answer, give it to me."

Jane pondered for a few seconds, and her face pinched. "I can't think of anything else, Kirkpatrick. Not even a courtesan could ask for more."

"We are betrothed, then?" He held his breath.

As small as Jane was, she suddenly seemed tall and strong. He must have imagined the regret in her face a moment before, for her smile was brilliant, and her eyes looked almost wild.

"Yes," she said. "I agree to your terms."

Thank God.

And God help him.

Chapter 3

Concerning the Uses of Gloves

If a man were asked to list his ambitions for his female relatives, Edmund knew that "devious proposal" and "hasty wedding" would rarely be at the top.

Therefore, when Edmund called at Xavier House the following afternoon to discuss the betrothal, he expected his old friend to make some protest. Though Xavier was a distant cousin of Jane's, the earl regarded her almost as a younger sister.

But Edmund had been away from Cornwall long enough to forget one key aspect of family relationships: exasperation. When he faced Xavier in the silk-papered study and asked for Jane's hand, the earl stared at him for a long moment.

"You want to marry Jane."

"Yes," Edmund confirmed.

Xavier sat back in his chair, his dark brows knit. "It's not even my birthday. Or Christmas."

"No, not for several more weeks. Do you require a calendar?"

Xavier grinned. "No, though smelling salts may be in order. I cannot believe you wish to marry Jane, but the chance to shake free from her schemes is most appealing. If you want the responsibility of her, she's all yours."

Simply as that, Edmund's sordid lamplit proposal was approved. Over the next few days, the marriage settlements were drawn up, and with a shake of hands and a flurry of signatures, the matter was arranged: Jane Tindall was to be converted into the Baroness Kirkpatrick in two weeks' time.

The next fortnight passed for Edmund in a soupy haze of plans and preparations. Refitting his house in Berkeley Square to welcome a bride. Accompanying Jane as she chose a modiste and a maid and a mare: the three essentials for any young matron of the *ton.*

Edmund welcomed the flurry of elegant industry because it kept him distracted. Almost distracted enough to catch a few hours of sleep at night; almost enough to forget the reason for the wedding.

Almost. But not quite. Every time he ventured into the heart of the city, he expected to come face-to-face with a nightmare two decades in the making. A nightmare cloaked in a lying smile and a lilting brogue. *Edmund, me boyo; to think of finding you here. All but a murderer.*

That letter he'd received the night of Sheringbrook's ball—the night of his own betrothal, as it turned out—had been hand-delivered. After twenty years in Australia, Turner was back in London, and he demanded a reckoning.

What form that would take, Edmund had no notion. But it would come, and soon. That certainty spurred him on through exhaustion, through the gnaw of pain in his abdomen. The days before the wedding were falling away, and soon he would take Jane to wife. And then . . . the getting of an heir. That part, at least, held the promise of pleasure; of a brief oblivion in his bride's arms.

If only he would feel safe once it was all done. If only Jane would be happy with the life he could give her, however long it lasted.

Edmund had no idea, truly, if any of these things would ever come to pass, or if he would ever be free.

The morning of the wedding, Edmund knotted his cravat with extra care and, with the help of his manservant, eased his shoulders into a new black coat.

"Gilding the lily, my lord," said Withey. "That young lady would marry you if you were wearing a farmer's smock."

"Silk purse out of a sow's ear," Edmund countered. He regarded himself in the glass: cheeks a bit hollow; shadows under his eyes almost as dark as his hair. "I look as if I've been out all night debauching myself."

"Night before your wedding? No one would blame you if you enjoyed yourself, my lord." The manservant looked Edmund up and down, then removed a bit of fluff from one coat sleeve.

"I would," Edmund said. "And Jane would. Or she ought."

Edmund was not surprised when Withey ignored this, as he did most of the unaccountable things Edmund said. The valet only pronounced his master acceptably dressed and summoned the carriage.

Now that the day was here, Edmund was eager to get the wedding over with before some accident could ruin everything. A bite from a rabid dog. A bolt of lightning. Collapsing buildings. A savage with a poisoned dart.

No one had ever accused Edmund of being unimaginative.

But the drive to Xavier House was blessedly brief and free from accidents. And as soon as he entered the house, he was greeted by a small group of familiar faces, none of which appeared to be rabid or lightning-struck.

Jane's ruddy little mother had trundled in from her country cottage, and in honor of the occasion, had stuffed her round body into a heavily starched gown. Xavier was here, of course, as dark and fashionable as always. His elegant wife, too: a quiet brunette with a mischievous smile. The Countess of Irving, Lady Xavier's aunt. Edmund had met her the previous year and had found her to be overly blunt and deeply loyal. Not surprisingly, Jane liked Lady Irving a great deal.

"Where is the bride?" Edmund craned his neck to look past the clergyman and the few other guests in the drawing room.

"Making herself beautiful," huffed Lady Irving. "None of us thought it would take so long."

"Aunt," hissed Xavier's wife.

Just then a light tread sounded at the doorway to the drawing room, and the guests turned toward it as one. Edmund followed their gaze.

There was Jane, whom he was accustomed to seeing in heavy, fussy gowns. Jane, who was rarely without a belligerent expression or a wicked gleam in her eye. She stood now in frail white silk and gauze, her light brown hair twisted back from a face as sweetly pale as a blossom.

She looked very pretty, and very unlike herself. As she accepted greetings in a quiet voice, she seemed fragile.

Yet Edmund knew she was not; not this woman who had tried so valiantly to forge her own independence, only to wind up in a leg shackle.

The ceremony was quick. The ancient vows made Mrs. Tindall sniffle. The ring went onto Jane's finger without a hitch. So they were married.

And then into the dining room for a wedding breakfast. Xavier was generous with the champagne and sweet-meats, and it wasn't long before the event turned rollicking. Lady Irving waved her champagne flute around while she held forth on how Xavier House ought to be re-decorated. Mrs. Tindall giggled at everything, then began the slow blink of tipsiness turned drowsy. A suntanned man in early middle age—Edmund had never met him before, so he must have been a guest of Mrs. Tindall or Lord Xavier—began regaling them with tales of life in India.

"*Droit du seigneur* is the way of things there," he said. "When a servant woman is to be married, her master visits her the night before the wedding."

Edmund had never heard of such a custom in India, but he was hardly an expert.

"As though a new bride doesn't have enough to deal with," said Jane to the man. Daniel Bellamy, that was his name. "Why must her master add to her list of chores? The timing is too burdensome. Let him visit her some other time." She took a sip of champagne. Above the glass, her cheeks had gone pink.

"It won't be a chore if he does his part well, my lady."

Jane blinked at him. "You called me 'my lady.' Oh, someone say that again. It sounds so strange."

The table erupted in a chorus of *my lady*-ing, and the salacious subject was left behind. Though the ghost of it

stayed in Edmund's head and drifted through his body—
the right of a man to his wife, the duty of a woman to her
husband. Could it be more than a duty and a right? Even
in a marriage of convenience?

Jane caught his eye then, and the look she gave him
was so *Jane*, so utterly wicked and laughing, that his
foggy thoughts cleared. Every time she smiled and
laughed, his relief grew. Something on this day had
brought her pleasure. Now he had only to continue it, not
create it.

The guests lingered long over breakfast, and it was
early afternoon before they began to disperse. As Edmund
shook Xavier's hand in thanks and farewell, he ignored a
quick gnaw of pain in his abdomen.

"I'll be good to her," Edmund assured his old friend.

The earl smiled. "I've no worries on that matter. You're
good to everyone."

The compliment made Edmund suddenly impatient.
You ought to trust me less and Jane more, he thought. But
the words didn't make their way anywhere near the tip of
his tongue. Because Xavier was right: Edmund was good
to everyone. He had developed the habit long ago. It
was . . . atonement.

The carriage ride to the house in Berkeley Square was
brief, though not silent. Edmund filled Jane's ears with
glib observations about the weather, the house, the guests.
Everything in the world came out of his mouth except for
what was important: that they were married, and that they
would soon get on with the business of becoming husband and wife in truth. Creating a child. An heir, he
hoped. Quickly, before Turner pounced on him; before
Edmund's dependents were left destitute.

The chain of thought was hardly conducive to passion.

He wished Jane would look at him in that wicked way again, as though their wedding was all a game and they were playing by their own secret, shared rules.

But her mind seemed elsewhere now. Edmund had no notion whether it was in the bedchamber, or a ballroom, or in Sheringbrook's card room before the moment of her ruin. When the carriage rolled up before the Berkeley Square house, she bounded from it as soon as the steps were let down. Up the stairs to the front door, and inside. In the entry hall, Edmund caught up to her.

She bounced on her toes before handing her cloak to a footman. "Kirkpatrick, it's beautiful. I couldn't even imagine how the work would look once complete."

This had to be an overstatement, because the only change to the entry hall was a coat of leaf-green paint that Jane had chosen to cover a glum lead-gray. Everything else was the same: a ceiling of delicate plasterwork and painted roundels. A dizzy-tiled floor with spiraling black and white diamonds. All had been cleaned and polished to a shine, though; the servants wanted the house to look its best for its new mistress.

Perhaps this was a sign that Jane would be good for his domestic peace. Or perhaps he was grasping at straws.

"The house looks well, does it not?" he said. "I'm glad your tastes are satisfied."

Satisfy. Would he be able to satisfy her? Would she know the difference?

"I didn't expect to enjoy it so much. Choosing colors for a house, I mean. I've never done such a thing before because my mother and I never had the money."

"Well, now you do," Edmund said lightly.

"Now I do," she echoed. She looked up at him, her expression covetous.

Holding his gaze with her deep hazel eyes, she began to remove her elbow-length gloves. Edmund watched as she took hold of the delicate kid leather between thumb and forefinger and pulled, releasing her fingers one by one from their sheath of propriety. Tugging the whole glove free, at last, revealing her pale arm in one slow sweep.

And then she did the same for the other glove, her eyes never leaving his.

Significance lay heavy in the air, as pungent as myrrh. Edmund watched, his throat dry, as Jane handed off her gloves to a servant. What would be undone next? The clasp of her necklace? Or she might remove the fragile high-heeled slippers on her feet, and he could carry her upstairs.

The idea was alluring.

Jane rubbed her hands up her just-bared arms, as if the feel of her own touch was an awakening.

And winked at him.

Just like that, it all made sense. She was acting a part again, this time for the ever-observant servants. Surely they had wondered what possessed their master to marry so quickly. Now they would know, for she had shown them the heat of a love match.

He grinned, then leaned close to her ear. "I know what you're doing," he breathed, setting her pearl earbob to dancing. "And I thank you."

She sucked in a deep breath. "That bit with the gloves was meant to be enticing, Kirkpatrick. How obstinate you are."

"No, it was very enticing," he reassured her. "I was highly enticed."

"I can see that," she whispered back. "Since we're still

standing in the entry of the house. Clearly you are so *enticed* that you have no choice but to ravish me with manners. If you thank me again in that seductive way, I may swoon."

A bizarre noise caught in Edmund's throat; a sort of cough and choke and laugh all together. He had no idea how to console a timid maiden, but he knew what to do for cynical, adventuresome Jane. All he need do was be good to her, just as he'd promised. So good that she would never regret marrying him.

Atonement. It had never seemed so sweet, or so sensual, as Edmund took his bride's ungloved hand in his. Her fingertips were calloused from needlework, the skin roughened. Her straitened life had formed her, this woman who would rather play cards than sew, who wondered at the miracle wrought by a new coat of paint.

He rubbed her fingers, and the touch sank deeply within him. She smelled clean like soap, her skin free from perfume.

He liked it, and suddenly it was not enough to hold her hand anymore. His body acted without orders, bending to sweep her up, catch her behind the knees and hold her lengthwise in his arms.

"Consider me enticed," he said. "Enticed, and entirely unmannerly." When Jane laughed, it felt like a victory.

"I should show you more of the house now," he said.

"You really should," Jane agreed. "Starting with the bedchamber."

And he carried her upstairs.

Chapter 4

Concerning an
Ill-Timed Confession

Perhaps the bit with the gloves had been too much. Kirkpatrick had not taken it seriously, and Jane could not recall ever being more serious.

It had been a great joke for him to carry her up the stairs, but as her new husband set her down gently on the carpeted floor of his—her?—their?—bedchamber, her smile felt ragged. The feel of his arms beneath her knees, wrapped around her chest—there was nothing funny in the slightest about that.

The room itself was dim, the inevitable fog and rain of late autumn tossing gray clouds across the window. She picked out a bootjack in a corner; a walnut vanity and wardrobe; a connecting door in the west wall. In the fireplace, flames devoured wood rather than coal—a special luxury in honor of their wedding day.

Blue draperies adorned the windows and curtained the bed. The bed itself seemed very large. Wood-framed and wide, its hangings were swagged back. Ready for two people to climb in.

Kirkpatrick faced her at the foot of it, his formal attire all stark blacks and whites. With his dark hair and light eyes, his fair Celtic skin, he looked crisp as a new pound note.

Or ten thousand pounds.

Jane shut her eyes and pressed at them with the heels of her hands.

"Jane? Are you fatigued?"

She kept her eyes covered. No need to look at Kirkpatrick; she could guess the expression on his face. Dark brows slightly lifted, mobile mouth ready to curve with sympathy. So many times, she had seen him direct that solicitous expression at a woman.

"I'm perfectly all right." She let her hands fall, her gaze trailing after to regard the toes of her high-heeled slippers. New white satin. Impractical and expensive.

For Jane Tindall, that is. But they were just the sort of shoe Baroness Kirkpatrick would favor from this point forward.

Her fingers trembled a bit as they lifted to the clasp of her necklace.

"Might I help you?" He took a step forward, then halted.

This careful courtesy would drive her mad. "No, I have it." She unfastened her pearl choker, then removed the matching earbobs. "I suppose I ought to keep these in some sort of case."

"I should think so," said Kirkpatrick. "Since they're only the first of many jewels, aren't they? That was one of the conditions of our marriage."

"Right. That's right." The smooth orbs felt heavy as a

chain in her hand. With a click and a clatter, she let them fall to the top of the walnut vanity. "Now what?"

"Now would you like me not to help you remove your slippers?"

"That would be acceptable." She bent to ease her heels free from the snug satin footwear, then kicked the slippers off. Without them, she stood a few inches shorter, and she seemed to look up at Kirkpatrick from a great distance.

"What next?" Her mouth felt dry.

He had to clear his own throat before he spoke. "Most likely you will need assistance with your gown. Shall I help you with that?"

"It should be my turn, I think. I ought not to help you with one of your own garments."

"Do you have a recommendation?"

"You wouldn't need any help with your cravat."

"Very true. I would not." His lips quirked. Clever fingers worked at the intricate knots of linen, and Jane watched, rapt and breathless, as he began to unwrap himself.

She stepped closer, standing at the foot of the bed facing him. A yard separated them, no more, and she could see dark stubble faintly shadowing his jaw. The cravat fell away and the opening of his shirt pulled wide, revealing the straight line of his throat, the chiseled hollow at his collarbone.

Jane wanted to put her tongue into that hollow, but she squelched the impulse. If a bit of glove-tugging had been too much for Kirkpatrick's composure, a sudden licking would doubtless send him into a fit of laughter.

So she gave him a cool smile. "Now you may remove your coat without my help."

"Actually, I'm not sure I can. It's very snug, and it took the assistance of my manservant to get me into it."

"Should we call him in?"

He tilted his head. Jane dragged her eyes up from the vulnerable line of his throat to see his face. He looked . . . damn it, he looked good. Patient. Kind.

As he always did.

"Jane, do you truly want us to call in help? Your maid and my manservant? Or—might we do for each other?"

Somehow, she managed to sound calm. "We could, if you like."

"What would *you* like?"

Anything. You. Anything with you. "Doing for one another would be fine."

They stared at each other for several seconds before she broke the silence. "Boots or coat first?"

"How about the coat?" His grin was a revelation, wry and sweet.

In her stockinged feet, Jane clambered onto the bed. Kirkpatrick turned to face her. "Ease it back from each shoulder first, then we'll tug at the sleeves." He shook his head. "Fashion can be a hindrance, can it not? But I couldn't be unfashionable on our wedding day."

Their eyes caught. Held. Her calm resolution vanished like smoke in wind. "I like your coat," she said. "And now let's take it off."

Kirkpatrick's own face looked a bit ruddy, if the gray-filtered light was to be trusted. She doubted he was a virgin—somehow, men never were—but he shared at least one characteristic with Jane: neither of them had ever had a wedding night.

She laid one hand, then the other, on the eggshell satin of his waistcoat. Palms flat on his chest. It was a strange sensation, to know that she might touch him as much as she liked.

Mine, she thought, *just as I've always wanted.* Her own heart hurried to match the thumping of his, a wonder beneath her palm. She could have remained thus for minutes, hours, allowing the realization to sink through her body and mind.

He wrapped his fingers around her wrists, slid them. Her palms skated up his chest; his breath hitched. Then her fingers caught beneath the lapels of his coat. With his coaxing grip, she pushed at the black superfine, easing it over the hard angle of one shoulder at a time. He released her then and turned to the side. The sleeves now. Jane caught each cuff in turn and tugged as he shrugged free. Broad shoulders flexed; his movements stirred her all up inside, hot and turbulent.

As he draped the coat over a chair, Jane watched the movement of his body, its every line revealed in the snug fit of trousers and waistcoat. Not a bit of spare flesh on his tall, solid frame. He was lean; maybe a little too much so.

Perhaps that was the effect of a sudden debt and betrothal on a man's body.

Ah . . . but his body also showed the effect of a woman waiting in his bed. Thanks to some lewd books Jane had found in her cousin Xavier's country house the previous year, she knew men had many names for the organ they valued so highly. But its real name was *penis*, and her husband's had grown large and hard enough to distort the line of his clothing.

She wasn't the only one feeling a bit turbulent inside.

"Boots next?" She was not entirely successful at keeping the quaver from her voice.

He shook his head. Silently over the deep-piled carpet,

he stepped back to the bed. Standing at its foot, he rested his hands on the counterpane, one on either side of Jane's kneeling form. "Your gown, if I may."

She shut her eyes. Already, it was a struggle not to grab for Kirkpatrick's body and pull him into her—though they were both still mostly clothed, and he wasn't even touching her.

That was about to change. "Gown, then," she said. She turned atop the bed, presenting him with her back. While he worked at the buttons, then found the laces of her underlying stays, she wadded up her silk skirts, stretched out her legs, and began unhooking her stockings from their garters.

Kirkpatrick's hands slid down her back. Spanned her waist. Trailed downward to the bundled fabric at her hips. "I like the scent you wear," he said, low in her ear. Heat clenched her belly.

"It's only soap," she said gruffly. "Ashes and animal fat. What is there to admire so much about that?"

"How poetically you describe it. Now I like it even more." He pressed his lips to the skin below her jaw, just once, like a punctuation mark to end his sentence.

Ah. For years, she had observed him as he flirted, pouring his sweet words into the ears of lonely widows and wallflower debutantes. What he did with them besides offer compliments and comfort, she'd no idea.

Now it was her turn, and he'd fallen silent. Not still, though; those big hands were sliding again, past the fabric, wadding it further, easing her toward him so that she rested with her back against his chest as he stood.

In this position, his hands could roam further, and they did. They slid upward, downward, finding entry to her loosened clothing. Tantalizing her bare skin, plucking and stroking and caressing. Her nipples; her navel; her hot, slick feminine parts. He had her writhing against him within moments, pressing herself into his touch with shameless fervor.

And then he stopped. "Excuse me," he said, and the heat of his hands was gone from her. An eddy of cool air raised gooseflesh on her half-bared back.

She folded herself up, knees against her chest, ankles crossed, trying to school her rebellious body into obedience. It was too much, this lust for him; she was certain to forget herself.

He returned to the bedside with a lamp, and she realized he had also removed his boots. He set the glass-globed light on a table close at hand, then pulled the bedcovers back. Jane scooted from the foot of the bed onto the cool crispness of linen sheets, then watched as he again began to divest himself of his clothing.

After sliding his braces from his shoulders, he hooked his thumbs into the waistband of his trousers and hesitated. "You can look away if you like. I won't be offended."

"Not likely, Kirkpatrick. We've bought and paid for each other, and I want the full show."

Though her face went hot, his expression looked pleased. *Oh, that Jane*, was how she would translate it into words.

That was fine for now. Amusement was fine. The trousers still came down.

He looked away, as though giving her a chance to express shock or horror without the additional embarrassment of his gaze. "No need to be bashful, Kirkpatrick," she said. "I've read some very scandalous books."

Not that woodcuts and etchings had prepared her for

the wonder of living flesh, of her big, handsome husband standing next to the marital bed with a massive cock-stand. The dark hairs that dusted his legs, chest, abdomen all seemed to guide her eyes—*there*.

"Dare I ask where you got hold of these books?"

"A lady must have some secrets," Jane said.

Gently trailing her fingers over his length, she explored him by lamplight and fire glow as the world went gray outside. His skin was hot and satin-sleek, smooth over a startling hardness. When she stroked up, then down, he gave a little moan and rocked on his feet.

Interesting. Enticing. Would he pounce upon her now? She unfurled from her huddle to face him, kneeling on the bed.

No, he eased himself into the bed slowly. Deliberately. As though he thought a sudden movement would make her bolt.

Never. She sank to one side, face-to-face with him, letting her loosened garments fall how they liked. This close, she could see him as never before. The lamplight pulled hints of red out of his dark hair. It revealed faint freckles across his cheekbones, plus one at the corner of his mouth.

She kissed it gently, placing her seal upon his lips.

When she pulled back to gauge his reaction, he was smiling at her. In the yellow-orange light of the lamp and fire, his blue eyes looked tawny as a lion's. "Thank you."

"There's nothing you need to thank me for." She paused. "Yet."

Kirkpatrick took this as permission to proceed, as she'd intended. He returned her kiss; first a peck, then a lingering press of the lips, and then a sweet, quick, open-mouthed kiss. She threaded her fingers into his hair and pulled him to her, and what was sweet and quick became long and hungry, and he covered her, bracing himself upon his elbows. Her gown and stays had worked their way into a pointless barrier of cloth, and with a few kicks on her part and shoves on his, finally, they were skin to skin all down their lengths.

His mouth was hot on hers; the hairs of his body tickled and woke her skin. The world fell away, so there was nothing but flame light and the bed and the inevitability of their joining.

When he entered her, it hurt. She could not suppress a gasp. But his fingers cradled her face and danced over her breasts, unknotting the pain. Soon it was entirely unraveled and a new kind of tension began to coil.

Lust. Passion. These words could not capture the wonder of the act. Each long slide of his body made her covet him more. She dug her nails into his shoulders, his back, pulling him ever deeper.

The pleasure built, slowly but inevitably, until it became quick, eager. Frantic. Before she expected it, it overpowered her, and she trembled from the shock of it, wrapping her arms around his sweat-slick back and crying out. "Oh, Edmund," she moaned. "Edmund, I love you."

He froze: propped on his elbows, half-in and half-out of her body. "What?"

At once, she suspected she had made an error. "Never mind. Keep going."

He did not. How could a man hold himself so still like that? How could he just . . . stop? If he had stopped before she reached her peak, she would have crawled over him, used him, done anything to find her pleasure.

His arms were corded with the effort of holding himself away from her. "You called me Edmund. You've never done that before."

"I've never done *this* before."

"You said . . ." He turned his head away. "You love me?"

"I believe people say all sorts of ridiculous things during intercourse."

"Is it untrue, then?" His eyes met hers, then slid away again. So blue; so beautiful.

"No," she said on a sigh.

The slick heat between them had turned clammy. He levered himself up, then slipped from her body. Jane caught a glimpse of his naked form before he tugged part of the sheet around himself. The long, hard staff had sunk, hardly rigid anymore.

So this was what the truth would do. She had meant to keep her feelings a secret until she was sure of his, but she hadn't expected the revelation to kill his pleasure so completely.

She shivered with what should have been the remnants of passion, but instead felt like a bone-deep chill.

He pulled in a long, deep breath, pressing a fist against his abdomen. "I didn't know."

Then he turned back to her, drew the sheet up over her nude body, and sat back against the high wooden headboard.

"I didn't know," he repeated, eyes fixed upon the bed hangings. "I'm so sorry."

Jane had not thought anything could increase her humiliation. It had grown so large and palpable, it was almost like a third person in the room. Lying between them, laughing at her. *Oh, you foolish girl.*

But she was wrong: the apology made the humiliation worse. The apology meant that he had not expected her to love him. That he didn't *want* her to love him. And why would that be?

Because there wasn't a prayer of him returning her feeling.

She needed every scrap of her acting ability to don a polite mask. "Don't worry about it, Kirkpatrick. It won't be a problem."

He rubbed a hand over his face. "You may say that now." His voice threaded, muffled, through his fingers. "But we will come to want very different things."

Jane would have very much liked to end the conversation right then. But just as at Sheringbrook's table, the game was not truly over, even after the cards had been played. There was still the question of payment. Kirkpatrick had gotten less than he should have in taking a wife with no dowry. But he had also received more than he'd bargained for when he'd learned that wife loved him. And it seemed he did not like the surprise.

So she must rake the coin of her love back. Hide it away like guineas in a miser's purse. "I shan't trouble you with messy emotions; you needn't worry about that. We can go on just as you expected." *Whatever that is.*

His hand fell to rest atop the sheets. His throat flexed, as though he was swallowing whatever he meant to say. Then after a long pause—"I'm honored. And I will do my best to make you a good husband."

Her smile felt fragile. "I've no doubt of it." No one doubted Kirkpatrick's goodness, or the fact that he always exerted himself to make women happy.

He returned her smile, looking relieved.

That same sweet, slow smile had captured her—what had it been, eighteen years ago? She'd been no more than three years old; her mother, newly widowed and grieving.

So Jane had been sent away, to visit her half-grown cousin Xavier while he was between school terms. A handsome friend was visiting him, too. Jane had been sad, and the older boy had been kind, and she had set aside the whole of her grateful heart for him.

She had been in love with Kirkpatrick for years before she realized he was just as kind to everyone else. By then, though, loving him was a habit she could not shake.

"Thank you," he repeated, and the politeness was just as dreadful as the apology had been.

He excused himself then, slipping from the bed to pass through the connecting door she had observed earlier.

This was to be her bedchamber, then. Not theirs.

As he left her behind, sated yet achingly hollow, Jane wondered whether being married to the man she loved was the best thing in the world, or the worst.

Chapter 5

Concerning a Pulverized Breakfast

They met again over breakfast.

Edmund had left Jane alone the night before. After the shock of her revelation, it seemed a great unkindness to return and try to pretend she had never spoken of love. Or to bring up the subject again, knowing that he couldn't reply with an honest "I love you" in return.

Love had not been part of their marriage bargain. In marrying her, he knew he was taking too much just by claiming her body; now her heart tipped the balance irrevocably askew.

He had no idea how to right matters. It was like being handed a chess piece and being told to strategize, when one had been expecting to batter one's body in a rousing game of cricket.

It was like being handed a flower he knew he could not keep alive.

But somehow he must make this marriage work. The morning would be different; better and easier. In the breakfast parlor, they had all the armor of daylight and clothing and food with which to busy their hands and mouths. Surely they could chatter and be friendly, just as they had for years.

As they faced each other, standing near the doorway, he mucked about for something to say. "Did you sleep well, Jane?"

She raised an eyebrow at him. "You want to discuss sleep?"

"I just thought you—"

"I'm fine." Her cheeks had gone a little pink. "The night passed tolerably well."

"Tolerably?" He could not explain why this pale word stung.

"Yes. Don't get huffy, Kirkpatrick. 'Tolerably' isn't so bad." With a fingertip, she scratched at the pin-striped wallpaper. "This room is pretty."

He accepted the offered turn of subject. "It's my favorite room in the house."

She regarded the row of gleaming salvers on the sideboard. "So I see. I never took you for a glutton."

A surprised laugh popped out. "Not because of the food. It's—well. I like the feel of the room."

Half an explanation, though in itself it was true. Cream-walled and high-windowed, the breakfast parlor managed to catch sunlight even on the smoky, dim mornings of late autumn and early winter.

But it was also the room in which he greeted each morning; the table at which he celebrated passing through another endless night.

Years ago, he had replaced the family portraits hanging here with some old flowery paintings that had been stored in the attics. The subsequent improvement in his mood was so great that he had proceeded to replace every portrait in the house with pictures of flowers, or dogs, or hunting scenes. Anything without a familiar face.

"A pity you like it so much." Jane's murmur broke into his thoughts. "I'd have liked to redecorate this room in the Egyptian style. Gold leaf and lacquer everywhere. Wouldn't you prefer salvers with Sphinx heads, too?"

His expression must have betrayed his horror.

Jane rolled her eyes. "Honestly, Kirkpatrick, you have no sense of humor before breakfast. Eat up, you old maid."

"There are so many things wrong with what you've just called me," he murmured in her ear. She turned still pinker, but shrugged him away.

Good. Friendly, just as they'd always been. Maybe— maybe this would work.

He turned his attention to the salvers. On his own, Edmund usually ate no more than toast; the pain in his stomach made him eschew richer fare. But this morning, the kitchen had also provided beef and eggs, muffins and ham, tea and coffee and chocolate.

Edmund realized that his servants had no notion what their new mistress preferred. Nor did he.

"May I serve you a plate?" He offered Jane a friendly smile.

She shrugged that off, too. "No need. I'm used to doing for myself." As she lifted each cover in turn, the sunlight through the east-facing windows caught the emerald in her wedding ring.

Edmund piled some of everything on his own plate, giving her implicit permission to take as much as she wanted. She settled on a boiled egg and a bit of ham, then seated herself at the foot of the small rectangular table. They could fit as many as eight around it; a man and wife and a healthy brood of children.

Pain gnawed at his insides with sharp teeth, and he nudged his plate away as he sat down.

A distraction, then. "You look lovely this morning," he said. "That color suits you."

Quick as a thought, she ducked beneath the table. "Does it? What color would you say it is?"

For a moment, he only blinked at the chair where his wife had been. "Um. Jane. Jane?" He tried to think how to tell her *baronesses don't climb under the table* without the footman overhearing.

Her voice sounded muffled from beneath the tabletop. "I just wondered whether you noticed what color I was wearing when you said I looked lovely in it."

"Most amusing," he replied. "Ha. Give your breakfast a try."

"You didn't really notice my gown, did you? You just said something that you thought sounded pretty."

He should have remembered this about her from the night he proposed: her intolerance of common compliments. Considering how willing she was to play a part, she ought to be more forgiving of such everyday deceit. Besides, what sort of woman questioned a compliment instead of accepting it?

Probably, said a small voice in his head, *the sort of woman who doesn't get many.*

"Your gown is green," he guessed.

Jane straightened up. Her light brown hair had become ruffled by her upside-down jaunt beneath the furniture; her expression was just as rumpled.

But her morning gown *was* green. A sort of pale apple-y color. "See? Lovely," Edmund said, hiding his relief.

"A lucky guess," she muttered.

He ignored this incisive comment; instead, he skimmed his eyes over her, looking for something pleasant to say that she would not be able to puncture or pick apart. The apple-green shade *did* suit her hair and skin, and the gown's simple line flattered her slim form. Had her maid advised her on its choice? He remembered Jane nearly drowning in ruffles and bright colors in the past.

"Your gown is cut well," he ventured.

It was more of a compliment to her modiste than herself, and perhaps that was why she accepted it. She lit up. "I know. I'm so glad to be free of those gowns my mother always chose for me. Wools in summer, and horrid glazed cotton. Enough ruffles to smother a horse."

When he smiled, she looked disgruntled and turned to gaze out the window. "I could almost spy into the drawing room of the house next door. Your neighbors in London are very close, aren't they?"

"*Our* neighbors," Edmund corrected.

"That's right. Our neighbors."

Thus the topics of clothing, compliments, and the neighbors were dispensed with. He had already inquired after her night's rest. And so a silence fell, broken by nothing but the busy clink of silverware on dishes. Edmund devoted intense attention to cutting his beef into small pieces. First cubes, an inch square. Then he halved them, then halved them again. This jolly family breakfast could take as long as one wished.

Why, they hadn't talked about the weather yet. They could do that next. November weather always offered Londoners plenty of opportunity for abuse. If it wasn't raining or sleeting, it was fog-choked. On dry days, coal smoke rose from the city like thunderclouds turned on their heads.

He opened his mouth, ready to say something about the chilly weather. The possibility of taking a drive later in his closed carriage.

When he looked at Jane, though, he had the sense that she'd just averted her eyes from him. And she continued Not Looking At Him so intently that the words took on capital letters; that the lack of attention became an intentional act.

It had to be. No one could devote so much time to cutting ham into little bites. Was she playing the shy bride? Was her silence meant to punish him for that thing he'd said about her gown? He had gotten the color right. Unaccountable woman.

Since Edmund's mouth was still hanging uselessly open, he put a bite into it, not caring what it might be.

Beef. Damn it. Who could bear to eat meat in the mornings? His stomach grumbled, threatening a rebellion.

Wonderful. He could not even spend his time at the breakfast table actually, oh, *eating breakfast.* And as Jane continued Not Looking At Him, the silence didn't feel mellow and friendly after all. This meal wasn't like sitting down at table with a relative or enjoying a postcoital repast with a lover. In the former, love might be taken for granted on both sides; in the latter, lust usurped the role of love, and most welcome it was.

This breakfast was both, yet neither. A strange, boiled-up amalgam of feeling. And the silence grew all out of proportion to the small breakfast parlor, until it seemed heavy and pressing.

A lump the size of a fist blocked his throat, and he felt that he could not have spoken even if Lord Sheringbrook offered to return his ill-gotten ten thousand pounds in exchange for a syllable.

After a tiny eternity, Jane broke the silence. "Kirkpatrick. Some couples travel after their marriage." She was still Not Looking At Him. With a spoon handle, she tapped at the shell of her boiled egg.

He gulped coffee until the lump in his throat dissolved. "That is correct."

When she didn't speak again, he realized that more was expected than an acknowledgment of a declarative sentence. "Some couples do," he added cautiously. "And some don't."

Tap tap tap. Jane frowned at the egg in its little silver cup. "Some couples go to Italy. Or France. France isn't far."

"You have pulverized that eggshell," Edmund pointed out.

"Well, you've shaved that beef to a powder."

Edmund looked at his plate. She was right; somehow, he had reduced his breakfast to a heap of stringy fibers.

He laid down his utensils. "Jane, might I assume you would like to travel, since you have introduced the subject?"

"I wouldn't hate it." At last, she met his eye.

"I'm sure I wouldn't either. But . . ." Edmund traced the crests on his blunt-handled utensils. The barony of Kirkpatrick, stamped on every piece. "I have responsibilities that keep me in London right now."

In truth, the idea of fleeing for the Continent right now was very appealing. Just to grab Jane's hand and run for Italy or France, leaving behind all the letters and threats and responsibilities that lurked in the city.

But someday he would have to return to them—and the burden, once laid down, would be unbearable to pick up again. Or worse yet, it would come rolling and crashing after him, and yet another part of the world would be despoiled. Cornwall and London had already been ruined for him; he could not bear to blight the loveliness of a summer in southern France, or the sunlit warmth of Italian vineyards.

"Perhaps next year," he said. "Next year, it might be different."

"Why should it be?" Jane picked up a knife and sliced the egg in half vertically as it sat within its cup. Then again, quartering it. "If a man won't turn his responsibilities over to his steward when he's newly married, why should he do so later?"

Edmund reminded himself that he wasn't the sort of man who poked his wife with a fork, no matter how annoying her questions.

"It's not that I'm unwilling, Jane." His voice came out too harsh; he paused, took a deep breath, and added more quietly, "I am unable. This is a matter none can handle but myself."

She blinked at him. Waiting for more. He should have known she would not be put off by vagueness.

"It's family business," he added. "Some long-standing arrangements are maturing, and I must oversee the process."

"Of course. You're very busy. Indispensable." She continued cutting, reducing the egg to a mass of crumbled yolk and shell before she spoke again. "But now I'm your family, too. The only member of it in London, unless I am mistaken."

He took another sip of coffee, hoping a brilliant reply would occur to him. Alas, no. "You are correct. But—"

"Could I help you, then? If this matter of business

requires"—she paused—"*ingenuity*, I might be able to move the process along."

So we can have a honeymoon.

The unspoken words fit neatly into the silence that followed. But the suggestion? No, impossible. There was no room for Jane in this ancient tangle of betrayal. Especially not if she loved him—or thought she did. Which for now came to the same thing.

As his silence stretched out, Jane turned to look out the window again. Her profile was as neat as a coin, her jaw set. Her eyes, though; her eyes betrayed her. She was blinking far too often. Tears? Surely not. Jane Tindall—no, Jane Ware, Lady Kirkpatrick—was far too strong to cry.

"Jane," he said softly.

Her jaw became still more set. "If you don't want me involved, just say so, Kirkpatrick. I'm strong enough to bear such a small revelation."

"I know you are."

As always, his agreement seemed to surprise her. She turned to regard him. "You . . . What?"

"I don't doubt your strength, Jane. Nor your ingenuity. This is simply . . ." He considered. "A confidential matter. I must respect the interests of others."

Perfect. He'd just made his family's sordid affairs sound like a treasure hunt for gold bullion. He must think of a way to describe this in the most boring fashion possible.

"You see," he began, "certain people have entrusted their . . . er . . . trust to me. And I must fulfill that trust. And now is the time that the trust which they have entrusted—"

"Oh, stop," Jane cut him off. "You'll do yourself an injury if you try to end that sentence."

Edmund blinked. "Ah. Well."

"So you're telling me it's a secret and I can't help you and we can't travel anywhere until it's all settled."

"To put it briefly, yes." She looked a little mutinous, so he added, "It's not much of a secret. Business, you know. Family . . . things. Why, you've got a few secrets of your own, don't you?"

She looked at him as though he'd served her a plate of horse droppings. "Not anymore."

Edmund, I love you.

They both turned scarlet at once.

"Maybe," he said in a rush, "we can do other things. Instead of traveling, I mean. Though this isn't a good time to leave England, surely we can find amusements in London. A ball. Would you like to attend a ball? Or—or visit the Tower of London."

Jane's hot color ebbed. "The Tower of London? Weren't people executed there?"

Edmund coughed. "Yes. Well. It was just a suggestion. I know it's not very romantic."

"It's bloodthirsty. I like it." She nodded. "But you're right. Maybe not during our honeymoon."

"I'm sorry about this. I'll do my best to wrap up the . . . family matter . . . quickly. As soon as there's a chance of travel"—*of escape*—"I will inform you, and you shall pick our destination."

"Will it be done before Christmas?"

Christmas. Seven weeks away. Could he stand seven weeks of this cat-and-mouse game with Turner?

If it meant seven weeks of respectability, yes. Seven weeks of safety for Jane, yes. Seven weeks in which to beget a child, innocent of all wrongdoing . . . God, how he hoped. "I'm not certain."

With a clatter, she shoved aside her egg cup. "But you *are* certain that it's not something your man of business could attend to? After all, he settled your last debt."

Sheringbrook's payment, she meant. "Unfortunately, no. The timing is inopportune, but—"

"—you didn't expect to get married this autumn. I understand." A smile clicked into place, and Edmund had the odd feeling that she was humoring him.

"Just because it was unexpected does not mean I am not delighted."

"No," Jane said. "But it also doesn't mean you *are*."

She shoved her chair back from the table, almost smacking into the footman who rushed forward to aid her. As she and the servant dodged one another, startled, she caught a foot in the hem of her gown and stumbled.

Edmund rose, striding the length of the table and catching Jane's arm. With a nod to the footman, he allowed the servant—still mumbling his apologies—to retreat. The man had only been doing his job; it was not his fault Jane didn't react as expected.

Come to think of it, Edmund could say the same for himself.

She struggled to shake him off, but his fingertips cradled her elbow gently. "As you are now a baroness," he murmured, "please do not cast aspersions on our marriage in front of the servants."

"Why? Because it will cause a scandal?" She narrowed her eyes. "I don't care about that."

"No, it probably wouldn't cause a scandal. But our servants work hard for us, and they will enjoy that work more if they think the household is harmonious."

Her struggling ceased. "You ask for their sake, then. Out of kindness. How am I supposed to argue with that?"

"I rather hoped you wouldn't." His stomach twisted, and he added, "I've promised that I will do my utmost to make you happy. Won't you allow me to try?"

Close enough to sense her every flicker of movement, to breathe in her clean scent, he waited for his wife's reply. For the battle or truce to begin.

Her gaze found his. Those hazel depths held such disappointment, such sorrow, that he drew back from her. *She knows.* She knew the truth somehow: that he would betray her, just as he had everyone else.

He shook his head, trying to rid himself of the thought. When he looked at Jane again, her eyes were clear; no trace of that deep, dark emotion shadowed them.

"Yes," Jane said, soft and low. "I trust you. And I'll do my best to be the wife you deserve."

Now, what sort of wife might that be?

"Thank you," he replied, and her expression turned wry.

"Always so polite," she said. "Well, then, husband. How shall you make me happy?"

He thought about this. Not the Tower of London, she had said. And she was no child, to be plied instead with sweets or a trip to the Royal Menagerie. She was a baroness. And she was ingenious.

Dumbly, he rooted about for ideas before seizing upon something that would please most young women. "Shall we attend a ball? Introduce Lady Kirkpatrick to polite society?"

Her smile was the brightest thing in the sunlit breakfast parlor. "Why, certainly. I'd love it above all things."

Chapter 6

Concerning Preliminary Attempts at Happiness

It was an excellent plan, this truce of theirs. But not even Kirkpatrick could conjure a ball for Jane at a moment's notice during the quiet of early November. London's elite was only just beginning to trickle back into the city for a special session of Parliament, and the first ball to which they had received an invitation—hosted by that determined matron of the *ton*, the Countess of Alleyneham—wasn't for another two weeks.

Two weeks for Jane to do—what? There was nothing but unaccustomed leisure. Kirkpatrick had kept every one of his promises to her.

She had a lady's maid, Hill, who arranged Jane's fine, sandy hair into elegant twists and somehow encouraged it to curl.

She had a set of emeralds, as well as beautiful gowns for every occasion. And when the weather turned cold and glum, there were fur-lined cloaks and warm capes and pelisses, as well as a carriage to shield her from the weather.

She had a mare, too; a bay with a white snip on the nose, kept in the mews stables behind Kirkpatrick's house. Since Jane didn't know how to ride, she visited the horse daily, but had a groom exercise Florence.

"One day," she murmured to the mare, who huffed warm breath over Jane's fingers. "One day we'll ride together. And one day I'll visit the city you're named for."

Florence bobbed her head, then took up a mouthful of hay. Jane smiled; the animal's contentment was refreshing.

She could have told Kirkpatrick that she needed someone to teach her to ride a horse. But she wanted him to realize it on his own.

He had kept all the promises she'd tugged from him in the forgotten little side parlor at Lord Sheringbrook's house. Jane realized now: Kirkpatrick would give her everything she asked for, and the best of it. But he would give her not an iota more.

When he'd made his proposal, she had not asked for time with him. She had not insisted that love be a condition of their marriage. And so these intangibles never came to pass. He had promised to try to make her happy—but what, after all, was trying? He hadn't promised to succeed. And she hadn't asked him to.

Perhaps she was not as ingenious as she had once thought.

After breakfast each day, Kirkpatrick disappeared into his study, a small room she had never yet entered. He had not said she couldn't, but she didn't try to cross the threshold. It would be too humiliating to be booted back.

So Jane spent the first days of her marriage without her husband. Instead of learning the corners of his heart or creating pet names for him, she acquainted herself with every corner of the house and every servant's name. She created menus for course after course.

No one had much appetite. But the food looked impressive.

Day by day, she felt Lady Kirkpatrick enclosing her, molding her into something quieter and sleeker than she'd ever imagined being. It was not unwelcome; it was simply unfamiliar. As little like her unmarried self as lilac was like hay. This was part of the bargain she had struck with her husband, and if he fulfilled his end so punctiliously, she could do no less.

So passed her days.

But when the sun slid beneath the horizon, the silence of the house softened. Not a brittle thing, but peaceful and gauzy. The servants vanished into their rooms, and the careful mask of propriety could vanish for a time, too, if Kirkpatrick would allow it.

Every night, a tap came at the door between their bedchambers, and he entered the room. There was never much talking. Clothes were shed, skin was stroked.

Each time, Jane tried to undo the harm she'd caused on their wedding day. She wanted to be rough and bawdy, to prove that she didn't mind that he couldn't love her back, that this clashing of bodies was enough for her. She wanted to press him to the bed and use him hard, until blessed oblivion could claim them both.

But Kirkpatrick *didn't* allow it. Night after night, he treated her with a politeness so complete that it became impersonal.

"Allow me," he said, pressing her hands aside with gentle force. Not allowing her to grab at him, pull him close. It was like a script: first he brought her to orgasm with his hands. Then he held himself high above her body as he stroked in and out. When he shuddered his completion, he pulled away at once.

The sensations were delicious, yet Jane felt soiled afterward. As though she'd breached their marriage contract when she'd admitted her love for him, and now he could hardly bear to do business with someone so untrustworthy.

She almost wished she had never agreed to marry him; that she had never gambled and lost her independence at Lord Sheringbrook's house.

Almost. For how could she lose an independence she'd never had, except as a dream? And how else was she to have Kirkpatrick—the deepest and sweetest and most painful of every dream she'd had?

Fool that she was, she still wanted him on any terms. Even these, which left her alone every night and every endless day.

Even these.

When the date of the ball arrived, Jane entered Alleyneham House on her husband's arm. As they queued in the receiving line, she watched the women before her and did as they did. Resting her fingertips on Kirkpatrick's sleeve with the correct featherlight pressure. Maintaining the perfect, proper distance between them so their expensive clothing would not be rumpled.

When it came their turn to greet their dithering hostess and stern-jawed host, she gave a careful nod to each. "Earl. Countess. How do you do?" To the angle and inch, it was a perfect copy of the greeting performed by the woman before her.

Except. From Lord Alleyneham's startled cough and his lady's wide-eyed flutter, she realized she had blundered.

Sweeping into a hurried bow, Kirkpatrick herded her on, his pressure at her elbow sudden and determined. A butler announced them to the room at large, and with more force than grace, they strode into the crowd, as though Kirkpatrick wanted to get them lost in the mill of guests.

When someone jostled Jane and a heavy boot ground down on her toes, she stopped walking. Kirkpatrick gave another tug at her arm; she tugged right back.

"Stop," she said through gritted teeth. She glanced around and spotted an alcove at the side of the soaring candlelit room. It was currently occupied by a potted palm.

Jane gave the palm a bit of company. Kirkpatrick followed, looking a bit hunted. "What's the problem, Jane? Don't you want to join the dancers?"

I would if I knew how to dance. But Lord Xavier's impoverished country cousin had never learned such social graces. "Not just yet. Out with it, Kirkpatrick. What did I do wrong?"

"I don't know what you mean." He became fascinated with the fronds of the palm.

"In the receiving line. I did something that horrified our host and hostess. What was it?"

His eyes found Jane's. "Ah. Well, nothing much. You gave a marchioness's greeting to a countess. The nod of a superior. But—well, Lord and Lady Alleyneham are good sorts. They won't mind it."

"They certainly looked as if they minded it."

"Mere surprise, that's all. Can I fetch you some punch?" He smiled, but Jane was not to be led astray.

"I didn't know," she muttered. "I should have curtsied, shouldn't I?"

It was a far simpler matter to ape her social superiors on the fringes of the *ton*, in places like Sheringbrook's card room, than in the heart of the polite world. And her cousin Xavier's country house party, which she had attended in past years, was a much different affair from a formal London ball.

In itself, this was neither good nor bad. It simply *was*. But not being ready for the new and next? Not even recognizing the boundaries of her own ignorance? That was bad indeed, and she thought she saw bright pity limning her husband's smile.

"I don't need any punch," she decided. "Only find me another baroness in this crowd, Kirkpatrick, and I'll copy her. I'll make certain I get everything right next time."

"That's what you want to do at a ball? You want to follow a perfect stranger around and mimic her?"

He made the behavior sound so odd. "Well, I won't let her *know*. She won't even see me. I can be unobtrusive when I wish. See?"

When she took a step back, her gown of dark green silk blended into the palm's fronds. Her ivory fan, snapped closed and held tight, was no more than a stick. And her hair could be anything, because on its own it was nothing. The dull shade of wood paneling or a dead frond.

Kirkpatrick's eyes lit with humor. "Are you considering the fact that if anyone sees you in there, you will have to make a swift explanation? I would dearly love to hear it."

Jane shrugged. "I'll say I dropped my fan and someone kicked it aside. I was retrieving it. Honestly, Kirkpatrick, do you think anyone is more interested in my doings than his or her own?"

He folded his arms. "This ball is our outing together. Something for you to enjoy."

"I realize that. But what I would really enjoy is not making another blunder."

He looked down at her for a long moment. Despite knowing him for most of her life, she couldn't read him as easily as she could most people. He was so carefully polite that it was impossible to tell what was flickering through his mind. Was he ashamed of her? Disappointed not to spend the whole evening together? Or relieved to extract himself from her company?

Finally he relented. "Very well, Jane. If that's what would please you. Watch the lady in the rose-colored gown, next to the third column. That's the Baroness Walling; she's a friend to the Patronesses of Almack's. Very proper."

"Sounds a bit too lofty for me."

Kirkpatrick reached out a hand. Jane thought for a dismayed moment that he was going to chuck her under the chin, but instead he traced her jawline with the pad of his thumb. "I don't think she is. But that's for you to decide, isn't it?"

Bewildered, she waved him off. "Thank you. Now. Go—go find someone to dance with." She didn't have time to pant after him now. No matter how many nice little things he did with his thumb.

She shuddered off a heated memory of an extremely nice thing he had done with that thumb the night before. It didn't matter. It didn't matter.

"All right," he said, "but just for an hour. Then I'll come find you. Yes?"

"Yes," she agreed. "That's fine."

When he vanished into the crowd, she settled in for

determined study. The Baroness Walling would show her what to do at a ball, just as over the years, Lord Xavier's guests had shown her what one might do—or ought not to do but still did—at a country house party.

She needed to learn how one acted in polite society. Unwittingly, she had bought herself a place in it the moment she clasped borrowed rubies around her neck and slipped out to Lord Sheringbrook's card party.

She had gambled and lost, and then she'd settled her debt. To protest now, if she were a gentleman, would be dishonorable. And Jane was far more than a gentleman.

She was a lady now. And a lady should always know what to do.

An hour and a half later, only sheer determination kept Jane's back straight and her chin up.

The end of their allotted hour apart had slipped by, yet her infernal husband continued to take to the dance floor with wallflowers and war widows. Either he had forgotten that he now possessed a wife to whom he had made a promise, or he simply hadn't cared enough to keep his word.

Something inside her felt tottery. She squared her shoulders to steady herself.

She hadn't wasted the time, at least. Her gambler's mind had gathered up gestures and phrases as easily as it did pips on a card. Slipping through the crowd, keeping Lady Walling in sight, Jane had observed a few tricks with a fan. The accessory was not, as she had presumed, to be used for cooling one's heated face. Instead, it was a signal for flirtation or rejection. The meaning was all in the wrist, in the placement, in the subtle way one fluttered it about.

Besides the language of the fan, Jane had taken in a fair amount of gossip.

"Yes, but Lady Alleyneham invites everyone. Desperate to marry off her daughters! I believe she'd take a shopkeeper at this point."

"Especially now that two of them have fallen ill. Lung ailment, she says? It's probably smallpox. Why, they'll be pockmarked as raisin puddings."

Yet much of the talk was nice:

"Have you seen the silk the Countess of Doverfield is draped in? Absolutely exquisite. I've been looking for that shade all autumn."

"My dear, your son has grown up so handsome. Have you given any thought to finding him a bride? That Miss Selby seems taken with him . . ."

Or just a simple *"I'm so glad to see you. Do come talk with me a while."*

Jane's heart had lurched when she'd heard a young woman speak those words in her direction. For a swooping instant, Jane thought this must be some friend of Kirkpatrick's, someone eager to know her better. But from behind Jane, the speaker's friend—the woman to whom she'd truly been speaking—had run up, and the pair entered into a giggling tête-à-tête.

Jane turned away, wishing her name was on someone's lips. Even to be gossiped about would be better than being forgotten.

Never mind that. Until Kirkpatrick found her, she would observe and learn. A likely looking subject meandered by: a laughing noblewoman in ivory silk and lace in conversation with a knot of friends. As Jane watched, she adjusted the angle of her head; the *beau monde* had beautiful posture, their chins always high. And the smiles—they hardly showed any teeth, did they? Smiles were mysterious; laughter was subdued.

And the curtsy; she realized now, there were infinite degrees of obeisance. She must bend her knees more—like so.

"Lady Kirkpatrick, you honor me."

Jane continued her observations for two full seconds before she recalled that she was Lady Kirkpatrick. And that she had just unintentionally greeted someone.

She turned and saw that man from India—Mr. Bellamy—who had been at her wedding. He had been speaking with one of Lord and Lady Alleyneham's daughters, and they were both standing near the refreshment table.

Jane's stomach gave a curious growl, and she realized she was as eager for lobster patties as she was for a test of her newly observed behaviors.

"Lady Audrina." With careful calculation, Jane made her curtsy. Her host's daughter did not appear shocked by the greeting; therefore Jane presumed she had performed it correctly this time. Or perhaps nothing shocked the youngest of the earl and countess's five unmarried daughters. Lady Audrina Bradleigh was dark and lively, a Mediterranean beauty in a season dominated by blond sylphs.

"Lady Kirkpatrick, how do you do this evening?" Bellamy looked elegant but old-fashioned. His silver-shot dark hair was tied back in a queue, and his tailcoat was accompanied by knee breeches. Above a snowy fall of lace at his throat, his deeply tanned face broke into a smile so bright that it was impossible not to reflect the expression.

"Fine, thank you, Mr. Bellamy." She extended her hand; instead of shaking it, he made a jostling bow over it. "I remember your exciting tales of travel from my wedding day."

"Indeed, indeed. And where is your noble husband? Surely he accompanied you. I hoped to see him again."

"Yes, he's here. Probably delighting the hearts of half the women in the ballroom." Jane used one of her new fan tricks to flutter her polite disinterest, as though an absent flirt of a husband must be perfectly acceptable to any newly wed bride.

"Fortunate women, and fortunate man." Bellamy bowed again. "Not that I mean to imply he is dallying with them. No doubt he has important things on his mind."

"No doubt." Jane's smile didn't even waver, though the innocent words felt barbed.

Lady Audrina laughed. "Kirkpatrick *is* rather dashing. But so is Mr. Bellamy. He tells the most excellent stories. Won't you tell us more about the people you met in India?"

"I shouldn't." He waved off the request. "Most of my tales aren't suitable for young women."

Jane protested. "That sounds like—"

"—the best sort of tale," Lady Audrina finished. The two women grinned at one another.

Bellamy raised placating hands. "I can see I'm in the company of true travelers."

"Oh, I've never traveled anywhere." Jane did another sort of fluttery thing with her fan.

"No matter, my lady. Traveling is a longing of the soul, not merely an activity of the body."

"A longing of the soul?" Lady Audrina's brow puckered. "I had thought of it as an entertainment. A pastime."

"It can be all those things," Jane replied. "Just thinking of other parts of the world—doesn't it make this corner seem larger?"

"My feelings exactly," Bellamy said. "Everyone hungers for novelty. Some find it in fashion or society; some by roaming the world."

Jane felt a moment of kinship with this sun-worn merchant. They were both outsiders to the polite world, weren't they? Living within its ranks like travelers in a foreign country; observing its customs; following its rules.

Sometimes causing unintended offense.

"A life in society can hold novelty indeed," said the earl's daughter. "If one knows where to find it. Or creates it."

"Do you create novelty, or do you find it?" Jane asked.

A wicked smile spread across Audrina's face. "The latter when I can; the former when I need to. And sometimes when I don't need to."

"Ladies," Bellamy said. "Might I get you some refreshment? Though you must have had any number of dedicated suitors retrieving dainties for you this evening."

"I've had as many suitors as I've had dainties," Jane replied. "None at all. I could kill for a beefsteak."

Lady Audrina laughed. "If you killed a cow, that would serve the purpose perfectly."

"As neither cow nor weapon nor beefsteak is at hand, Lady Kirkpatrick, I fear your wishes are to be thwarted," Bellamy said. "But I'll see what else I can find."

With a shove of his shoulder, he broke the ranks around the table of refreshments. Jane's fingers worked on the handle of her fan. A silly little ivory thing; she'd already cracked the sticks simply by holding it too hard.

"Your gown is lovely," said Lady Audrina, nodding at Jane's dark-green silk. "I thought you preferred bright colors, but this suits you beautifully."

Jane hesitated, then explained, "My mother chose most of my gowns before I was married. Now my lady's maid advises me. Their tastes aren't much alike."

"They had a different purpose in mind, didn't they? Your mother wanted you to catch the eyes of a handsome gentleman. Now that he's already caught, well . . . the dress must show your triumph, yet keep up a bit of mystery." The young woman gave such an extravagant waggle of her eyebrows that Jane had to laugh.

"It's not like that," she said.

"Right, right. I'm certain it's not," replied Lady Audrina. "Newly wed to Lord Kirkpatrick. You don't have to tell me a thing, Lady Kirkpatrick. I can imagine all I need to."

Jane refused to blush. Especially over the truth of her marriage. So she simply said, "You may call me Jane if you like, Lady Audrina."

"Oh, I'd like it very well, Jane. And in return, you mustn't bother with that 'Lady' before my name."

Bellamy returned just then with a plate of tiny, fussy foods. "Now, Lady Kirkpatrick, it will be supper before long. If you can manage not to commit murder for the next half hour, I think you'll make it through the evening right enough."

Jane accepted the plate and began to eat. The offerings were the most delicious dainties she'd ever tasted, the lobster patties buttery and pleasantly rich. "Thank you," she managed to say when the food had all but vanished. "For the plate. Thank you."

"Very welcome, my lady. It's the least a gentleman can do."

Jane wondered whether he was taking a poke at Kirkpatrick's absence from her side. She shrugged, then looked around for a place to set her plate. Laying it on the seat of a chair, she said, "I hope no one sits without looking at the chair first."

"I hope someone does," Audrina replied. Before she could say more, her gaze caught on something over Bellamy's shoulder. Her lips pressed together. "Would you please excuse me? I see some . . . novelty . . . I must attend to."

She disappeared into the crowd before they could see to what, or to whom, she was referring.

Jane faltered, but only for an instant. She was a baroness. Married. With the soul of a traveler. She affixed a confident smile and turned back to Bellamy. "I'd still like to hear more about India. One day I might go there myself."

"Do you know much of it?" Bellamy plucked a flute of champagne from a passing footman's tray, then handed it to Jane.

"No, nothing. I've seen only the south of England and read about little more. Italy, France, Spain. I'm an ignorant but eager pupil."

"The best possible sort."

His tanned faced creased with concentration. With hair graying at the temples and that devilish smile, he looked like a scandalous diplomat. "What shall I tell you about first? The elephants, I think. They're so common in India, the natives keep them like Englishwomen keep pugs. One for every household, no matter how poor, and as gentle as you can imagine. Why, I once saw an elephant lift up a child in its trunk . . ."

The story wrapped around her, tugging her from the crowded ballroom to the sultry sun-baked ground of a faraway land.

Jane cradled her untouched flute of champagne, drinking in Bellamy's words instead. Her hands were covered with expensive kid gloves, wrapped around costly crystal. She might dress the part, but she felt herself as much an outsider in this ballroom as she would be in India.

For the first time this evening, it felt like an adventure, and not just a happenstance.

Chapter 7

Concerning the
Purpose of Flirtation

"You dance like an angel, my lady."

As the last notes of the quadrille dissolved, Edmund uttered this complete falsity with a brilliant smile, bowing over the hand of his hostess. Lady Alleyneham's awkwardness during the lively dance had made a catastrophe of his boots, but he had managed to weave her through the other couples well enough to keep the dance moving.

"Dear me, Kirkpatrick," the countess fluttered, taking his arm and accompanying him through the crowd. "I can't think of the last time I've danced a quadrille. Not this year, I vow! Why, I hardly remembered a one of the figures."

"Surely not," he lied. "You were as light on your feet as a cloud. Or—'a host of dancing daffodils.'"

A rather muddled compliment, but the Wordsworth seemed to please the countess. With five unmarried daughters—two of whom were presently in the country, recovering from some lung ailment—the countess deserved a bit of fun. Even if it came at the price of a few bruised toes.

Edmund smiled down at the plump countess as she chattered about the complexities of planning a ball, but with his peripheral vision, he scanned the crowd. Whom should he approach next? This would be the supper dance, so he would be paired with the lady for quite some time.

A laugh floated above Lady Alleyneham's wall of prattle.

His head snapped up. He knew that laugh: too loud for politeness, but lusty and genuine.

Jane.

And he realized in a flash that he had promised to return to her. And he was probably late.

When she had released him for an hour, he had fallen into his usual habits at a ball, capturing the loneliest-looking women for a series of dances. Spinsters, widows, even a chaperone or two. Harassed companions used to following the whims of the wealthy and doing without pleasures of their own. He parceled out his evening for them, brightening their spirits a few minutes at a time. Delivering the most outrageous compliments he could think of, just to make them smile.

What had Jane done with herself during that time? Surely he owed his wife the same amount of courtesy that he had extended to near strangers tonight.

Lady Alleyneham was running through a lengthy account of how she'd chosen an engraver for the ball invitations. "So we chose the eleventh design," she concluded, "because the gilding was so smart. Didn't you think so?"

"I certainly did." Edmund had no idea what he was

agreeing to. "Would you excuse me, my lady? I believe my wife needs locating."

Lady Alleyneham batted him on the arm. "You newly wed couples. So devoted! You must run off and find your bride, then. You were very good to give me a dance, Kirkpatrick."

Of course, my lady. I'm good to everyone—except the people who deserve it most.

"It was my very great pleasure," he said instead, then went in search of his baroness.

Despite her lack of height, she was easy to find, for at the moment she possessed no corresponding lack of volume. Once more, her laugh rang above the chatter in the ballroom, and he soon found her in conversation with a familiar man. Edmund pawed through his memories, trying to place the square-jawed fellow before him.

". . . slid directly into the Ganges," said the man to Jane. "Can you credit it? A river of mud, and I was riding atop it just like a child sledding down a snowy hill."

Bellamy, that was who it was. The *sahib* who had attended their wedding. That friend of Xavier's or whatever the case might be.

Edmund lurked at Jane's side, waiting for her to notice his presence as her companion continued his thrilling tale about surviving a mudslide into the Ganges River.

"Again, though, an elephant came to the rescue," said the older man. "It wrapped its trunk about me and lifted me as if I was no more than a baby. I rode back to my home on its back and kept it as a pet. Why, the beast followed me everywhere, it was so devoted. I do believe it was sadder than I when I had to leave it behind in India. But one can hardly bring such a pet to London."

Edmund had to interject at this point. "You kept an elephant as a pet? Don't they eat a great deal?"

Jane turned to him, her expression turning from rapt attention to reproach at once. "Hallo, Kirkpatrick. You've missed the beginning of the story."

"Not at all, not at all." Bellamy's teeth flashed brilliantly white against his sun-browned skin. "Unless you've been to India, my lord, you wouldn't realize just how easy it is to care for an elephant."

"I've not had the pleasure of going to India." Edmund shrugged off the subject. "Jane, would you care to join—"

"Do you recognize me, my lord?" The man's smile widened.

"Yes, you were at our wedding." Edmund quashed a flicker of annoyance at the man's interruption. "Bellamy, isn't it?"

"Indeed. My congratulations on a most lovely bride, my lord." Bellamy turned to Jane. "I was just about to ask Lady Kirkpatrick if she would do me the honor of joining me for the supper dance."

Edmund frowned, but before he could protest, Jane spoke. "I'm sorry, Daniel. I've already promised my husband."

"Ah." A flash of regret crossed the man's face; Edmund wanted to wipe his features clean for him. *Daniel.* "Well. Such devotion is to be expected in these early weeks. Enjoy it while it lasts, my lord. Lady Kirkpatrick."

With a bow to each of them, he slipped away through the crowd, and Edmund rounded on Jane. "You call him *Daniel*? He's all but a stranger, Jane. You don't even call *me* by my Christian name."

She shot him a Look. "I did once. You didn't seem to like it."

Edmund, I love you.

"I liked it fine," he said, keeping his voice gentle with an effort. "Henceforth, please address me with at least the same degree of intimacy that you use with recent acquaintances. Especially those who spout ridiculous tales about elephants."

"They were *exciting* tales. Since I'm interested in travel, he was telling me about his life in India. And he offered to let me use his Christian name. Did you notice, *Edmund*, that I did not make the same offer to him?"

Edmund felt every sentence as a reproach. This odd wedding guest had captured his wife's imagination, swiftly endeared himself to her. With his stories, he had brought her to India, while Edmund had taken her nowhere but a ballroom.

"Besides," she added, so low beneath the hubbub that Edmund bent his head to catch her words, "it was not as though you required my company. You were dancing holes in your boots with every other woman here."

"Are you jealous?" His brows knit.

"What do you care?"

"I care a great deal," he said stupidly.

She made an impatient gesture. "If you insist. Look . . . Edmund. I didn't ask you for any of your time this evening. You volunteered it."

"Yes," he said. "And I wanted—"

"You wanted to dance with everyone else and leave behind your absurd little wife who doesn't even know how to curtsy to a countess. Fine, Edmund. That's fine. I don't expect anything different."

This was so unexpected, so suddenly vehement, that he could only stare at her. "No. I never—"

"I never asked you to make me any promise at all. So don't go out of your way to make one if you won't keep it."

If she didn't let him complete a sentence in the next *five seconds*, he would cover her mouth.

"I get the distinct impression," he said in a carefully restrained voice, "that you are displeased with me. I'm sorry I didn't return at the precise moment I said I would. And I'm glad you found someone congenial to speak with."

"Ha." She wrapped both gloved hands around her folded fan, holding to it like a sailor might clutch a rope.

"I'm sorry, Jane."

"That's your answer to everything, isn't it? 'I'm sorry.' That doesn't make it right."

"No. It doesn't." He had the feeling that she, like he, was talking of much more than an evening's entertainment. But what was on her mind, he had no idea. "Come, Jane. Join me in the supper dance, won't you?"

All the fight went out of her. "I can't. I don't know how to dance."

He blinked at her. "Come now. Surely you—" This time, he cut himself off before Jane could. Surely she . . . what? If Lord Xavier's country cousin, who lived alone with a widowed mother, had never learned the intricacies of social greetings, when would she have learned to dance?

Even so, this made no sense. "You never learned to dance, yet you encouraged me to bring you to a ball."

She grimaced, then nodded.

"Jane, how would attending a ball possibly be an

amusing evening for you? I'd never have suggested it if I'd known."

She muttered something he didn't catch, though the movements of her lips hinted at impolite terminology.

"What was that?"

She looked away, hands clutching her fan tight. "Since you offered to bring me to this ball, I was willing to come along. It was nice to have you suggest something you wanted to do."

Oh.

She had been trying to please him, as he had tried to please her. As he'd tried to please every woman sitting on the fringes of the ballroom.

They probably *could* have worked more at cross-purposes if they had tried. But for an unintentional effort, it had been most effective.

"Let's sit out this dance, then," he suggested. "I'll still take you in to supper."

"If you don't care to, that's fine. I could easily fake a sick headache or a torn flounce and disappear for a while."

"Nonsense. You'll join me for supper, or I'll fly into a towering rage."

Her smile looked sad. "We can't have that."

They stood at the edge of the ballroom, not far from the refreshments and near a line of gilded chairs that held many of the same ladies with whom he'd stepped through dances earlier. With nods and smiles, he acknowledged them as he handed Jane into a chair.

"Not that one," she muttered. "Someone left a plate on it."

She sidled to an empty chair; Edmund seated himself next to her. Once side by side, though, she avoided his eyes. Looked at her gloved hands and her fragile little fan. Down the row of chairs. Anywhere else.

"Something still weighs on your mind, Jane."

She shook her head. Jerked her chin in a nod. Then blurted: "Why do you flirt with all those women?"

Her question surprised him as much as her hesitation, and he parried it with one of his own. "Do my attentions to them bother you?"

"No. I just wondered why you bother paying them so much notice. They're the women that no one else flirts with."

Edmund tried to settle back in the chair, but it was spindly and frail. "Just for the reason you said: no one else pays them any heed. They like knowing that someone remembers them once in a while. And really, it's the least I can do."

Fortunately, she seemed too distracted to press further. She smoothed her skirts over her thighs—Edmund shook off a sudden flare of heat—then regarded him again. "What about what *I* like?"

"What *about* what you like?" Edmund repeated. "What do you mean? We came to this ball because you said you would like to attend a ball."

"No, I agreed when you suggested it. It's not the same thing."

"Explain to me what you mean, please."

"I already did." She sighed. "Never mind. We don't have to talk about it anymore."

Edmund counted to ten before he spoke. "Do you mean that you were trying to please me by agreeing to attend tonight? And that I have not yet found an activity that will please you?"

"Not an activity, exactly." She looked up at him, her

eyes tawny as topaz. "You give a piece of yourself to everyone who sits at the edge of a ballroom. But . . . Edmund . . . you married *me*."

"True."

"So. Don't you think we . . ." She trailed off. When she spoke again, her voice was carefully flat. "I thought we'd be together this evening. Not for the whole evening. Just part."

"I'm with you right now."

"Are you?"

Her gaze held him, deep and skeptical, and his stomach gave a twist of pain. No, he wasn't with her. He was always half in Cornwall and half in the past, which left nothing for Jane, here and now.

If only she didn't love him, he could have made her so happy.

"Of course I am." He was certainly lying a great deal this evening, but as the lies were kindly meant, he hoped the Almighty would forgive him.

"I would have been one of those women, too, Edmund," she said. "If I'd ever had cause to attend a ball before, I'd have been sitting at the side of the room. Would you have given me a bit of your time?"

"I did at the beginning of the ball. Then you told me to go away."

From the way she pulled in a deep, impatient breath, he guessed that this response was not to her liking.

He tried again. "You're the cousin of my old friend Xavier. It would have been my pleasure to look after you."

She made a choking sound. As she didn't fall upon him and smother him with kisses, he assumed this was not the good sort of choking sound. As she hadn't been eating, it couldn't be the dangerous sort. Which meant . . .

"You're angry with me." He turned his head, studying her from the corner of his eye. "Why?"

"If you don't know—"

"Please, I beg of you, do not let the ending of that sentence be, 'I'm not going to tell you.'"

Jane went white about the nostrils. "As a matter of fact, it was going to be, 'then you're a bigger fool than I thought.'"

His head reared back. "You think that of me?"

Her posture crumpled. "No more than I think it of myself."

That was not precisely the robust denial he'd been hoping for.

Nor was it any assurance that he had made her happy, as he'd promised. As he'd tried to do.

Sort of. In easy ways.

"Jane," he said softly. He knew she was listening to him; her head turned, just the slightest amount, toward him.

The sliver of movement reminded him of a flower tilting toward the sun. But she was hardly so fragile, and he, certainly not that bright.

How to finish the sentence? How to fix this new hurt, however he had caused it?

She had asked him to consider what she liked. A ball wasn't the right answer; it had only reminded her of how recent a graft she was onto the spreading branches of society.

What else, then? She liked the truth. And travel, apparently. Two things he couldn't give her right now.

But he could give her clothing. Jewels. Anything that could be found in a shop, in these weeks before Christmas. He could wrap her in luxury so she would never have cause to regret choosing him. So she would enjoy their life together, while it lasted.

"Tomorrow, Jane," he said, "we shall go driving in Bond Street, and you shall pick out whatever gift you like. Spare no expense."

When he finished speaking, she looked up at him. He smiled, waiting for her to brighten, but her expression was a cipher.

"Do you know," she finally said, "I don't believe I'm hungry after all. You need not accompany me in to supper. If you'll excuse me, my lord, I'll have the carriage summoned to take me home."

He felt as knocked off balance as if she had slapped him. Still, the reflex of manners made him speak. "Please, allow me."

When she nodded her assent, those same manners lifted Edmund to his feet, bent him into a bow, and carried him off into the crowd before deserting him. Puzzled and more than a little annoyed, he looked back over his shoulder in Jane's direction.

Her back was straight, her gaze fixed on some point in the middle distance. In her green silk, with emeralds clasping her ears and throat, she looked as confident and proud as she had in Sheringbrook's makeshift hell. When she had pretended to be a countess. When she'd lost a fortune.

As he watched, her jaw clenched; she swallowed. And then she drew herself up even straighter.

Such pride. Such terrible pride. Edmund turned away, his annoyance melting. As it vanished, it left behind a hole, an aching sense of failure.

He kept going wrong with her, and he'd no idea how. Did she want more from him, or less? She let him into her bed each night, yet during the day, she rejected his every polite attention.

If she truly loved him, why would she not take everything he offered?

He had no answer to that. And perhaps he shouldn't hunt too hard for a solution. As long as she allowed him to bed her, he might get an heir from their dreadful bargain. He had hoped to give her something she might want in exchange, but she'd just made it clear he had no inkling how to do that.

He had the carriage summoned for Jane, but in a fit of pique, he declined to accompany her home just yet. Instead, he found the homeliest, poorest, plainest widow at the ball and danced with her until her thin cheeks grew rosy and her hard mouth relaxed into a smile.

The horrid ache within him dissolved a bit—just a bit—at the sight.

When he arrived at the house in Berkeley Square, he made his way to Jane's bedchamber to apologize for his latest wrong. He would begin by praising her appearance; she had looked rather pretty tonight, and he should have told her so. A few compliments never went amiss, did they? And then, the nightly act: a few orgasms never went amiss, either. He'd take all the time in the world; make her feel treasured. Make certain she found her pleasure—twice, even.

Yes. That was a good plan.

But when he tried to turn the handle of her door, he found that she had locked it.

Chapter 8

Concerning an Unexpected Caller

Under most circumstances, it would be considered impolite for an unknown gentleman to call on a couple during their honeymoon.

But as Edmund and Jane had already ventured out in company, and as Jane had closed her door to him last night, Edmund couldn't help but feel that the honeymoon was over. If they had ever had one at all.

It was a relief, then, when Edmund's butler, Pye, scratched at the door of Edmund's study the following morning to inform him he had a caller.

"My lord, a Mr. Bellamy to see you." Pye spoke the name as though he doubted its veracity. Pye always sounded that way, though: starchy enough to stiffen a year's worth of cravats. Of middling height, spare of build, and nondescript in his coloring, Pye blended into any space. The perfect butler.

Edmund looked up from a letter he'd read six times without taking in its contents. "Bellamy wishes to see me? It was Lady Kirkpatrick he spoke with last night. I hardly talked to the man."

"If your lordship wishes, I can inform the caller you are not at home."

Edmund considered. Jane hadn't yet emerged from behind her locked door, and he had no idea what they would do together when she awoke. Invitations were thin for a newly married couple, since the *ton* assumed they would be basking in delights of the flesh. And it wasn't as though Edmund was accomplishing any work while left to his own devices.

"Send him in," he decided. "I don't mind seeing what the man wants."

He spent the few minutes before his caller entered tidying up the litter on his desk, covering private documents. There were always papers and accounts and bills to attend to when one possessed a barony that one never visited. From afar, he had to ensure that everyone in his care was prospering. Browning, the estate's steward—a scrupulous young Londoner whom Edmund had placed in the post three years earlier—sent a positive flood of news his way. Edmund read everything carefully, then ended by approving nearly every request.

It was good to have one person in the world whom he could trust.

Just as Edmund finished squaring away his papers, Mr. Bellamy entered the study, a genial smile on his sun-browned features. He was dressed nearly as formally as he had been at the ball the previous night, though he'd exchanged his old-fashioned knee breeches for loose trousers. Ruby rings winked on both of his little fingers, and his cravat was an elaborate arrangement of starched linen and lace.

Edmund shrugged off these oddnesses of dress as a likely result of the man's years away from England. "Good morning to you, Mr. Bellamy. Do you care for spirits? Or some coffee or tea?"

Bellamy waved a hand. "Nothing, nothing. I don't intend to stay long."

Edmund indicated a seat for his caller across his desk. Rightly, he should have inquired about Bellamy's business, then sent the man on his way. But it was so good to see another human face—a face he hadn't disappointed, a face that smiled at him—that he drew out the call. "Will you be staying until the Season, Mr. Bellamy? I imagine a London ball is quite different from the amusements of India."

Bellamy chuckled. "It's a bit odd, all those white faces in one ballroom. Haven't seen so many in decades, especially not female ones." He tapped his nose. "I'm not sure how long my business will keep me here. I've a nose for the main chance, my lord. That's all the amusement I've ever required, no matter the continent."

"The main chance?" Edmund turned his head, the better to examine Bellamy in his peripheral vision. Jane seemed fascinated by the fellow; why was that?

"It's but a matter of business, my lord. Men of the world, men of the world. We must have our secrets, mustn't we?" Bellamy looked around the study as though appraising the dark wood and battered antique furniture.

Edmund was glad he'd covered the papers on his desk. "I suppose."

"Good to be back in the city," Bellamy continued. "Especially this time of year. Chilly rain, gray sky—gad, a man gets to miss Merry Old England when it's nothing but sun, sun, sun, all year. How is one to know what season it is when every day is the same?"

"I suppose," Edmund said again. This must be what Jane liked: that sense of foreignness about Bellamy. His accent was as odd a cobble as his clothing. It rang flat, as though he'd heard so many different ways of speaking that his own speech had been altered.

"Well." Edmund drummed his fingers on his desk. "What brings you to my house this morning, Mr. Bellamy? Is it a matter of business? Or something to do with Lady Kirkpatrick? Thank you for entertaining her so well at the ball last night, by the way."

Bellamy turned his scrutiny from the room to Edmund himself. The focus was unsettling, especially when Bellamy smiled. A wide, confident, adventurer's grin. "No, no. She's not the one I'm interested in, except as . . . ah, well. Collateral, I should say."

And then he changed.

With a lift of his shoulder, a narrowing of his eyes, his charm dropped away. His flat accent became a lilt: "Don't you know me, boyo?"

Edmund fell into a nightmare.

"That's not possible," he managed to say, even as his heart began to hammer furiously. *Get out get out get out of here while you can.*

Over the past twenty years, Turner's face had blurred in his mind, until now it was only an impression of spare features held together by a sense of revulsion. The man across from him was sturdy, blocky, genial. Every inch of his face and dress proclaimed him a merchant who'd built a fortune overseas, just as he'd said.

But the voice—oh, Edmund knew that voice as well as his own. Behind the flat tones of the *sahib*, the gentle hills of Ireland unrolled. The hills Edmund's mother had roamed with Turner before she'd been trussed into marriage and sent across the cold sea.

Turner, here, in Edmund's house. After all this time.

"Sent you a letter, didn't I, last month?" Turner's smile was back. Unlike his smile as Daniel Bellamy, it was lazy, devil-may-care. "I don't see such call for surprise, Edmund."

Edmund's stomach gave a warning lurch. He tightened his fingers on the edge of his desk. "I beg your pardon, Mr. Bellamy. You appear to think we are acquainted."

The man across from him made a dismissive sound. "Trying to brazen it out? But you know me as well as I know you. And now you know, too, I can get to you whenever I like."

The man leaned back in his chair, studying Edmund with some interest. "You turned out looking like your da. May he rest in peace."

"You've no right even to speak of him. I—" Edmund cut himself off. He must stop. Think. He had known this confrontation would come someday, and now it was here. "Turner."

Slowly, the man nodded. "Asked you if you recognized me, didn't I? Last night?"

Edmund pulled in a deep breath. Another. And another, until his heart slowed from its frantic pace, leaving him winded. "I do now."

For a minute—surely one that lasted much longer than sixty seconds—the men watched each other across the desk. Finally, Turner broke the silence. "I wonder if you ever thought of how I'd spent my years."

Every day. "Why have you returned?"

"Reasons on reasons on reasons. You've got some

explaining to do, boyo. And some . . ." Turner pursed his lips. "Some atonement."

Later Edmund might laugh, that he and Turner—so long separated by an ocean—had settled on the same word.

But for now, he drew himself up straight, ignoring a chill that raced down his spine. "You may refer to me as 'my lord.'"

"You're off your arse if you think that's going to happen."

"No? Then perhaps I'll refer to *you* as Turner. You've been cutting a swath through the *ton* over the past month, haven't you? How would you like the polite world to know you spent the last twenty years in a penal colony, *Mr. Bellamy*?"

"How would you like the polite world to know why?"

No. The polite world could never be permitted to know. And Turner knew that as well as Edmund.

Turner was watching him, brows lifted, and Edmund wondered how he hadn't recognized the man before. That considering expression; how many times had he seen it? *Try again, boyo. These sums won't figure themselves.*

Or when he was a bit older: *No lessons today, Edmund. Just me and your mam. Leave us alone, there's a lad.*

So long, Edmund had thought of him as a monster. Now he appeared in lace and gold; no knives or weapons in sight.

Yet Turner had never needed weapons to cause damage. Edmund might have forgotten the man's face or failed to predict how twenty years would change it, but he would never forget that. Turner had sunk claws into their family, so deeply that they mistook the intrusion for roots and allowed his hold to strengthen. When he was finally—fortunately—ripped away, he had torn the family to ribbons. It had never healed.

"We are in a stalemate, aren't we?" Edmund felt more tired than he could ever remember. "I presume you intend some sort of revenge. Blackmail? Murder? Or is theft still to your taste? Whatever you've in mind, just have done, Turner."

"Is that an order?" Turner folded his hands over his belly and studied him, every bit the tutor regarding a student. "I don't think you've the right to give me orders. Not after everything you've taken from me."

"I only did what had to be done. I took nothing from you that you didn't deserve to lose," Edmund said. "And I certainly gained nothing in return."

"If you didn't gain," Turner said slowly, "at least you kept what you had."

"No, I didn't." Edmund rubbed a hand over his face. His eyes felt gritty. How long since he'd enjoyed an untroubled sleep? "You took my family and rent it apart. I haven't been to Cornwall in twenty years."

Unseen, the man across from him drew in a deep breath. "Likewise, boyo. Likewise."

Maybe it was the childish nickname. The arrogance of Turner's approach. Or the shock of knowing that Turner had been part of his entire marriage, beginning with his wedding day. It all roiled together inside Edmund like acid, and his weary lethargy snapped, unleashing sudden anger.

His hand formed a fist; it thumped to his desk. "How well I know your arrogance," he said in a controlled tone. "Even so, you've surpassed yourself by coming to *my house* and accusing *me* of wrongdoing. You deserved your punishment, and worse—why, you could have been executed for the amount you stole. Especially if it became known you planned treason with it."

"Money. Trash." Turner lunged forward, almost in Edmund's face. "It would have come to nothing if you'd kept your nose where it belonged. And your father would have come to nothing, too."

Again, the mad urge to laugh. *Nothing:* that was as apt a description of Edmund's father as any other. The man had had no will of his own. Left to his own devices, he would have been the ruin of his entire lineage.

Instead, his only son had ruined *him.*

Turner sat back in his chair, a sneer on his face. "But it's not the money I've come for. Nor to hurt your precious body, *my lord.* I wouldn't hurt a hair on your head. There's people counting on you to stay healthy and take care of them." He smirked. "Not that you're doing such a job of that. You look skinny as a wet cat, and about as happy."

Edmund stared at him. "You're saying you don't want money. And you don't want to hurt me."

"Have we a problem?"

The situation suddenly struck him as absurd. "I'm certainly not going to try to talk you into it."

Turner smiled. "I've got another reason for calling on you, boyo. Got yourself married, didn't you?"

A prickle of foreboding raced down Edmund's spine. "You know I did. You were at the damned wedding."

"Lady Kirkpatrick seems rather fond of you. Just how fond *is* she?"

Edmund, I love you. He shuddered off the thought. "She's under my protection."

"Is she, now." Turner opened the inkwell. Closed it again. "Is she, now. I wonder what that's worth?"

He shoved back his chair and rose to his feet, strolling the length of the room. "I've been thinking for a long time what I'd want to do when I was free again. How to respond. What to do to you for your interference."

Edmund's fingers clenched the arms of his chair.

"We both lost our way of life, young Edmund. But I had no choice about it. So I'll take a choice away from you. Only justice, isn't it?" Turner paused. Trailed his fingers over the spines of the books. Edmund had to quash the command *stop—stop touching my things.*

The next words were tossed lightly over Turner's shoulder. "The wife you chose."

Edmund fumbled for understanding. "What do you mean? A person can't take away a wife."

Oh. Yes, one could. Long ago, Turner had demonstrated that.

"You intend to try to make Lady Kirkpatrick love you?" The idea was nonsense.

"I don't have to, do I? I just have to take away her love for you. And with what shall I replace it?" Turner's blunt fingers tugged on a book, stretching the leather at the top of the spine. "Hate?"

He knocked the book back into place, then turned to face Edmund. "No. Indifference would be better, wouldn't it? When I'm done with her, she'll never think of you at all, unless it's with disappointment."

"You won't be able to trick the baroness."

"Already have, haven't I? She thinks I'm Daniel Bellamy, full of stories and charm."

"You're certainly full of sh—"

"Tell me, boyo," Turner cut him off. "Do you know where she is right this very moment?"

Edmund frowned. "The location of my wife is no business of yours."

"You don't know, though, do you? She could be anywhere. She could be in her bedchamber. She could be fiddling about in the kitchens. She could be . . ." Turner's eyes narrowed. "Meeting a lover."

"She's not."

"Maybe. Maybe not. But you don't know. And you'll think about that now, won't you? I'll work at her the same way. That's all the beginning I need—the not knowing. Then comes the not trusting. And then comes the not loving." Turner shrugged. "Simple as can be."

Acid rose into Edmund's throat. With an effort, he forced it down. "I would consider such games a great wrong against a woman who's done nothing to harm you."

"Chose you, didn't she? People are punished every day for their *dobhránta* choices."

Stupid. Edmund knew that word well. Turner had once been his tutor, after all, and not overgenerous with praise.

Yet he could not let this stand. "Lady Kirkpatrick had no choice but to marry me. She is innocent."

"Just depends on how we define innocent, doesn't it?" Turner considered. "If she'd no choice in the matter, mayhap she'd already given up her innocence."

"I won't discuss it."

The man laughed so hard that his queue shook like the clapper of a bell. "So she did, did she? Hope she was good enough to be worth a leg shackle."

"This marriage was my decision," Edmund said through gritted teeth. "It's a way to take care of my own."

Turner's laughter cut off abruptly. "Your own. Ah, yes. That's the heart of the matter, isn't it?"

Again Turner paced the small confines of the study.

Corner to corner, back again, as though trailing a web behind him. Edmund felt like nothing so much as a fly, wrapped and trapped. "*You took my family and rent it apart. I haven't been to Cornwall in twenty years.*"

"Is there some reason you're repeating my words?"

"Yes. Yes." Turner stopped his pacing and turned on his heel, facing Edmund. "I told you 'likewise,' didn't I? You could have gone back anytime you wanted. Me, I'd no choice but to stay away."

"You made the choices; the law kept you away." Fury knotted his stomach. "You should never be allowed to touch them. If you leave England, I'll give you sufficient money for—"

"I don't want your money," Turner said quietly. "I want your family. *My* family."

"What?" Edmund's lips felt so cold, he could hardly speak the word.

"Your sisters," Turner said. "They're my daughters. And when I've done with you and your wife, I'm going back to Cornwall."

Chapter 9

Concerning an Apology
and a Local Journey

Jane spent the morning waiting.

After arising from a broken sleep, she waited as her maid took the curl papers from her hair and coaxed it into a fashionable twist. Then she waited upstairs for her husband's morning caller to leave.

Now she waited for Edmund to answer her scratch at the study door. She knew he was in there; why didn't he answer? She needed to tell him something important, and the delay was causing it to grow heavier on her shoulders.

Her nerves were fairly strong as a rule, but she couldn't keep herself politely still right now. So she kicked the door.

"Come," he called at once.

Hmph.

When she turned the handle and stepped into the room, the small size of the study surprised her. It was dark, too; a high-ceilinged, narrow space paneled in varnished wood. The study was dominated by a massive desk, the wood glossy but scarred. Bookcases set into the walls held a jumble of volumes. It looked like a room both well used and ill cared for.

And behind the desk sat Edmund, scribbling away at a letter. "Pye," he said, "see that this is posted at—oh. Jane?"

He squinted up at her, as though he might possibly have mistaken the spare figure of their butler for Jane's much shorter form.

"Yes." An unnecessary reply, but she couldn't just stand there like an unneeded piece of furniture. She booted the leg of the desk with her slippered toe. This was a fine morning for kicking things.

He stood—manners, always manners—and indicated a seat across the desk. "I wish I had a different chair to offer you," he murmured. "What brings you in here? Are you all right?"

"Yes." She looked him up and down. "Are you?"

At the moment, he looked as ill cared for as his study. He must have tugged his cravat loose while writing, because it was flecked with ink and the careful starched folds were crushed. Under his eyes were dark shadows—or maybe that was only the effect of the lamplight and the inevitable gray sky.

"Fine, fine. Just thinking over a letter."

"Do you need me to come back later?" She scooted to the edge of her seat. *Coward.*

"No." He sanded and shook off the letter, then took up the seal and wax. "I've written all that needs to be said."

"Is it something important?"

His hands fumbled the letter; a blob of wax fell on it an inch away from the folded edge. Edmund frowned, dropping more wax over the fold and pressing his seal on it. "Nothing you need concern yourself with. I'm asking my steward in Cornwall to look into a few questions that have suddenly come up."

When he looked up at her, he smiled. That sweet, lovely, I'm-thinking-of-nothing-but-your-pleasure smile. "We needn't talk of that. How are you, Jane, after your first London ball?"

"I'm fine." She took a deep breath. "And I owe you an apology."

The ball the previous night had shown her the greed of her own heart: she wanted more from him than the kindness he shared with all others. Exactly as Edmund had predicted when she'd first admitted her love; exactly what she'd assured him would not happen.

Yet he had done everything he promised for her—everything, that is, except return to her side after precisely one hour. And considering how far in his debt she was, that was hardly a trespass at all.

So she had decided on a reasonable course of action. No fussing; no demands. Just simple friendship and separate lives, with the hope that one day soon, she'd stop hoping. If she didn't speak of her unwanted love, or act on it, it would become a back-of-the-mind family secret, rather like having a mad aunt in the country. A bit embarrassing, yes, but certainly nothing that need interfere with their daily life.

As though she hadn't spoken, his hand still pressed the seal to his letter.

"Edmund. Did you hear me? I apologize."

"For what?"

She chose her words carefully. "Because I left the ball without you. Because I was jealous. Not in the way you assumed," she added in a rush. "It's not because I mind your attentions to other women. I know you're being kind."

When he lifted his seal, the Kirkpatrick crest was imprinted clearly in red wax. "Oh? How do you mean it, then?"

"I've never had a suitor, Edmund. I've never been to a ball, or anything more than one of Xavier's country house parties. After my father died, I had a quiet village life. No lessons or instructors. Horrid clothes." She gave him a thin smile. "I just felt I didn't belong last night. And you always know how to set people at ease. I'd have liked your company. That's all."

Wariness fled his face; sympathy took its place. "I understand. And you've every right to expect that sort of consideration. I simply didn't think."

"Well. Marriage is new to us both."

"You're right. And we ought to do something more to celebrate it than we have." When he stood, the clean scent of soap and starch caught her, made her want to bury her face in the hollow of his neck. "I can't take you out of England right now, but is there somewhere in London you'd like to go?"

"Vauxhall Gardens," she said promptly.

He looked at her with mock severity. "Yes, I can only imagine what you'd do with a cloak of shadows and a park full of drunkards. It's a fortunate thing for the world that your taste for adventure stopped with gambling and never turned to pickpocketry."

"You'll give me the vapors with such praise." How she hoarded these signs that he knew her, even a little.

"I regret that Vauxhall Gardens is closed in autumn and winter. Perhaps we can go in the spring." His voice trailed off, and he straightened the items on his desk before adding, "Is there anywhere else?"

She considered. "Yesterday you suggested Bond Street. Why not there?"

As he stood, his answering smile was worth the heartburn of all her swallowed pride. "An excellent plan."

"We don't have to," she said. "I know gentlemen don't like to go to Bond Street until after dinner, when they can buy themselves a . . . um, fancy lady."

"Do you honestly think I would do that?"

"No, I guess not." Jane scuffed the toe of her slipper on the carpet, then made herself stop. "But. Well. I don't mind if you don't want to go."

"As it was my idea, I fully intend to accompany you. A lady of quality must have a chaperone, and I know of no lady of better quality than yourself."

A few steps brought him around the desk to face her; then he raised her hand to his lips. Just a quick brush, light as a moth wing.

Jane felt as though she had fallen into a flame.

His hand on hers; those sweet words; his mouth. This tiny politeness seemed more intimate than the marital acts they had engaged in over the past weeks.

She drew her hand free of his grasp. "Don't be ridiculous." She must convince him that he didn't need to reassure her. If she were strong enough to lean on, one day he might rely on her. And that—that would be enough.

She could hope.

"I'll get a bonnet," she said. And before she could say something else, something that would ruin the moment, she darted from the room.

* * *

"I've had the carriage brought around," Edmund said when she joined him in the entrance hall a little while later, a drab-colored poke bonnet now atop her head. Jane noted that he had used the time to put on a fresh cravat. Thoughtful of him.

She hadn't expected the carriage, though. "You don't want to walk?"

"In late November? You'd be chilled in an instant. As it is, you can hardly be warm enough even while we're in the house." His fingers stroked the fur cuff of her long sleeve. "This is nothing like enough covering, is it? Your hands must be cold. Or your neck, with your hair piled up under your hat like that."

"It's not a *hat*. It's a bonnet. And it's meant to be fashionable. Comfort has nothing to do with it."

He frowned. "Surely you could have both fashion and comfort."

She had gooseflesh on her arms, less from cold than the fact that he sounded genuinely interested in her welfare. "You think so? Then talk to the modistes of the world about that. In the meantime, I need my pelisse."

While she wrapped herself up, Edmund said, "You must be wanting new clothes, though. We could visit a modiste's. Or a milliner's?"

"Why must I be wanting new clothes?"

He looked at her askance. "Women always want new clothes."

She looked askance at him right back.

He tilted his head. "Don't they?"

"I *have* new clothes. Don't you remember? I had them made before we were married."

"Well, you could get more." At her ferocious expression,

he lifted his hands. "All right, Jane. It's your outing. Let us go to Bond Street and see what strikes your fancy."

Edmund gave instructions to the coachman, and off they rolled. Rather than sit on the backward-facing seat, he sat next to Jane on the plush squabs of the closed carriage.

She flinched when his sleeve brushed against the edge of her breast.

"I'm sorry, I should have asked if I might sit by you," he said. "If it doesn't crowd you too much, may I?"

Yes yes yes yes yes. "If you like."

"We can talk more easily if we're next to each other."

Jane disagreed with this about as much as a person could disagree with any statement. When Edmund sat this close to her, her senses became so full of him that talk was impossible. The faint shush and thump of his boot heels shifting on the carriage floor. The shadows that his tall form cast in the carriage interior. Even a hum of heat as he sat close, as her body yearned toward his.

She made herself pull back. "Is something on your mind, then?" she asked lightly.

"Not at all," he said at once. "I just want to make certain you have a nice time. Are you having a nice time?"

"Er. That's not your responsibility, Edmund."

Her blunt words must have startled him, because he leaned away from her so he could look her in the face.

The small distance made it easier to muster an explanation. "You're taking me to Bond Street, which is very kind of you. But if I should decide to be in a temper, that wouldn't be your fault. Nor could you likely talk me out of it. And if you keep asking me whether I'm having a nice time, I *will* be in a temper."

He considered this for a moment. "Fair enough. If

you should begin *not* to have a nice time, I'll trust you to tell me."

"I should hope so."

Edmund drummed his fingers on his thigh, then nodded. "All right." *Drum drum.* "Jane. Who invited Mr. Bellamy to our wedding?"

"Mr. Bellamy?" This ranked very low on the list of questions she might have expected him to ask. It took her a moment to think through an answer. "Probably my cousin Xavier asked him. Why?"

"I just wondered. You don't know him well, do you? Bellamy, I mean. Not Xavier."

"Not well, no." She smiled. "Bellamy, I mean. Not Xavier. I know my dratted cousin far too well."

He didn't respond to her attempt at humor. "Bellamy doesn't strike me as a good person to associate with." His profile was to her, but she caught the flicker of a glance from the corner of his eye.

Her insides fluttered. "You don't have to be jealous," she blurted.

His jaw tightened. "I'm not."

"No, of course you aren't," she muttered. "How stupid of me."

He seemed to realize he had been ungracious. "Not that I doubt your appeal to middle-aged men of questionable background, Jane. Because I certainly do not."

"Oh, stop." She sank back against the squabs. "You're only making it worse. Forget I said anything."

"Please *don't* forget I said anything," Edmund said quietly. "Don't let him catch you alone. And don't believe his tales."

"Tales? Do you know something about him that I don't?"

His eyes met hers and held. "No." He laced his fingers

through hers. "I'm only thinking of propriety. Now, where shall we stop first? Your wish is my command."

She wished that were true. More than wished: she yearned, pined, hungered. Every pitiful overwrought urge that a poet could dream up.

But she had apologized, and she had made him—and herself—a vow. There would be none of that nonsense.

She looked out the carriage window at the jostling crowds. "It doesn't matter." Somehow, she sounded calm as she eased her fingers from his grasp. "How about a bookshop?"

"Your wish," he said again, "is my command."

The pallid sunlight peeking through gray clouds drew out crowds of shoppers in full force. Throngs slowed Jane's progress along the pavement at her husband's side, and she welcomed the chance to look about. The busy streets of London were as much a novelty as the goods in shop windows.

Jane hadn't realized how different the winter was in London than the country. Living on the fringes of the village of Mytchett, Jane and her mother—like the other scattered villagers—hoarded coal and wood and preserved food each autumn. Not because they were unwilling to rely on their neighbors, but because they knew distance and weather might make it impossible. Londoners had no such fear: the world, they seemed confident, would come to them.

Jane was beginning to like London more and more.

The decision to go hunting for books, rather than ribbons or slippers, had required a turn of the carriage from Bond Street into Piccadilly. The road was blocked by a wagon with a broken axle, so Edmund and Jane disembarked shy of their destination.

He drew her gloved hand onto his arm once they stood on the pavement. "I won't ask how you are because you've threatened me with a tantrum. Only you must tell me if you get cold."

"What would you do if I was?" Wind snagged a wisp of hair on Jane's forehead, ruffling it against the broad brim of her bonnet.

"I'd buy a hot potato for you to hold." He grinned. "Or get you into someplace warm. The shops will be crowded enough to keep you well toasted."

Jane could believe it. Each one seemed crammed with shoppers, wealthy men and women looking for any excuse to spend their coin. More likely they were preparing for the opening of Parliament in a few days, the beginning of society's extended social whirl, than snapping up the perfect Christmas gifts for loved ones. But Jane could pretend: that it was nearly Christmas, that she was beloved, and that she would get the gift she wanted most.

She could pretend. *Could*. But she wouldn't.

As they made their way toward the windowed front of Hatchards, the wind's breath came sharp and chill. Jane heard a woman cry out, "Oh! My bonnet!"

Tumbling atop the crowd from head to shoulder, person to person, came a woman's hat topped most improbably with a stuffed pigeon.

With a quick catch, Edmund grabbed it before the wind could whirl it away. Its owner—a buxom, well-dressed young woman—was upon them in a few seconds, stammering her thanks. "The ribbon parted from the brim," she explained. "I can't think how. I should have been so sorry to lose my favorite hat."

"And rightly so," Edmund said with a bow. "It looks good enough to eat."

The woman laughed, her cheeks pinker than the snap of wind would warrant, and went on her way.

Jane took Edmund's arm again. "You shouldn't have saved that hat. It was horrible."

"She didn't think so." His gaze roamed over the crowded street. "And since I could catch it, I did."

Though he spoke mildly, Jane had the feeling she'd been put in her place. And it wasn't a place she particularly liked. She took her hand from his arm.

Not that he noticed. His eye had been caught by a hackney a few steps farther on. A woman hesitated in the hired carriage's open door, unwilling to venture into the muddy slush at the edge of the pavement.

"Allow me, madam." Edmund extended a hand to help her jump to dry stone, then assisted her maid. "Such angels should float above the muck of the streets."

With a tip of his hat, he moved on. The sound of a maid's giggles and a surprised *thanks* floated after them.

"Angels," Jane grumbled.

Edmund shot her a sidelong glance. "Well, I could hardly call them devils. I don't know them at all."

"Why did you have to call them anything?" Jane bit her lip. *Remember: just a good old chum.* "Never mind. I can see that they liked it."

"Most women like being called angels." He took her arm again as though there had been no interruption, and certainly not two.

"What would London do without you?"

Edmund looked down at her with some surprise. "Whatever do you mean?"

"You seem to find many ways to do things that people like."

"I do little enough. It could be more." His mouth pulled tight, and without another word, they continued their walk.

It could be more. Yes, he was right about that.

Jane was torn between wanting to kick him—since this was, after all, the day for kicking things—and wanting to press kisses all over his face.

But. Maybe it was a good thing that he didn't treat her with swooning solicitude. Maybe that meant he thought she was strong enough to fend for herself.

Or maybe he simply forgot about her.

She hoped it was the former, and that in some way— even if not the way she wanted—she was special to him.

Chapter 10

Concerning Cartography and Selfishness

They reached Hatchards without further interruption by wayward hats or street-shy angels. Without waiting for Edmund to usher her inside, Jane flung open the door to the bookshop and pressed into its crowded confines.

A stack of little rooms around a tightly coiled staircase, the space was edged with counters interrupted by ceiling-tall bookcases. Every inch of shelf and table space was full of books in boards and bindings. Clerks with a sheen of perspiration on their brows, handing over volumes or jotting notes. Patrons with clucking tongues or triumphant smiles.

"I'll wager you're not worried about me being cold anymore," Jane murmured to Edmund, who had jostled in behind her. He chuckled.

Jane felt crushed in on all sides, and for some reason, this made her feel bigger. She was part of the crowd, part of London now. As she swept up the stairs with no partic-

ular destination in mind, she became separated from
Edmund, but it didn't matter. She was a baroness, out
for a little shopping, with pin money and credit and infinite leisure.

Turning a bend in the staircase, she found herself in a
less-full part of the shop. In a side chamber, a large table
dominated a small space. And scattered over its surface . . .

Maps. Stacks and sheaves of maps on parchment and
paper and vellum and linen. Large maps, rolled up and
tied with cords; small ones, inked and beautifully hand-
colored. The whole world had been tumbled onto that
single table, and it drew Jane as if whispering her name.

Atop the messy stack was a small watercolor of an
island, a hand-drawn antique labeled *La Sicilia* in an
elaborate script. Jane took the corner of the paper in her
fingertips, then drew her hand back.

She looked around. No one paid her any heed. Strip-
ping off one glove, she touched the corner of the map
again. The old paper was hand-laid, thick as cloth. Faint
lines crossed it where the fibers—linen, cotton, Jane
couldn't tell—had been pressed dry; she felt them as tiny
ridges.

Had the person who drew and painted this map ever
been to Sicily? Basked in the sun and eaten olives and
oranges straight from trees? Or was the artist, like Jane,
simply someone who wished for faraway places?

Even if she only found bits of the world in London, it
was better than having none of the world at all. And even
if only on a map, she could see places she'd never seen
before.

"How can I help you, miss?" A clerk had come up
beside her, the sound of his footfalls lost in the noise that

leaked upward through the staircase. He was a young man in a dark coat, his expression slightly harried.

Jane folded her hands behind her back. "Lady Kirkpatrick," she corrected him.

"My lady." He bowed, turned red, and made a gulping sound all at once. "I beg your pardon."

"That's all right." Jane realized she rather enjoyed the whole business of surprising people, then being gracious to them. And then she hit on an idea. "Could you show me where the atlases are kept?"

By the time Edmund rounded the third turn of the hairpin-tight stairway, he was perspiring. Yes, it was damnably hot and crowded in the bookshop, but the real problem was that he'd lost his wife. And if he couldn't see her, then maybe Turner could. Maybe Turner was here, and he . . .

No. Edmund had to find Jane, and when he did, he had to keep a daft smile on his face.

The press of the crowd lessened as he climbed into the upper rooms of the shop. When he rounded one more turn of the little wood stairs, there she was. No Turner in sight; just a small woman holding a medium-sized book, standing behind a large table. The dark green of her pelisse made her cheeks rosy, and wisps of her light-brown hair sneaked from beneath her pale bonnet.

The smile that crossed his face might have been daft, but it was also genuine. "Jane. I thought I'd lost you."

"I'm not lost." She turned a page, not looking up from her book.

"What have you found there? Something for Louisa?" Lord Xavier's wife was known to be quite a scholar.

"For me. I think." When he reached her side, she looked up. Her hazel eyes were bright, crinkled at the corners with excitement. "It's an atlas. The maps are beautiful, and there are color plates, too. Scenes of cities and people."

"May I see?"

She extended the opened volume to him. "This plate shows a street in Bombay."

The aquatinted drawing spreading over the page contained a crowd of neat white buildings with red-brown roofs. A clutter of people walked between them down a narrow street, separated by the occasional carriage or cart pulled by a tiny figure in a broad-brimmed hat.

The scene could almost have been from London. In some ways, a city was a city, no matter where in the world it was found. Yet in the wide-hipped roofs and stretching awnings, there was a suggestion of something unfamiliar. *Things are a little different here.*

Was it because of the heat? The brightness? How did it change a person's heart, to trust in the sun?

Only when Jane tugged the book away did Edmund realize he had been staring at the image for a long time. He blinked, trying to clear his head. He seemed to have traveled away from the second story of Hatchards, and his mind fought the return to his body.

"You like it, too, don't you?" Jane's fingers hovered over the picture.

His throat felt dry. "Is there something about India in particular that you like?" He swallowed. Coughed. "Because of . . . of Bellamy?"

Not that Bellamy—Turner—had a damn thing to do with India, in truth. His stories were nothing but false tales from his fevered imagination.

"Not only India. Anywhere. Everywhere." Her fingers

trailed over the illustration. "I just want to know more. I don't want to have a small life."

Oh.

It wasn't Bellamy, or India, or disappointment in Edmund. It was her own wish, untainted and sincere. And how could he argue with a wish like that?

His face must have changed, for she closed the atlas. "I'll put it back. It's rather expensive."

He took the volume from her, but instead of returning it to the shelf, he handed it to a nearby clerk. "Please charge this to Lord Kirkpatrick's account and have it wrapped up. We shall take it with us."

When he turned back to Jane, he took her hand and gave it a quick squeeze. "I wish I could give you more than a book."

"A book is enough." God bless the woman; she even met his eyes when she said it.

Now that he'd found a way to please her, his body unknotted. A ridge of tension between his shoulder blades began to relax; the constant twisting feeling of his stomach began to ebb. This was . . . good. This was marriage as he'd never seen it: friendly and comfortable. As long as there was amity, they could rub along well enough without love.

He cleared his throat. Onward. "Will you help me choose a few Christmas gifts for relatives? They'll need to be sent to Cornwall, so it's best to buy them now."

Jane's brow furrowed. "Cornwall? You still have relatives living there?" She shook her head. "Yes, I knew that. It can't be your father, but . . ."

"My mother. Two sisters."

"And they won't come to London for Christmas?"

He forced a smile. "They don't travel, and I don't either."

"Yes, I know that well enough." Reaching for the shelf at her side, she took down a volume at random, then put it back. "My mother is the same way. She likes to stay close to home, and she doesn't like venturing into London. I was almost surprised that she came to our wedding, but she couldn't ignore the marriage of her only child."

"I'm glad she did not," Edmund said.

Jane seemed not to hear him; gently, she stroked a hand-painted map labeled *La Sicilia.* "I said I didn't want a small life, but that's all she's ever wanted. After my father died, so long ago I hardly remember him, it was just me and my mother and a sniffle-nosed maid-of-all-work. We lived on the fringes of a village, with enough shabby gentility to—"

"Carpet an estate?" he teased.

"With a very threadbare carpet." Tracing the shapes on the map, she added, "I always knew that life wasn't what I wanted for myself."

Edmund opened his mouth to reply, then closed it again. Formulating some sort of flowery compliment was much more difficult when one was given honesty rather than flirtation. "I understand."

"Do you?" She gave a dry laugh. "I'm a baroness now. Lady Kirkpatrick. I certainly don't understand it myself."

"There's no mystery to it," he said. "Baroness or beggar, one just does what needs to be done. As sharp-witted as you are, I've no concerns about what sort of baroness you'll be."

"Sharp-witted," she repeated. "I like the sound of that."

"It's the truth. Sharp-tongued, too."

"Do you know, I think you're being sincere." She smiled at him.

Jane had quite a pretty smile, really. Her teeth were straight, and her chin came to a sweet point. In past years, he had tended to be wary of her smiles, which were often coupled with a wicked plan certain to result in ruined clothing or physical injury.

But she'd been very young then. And so had he. And now . . . her smile was lovely.

It was easy to return a smile to her.

"Well, let's find those books you want." All business, she broke into his musings. "Downstairs?"

"Yes. Have you found everything you want up here?"

"For now." She looked down at *La Sicilia* once again. "Thank you for the book."

"Don't start thanking me again. You should say, 'About dratted time you bought me a good present, Edmund.'"

Ah. That smile again. Good.

She led the way down the stairs. As soon as they rounded the first curve of the staircase, the clamor increased. They shouldered their way to a tall case of bound volumes. Edmund looked at the shelf before him, wishing the right book would leap into his hand. "Do women like novels?"

At his side, Jane scanned the shelves. "Some do. Do you think your sisters would like something humorous? Or something chilling and Gothic?"

"I'm not sure. Catherine used to like horses. And Mary liked flowers and things."

"She liked 'things'? Wonderful. Let's find the section of books about 'things.'"

Edmund poked her in the arm. "Minx. You know what I mean. Bright things. Butterflies. Fairies. Folk tales."

Her mouth curved. "We can find her a book about 'bright things,' then. With nice illustrations."

He caught her arm before she could seek a clerk. "Wait. Jane. I don't know if she would enjoy that sort of book now. She—well. She liked all of that when she was a child."

"Oh." Jane tilted her head. "How old is she now?"

"Twenty-three. And Catherine is twenty-five."

She paused. Blinked. "All right. Then they could do with a good novel."

Jane began tugging down bound volumes. Green leather; black bindings; morocco and kid. She handed them to him, making a pile in his arms, and he felt relief at her quick decision.

And at the fact that she hadn't commented on his being twenty years behind in knowing what his sisters liked.

"That should be enough," she said when the pile of books reached Edmund's chin. He set his jaw atop the stack to hold them steady. "Several Waverley novels. Your mother will probably like those, too. Besides that, *Tom Jones*. Send that one separately so your mother doesn't know they have it, or she might be shocked."

"I doubt much of anything could shock my mother." If Turner was telling the truth about his sisters' parentage, that is. His letter to his steward Browning, sent that morning, contained a few judicious questions. The younger man might infer their true meaning, but Edmund trusted in his discretion.

"Better to be safe than to get your sisters in trouble." She winked at him; her smile had taken on the familiar mischievous twist. It brought out a dimple at one corner of her mouth.

His throat closed tight. "Where would you like to go

after this?" He croaked as a clerk wrapped their parcels. "Name the place."

He almost wished she would suggest someplace far away. France. *La Sicilia*. He wouldn't leave London for his own sake, but he would do it for hers, even knowing Turner would chase them.

Edmund owed him a debt of blood? Well. Likewise. Only Edmund had never intended to collect.

Jane took so long to answer that Edmund wondered if her mind had flitted back upstairs to the table of maps. Finally she said, "Let's keep looking together and see what we find."

Christmas had come early.

Oh, the calendar said it was still a month away. The shops hadn't yet trimmed their windows with garlands. The weather was stubbornly gray, the rooftops wet with drizzle rather than snow-frosted.

Still. As far as Jane was concerned, Christmas had nothing more to offer than this day. Not gifts, not gratitude, not triumph over her own rebellious self.

She had succeeded in spending the afternoon with Edmund without the dreadful subject of love being brought up. She had even managed to tell him something real. How she felt about travel. About her mother. Her tiny little life.

She had managed to make him laugh. As though he liked being with her.

After completing their purchases at Hatchards, they wandered next into a shop of furnishings and decorative trinkets. Jane found a vase that purported to be from China, though for all she knew, it could have been painted up in the Wedgwood pottery the week before. It had a pleasing look of far-traveled splendor about it, though: nearly two feet in height, rectangular in form, with gilded handles in the shape of sinuous dragons. Each of the four sides was enameled with complex scenes of buildings and people and animals, trees and clouds and sky, all stacked in severe perspective and colored with tints brighter than nature.

As she studied it, Edmund found his way to her. "You like it."

"I could look at it for hours and still find new things to notice. It's like being in China. Or seeing what people in China think is beautiful."

"I don't think anyone could disagree with the beauty of this vase."

She looked up at him. "Do you think it's real?"

"From China?" He touched a dragon-formed handle with one gloved fingertip. "Most likely. I've never seen a vase like this before."

"I'll get it," she decided. "I can use this quarter's pin money."

"Nonsense. I'll take care of it."

In a high-handed instant, Edmund had found a clerk and arranged for the billing and packaging of the vase.

When he returned to her side, she asked, "Why do you even grant me pin money if you never allow me to use it?"

His brows lifted. "It's for when you want something so frivolous that the very idea of spending money on it makes me shudder."

"Such as?"

"A bonnet with a stuffed pigeon on it?" His eyes crinkled, attempting a shared joke, and she couldn't help but relent. Though she managed to thank him, a slight sense of injury lingered, as though he had taken away something she wanted very much for herself.

She was not to be trusted with money, her cousin Xavier had once said. But what he meant was that she was not to be trusted to spend it as she wished. Now Jane had money in her pocket, yet a man still held her purse strings and kept her from buying anything for her own.

Her spirits revived as they meandered through the shop, poking through boxes of precious-stone scarabs and admiring Dutch paintings. They both squeezed onto a tiny French *fauteuil* and stood, quickly and guiltily, when its old wooden bones creaked a loud protest.

Next they drifted into a milliner's shop, a narrow space crowded with bright fabrics and plumes and ribbons, with finished hats lining shelves and resting on stands. Edmund chose three of the most lavish affairs—a silk turban trimmed with plumes, plus two high-crowned bonnets with ruched velvet and lace trim—for his mother and sisters. Jane found a length of lace for her mother; Mrs. Tindall could trim a cap with it and feel herself the belle of her village.

"You can't always be giving things to other people," Edmund said. "You must get something for yourself now."

Jane laughed. "I've bought enough already. But if we're keeping track of purchases, I haven't seen you get anything for yourself yet."

His own expression remained solemn. "A new bonnet, maybe. You could do with a new bonnet, couldn't you?"

"Surely a man of society needs a new beaver hat. Or a snuffbox."

Edmund pulled a face. "I have enough hats. And snuff? No."

"A quizzing glass, then?"

"Jane, stop. My eyes are fine on their own. I don't need anything. Now, what bonnet are we going to choose?"

"We are not talking of a matter of *need*. I don't *need* a bonnet. I've already told you, I had all new clothing when we were married."

He turned his face to one side, giving her his profile; a sculptor's fantasy of clean lines. "We didn't come out today so I could buy something for myself. Please, choose something."

"I don't want to, Edmund. Christmas is still weeks away. And I've already got a new atlas. And a vase."

"It's not enough."

"It's enough for me."

"It shouldn't be."

Jane pressed her lips together. Not only was he not even looking at her; he wasn't *listening*. "You want me to choose something? Fine. A bonnet will make you happy? Fine. You'd look lovely in red."

He turned back to her, eyebrows arched. "A charming offer. But the bonnet is to be for you."

"Who are you trying to please here? Me, or you?"

He blinked at her. "You, Jane. It's for you."

All she could do was blink back.

He thought he was being kind, but forcing unwanted gifts upon someone wasn't kindness at all. It was selfish for him to press her like this. Was this because he felt guilty over neglecting her at last night's ball? Was he trying to make her feel better?

If so, then he ought to atone in the manner of *her* choosing. Not force her to allow his own chosen atonement.

It had never occurred to her before that kindness could

be selfish, yet this was. And he'd been selfish at the ball, too, hadn't he? Spinning woman after woman onto the dance floor, ignoring his promise to her. Just as it had been lightly made, so had it been lightly discarded.

Not that she was going to say any of this in the middle of a shop. But the only person who was going to feel better after this purchase was the shopkeeper.

Skimming over bright ribbons and soft-crowned caps, satin turbans and silk-velvet bonnets, she looked for— *aha*. Tucked up in the corner of a shelf, half-hidden behind gaudier companions, was the bonnet of Jane's choosing.

"That one, please. No—behind the plumed turban— yes, that's right. The straw."

A plain. Straw. Bonnet. That would show Edmund.

She put the bonnet on her head and regarded herself in the hand mirror the shopkeeper pressed upon her. The simple hat was prettier than she had expected, like a promise of spring in this drab wintry season: pale-blue straw, wired and shaped into a rounded frame around the face. The inside brim was edged with ivory silk, and a fat brown bow tied beneath her chin.

As she considered her reflection, Edmund's face appeared over her shoulder in the glass. "'Shall I compare thee to a summer's day?'"

"No." Her reply surprised even Jane.

"'Thou art more lovely and more temp—'"

"No."

"Not in the mood for poetry?"

"No."

When he stepped out of the glass's view, she glared at the face framed by the bonnet. Muddy eyes, obstinate mouth, slashing brows. A regular crab apple, with a hopelessly prosaic soul.

Carefully, she set the small mirror down on the shop counter. She'd seen enough. "I'm sorry, Edmund. I know you were trying to be kind."

"Don't be ridiculous; I was trying to be poetic. Kindness had nothing to do with it."

"Why bother trying to be poetic?"

"To make you smile." He touched the point of her chin. "I should have known, though, you can't be persuaded to do anything you don't want to. Even smile."

"I want to smile. Sometimes." She just didn't feel like it right now. Not after so much time together, with such elusive sweetness, with disappointment inevitable on both sides.

No. Enough of that. No one liked a gloomy crab apple, especially not the gloomy crab apple herself. She tried a smile on.

Edmund covered his eyes and shrank away. "She snarled at me! Help! She showed her teeth like a wolf!"

Jane folded her arms. "Who is ridiculous now?"

Sober in an instant, he folded his arms in return. "Me, I suppose, for putting forth the effort. Yet you still won't smile. And you won't let me ask you if you're having a nice time, or if you're cold. How stubborn you are."

She felt the point of her chin where he had just touched it. "You think I'm stubborn?"

"My dear lady, the whole world *thinks* you're stubborn. But I *know* you are stubborn. And I'm certainly not going to buy you any more gifts today. Now are you going to purchase that hat for yourself or not?" The clownish grin had vanished. Instead, his lips pressed together, curling up at one side. Not a smile, but an expression of exasperation.

Triumph made her hands unsteady as she undid the bow at her chin. In some small way, she had forced him to see her clearly.

"Yes," she decided. "I will buy it, after all."

As Edmund helped Jane back into their carriage, freed from the snarl of traffic and half-filled with packages, there was only one question on his mind.

Why was she so obstinate?

She would not take what he offered in the intended spirit. He'd had to browbeat her into picking out something personal, not just something for the house or the library.

He had warned Jane against the so-called Bellamy as much as he could without telling her the full shameful truth. Now it was up to Edmund to protect her. To do so, he must keep her happy, wrapped up in threads of joy, cocooned from the man's poison. More outings like today's; that would be the answer. Little gifts. Books that pleased her.

Yet she had said she didn't want a small life, hadn't she? And there was not much that was smaller than a cocoon.

But how could he keep her safe if she wouldn't allow him to make her happy?

All right, that was much more than one question. In truth, the uncertainties seemed infinite.

Jane shifted on the seat, elbowing him in the ribs. "Pardon me. We're in tight quarters."

It would have been more convincing as an accident had she not used so much force.

"Think nothing of it," he replied through clenched teeth. A wet blanket of silence settled over them, heavy as the afternoon fog now drifting over the street.

"Last night." Jane cut the silence. "I shut my door to you."

His solicitous voice clicked into place at once. "You may do that whenever you wish."

"I shut my door because"—she paused—"I'm having my courses."

"You're—oh."

"Yes. Right."

"I see."

In the light from the carriage window, he could tell her cheeks had flamed hot. An endless pause succeeded their pointless stammering.

This silence was of a different sort, though. It was a space full of sounds: the soft pull of her breath; the rustle of paper-wrapped parcels sliding on the floor; the dim clamor outside the carriage. Impossible, amidst all these little noises, not to be aware of how alone they were, together. Impossible not to recall the ways they'd been utterly naked with one another, as well as all he withheld from her.

Edmund, I love you, she had told him. Then she had sworn it wouldn't be a problem, and she was as good as her word. She intruded little on his life, so little that every night he felt he was an intrusion on hers. She took nothing from him without begrudging the gift.

But whatever he could give her wouldn't be enough.

"Thank you for telling me," he managed to say. "I wondered if I had somehow displeased you. At the ball."

"You did, but that doesn't matter now. We already talked about that in your study. And what I said is true. That I'm having my—well."

"Oh," he said again.

They hadn't managed to create an heir, then—or a little daughter, either. Much as he'd tried to force a child into existence, with all the urgency of the past snapping at his heels, he had failed.

He wasn't sorry, exactly. Being created not out of love, but out of desperate necessity, was no way to begin one's life. He wished his nonexistent offspring better than that.

As long as he was wishing, he wished himself better than that, too. His parents' marriage had been arranged, with no purpose but the creation of an heir. Now he was repeating their mistakes. It was all he knew.

That, and the fact that marriage was somehow wondrously different for some people.

There was no point in wishing, though, was there? Sometimes things simply *were*, and all one could do was deal with what came next, and next.

"Jane. When you wish me to return"—there was that word, *wish*, again—"just leave your door open."

"All right." Her face was still flushed.

Edmund let the subject drop. Either she would open her door to him, or she wouldn't.

He rummaged for a new topic. A new way to keep her close. "Until then—I remember you mentioned you didn't know how to dance. Would you like me to teach you?"

"Would you really?" She looked at him for the first time since they had clambered into the carriage.

"Yes, I really would. If you want me to."

"I'd love it above all things."

Her smile was bright, but he remembered that she had

used the same words about attending a ball with him. Now, like then, did she agree simply to humor him? He didn't know.

That's all the beginning I need—the not knowing. Then comes the not trusting. And then comes the not loving.

So Turner had said.

And to hear Jane use the word *love* when she meant it not at all—well. Perhaps she had never meant it very much, even when she'd directed it at him.

He didn't know; he didn't know. And he couldn't help but wonder if she was beginning to slip away before he ever figured out how to hold her.

Chapter 11

Concerning Secrets,
Both Likeable and Otherwise

The following day, Lord and Lady Kirkpatrick were invited to a dinner party at the home of Jane's cousin, Lord Xavier, and his wife. On the small scale of this event, Jane was confident she could avoid major social trespass.

Xavier House was a thick slice of dark brick and pale-trimmed stone on the west boundary of Hanover Square. Jane had visited many times before, of course; most recently, to get married in the drawing room. As she proceeded after Edmund into that same room, she wondered at the effect of marriage on a house. Edmund had lived with morose gray walls until Jane splashed green up in their place. During cousin Xavier's bachelor days, he had followed every fashion in décor, most recently surrounding himself with the chilly splendor of gilt and lacquer. Men, on their own, had no notion how to create a true home.

Now the gilt had been relegated to the scrolls and roundels of plasterwork, bright flashes in the candlelight, warm on yellow-papered walls. Instead of lacquer's cold gloss, all the elegant old furniture Xavier had shoved up in the home's attics was back in the drawing room. A warm antique carpet stretched underfoot. Tapestry-covered armchairs; a painted and caned sofa with scrolled arms and a silk cushion. The dinner guests were perched on cushions or toasting themselves before a generous fire.

Xavier came over to greet them, tall and confident, a pucker tugging at his brows. Louisa—his wife and Jane's friend—caught up to him, stately in a long-sleeved gown the purple-blue shade of a bachelor's button. She laid a hand on her husband's sleeve and whispered something in his ear that made him jerk with surprise, then grin.

There seemed to be enough of that grin to share, for Louisa was wearing it too as she shooed him and Edmund away. "Alex, why not find a masculine beverage for your new cousin? Lord Kirkpatrick would undoubtedly like to admire your port bottles."

"You are chasing me away, aren't you?" Xavier dropped a kiss on his wife's head.

"Maybe."

"Don't let Jane be a bad influence on you."

"Perhaps I shall be a bad influence on *her*," Louisa said, waving them off. Then she turned toward Jane. Without preamble, she said, "Your cousin is worried that marriage doesn't suit you."

"He's such an old woman." Jane snorted. "What on earth gives him a reason to think that?"

Louisa let pass the fact that Jane hadn't denied the statement. "He worries because he loves you."

Jane let pass the fact that Louisa hadn't answered her

question. "How sentimental he is. And what did you say to make him smile?"

Louisa went slightly pink. "I reminded him that we got an early start on figuring out . . . ah, certain aspects of marriage. But not everyone does. I think you and Kirkpatrick will deal well together in time, with feeling such as yours to guide you."

Feeling such as hers. Ha. Jane's stomach felt as though she'd swallowed a stone.

Though Jane and Louisa had once discovered a cache of bawdy books together—though they'd talked over their ideal men, and though Jane had first admitted her feelings for Edmund to Louisa—some secrets were too private to share with a friend. Among this number were included the fact that Jane's feelings had led her horribly astray, and that *certain aspects* were the only bits of her marriage that seemed to be going well right now.

Jane caught sight of Edmund, now in conversation with Xavier on the other side of the room. He appeared to be reassuring her cousin, all friendly nonchalance. In the light of an Argand lamp, his fair skin was gilded, his hair darkened, the beautiful bones of his face thrown into highlight and shadow.

Lamplight brought out the best or worst of people; Edmund had only the best to bring out. Her chest squeezed, desire holding her heart in an unyielding fist.

Oh, those *certain aspects*. Oh, how she wanted more, though she'd never even expected to have so much. This careful marriage was like giving an addict only the sweet scent of opium, but none of its smoke. Having Edmund's body was nothing compared to possessing his heart.

At least no one else had his heart instead. She ought to be satisfied with that.

She didn't realize she'd muttered this aloud until Louisa asked, "What did you say?"

Jane met her friend's dark eyes. Louisa's laughter had vanished, now replaced by the same pucker that had creased Xavier's brows.

No. They would not be permitted to worry about her, and they would not pity her. This was a private matter, not even between Jane and her husband. This was a battle with herself, which meant that she alone would win.

"I said . . ." Jane thought quickly. "'At least no one else heard what you said.' Because I would be embarrassed. If someone knew you and Xavier were talking about me."

Louisa relaxed. "Nonsense. We're family, and family cares. But I'll confine my bawdy comments to a mere whisper."

She leaned closer to Jane. "By the by, I asked Xavier to invite Mr. Bellamy, since he is such a particular friend of your mother's."

"My mother's? I thought he was Xavier's friend." Jane frowned. "Maybe Bellamy knew my father before traveling to India." She knew little about the interests of the man who had helped to give her life, then died in her early childhood.

"Bellamy has been a busy man over the past month or two," Louisa said. "Such a far-traveled man fascinates the polite world; I think he's had an invitation almost every night. Lady Alleyneham even held a picnic *al fresco* in his honor."

"What, they ate outside in autumn? The guests must have been half-frozen by the end of it."

"Doubtless they thought a cold rear was not too high a price to pay. No one wishes to miss his thrilling tales." The young countess hesitated. "Jane. I don't mean to question the reputation of any friend of your family. But are you certain all Bellamy's tales are true?"

"I don't know. I've never been to India."

It was a stupid answer, but Louisa let it pass. "Few people in London right now have. And I haven't read much on the local customs, yet it seems—"

"I got a book," Jane broke in. "Well, Kirkpatrick got it. A book about India. When I read it, I'll know more."

Louisa looked relieved. "Good. So Kirkpatrick is wondering about him, too? It's important to—well. Bellamy is a friend of your mother. So. We'll leave it at that."

"Yes," Jane agreed vaguely. All her attention seemed required for keeping a pleasant expression on her face. For neither ignoring Edmund, nor hunting him with her gaze. For being just the right sort of baroness.

The light chatter continued until the guests were called down to dinner. Not sticklers for a strict order of precedence, Xavier and Louisa allowed everyone to walk in as they so chose, and couples took one another's arms in a casual fashion.

Edmund came for Jane, his smile warm. "Having a nice time?"

"I always like to see friends," she replied. So many lies of omission, but they were necessary to win this battle with herself. Looking ahead down the echoing years of her marriage, she would far rather fill the space with friendship than unrequited yearning. She would triumph over her desperate love.

Her body hadn't received notice of this determination: as she hooked her hand around Edmund's arm, sweet heat arced through her.

And it occurred to her that in a battle with herself, she was guaranteed a defeat along with her victory.

* * *

Whether by accident or some design on his part, Bellamy seated himself next to Jane at dinner. Jane wasn't unwilling to speak to him; in fact, she had a topic of conversation at the ready. "Mr. Bellamy, I've recently gotten a book about India. Once I've read it, I'd like to discuss it with you."

He smiled. "I thought we agreed it was to be 'Daniel.'"

She remembered Edmund's cautions and Louisa's doubts. "I don't even call our host—my cousin—by his first name. I think it ought to remain 'Mr. Bellamy.'"

"You called me Daniel once."

"I'm rather impulsive," she said. "Which means I also change my mind."

"A woman's prerogative. Do you change your mind about everything?"

His eyes had gone hard; Jane recognized the signs of frustration. Many times, she had seen that look in the glass. "As much as I need to," she said. "Don't take it to heart, Mr. Bellamy. We're both new to society. We're bound to make a misstep now and then."

"You are right." He forked up some chicken; the meat fell from the tines and he scooped it up with the flat of his knife. "I am honored to be admitted to your inner circle of acquaintances, Lady Kirkpatrick. Especially if your husband proves unforgiving."

"I never said—" Jane glanced at Edmund, several places down on the other side of the table. The look on his face could only be described as a glare: eyes narrowed, lips curled.

In other words, unforgiving.

When his gaze met Jane's, the expression was instantly

wiped from his face. He tossed her a doting smile, then turned his head to the side, as though very interested in what was going on at the head of the table.

"You don't have to say anything about your husband," Bellamy murmured. "Word gets around all the same. He's got a way with the ladies, hasn't he? Always with a beauty or two."

"Not always." Jane stabbed her meat harder than was necessary. "Not this evening."

"You are too modest."

"No. Honest, that's all." Jane laid down her utensils. "Let's not talk about Kirkpatrick. Let's talk about India instead. Won't you tell me another of your stories?"

"Ah, I've no doubt my adventures will seem pale in comparison to the book you've just bought. I shouldn't open myself to criticism like that. My reputation is very fragile, you know."

Jane made a dismissive noise before it occurred to her that baronesses probably didn't make dismissive noises. "I mean," she corrected herself, "That can't be. You must have met half the *ton* by now. Whatever your business, it's bound to be a success by now."

"Why would you say such a thing?" Bellamy studied her closely.

Probably baronesses didn't let a what-the-devil-is-wrong-with-you expression cross their faces either, so Jane managed bland politeness instead. "Only because the *ton* seems very ready to like you. Why, what else could I possibly mean?"

What else, indeed? Behind her sweetly blank face, her mind began to grasp at possibilities. Bloodthirsty, ingenious possibilities. Maybe Bellamy was a pirate? No, more likely a smuggler. Maybe he was a smuggler who was selling things to Edmund, which was why Edmund wouldn't tell her about his business but *would* tell her to stay away from Bellamy.

She smiled. Bellamy relaxed, his sturdy frame sinking against the tall, carved back of his chair. "Nothing at all, dear lady. We men of business get so wrapped up in our plans and schemes that we forget about simple good manners."

Between their plates, his hand found Jane's and closed over it for a moment. Before she could draw it away—or wonder if she ought to—he released it with a friendly pat and picked up a utensil.

Jane shrugged off this odd exchange. Likely he had little notion of what constituted good manners in London; not that Jane herself was much better off. She ventured a glance at the foot of the table, noting which fork Louisa was using and how much of each dish she had served herself.

As she followed the example of Louisa's manners, she said, "You mentioned your business, Mr. Bellamy. What sort is it? I keep thinking of you as a traveler, but it must be for a reason."

"So it is. I trade in whatever will keep me. I've bought and sold things you wouldn't believe. London's an excellent market for—well, let's say, unusual items."

She batted her lashes at him. "How mysterious. Like what?"

He raised his brows. "Do you like secrets, Lady Kirkpatrick?"

The question chased away all her curiosity. Her thoughts tumbled, and she felt as though she were rolling down a hill right after them. *Gambling—love—ten thousand pounds—our swift wedding.* "I used to. I don't like them much anymore."

"Most are hardly worth the telling." Bellamy speared a single pea on the point of his knife. "But they get to be a habit. For some people." He popped the pea into his mouth.

"I can imagine."

Oh, she could. Until recently, she hadn't realized how many secrets of her own she held. For all the years of her upbringing, she had hidden her impatience with village life. She had concealed her ability to count cards from one gambling partner after another. Year after year, she had kept her love for Edmund a secret without even meaning to.

She didn't have any secrets left now. Shouldn't honesty bring people together? Yet she felt farther away from Edmund now than she had on the evening he'd blundered into Sheringbrook's card room. Her name on his lips; her heart—though he'd no idea of it—in his keeping.

She glanced at Edmund again. He still had his head turned to the side away. Not looking at her. Not eating much. But he was doing a damned lot of talking. Not to a beauty, though; to Louisa's aunt, Lady Irving. A woman many would describe as *formidable* or *terrifying*. Yet Edmund had her smiling. Hooting, even.

Jane wanted a little part of that joy. She had a sudden devilish urge to call across the table, *Edmund dear, if you should begin not to have a nice time, I'll trust you to tell me.*

But with Xavier at one end of the table and Louisa at the other, and with a motley yet gracious variety of guests in between, she decided against making a spectacle of them both.

"Do you think your husband—" Bellamy began, then paused. "I'm not sure how *ton* marriages work. Do you think he keeps secrets from you?"

With an effort, Jane tugged her gaze back to her dining partner. "I've no doubt he does," she said airily. "But they don't matter."

"You are a remarkably tolerant woman, then, aren't you?"

"No. I'm not." She considered her reply. Knowing Edmund didn't care for Bellamy made her a little more cautious. "Everyone has a right to privacy," she finally said.

Bellamy merely looked skeptical and started fooling about with his utensils.

"That knife is for fruit, I think," Jane murmured.

"Are you certain of that?"

"Mostly."

Lady Alleyneham, blithe and breathless as always, spoke above the quiet chat around the table. "How I do admire those pearls! And it's so good to see you out and about. Are you feeling quite the thing, Lady Sheringbrook?"

At the sound of the name Sheringbrook, Jane dropped her fork. But the voice that replied to the name was cultured and female. "I am well, thank you."

Sanity returned in a quick flash: *Lady* Sheringbrook. The mother of Jane's nemesis. Dowager viscountess and unfortunate mother to a card cheat, she sat close to the head of the table: a woman in late middle age, her hair prematurely snowy, her posture straight and proud. Gray silk and a set of large and beautifully matched pearls added to her dignity.

Yet as Jane watched, a tremor shook the woman's

hand, and her fork clattered so that all the food fell from it.

"I do beg your pardon," she said. The statement sounded tired, as though it had been trotted out too many times.

Freddie Pellington, a friendly young dandy to the dowager's left, said, "Dash it, Lady Sheringbrook, won't you allow me—"

"I'm fine, Mr. Pellington, as I have told you before." The woman's voice was steel beneath velvet-soft diction. "Simply because my hands grow disobedient does not mean you need be."

Abandoning her fork, she clasped her hands together. Twitches racked the folded fists every few seconds. She had no more control over her own extremities than she did over her son. Yet she sat straight, her face serene.

Pity was too small an emotion for a woman with such determined dignity. Jane decided on respect instead.

Louisa broke the awkward silence. "Will you try the brioche, ma'am? The pastry cook is most eager that we should admire his talents. I believe he uses cheese curds in the making of it." At the foot of the table, Louisa took a bit of the rich bread for herself, then motioned for a footman to hand the platter around.

By tacit agreement, brioche became the new staple on everyone's plate. When everyone was crumbling bread about, the viscountess's hands might do what they wished, and she need not go hungry.

Well done, Louisa. Jane grinned at her friend and stuffed a bite of the buttery bread in her mouth. The crumbs melted on her tongue, salty-sweet.

In the delight of eating delicious food and admiring her friend's perceptive manners, Jane had forgotten her dinner companion. "You seemed startled, Lady Kay, to see Lady Sheringbrook here."

She turned back to Bellamy to see him regarding her closely. Close indeed; their faces were but a foot and a half apart. She had never noticed before how much gray threaded through his hair. Though she had assumed he was in his late thirties, he must be older.

The notion that she had seen him incorrectly unsettled her, though it was none of his doing. "Not at all. I've never met the lady before."

"Yet her name means something to you?"

Jane waved the hand that held her brioche. "I've met her son before. That's all. I think everyone's met her son." She gave a little laugh to show that the subject was of no importance.

Bellamy seemed interested, though. "Her son? He's— oh, what's the popular cant now? *Not the thing*?"

"I would hardly say so, with his mother sitting at the same table." Jane kept her voice low.

"But in private company . . ."

She gave in. "Private company with Lord Sheringbrook is no place to be."

Bellamy settled back in his chair. "Please forgive my curiosity, Lady Kay. I simply don't want to make a blunder by falling in with the wrong sort. A man of business must be careful. You understand?"

"Oh, I do indeed. A woman of not-business must be careful, too." She paused. "You'd best call me Lady Kirkpatrick."

"Your wish is my command." His smile was all white teeth and roguery.

When Edmund had spoken that phrase—*your wish is my command*—Jane had wished for him. Now the phrase itself reminded her of her husband. How unfair, that he should take ownership of simple phrases when the world already contained far too many reminders of his presence.

Such as, well, his presence itself. Jane peeked at him beneath her lashes. He was still in conversation with Louisa's aunt, Lady Irving. Whatever she was crowing about, he gave every appearance of being fascinated.

Lord, he had good manners.

Jane turned away from him. "Tell me, Mr. Bellamy. How long were you in India?"

His smile slid to one side. "Would you care to make a guess?"

"I shouldn't. I don't want to sound insulting or ignorant, and I don't have enough knowledge to avoid them both."

"The two greatest sins of society. You are right to avoid them. As a matter of fact, I've been away for twenty years."

"You must have been very young when you left."

He shrugged. "Some would say I was old enough to know better. Though some would say I never learned to act my age."

Jane cast another glance in Edmund's direction. Now he had the countess pounding his forearm and chortling.

"Age doesn't matter at all," she said. Certainly Lady Irving had more energy than any young woman Jane had ever met.

"Ah, you are flattering me!"

Jane turned back to Bellamy with some surprise. "No, I wasn't speaking of you." She realized this wasn't precisely polite. "I mean, I'm sure it's true of you as well. As it is of . . . many people."

He let her floundering pass. As the meal meandered

on, the hard look never returned to Bellamy's eyes. Instead, as he spoke with Jane—asking her questions about London, tugging forth her opinions—he seemed to soften. There was something lonely about the man. He'd been gone for so long, England must now seem foreign to him. Perhaps he had even left behind loved ones in India, though he never mentioned a family.

"Do you have a family?" She couldn't resist asking, though the question had nothing to do with his just-completed tale about an elephant that had been trained to pick peaches and drop the food for poor children.

"Ah." He shifted topics smoothly. "You are the first to ask me such a question, my lady."

He looked up and down the length of the table; Jane couldn't tell if his gaze snagged on Edmund, or if it only seemed that way because hers did. "I had a family once, long ago. Before I left for India. But they were lost to me."

"I don't mean to pry." Jane paused. "Well, yes, I do. Did they meet with an accident? I only wonder because you seem to be missing them. Or someone."

"Yes, they met with an accident, and I lost them all at once." He smiled. "But it was so long ago. We should not allow the events of decades ago to spoil our lives now." He raised a wineglass, which he'd had filled rather a lot of times. "If there's anything I miss while I travel, it's good company. And that's not found by poking through old memories. It's found at table."

As he spoke, his voice rose, drawing more than a few curious glances. "Hear, hear," chimed in Freddie Pellington, who clinked glasses with Lady Sheringbrook.

As others followed suit, a round of impromptu toasts circled the table. Lord Weatherwax, a cheerful inebriate with wild white hair, toasted the drink itself. Lady Irving toasted Louisa and Xavier, calling the latter a "rapscallion."

Jane approved. Raising her own glass, she announced, "I don't have anything to say. But I've never given a toast before, and I wanted to."

"A good enough reason. Drink up, everyone," barked Lady Irving.

Xavier shook his head. "Jane, you are a rascally imp." He lifted his glass. "To my rascally imp of a cousin, and my old friend Kirkpatrick. I can think of no one in whose hands I would rather have placed Jane, except for those of a madhouse keeper."

Jane frowned. "Wait. Are you giving me a compliment or him a curse?"

"My dear cousin, it is a fervent hope for your future happiness."

"Then just say that instead."

"Now it won't sound original." Xavier regarded his glass with some doubt. "Ah, well. For a good cause. Best wishes for future happiness to our newly wed pair. And to the rest of you, too. Why should all of you be denied my best wishes, simply because you didn't happen to marry my cousin Jane?"

At the opposite end of the table, Louisa added, "Very diplomatic, and sensible, too. Good wishes cost the giver nothing, but may mean everything to the one receiving them."

"Lady Xavier is always saying wise things like that," Xavier said.

A small smile touched Louisa's lips. "Lord Xavier thinks he can discomfit me by analyzing everything I say.

But if he recalls the fact that I married him, he will surely realize that I cannot be discomfited."

Jane said, "Xavier, I think she just gave you a compliment *and* a curse, all at once." The rest of the table relaxed into chuckles and chattering.

"Happiness in marriage," Bellamy muttered at Jane's side. "There's a fable as sure as the City of Atlantis."

"Not at all. Why, just look." She indicated the foot of the table, from which Louisa regarded her husband with a smile. It was the sort that ought to be reserved for private moments, intimate pleasures. There was nothing salacious in it; it was just so honest. The smile of a woman delighted to be in company with the man she loved; the smile of a woman in love.

"Miracles do happen," Bellamy admitted. "Families are lost, then found again. Men are born who change the course of a nation. Today of all days, we should remember that."

"Why today?"

He blinked at her. "Why? Well—because. We're drawing near Christmas."

"Then why today? Why not . . . oh, five weeks from today, or however long it is?"

"Ah, Lady Kirkpatrick, when you reach my age, you'll regard every day as an opportunity. To right a wrong, to do one's best."

"I'll drink to that," Jane decided.

The meal continued with toasts and brioche and the promise of new day after new day. It was all going rather well. Eventually she would master this life as a baroness.

Since she wasn't given all that much to master, it ought to be within her power.

Again she searched out Edmund across the table. He was in full bloom, bringing a laugh to Lady Irving's lips and a smile to the watching Lady Sheringbrook.

His mouth made all the right shapes, but there was no joy in his eyes. Had they always been like that, or had she never looked closely enough to notice before?

Jane wondered whether happiness in marriage—though not a fable—was a rarer miracle than she had supposed.

Chapter 12

Concerning Revolution

All through dinner, Turner had chatted with Jane, playing the man of business, the world traveler. And all through dinner, Edmund had been forced to play a part, too: the friendly bridegroom who had nothing on his mind but the meal before him. And the conversation of his hostess's blunt-spoken aunt, Lady Irving, who sat at his right.

"You'll never keep that wife of yours satisfied if you can't keep her closer than this," the widowed countess said after two glasses of wine, not that she needed the assistance of spirits to speak her mind. "Brides need a lot of tending, you young rogue."

"Tending? Like gardens?" Edmund blinked innocently at his dinner companion.

"I thought you'd enough experience with women not to be such a ninny." With a practiced hand, she straightened her bright orange shot-silk turban. "*Tending*, man. Tending. Make her feel—hmm."

"Treasured," said Edmund, just as Lady Irving added, "Pleasured."

They looked at one another and grinned. "Treasured would work, at that," the countess granted. "But she's neither treasured nor pleasured while she's sitting next to that jumped-up ninny of a tradesman."

Edmund could hardly disguise his pleasure in hearing Turner called a jumped-up ninny. "Perhaps," he replied, "my wife is so well satisfied with my company that she has no need for large doses."

The countess's smile vanished. "It would be dangerous to think so." She set down her wineglass, turning its stem between her fingertips. "Dangerous to take a wife for granted, especially at this early stage of your marriage."

"Dangerous? How so?" Edmund tried for a light tone. From the corner of his eye, he watched Jane and Turner. The false Bellamy. The liar who held Edmund's past and future in his blunt-fingered hands. Hands that he had just lain over Jane's.

Edmund's insides felt knotted and acid-burned. Somehow, he had to get Turner out of his life and away from those who relied on him, but he had no more notion how to do that now than he had twenty years before.

Lady Irving rested her hand on his arm, drawing his gaze back to her. "Think about the sort of marriage you want, young man. If you'd like to whore around London, coming home only to get an heir, then by all means, carry on."

"I would never treat my wife thus." Well, not the whoring-around-London part.

Spin spin spin. Lady Irving rotated her wineglass by its stem again, then folded her hands in her lap. "I suppose not. But Jane is my niece's cousin-in-law, which makes her almost my family. I would hate to think she married a damned fool."

"So would I."

With a low bark of laughter, the countess said, "That's a start, young man. That's a start. Now, mind you keep her pleasured and treasured."

"I'm trying," Edmund muttered. "If she would only let me give—"

He cut himself off, not wanting to discuss the failure of his usual being-good-to-everyone methods on Jane, but the countess seemed to understand. "It's like that, then; I see. Jane can be a stubborn wench. Just like her aunt-in-law, or whatever relation I am to her."

Her garish orange turban slipped, loosing a few strands of auburn hair. "I might have spoken out of turn; I can guarantee it won't be the last time I do so. But mind you think less about what she won't allow and more about what she will. Don't give up on that wife of yours. She's a girl after my own heart, and that means she won't give hers lightly."

"Yes," Edmund said, not knowing exactly what he was agreeing with. Jane had told him—once, only once—that her heart was already his. But for how long if there was always a wall between them, whether of plaster and brick or of deathly politeness? How long could love last, unfed and unwatered? And did he even want it to?

At the mere thought, *fed*, his stomach wrenched with a protest. With Turner across the table, and Lady Irving testing his resolve to keep a damned smile on his face, he regretted every bite he'd choked down.

Fortunately, the conversation around the table took a turn then, and the group started toasting one another. By the time the women rose to leave the dining room,

Edmund had put a lid on the dreadful feelings Turner awoke. He had slipped once, early in the meal; Jane had caught him glaring at Turner. She could not have known why, yet the distance that slivered between her and Turner had pleased Edmund.

She came no closer to Edmund, but as long as she was farther away from Turner, he would settle for that. And though there was no opportunity to speak to her before the women trailed into the drawing room, leaving the men behind at table, her departure placed walls between her and Turner. Physical walls, surely more of a barrier than the one between her and Edmund.

He would settle for that, too.

Around the long wooden table, Xavier offered cigars. "From Fox of St. James's," he said, naming one of the *ton*'s favorite tobacconists. Port came next. The ever-tipsy Lord Weatherwax, whose blunted nose was already beginning to redden, took a glass in each hand and had drained both before the other men had laid hold of their own port.

"Dreadful weather and whatnot," said cherubic Freddie Pellington, standing before the fire and rubbing his hands together. "Dash it, London's no place for a gentleman in autumn. Can't keep my cravat starched properly with all the mist in the air."

"Damned nuisance to come back to London so early." Lord Alleyneham, a stern-faced earl, hooked his ebony-headed walking stick on the back of his chair, then belched and stretched out a hand for a glass of port. "Ought to be in the country shooting, what? I would be, but for the damned rebels at Peterloo. Bloody traitors."

Ah, the Peterloo massacre, as the papers were calling it. Edmund had lately been so caught up in his own problem—the problem that now stood in the corner of the dining room, playing with a gold cigar case—that he'd forgotten the lords who had left town had been recalled for a special session of Parliament. Over the summer, a peaceful worker protest in Manchester had been broken up by cavalry, with gruesome results. The Prince Regent and Home Secretary were determined such a thing would never happen again: not the attack, but the very act of protest.

"Ought to have been shot, the lot of them," Lord Alleyneham was now adding. His tongue chased the last drops of port around his glass.

"Many of them *were* shot," Xavier said. "Yet they were not armed, were they? They were simply hungry. On the backs of people like these rests our livelihood; should we not lessen their burdens when we can?"

Lord Alleyneham's mouth went flat. "Sounding rather Whiggish, aren't you? Thought you were a good Tory. Member of White's and all that."

"Goodness has nothing to do with one's political leanings." Xavier bowed his head to the older earl. "Though I am honored that you should associate goodness with me in any way."

Turner flipped open his cigar case, then snapped it shut. "If the Peterloo crowd had gone at the cavalry with bricks and bats, there would be none of this puling. Either they'd have got what they wanted, or they'd be punished right clear."

"Damned lucky they didn't rise up," Alleyneham said. "There were what, fifty thousand there? They'd have overwhelmed the cavalry in a second. But then you can't expect peasants to possess an understanding of arithmetic." He leaned back in his chair, setting his walking stick to swinging like a clock pendulum. *Tick*, it went, as the ebony head of it rocked back and forth. It seemed the voice of time itself, tugging on Edmund with dreadful force.

The subject was all too familiar to Edmund. Too familiar, the protests by a desperate crowd; too familiar, the violence and blood. More than twenty years had passed, yet it was not long enough to forget.

He tried for a calm voice. "It had less to do with arithmetic than human decency, Alleyneham. Even a child can tell that a crowd is more powerful than a few mounted riders. The workers wanted to be heard, not to hurt."

Turner raised his brows. "What does a child know of revolution?"

Edmund wished that his pale skin didn't flush so easily. They might attribute it to the port; Alleyneham and Weatherwax had already grown ruddy. "In an ideal world," Edmund said, "a child would know nothing of revolution at all. But this is hardly an ideal world. Sometimes children are pulled into the struggles of adults, and they must cope as best they can."

Xavier looked at him oddly; then an expression of amused tolerance draped their host's features. "Indeed, Kirkpatrick. In comparison, adults are damnably complacent—at least, we often are in Parliament. I've no idea how the voting will shake out, but we wouldn't be having a special session of Parliament if the Prince Regent wasn't a bit nervous."

"Quite right." Alleyneham blinked pouchy eyes. "Think of that Irish uprising in, what was it?"

"1798," Edmund supplied. His fingers went cold, and he set down his port glass. At once, he picked it up again so his hands would have something with which to busy themselves.

Alleyneham's walking stick clattered to the floor. "Right, right, 1798," he said loudly as a footman raced to pick it up. "Those rebels killed thousands, didn't they, and laid waste to half of Ireland. And how did it all turn out? With their leaders executed and their Parliament dissolved. People who can't rule themselves must be ruled with an ever-tighter fist, and there's an end to it."

"Ah, but that wasn't an end to it." Turner opened his case again, taking his time selecting a cigar.

"How do you mean, sir?" Alleyneham was looking still redder.

"The spirit of revolution survived." With a tiny blade, Turner lopped off the end of his cigar. "If the government tightens its fist too much, people become accustomed to slipping through its fingers, don't they?"

"You are right," Xavier admitted. "There was another uprising in the early 1800s, wasn't there? Around—oh, I'd say 1803. I had just gone to school when it took place."

"It went nowhere. Quickly quashed, just like this Peterloo nonsense." Alleyneham eyed Turner's cigar case with some interest. "Having one of your fine Indian cigars, Bellamy?"

"Indeed, my lord." The so-called Bellamy walked over to the earl, holding forth the case. "You're welcome to one."

"Don't mind if I do."

Edmund watched as England's greatest fraud handed off a cigar to England's most complacent old lion. What would Alleyneham do if Edmund were to shout, *he's lying to you; he's as bad as those you've called traitors. Worse, far worse.*

And those cigars could not *possibly* be from India.

He couldn't shout it, though; it would be the work of a moment for Turner to spit his own truths right back. The man hadn't plotted treason alone, nor committed adultery by himself. Edmund could never implicate Turner without destroying what was left of his own family, himself, and now—Jane, too.

Inside, he boiled; a boiling that tightened his fingers on the curve of his glass and made him wish it was Turner's neck. He wanted to crush the man who had taken so much and who was back now, cheerful and vile, to take everything else.

Snip. Turner cut off the end of Alleyneham's cigar. "There you are, my lord. Enjoy it."

"Indeed. I thank you, Bellamy." Lord Alleyneham took a puff, and an acrid smell like burning manure wafted from the end. "It has an interesting bouquet, hasn't it?"

Again, Xavier offered his own sort, and the conversation was directed from politics to tobacco before a towering argument took place.

Edmund made his way to the fireplace. Setting his glass on the mantel, he rubbed his hands together. Either the autumn weather was bleeding into winter as November fled by or the chill came from within, as Edmund was forced to keep a damned smile on his face while Turner lied and lied.

"Enjoying the conversation, my lord? It's a fine day for talk of revolution."

Turner. Of course, Turner had followed him to the edge of the room. His flat voice was unmistakable, as were the scents of pomade and cheap cigars.

"Not now, please," Edmund said without turning. "Really, not ever."

"Wolfe Tone," Turner continued, "died on this day twenty-one years ago. Finest of the Irish revolutionaries. It's fitting we should talk of his cause today, don't you think? So much to celebrate and mourn."

Edmund turned. "Is it his cause, or yours?"

"Hmm." Turner shrugged. He was still working his cigar cutter, probably liking its clean sound of destruction. *Snip snip.* The tiny blade winked sharp and gilded in the candlelight. Edmund wondered, dimly, where the man got all his money.

No. No need to wonder. He was brilliant at persuading money from people, and if that failed, stealing it. The ends justified the means, so far as Turner was concerned.

The idea made Edmund's knees watery. The ends justified the means, and Turner's end now was turning Jane's loyal heart away. So what would the means be?

Anything. Anything. But this time, Edmund was a grown man, not a boy, and he would protect his own. "Go away, Turner. You've already inflicted far too much of your presence on me."

"Tut, tut. Just inquiring after your welfare, I was."

"My welfare would be significantly improved if we were never in one another's presence again."

Turner clipped the end off a cigar. "Likewise, boyo. Yet here we are. Neither of us can leave unless the other gives in."

"Ah, Bellamy, are you sharing one of your good Indian smokes?" Lord Weatherwax called in a voice thick with drink. "Enjoy it, Kirkpatrick."

Edmund offered what he hoped was a careless grin. "Never know when we'll find a new favorite, do we, Weatherwax?"

He waited for the nobleman to continue drowning

himself in port before turning back to accept the unwanted cigar, now lit, wrapping him in its acrid odor.

"This smells of the stable yard," he muttered. "Hardly a fine imported cigar, is it?"

Turner took up a glass of port, then smiled. The same diplomat's expression that had once eased him through negotiations with Edmund's father; through lover's quarrels with Edmund's mother. "It amuses me," he said, letting the words lilt in his true accent, "to see a lord puff away at the worst sort of mundungus, simply because he thinks it's from another part of the world."

"There's nothing wrong with wanting to try new things." In Edmund's mind's eye, he saw Jane's face, eager as she asked if they might travel. "It shows openness of character."

"It shows foolishness, to believe everything one's told." He looked Edmund up and down. "But then, you've always been that way. *Dob*—"

"*Dobhránta*. Yes, yes. Get a new word, won't you? I think you've done all you can with that one." Edmund motioned for a footman and handed off the horrid cigar. When he turned back, his former tutor was staring at him with grudging approval.

"What?"

"You could've put it out in my port, couldn't you?"

"That would have done a disservice to the port, besides drawing unwanted attention to our conversation."

Slowly, Turner shook his head. "Unaccountable lad."

"I'm no more a lad than that was an Indian cigar." He paused. "Turner, if you keep up this ruse of life in India, you'll be caught out soon. Not everyone is credulous or untraveled—which are *not* the same thing, nor anything to be ashamed of," he added when a smirk began to form on the man's features.

"Hasn't happened yet, has it? People believe whatever they're told. Why, I got your wife's silly little mother to invite me to the wedding, didn't I? Swore I was your father's oldest friend —"

Edmund spluttered.

"—but I told her I couldn't possibly intrude when you hadn't known me well yourself. No, no; not even for the sake of family." He put a hand over his heart, his expression a mockery of sentiment. "The more I insisted, the more she did, too. Ah, Mrs. Tindall, the good-hearted dupe. I can see why you settled on her daughter."

"Don't," Edmund said low, "talk of my wife or her family."

"Why not? You talk of my family all the time."

"They were *my* family." Edmund caught himself. "Are. They *are* my family. Not yours. Not in any real sense."

"What's a real sense to you?" Turner sipped at his port, then set his glass on the mantel beside Edmund's. "A blood tie? I've that as much as you. You can't say it's spending time together, for you've admitted yourself, you've not been back in twenty years."

How could Turner speak so calmly? How could he claim a right to any piece of a family he'd done his best to ruin? If they hadn't been tucked into the corner of a dining room, Edmund would have called him out for sheer gall.

But he couldn't. He couldn't even raise his voice. More reputations than his own were tied to the way he behaved. Again, Edmund felt his dreadful connection to Turner.

They could hold one another at the edge of the cliff, or they could both tumble from its edge.

The edge lured him with a keening siren's song. But Edmund stepped back. This time.

In a low voice choked with anger, he said, "I consider that a family is made up of people for whom one takes responsibility. In that sense, you've never had any family at all."

"And whose fault was that?"

Edmund didn't hesitate. "Yours. You could have done the honorable thing before my parents were married. Stayed behind in Ireland. Accepted that there was no place for you in England."

Turner took out another cigar and snipped off the end with a brutal gesture; then another section, and another, before tossing all the pieces into the fire. "Your mum and I had love on our side. What was a marriage of convenience compared to that?"

"Everything. Once she took her vows, you should have left her alone. Love had nothing to do with it."

"Is that what you tell your wife? When you take her every night, all business and duty? 'Love's got nothing to do with this, Lady Kay. Now spread your legs.'"

Disgusted, Edmund shook his head. "How foul you have become. My marriage has nothing to do with this conversation, or with you. And neither will my wife."

"You keep wishing for that, and see how it works for you." Turner clapped him on the back. "Pardon me, boyo. Lord Weatherwax!" he called in his horrid, flat Bellamy voice as he began to move away. "Care for another of my Indian cigars? How about you, Mr. Pellington?"

Edmund grimaced. Shuddered, like a dog shaking off

a chilly drenching. He reached for his glass, ready to toss back the warming spirits and chase a bit of oblivion.

But there were two cut-crystal tumblers on the mantel. He couldn't remember which glass was his and which Turner's.

Never mind, then. Instead, he leaned against the wall next to the fireplace, pasting a sleepy smile over his features so the other guests would ignore him.

Turner was right: they were bound together. Perhaps if he had been able to expose the man's false identity at once, he could have prevented this terrible charade. But he'd been blind. Stuck too deep in the past to recognize how it appeared here and now. And Turner had become a novelty, lifted up and held to the light by the *beau monde*, just like a glass ornament. If Edmund smashed it, he— as much as Turner—would be injured. And so would his family. They were all living a respectable life only because no one knew the truth.

It seemed secrets had become a habit he couldn't shake, like other men became steeped in drink or fascinated by whores. Edmund could almost wish for such an escape; to forget oneself, even for a few minutes, in a bottle or a bed.

When the men heaved themselves from the table and lurched upstairs to the drawing room, Jane's was the first face Edmund sought. And when she smiled at him, he smiled back.

There were, as yet, a few things Turner hadn't spoiled.

When they returned home that night, Edmund bade Jane farewell until the morning. The door of her bedchamber closed him out with a soft sigh of hinges. This time, though, Edmund knew why there was a wall between them. And in a few days, it would come down.

Until then, and ever after, he would devote himself to making her the happiest of women. Pleasured and treasured. Somehow, he would find a way.

Such a victory was essential.

Chapter 13

Concerning Theft, Pain, and Sleep

A few days later, Parliament began its special session, and Edmund spent long afternoons away in the House of Lords.

Jane found these afternoons endless. In the country, one might tear about, clambering over ruins or shooting at any furred creature unwise enough to poke its head from its burrow. Then return home, heart pumping with joyous exertion, for an early supper of hearty meats and cider.

In London, the hour was too early to dine and too late to pay calls. And shopping seemed a waste of time when Jane had already been given every item she wanted and many that she didn't. She tried to amuse herself with her new atlas, but the bright-tinted maps seemed to taunt her, and she soon closed the book and laid it aside on a drawing-room table.

For the first time, London had failed her. So she would have to make her own diversion.

It was the work of a few minutes to send a messenger

to Lady Audrina Bradleigh, and within an hour, the two women met for an outing in Hyde Park.

The winter sky was gray and hazy, greased by coal smoke and made surly by clouds hanging low overhead. Though they threatened rain, the weather kept its peace for now, and Jane and Audrina were two among many of the quality who took the chance to promenade.

"I'm glad you wanted to walk out today," Audrina said. "My parents are being intolerable. Papa has been ranting about scoundrels and ruffians and revolution for days on end. With the opening of Parliament, he'll finally have new people at whom to rant."

"Lord Kirkpatrick has taken up his seat, too. Probably without quite so much ranting."

"If he can't froth at the mouth a bit, he'll never make himself heard. No one listens to anyone else. Or such is my impression of Parliament."

"What's the fun of shouting if no one hears? I used to be annoyed that women couldn't hold seats in Parliament," Jane mused. "But maybe I won't bother anymore. There are so many other things to be annoyed about instead."

Such as the fact that walking next to her taller friend made her feel like a bit of broccoli: a little sprout, all in green; her pelisse in a dark shade, her gown in a pale color. She had preferred the color to all others since Edmund once gave her a compliment. The morning after their marriage, when she had felt as though she had to leave or cry, yet neither was an option.

And then he had told her he liked her dress.

Silly of her to care, when he said that sort of thing all the time, to all sorts of people. Yet one's clothing had to be some color, didn't it? So it might as well be green.

Draped in a cloak of deep red wool and velvet, Audrina looked as beautiful as a hothouse rose, all deep colors and sweeping curves. A bit thorny, too, in the way she swept along on the park paths, scattering those who sought her attention.

"If you want something else to annoy you," Audrina grumbled, "do allow me to suggest my mother. I mentioned that *both* of my parents were being horrid, didn't I? She gets as fussed as my father does. Look."

She pulled back the edge of her cloak to display a gown fairly spangled with brooches and pins.

"Er," said Jane. "She wanted you to wear an entire jewel box at once?"

As Audrina let the cloak drop again, Jane noticed it was closed with not one pin, but three. "Aren't those evening pieces? With real stones?"

Audrina's gloved hands covered them, then clasped together in a gesture of frustration. "Yes. It's silly, isn't it?"

"Wearing evening pieces during the day? Well. Not if you like them."

"Three at once. On a cloak." The earl's daughter blew out an impatient breath. "It *is* silly. But Mama insisted I wear everything today."

"Are you for sale?" Jane teased.

"You're more right than you realize," Audrina said drily. "What's a dowry, after all, but a sale price?"

"Oh." Jane didn't precisely adore the subject of dowries.

"But as to the jewels," Audrina continued, "I'm to wear them for safekeeping. Ever since Lady Sheringbrook's pearls were stolen—"

"What? When?"

Audrina's brow furrowed. "A few days ago. The day after that dinner party at Xavier House." She lowered her voice below the crunch of their feet on the graveled path. "They were stolen out of her very house, from some safe or locked cupboard or whatever it was."

"Oh! Those beautiful matched pearls." Jane remembered how they had clasped the neck and wrists and ears of the dignified viscountess. Each was perfect: gray-tinted and iridescent like the throat of a pigeon.

Jane wished she could recall society's rules, like the depth of a curtsy to a countess, as easily as she remembered cards and gems. Alas, she seemed to have the mind of a pirate.

"At least Lady Sheringbrook knows where to look for the thief." Jane's fists clenched. "Considering her son is a—"

"I know what you're thinking." Audrina shook her head. "That her awful son took them. But it couldn't have been him because he was in company. Playing cards for an entire day and night."

"It was simply some chance thief, then?"

"I doubt it was chance." Audrina's gloved hand covered the top brooch pinning her cloak, a sunburst of rubies and topaz. "Lady Sheringbrook's pearls are famous, and nothing else was taken."

"She was lucky, then."

"I don't think she feels lucky." Her friend's hand tightened about the jeweled piece. "I think she feels violated. Someone came into her home without her knowledge and took something of far more value to her than money."

The hoarseness in Audrina's voice caught Jane's notice, but her new friend only looked away to the rippling grass at the edge of the path.

"You may be right," Jane said. "I hadn't thought of it like that."

"I hadn't thought of it any other way." Her clenched hand flexed, fluttered, fell to her side. When she looked back at Jane, her gaze slid off after only a moment.

Jane narrowed her eyes. Something was bothering Audrina, that was obvious. Their acquaintance was a bit new for painful truths, but Jane decided to make the venture. "Is something bothering you?"

"I'm fine." The smile that crossed the taller woman's features was as lovely as it was false. "Just feeling ridiculous, draped in every bit of jewelry I own for a simple walk in the park. But since the theft, Mama insists that the only safe place for jewels is on her person. She has been dripping with gemstones ever since and insisting that we daughters do the same."

"Isn't she worried about pickpockets?"

"I'm in no danger from thieves." The autumn breeze had brought high color to Audrina's cheeks; a flare of sudden emotion made them still more ruddy. "Did you not observe our company? I'm followed by a maid, a groom, and a footman."

Jane glanced around, catching sight of two burly men, one in livery, slipping along behind nearby trees. "Lord. Your parents really do want your jewelry to be safe."

"This is how I'm always made to walk out, jewels or no."

"With three servants?" At her friend's nod, Jane said, "Then your parents want you to be safe, too."

"No, they want to keep me under watch. They don't trust me."

Jane choked. "Ha. What a coincidence. No one trusts me either."

Audrina raised a brow. "What did you do?"

Gambled away my dowry. "Oh, nothing so very bad," Jane said lightly. "You?"

"Something very bad indeed: I was born a daughter when there were already four in the family. My sisters have been bad, too, since none of them has married a duke yet, as my mother wishes. Now we're all on the shelf."

"I don't think you're on the shelf at all. But if you were—well, from a shelf, one can see everything that's going on. It's an excellent place for the curious."

"I'm not curious anymore," Audrina said. "I'm desperate."

She stopped walking, her hand catching Jane's arm. "Forget I said anything, won't you? It's not bad. I could be much less fortunate. I know that."

"Yes," agreed Jane. "But just because things could always be worse doesn't mean we can't wish them better."

"Why, Jane, you are a philosopher."

Jane waved a hand. "No, that's probably the only wise thing I've ever said in my life. Don't tell, please. Lord Kirkpatrick is convinced I'm bloodthirsty and impetuous."

"I can only hope," Audrina said, "to meet a man someday who thinks me bloodthirsty and impetuous."

"There are better things to be thought."

Audrina looked puzzled. "Surely Lord Kirkpatrick has made you a good husband."

Jane would not cast aspersions on her marriage. Not in front of the servants; not in front of the daughter of an earl. "I cannot imagine him making anyone a better husband."

How could he? He didn't love anyone—or, just a little, he loved everyone.

* * *

"I met a friend today," Jane told Edmund at dinner late that evening.

He looked up sharply from the soup he'd been stirring. "Bellamy?"

"No. Lady Audrina Bradleigh." She frowned at her husband. "You always bring up Bellamy. Why?"

"Never mind." He swallowed a huge spoonful of soup, then choked. "Nothing. No reason."

When she slammed down her silver spoon, it echoed her aggravation with a satisfyingly loud *clack*. "There must be a reason. Now. Is it to do with me, or to do with him?"

"Him," Edmund wheezed. "Excuse me." He coughed into his napkin. "I beg your pardon. I'm not accustomed to—"

"Eating at mealtimes?"

He narrowed his eyes. "Swallowing half a bowl of soup at once."

"What about Bellamy?" Jane refused to be diverted.

"I think." Edmund fiddled with his spoon, then pushed aside his bowl. "I think he has a *tendre* for you."

"Impossible."

Edmund raised an eyebrow. "Who sat next to you at dinner at Xavier House? With whom were you in conversation at the Alleyneham House ball?"

"He's just lonely. I'm the only person in the *ton* who's as much of an outsider as he."

"I sincerely doubt you have much in common with the man."

"I never said I did." Wariness prickled between her

shoulder blades. Had she encouraged Bellamy's attention through her friendliness? She knew that many of the quality took their marriage vows lightly; perhaps he assumed Jane would be the same way. "I don't think I've ever done anything to encourage him. Have I?"

"Bellamy doesn't require encouragement to be encouraged." Edmund said as a footman collected the soup plates. "I've observed that his encouragement comes from—"

"Is this to be another of those sentences where you wind yourself up in knots by the end?"

He smiled. "I think not. But it's better I put an end to it all the same. Nothing more about Bellamy; tell me about your meeting with Lady Audrina. Is this the first time you've seen her since the ball at her parents' home?"

"It is." Jane waited until the soup plate vanished and was replaced by a dinner plate of crested china. She chose sauced beef and honey-glazed carrots before adding, "She's the first friend I've made in London."

A strange sound issued from the other end of the table. It sounded like "wwww" but ended in a clearing of the throat. "Very nice, I'm sure."

"Were you going to say, 'what about Bellamy'?"

"I thought better of it just in time." Edmund poked through his own carrots with a fork. "It's not your fault if someone chooses to take a liking to you."

"No," she said faintly. Such a statement could not help but remind her of her own foolish regard for the man at the head of the table.

But she would *not* think of it. With determined force, she stabbed circles of carrot and shoved them into her mouth. The honey glaze was cloyingly sweet, and she let herself grimace.

"When someone does take a liking to you, though," he continued, not commenting on the bizarre workings of her expression, "I can only assume they have great good sense."

"What?" She didn't mean to drop her utensil again. This dinner came with a percussion accompaniment.

He brandished a carrot-carrying fork at her. "You. People *should* like you."

"In the same way people should wear cloaks outside in winter? For self-preservation?"

"Not at all." He considered. "More like in the way people should arrive at the theater on time. Because if they do not, they will miss a most entertaining experience."

"You think I'm entertaining?"

He shot a look at the fork lying tines-down at the edge of her china, where it had clattered from her fingers.

"Oh, hush." She tried not to smile, yet she felt all fluttery inside.

After dinner, they drifted into the drawing room. Without guests, there was no reason to separate after the meal.

"You may have your cigars and port in here," Jane said.

"How magnanimous," Edmund replied. "I suppose you want some."

"Not a cigar. But I'd rather like to try port."

"How about brandy instead?" Moving to a cunning sideboard, L-shaped to tuck into the corner of the room, he opened one of its cupboard doors and drew forth a decanter. Once he had located a snifter, he returned to Jane with a glass of the amber liquid. "Sip slowly. It's much stronger than sherry or port."

"I *know*. I'm not an idiot."

"I never implied anything of the sort. Only that you weren't a hardened souse."

With a sniff of stifled laughter, she took a sip of the brandy as Edmund watched. "What do you think?" he asked.

Nothing. She couldn't think at all. A freezing wash in her mouth, then scalding heat. Sharp. Astringent. She wanted to cough and splutter and spit it out.

With choking difficulty, she swallowed the brandy. It burned its way down her throat and settled, hot, in her stomach. "Very nice. I like it."

"Liar." He smirked. "Your eyes are watering."

"Only because I'm so delighted to taste brandy."

"You don't have to drink it, you know." He extended a hand, as though to take back the snifter.

The bite of the alcohol was fading now, and the flavor on her tongue had turned slightly sweet. A little spicy. Buttery, even, if a liquid could be buttery. "I think I want to."

She took another sip. This time, she knew what to expect, or she was numbed from the first sip. The full taste of the brandy filled her mouth, then spread its warmth into her arms and legs.

"I do want to drink it," she decided. "Maybe if I drink enough, I'll stop wanting more."

"More to drink?"

"Yes. More to drink. What else could I possibly mean?" Another sip burned her mouth. "Will it make me drunk?"

"Not in that amount. You've just eaten a meal, so the brandy won't go to your head right away."

"Will you have some, too?"

"I don't care for any." He returned to the sideboard and closed up the cupboard doors, then ran his hand over the sleek right angle of the mahogany top. "Best not to tempt fate."

"In what way?" She was beginning to feel very warm now. Waving her free hand before her face like a fan, she took another sip. Wisps of hair danced and tickled her forehead.

"Nothing much. Just a sensitive stomach." This comment was tossed over his shoulder as he walked to the fireplace and poked up the fire. "Warm enough?"

"Yes." She sank into the nearest chair, a painted spoon-backed affair with a woven seat. A rosewood-topped occasional table stood next to it; she set down her snifter upon it. Enough brandy. Edmund had just admitted something rather interesting.

"Edmund. Your stomach bothers you?"

Jab, jab went the poker, turning coals until they glowed. "Oh. Well. Sometimes."

His shoulders shifted, broad and capable; his coat lay snug over the hard lines of his body. It was a pleasure to watch him; still, surely it didn't take that long to poke up a fire.

"Edmund?"

One more jab; then he returned the poker to its place. "Sometimes I want to be careful about what I eat and drink. That's all."

She recalled their first breakfast together as a married couple, when he had shredded his food. At dinner, he toyed with his spoon so no one would notice he wasn't eating soup. He cut his meat very fine and shuffled it around his plate.

"Not sometimes," she realized. "All the time."

She rose from her seat to join him before the fireplace. Laying a hand on his forearm, she looked up into his face.

"You're careful all the time, aren't you? You hardly ever eat or drink in company. I should have realized sooner."

He gave her a tight smile, then turned to study the ornaments on the mantel. "I've gotten good at little tricks to keep people from noticing."

"Even so." Once upon a time, she had prided herself on spotting little tricks. A woman played cards with much more success if she read her opponents along with the hand dealt to her. Instead of noticing her own husband, though, she had been busy noticing her house, her own behavior, her own chagrin at the mistakes she had made. Perhaps this was understandable. She had never thought of Edmund as an opponent, so why should she watch him as closely as she once had Lord Sheringbrook?

"What does it feel like, Edmund? Does it hurt very much?"

He nudged an alabaster jar ever so slightly to the left, then made its fellow on the right side of the mantel match. "Some. It depends on what I'm doing."

"What makes it not hurt?"

He looked down at her, eyes deep and shadowed. "Such solicitude all of a sudden. What has happened to my bloodthirsty Jane?"

"I can't possibly be bloodthirsty all the time. It's so exhausting. Even if by accident, I'm sure to be polite every once in a while."

"You don't have to." He turned away from the fire and motioned toward the rosewood-topped table. "Don't you want to finish your brandy? Come, it's a fine vintage. You mustn't waste it."

"I don't want any more."

"You said you liked it."

Jane shook her head. "Not five minutes ago, you told

me I didn't have to drink it. What is the problem? Do you so badly not want to talk about your stomach pain? Just say so, and I'll drop the subject."

His hand fell to his side. "It's not that, exactly."

"What, then?"

"It's the kindness. The . . . wifeliness. You don't have to pretend like that."

Stung, she retorted, "I'm not pretending anything. If you can't even eat your own food and drink your own brandy, I want to know how I can help."

He blinked at her. "Really."

"Yes." She lifted her chin. "Really."

"Well. If I have rather a lot on my mind, there's no room for food in my stomach. Something like that."

"That makes no sense at all. You can't eat your own thoughts. Though I'd rather like to give you a piece of *my* mind right now."

He smiled, as she hoped he would. "I have the distinct feeling it would not improve the state of my digestion."

"You're right about that." She walked over to her vase, her beautiful faraway Chinese vase, and touched the smooth glaze.

"Jane. May I come to you tonight?"

The words made her freeze, her finger in the act of tracing the purple-tinted river winding through knobby brown mountains.

"Not for—well. I don't mean to press any attentions on you." The words stumbled from his tongue.

She turned from her vase to regard him, only to find that he had drawn close.

"What do you have in mind?" Jane liked the idea of him *pressing his attentions* on her, except for the fact that he described it like unwanted business.

"Simply a bit of companionship. Simply—well."

"Say what you mean at once, or I will throw a shoe at your head."

His mouth curved in a half smile. "I thought we could sleep together. Not for any reason except rest."

"No reason other than that?"

"I thought you would like it?"

"Why does that sound like a question?"

"I thought you would like it," he amended. "It's not a question. That's what I thought."

Nonsensical man. He offered her this instead of a few words about what was on his mind. "Would you like it?" She was beginning to want to throw a shoe at his head again.

"I think so," he said. "I've never done such a thing before."

"Slept with your wife? I know you haven't. I'd have been there."

His smile melted away. "Not to be impolite—"

"I would give you ten thousand pounds to be impolite just once."

"A gross overpayment," he said lightly. "I don't mean to be indelicate. What I mean is that I've never stayed all night with any lady."

She had assumed he'd had other women, but the very thought made her feel jealous and contrary. "Why not?"

"It never seemed to serve a purpose."

"What sort of purpose?"

"Jane, I don't wish to discuss this with you—"

"Discuss it." She knew she was being rude. But he hadn't told her anything about his thoughts, his tensions that kept him from eating a decent meal. She felt as though she had to follow some thread through to its honest end, even if it became dirty and frayed.

He sighed. Taking her fingers in his, he pulled her to a seat on the drawing room's long sofa, then sat next to her. From here, she could see her painted Chinese vase. *Escape escape escape.*

"Discuss it, Edmund," she said through gritted teeth.

He pulled his hand away, then rose to his feet. "Fine, Jane. Fine." He paced away, then back, catching and holding her gaze. "There is no reason to stay the night when one only wishes to give pleasure to one's partner. Once the pleasure is done, the encounter is done. Sleeping is not to the point."

"Oh." The words hurt; the vehemence hurt. Yet she took satisfaction in his painful honesty. "What if"—she swallowed—"what if the closeness itself gave the woman pleasure?"

"I have my limits." He stopped his pacing. For a moment, he stood still, as though he'd forgotten his destination; then he sank onto the sofa beside her again.

And Jane realized: this talk of pleasure was carefully meted out, just as the pleasures themselves were. He wanted to spare Jane any discomfort or jealousy, just as he had wanted to fulfill the desires of those other women.

But that sort of fulfillment was all about quantity: meet the goal, move along to someone else. He wanted to help as many people as possible, which meant he had little time for any one individual. A wife was no exception. At the moment, he thought he could best please her by ending the conversation.

Wrong. Though she might end by taking no pleasure in it, she was determined to tug him beyond his careful boundaries. "What about me?"

Leaning back against the unyielding cane and silk of the sofa, he shut his eyes. "My limits are different with you."

"In what way?"

"In every way." His hand fumbled for hers; she let him take it, but she didn't close her fingers around his.

"You're offended." Before she could reply, he sat up, making a noise of impatience. "I knew I shouldn't have talked about this. I told you, Jane, it doesn't have anything to do with us."

How entirely he missed the point. But she was done with explaining; done with hoping, even if not with wanting. "Pleasure does not?" A polite expression was pasted onto her features.

"That's not what I meant, though I'm not sure that it does. We married out of good sense. And pleasure hasn't gone all that well for us, has it?"

"If you except our first encounter," Jane said primly, "then it's been all right."

"'All right.'" If another man made the ensuing sound, Jane would have called it a snort. Never had she known Edmund to do anything so impatient or cynical as snort.

"Yes," she repeated. "'All right.' I don't know another description. I have no other experiences to compare it with."

"I rather hoped for 'marvelous' or 'earth-moving.'"

"How astronomical of you." She fixed her eyes on her vase. Over its antique glazed surface, the river flowed purple and winding. "Have you given me your best, then? Leaving as you do each time?"

The silence before he spoke was long and hollow as an echo. "I give you the best I can."

"And I say that it's all right."

He touched the point of her chin, then turned her face

to him. "Jane. I asked if I might come to you tonight. I'm offering you something different this time. Just sleep, and I won't leave until morning."

The offer was intoxicating in a way even the brandy had not been. Where he touched her chin, her skin tingled, tempting her to relent. "I *am* very tired."

His finger traced the line of her jaw. "I am, too. Shall we?"

A swell of sharp-sweet hunger made her catch her breath. "Yes." She slipped her loosened shoe back on and stood.

As they walked up the stairs to their connecting bedchambers, her heart thudded as it hadn't since her wedding day. He didn't intend to touch her in a sexual way. Yet the idea of sleeping together seemed more intimate than sex, and in a way, more pleasurable.

I won't leave, he had said. He had chosen her, only her, all night.

Not just over another woman, or all the women of his past, but over the responsibilities that split him from her during the day. The sense of obligation that drove him toward, then away from, her bed. He might not desire her, yet he gave her this piece of himself: this time, this closeness, that he had never before shared.

She wasn't lying about being tired, though as she undressed and pulled on her nightclothes, the fatigue was limned with nervousness. Did he mean it? Would he really join her, and stay all night?

The door opened with a quiet sound that seemed loud. Lying beneath the coverlet, Jane's breathing seemed loud, too. Edmund's footfalls on the carpeted floor marched toward her like drumbeats, and when his hand tugged back the covers, the rustling fabric sounded like a howling wind.

He pressed his body behind hers, full-length, and encircled her waist with an arm. "Good night, Jane."

"Good night." Her voice was oddly bright.

For a minute, he held her tight, then his arm loosened to curve gently over her waist. "Sleep well."

"You, too." That stupid bright voice again. She couldn't help it. She was nervous about this new, odd intimacy, even as he still kept his thoughts locked away.

But that was that: two short sentences apiece. He didn't speak to her again, and within a few minutes, the soft, slow sound of breathing told her he had fallen asleep—or he was better at pretending than she was.

After some minutes or some hours, when the sky was black outside and the world had gone quiet, Jane fell asleep, too. When the sun reached through the bedchamber window at dawn, she was still within the circle of his arm.

But when Jane stretched out and turned over an hour later, she was alone but for an indentation in the soft mattress.

Darling Edmund. Damned Edmund. Once again, he had fulfilled his promise, and nothing more.

Chapter 14

Concerning the Proper Steps

All things considered, Edmund thought that whole business of sleeping with his wife had gone rather well. When the sun rose, he had awoken, refreshed as he rarely was after a night alone.

Maybe because, holding Jane within his arms, he knew he kept her safe. Maybe because the lithe warmth of her body was a balm to him, too. At last, he felt he'd done something right, and the following morning, he couldn't resist prolonging the pleasant sensation.

He located her in the breakfast parlor, where she was crunching through a heap of toast and sweetening a cup of coffee.

"Jane, I have a wonderful idea for this morn—*how* much sugar are you putting in that coffee?"

She lifted her brows. "Enough to make it taste good. I think it's been scorched." Watery sunlight painted her face, gilding the tips of her lashes. Her eyes looked woodsy-green this morning, reflecting the shade of her gown.

Long familiarity had led him to take her appearance for granted, but now that he looked her over again—why, she was lovely, wasn't she? It was more than just her form and features; it was her vitality. She was curious and lively, bringing him out of himself with her teasing ways.

"You look pretty," Edmund blurted. "This morning. You—you know. Look pretty. Did you sleep well?"

She set down her slice of toast. "For a while." She frowned, as though his words made no sense to her.

"You look pretty," Edmund said again. It seemed important that she understand this.

"Why?"

"Why do you look pretty? It's hard to explain. Something about your expression."

She kept frowning.

"You still look pretty when you frown," he added. "It's just the way you're made."

Her frown quivered and changed direction.

"And when you try not to smile, you're even prettier."

"There's the blarney from your Irish blood." She picked up her toast again. "Stop it. You're being ridiculous."

He drew out a chair and sat at her left. The pile of toast looked rather good. "May I?" When she nodded, he grabbed a slice.

"So," he said between bites, "what am I to say when I think you look pretty, if not that you look pretty?"

"Just stop saying it." She looked puzzled. "You don't have to say anything. I wish you wouldn't."

"Because?"

She crumbled the crust of her toast to powder. "Because it sounds like exactly the sort of thing you say to everyone else. So it doesn't mean anything."

So simply stated. So well aimed; so dreadful. Their brutally honest conversation yesterday had cracked something that lay between them. He had thought that *something* a wall that separated them, coming down. But maybe she saw those little truths as betrayals, breaking her trust in him.

Some reassurance, then, that he was all hers now. Edmund pasted a rakish grin on his face. "If I can't talk about the way you look, am I at least permitted a few impure thoughts?"

A tiny smile crossed her features. "I can't possibly control your thoughts."

"Nor can I."

"Edmund, when you came into this room, were you going to tell me something?" Abandoning her scorched coffee and toast, she stood.

He followed suit, brushing crumbs from his fingertips. "Yes. Well—no, I was going to suggest something. So it was actually more of a question than a statement. Or more of a suggestion than a question. An offering of—"

"Oh, stop, and just tell me what it is." With a smile, she slid her hand into the crook of his arm.

"I have a free morning, and I thought we could use it to practice dancing."

She went still. "Dancing."

"Do you dislike the idea?" The few bites of toast in his stomach became lead.

"No. I just didn't expect that you'd really teach me."

He caught her under the chin, tilted her face up to look him in the eye. "I said I would, and I will. Jane. I always keep my promises to you."

"I know," she sighed, patting his hand where it touched her jaw. "I know you do."

This didn't precisely sound like the yipping delight he had hoped for. Still, he led her into the drawing room, in which a pleasant coal fire glowed. To clear a space for dancing, he pushed aside a small table on which her recently purchased Chinese vase teetered, and Jane heaved a striped ottoman out of the way.

"We'll try a waltz," he decided. "That's the only dance I can think to teach you without the help of others. A quadrille or a reel have such complicated figures that we'd need a whole dancing school to sort them out."

"A waltz?" She quit shoving at the ottoman and marched to stand before him. "I know how that works, sort of. I slap my hands all over you and we twirl around to the count of three."

"Yes, that's right. And I slap my hands all over you, too."

Jane held up her hands. "Where do they go?"

"My dear, they can go wherever you like." At Jane's snort, he added, "But for the sake of a waltz, your left hand can go on my shoulder. Your right hand holds my left."

"And yours?"

"Mine goes here." He laid his right hand on the curve of her waist.

Hardly an intimate touch for a husband who had seen and stroked all of his wife's body. He could scarcely feel the shape of her form beneath gown and stays and chemise, so many layers of fabric separating them. Her hand on his shoulder felt featherlight atop the woolen bulk of his coat, the spiderweb of linen shirt. Yet such touch was forbidden in the cold stare of public view, unless it came in the course of a dance.

"Now we're settled," he said lightly. "I'll count for us and spin, and you let yourself be pushed about backward."

"How delightful," Jane grumbled. "Pushed about backward like a broom. I can't imagine why I haven't learned this before—*oh*."

For with a quick one-two-three, Edmund had swept her in a wide circle, and when she stumbled, she pressed against the full length of his body. Her hair smelled so good, soapy-clean and smooth in its simple twist, that he dropped a kiss on top of her head.

She shivered, an enticing frisson against his chest, and his hands rearranged themselves into a position decidedly unsuited for waltzing in public.

"I am quite sure," came her muffled voice against his chest, "that is *not* where you said you'd be grabbing at me."

"Well, if you're to tumble against me, I owe it to you to steady you. At all bendy bits of your form."

She slid free from his embrace and stepped back, cheeks pink. "My bottom is *not* bendy."

"Correct. Not if I have my hands on it."

"Not at *any* time. Edmund, why did you . . ." She trailed off, looking around the room as though her words had scampered away and hidden under the ottoman.

From experience, he knew *I thought you'd like it* was the wrong answer. "Because I wanted to put my hands on you," he said firmly. Truthfully.

They looked at one another with some surprise.

"I did," he said. "And I'd like to do it some more."

"I believe you." She looked still more surprised, but pleased, too.

He hoped.

He hoped for many things, though. Her happiness. A return to her bed.

He hoped for too much. He'd no right; there were walls between them that he could never tear down.

"Here's what else I want," he interrupted his own thoughts. "To take you to a masquerade. Lord Weatherwax is hosting one on the first of December. His masquerades are notorious and usually lead to a scandal or two."

"Scandal? Are you flirting with me?"

"If I know you at all, you wish to flirt with scandal. I am merely stating the enticing truth. So practice your waltzing, Lady Kirkpatrick. And come up with a costume. And be ready"—he patted her rear—"to have a handsome man put his hands all over you. Within the context of a waltz, of course."

"This is what you want," she mused.

"Yes," he said. "Especially the bit about putting my hands on you. Because, by the way, I'm the handsome man I mentioned."

"Yes, I figured that part out." She smiled. "All right, my lord. I'll come up with something very grabbable. In case there are dark paths to wander down."

"There will be. It wouldn't be a proper masquerade otherwise."

One step brought him near her; now only a few inches separated them. He traced the slope of her nose, then feathered a touch over her cheekbone.

She drew back at once. "What? Do I have a smut on my face?"

"No. You look fine." He settled for a kiss on the forehead, less like a husband or a lover than a proud tutor.

Not that he had really taught her anything.

"You look fine, too," she muttered, sounding as though she meant exactly the opposite.

"Wait until you see me in my costume."

Just for one night, they could sink into the darkness of a masquerade. And in masking themselves, maybe they could lose themselves; leave their unspoken wounds behind. Maybe their troubles wouldn't find them.

Just for one night.

The first of December was always an odd day for Edmund. When he was a boy, his mother told him that she'd named him for a long-ago martyred priest, Edmund Campion, who had lost his life in a horrible way on this date. Why the baroness had named her son for a man whose secret ministry led to his execution for treason, Edmund had no idea.

Well, once his mother's relationship with Turner became more clear, Edmund had a *little* idea. Still, knowing that his mother associated him with betrayal was hardly the sort of comfort he sought when inquiring after the history of his name. He had often wondered what it would be like to live a life free of secrets and shame. But such musings were idle, like wondering what it would be like to be Russian. Or to breathe underwater. Unimaginable, such realities.

Edmund was glad for the distraction of tonight's masquerade, a lavish wintry affair to be held at the mansion of Lord Weatherwax. The cheerful inebriate was sure to provide ciders and ports and mulled wine aplenty, and after a long week of Parliamentary debate, London's lords were ready to escape into other selves beneath the silver of a full moon.

He dressed with the help of his manservant, Withey, in a costume chosen to appeal to Jane. A makeshift uniform aping that of a naval officer, it was a see-the-world costume. A man dressed as he was—cream-colored knee breeches and white stockings; polished black shoes and a deep blue cutaway tailcoat—ordered his life around exploration. Curiosity. Knowledge.

A man like this could capture the notice of Lady Kirkpatrick.

It wasn't a perfect simulacrum. The buckram hat was a too-plain cousin to the great cockaded semicircles worn by England's naval heroes. But then, Edmund was no hero. He was just a man in a costume, hoping to make his wife smile when she saw him.

When she twirled into the entry hall of their house, he caught sight of her costume for the first time. And *he* was the one who smiled.

And looked, and looked, and looked.

Under his gaze, she grinned back. "I look a right jade, don't I?"

She had dressed as the sort of serving wench one might have found at a wayside taproom in a bygone era. Over a full-sleeved chemise, she wore a kirtle, tight beneath her breasts and, oh, so low and loose over them. Her skirts nipped at her ankles, shorter than fashion decreed today. What did fashion know?

Her kirtle and skirts were a respectable brown, yet just the burnished shade to brighten her hair: a study in gold and copper and wood-dark brown, all rag-bagged together. Yet she was no precious metal, to be hammered into a delicate form. She was vivid and strong, like earth itself, and her mouth had been painted the red of sin.

He had a sudden, vivid urge to tip her over a table, tumble up those skirts, and drive into her from behind.

He shut his eyes. When he opened them again, she was looking at him with much curiosity.

"I wonder," she said, "what on earth was on your mind just now. You got the most interesting look on your face."

"Perhaps you'll find out later," he said in a hoarse voice.

"Oh, so it's like that?" She grinned, saucy as any serving wench, and he had to remind himself rather aggressively that she was a baroness, and he was a baron, and they were in the entrance of their house with a footman standing by.

He held out a black demi-mask. "Put this on, please."

"I will when we get there. Until then, I want to see your face." She slipped her hand into his. "In case you get an interesting look on it again."

"The punch is notoriously strong," Edmund murmured in Jane's ear. "I think more people are waiting for refreshments than are dancing."

In a glance, he took in Lord Weatherwax's ballroom, all Georgian splendor in its gilt trim and glistening rose-dark porphyry columns. Every inch of the ceiling was painted with lush figures from mythology, and the marble floor gleamed. Though a small orchestra played on a dais festooned with evergreen garland, most of the masked and costumed figures were lurking around the refreshment table rather than the dance floor.

"I wonder if those couples learned to waltz the same way I did," Jane whispered back. "In another instant, will they be grabbing at each other's—"

"Shh, now." Edmund gave her hand a squeeze, chuckling. "The appeal must be Lord Weatherwax's punch. If anyone knows his spirits, it's our host."

Not that Jane had ever required liquid courage, to his

knowledge. The last time they had entered a ballroom together, she had blundered in her greeting, yet instead of retreating, she had marched onward through polite society. Since then, she'd become a correct baroness.

And a wench.

He rather liked the wench. And he liked the ill fit of his black demi-mask with its poorly aligned eyeholes. He could peek down Jane's bodice, and she was none the wiser.

"I can tell you're peeking down my bodice," she muttered. "Stop it. You're making me feel silly."

He covered her hand with his, guiding her through the crowd to a clear area of the floor. "I had rather hoped that it would make you feel irresistible."

She snorted. "Men have spent their lives resisting me, Edmund. I've no illusions that a few feet of cheap cloth will change matters."

"Tut, tut. This from a woman whom I once found playing cards for shocking stakes, enthralling four men at once with nothing but the power of her words and—"

"A fortune in borrowed jewels?" She shook her head. "That *was* fun, until I lost. I can't seem to cast that sort of spell anymore."

"You could indeed. You just haven't tried."

"That sounds like a challenge."

"It is. I challenge you to be at least as wenchy as you were, ah, borrowed-jewel-y."

"Hmm." She looked him up and down. And then she tipped him a curtsy, somehow managing to stick out her chest and bottom at once. "Get you a tankard o' somethin', milor'?" Adopting the consonant-dropping shambles of a serving wench's speech, she waggled her bosom at Edmund.

"I'm keen on a jug, sweeting," he played along. "But it's a different sort of—oh, I can't even finish the sentence." He laughed. "Sorry, Jane. I could quote you a poem, but I can't talk about you like you're food."

She straightened up, all Jane again at once. "You're not very good at the wenching game."

He laughed again. "Not nearly as good as I once thought, my darling difficult wife. But I *am* good at waltzing. Shall we have a dance?"

A few other couples were twirling tipsily to the one-two-three of the musicians, who seemed as unsteady on their feet as the people for whom they played.

Considering Jane's waltzing lesson had amounted to little more than a stumble and a grope, he was relieved that tonight's guests seemed more inclined to drink than dance. "I *must* try our host's punch," Edmund muttered.

He drew her closer, so that the gentle curve of her breast pressed against his arm. Even in this crowded room, hot and evergreen-spiced and heavy with alcohol, he could smell her clean scent. Just Jane and soap: no fuss, no perfume; enticing as she was.

"Ready?" When she nodded, fitting one hand to his shoulder, he swooped her other one into his and stepped forward. "Here we go. One-two-three; hold my hands; let me shove you about."

"Like a broom," she confirmed, following his lead. Her hands gripped tightly at first, tense within their short, kid gloves. Edmund guided her with a gentle touch at the waist, stepping back and forth, sideways, an occasional twirl. The simple pattern of the waltz. They had all the space they needed, and wheezing music that made him smile, and sweet candlelit time that unfurled slowly; Jane relaxing, him holding her ever closer.

A wife in his arms. He'd never thought to wish for this, and now that he had it, it seemed a greater gift than he could ever have hoped for.

"I like dancing with you," he said. Inadequate, but true. Jane liked things that were true.

She nodded, performing a half turn with new confidence. "I like this, too. We're doing well, aren't we? I haven't fallen onto your feet yet, and you haven't grabbed my—ah."

Ah indeed. She was talking about the dance, and the dance alone. He replied in kind: "It was a selfless maneuver to help you keep your balance. I've told you before."

"I feel like I'm losing my balance now." Indeed, she wobbled, knocking her shoe against his.

Edmund tightened his hand on her waist. "Steady, Jane."

"Don't call me by name," she whispered. "It's a secret. I'm a wench and you're a sea captain and we don't know each other."

"So that's how it is. You want to play a part?"

"Yes." She nestled against his chest, head tucking neatly beneath his chin, her hair a soft tickle against his jaw. "Yes, just for a little while."

She wanted it, too, then: to leave themselves behind. This was the appeal, the temptation, of a masquerade, and a few words sprang to mind.

"'To-morrow when thou leavest,'" he spoke quietly, lips moving against the braided crown of her hair. "'What wilt thou say? Wilt thou then antedate some new-made vow? Or say that now—we are not just those persons which we were?'"

Her mask fit better than his, because when she tipped up her face to his, he could see her roll her hazel eyes.

"You've made good on your threat of a poem. What was that, Shakespeare?"

"John Donne."

"It doesn't sound very nice."

Edmund's hand at her waist drifted—not down to cup her rear, but up, to stroke her back in a gesture of comfort. "It's nice. I meant it to be nice. It's about vows and changes and . . ."

He trailed off. The poem was called "Woman's Constancy," and it dealt with doubt. Doubt in a woman's love, and lies, and . . . hmm.

"I meant it to be nice," he repeated with more force than pleasantness.

Just then, a turbaned figure, masked and cloaked, glided up behind the pair of them and tapped Jane on the shoulder. "May I have the rest of this dance, miss?"

Never were they to be granted more than a moment's peace.

The odd, lax manners of masquerades demanded that Edmund turn Jane over to this new partner. But then the cadence of the interloper's voice finished its ringing through Edmund's ears, dreadfully familiar.

It was Turner. Here.

No, never were they to be granted more than a moment's peace.

Chapter 15

Concerning Secret Identities

Edmund tightened his grip on Jane's hand and waist. The mere thought of doubts and lies must have summoned Turner.

The man spoke in his natural brogue; Jane wouldn't recognize his voice. But no matter the voice, Edmund would know who stood behind his wife. The shape of this particular threat was unmistakable.

"No, you may not have this dance. The lady is already dancing with me." Edmund held Jane's fingers tight; his hand clasped her more closely about the waist.

"But you hide your face behind a mask." Turner's voice flowed low and liquid beneath the squeaks of the reedy woodwinds. "How is this delightful lass to know if she's found the man she wants?"

He ought to have appeared ludicrous in his turban of red silk. But somehow it looked a little mad, adding menace to his black demi-mask and sweeping cloak.

"The lady has found the man she wants," Edmund

ground out. He wished he didn't feel the old twinge of guilt as he said this. "There is no need for your presence."

Jane piped up. "Oh, I'm sure this fellow is decent enough for a—"

"The lady is taken." Edmund glared at Turner, but the eyeholes of his mask were still misaligned, and the black cloth probably received more of his fury than Turner's own gaze.

As Edmund turned Jane away, she trod on his feet. "I beg your pardon," she said sweetly. "I lost count of the steps while you were talking to that gentleman."

"I sincerely doubt he's a gentleman."

"Edm—" Jane pressed her lips together, cutting off his name just in time. "What do you mean? We've just met this person."

He raised his index finger to indicate that his reply must wait, then led her from the dancing area to a quieter alcove.

When he looked over his shoulder, Turner, turbaned and smiling, was right behind them.

So. He wanted a confrontation in Jane's hearing. He wanted to break their peace, then flit away with no consequences. Never would Jane suspect that this was her favored Bellamy, or that he was really an Irish traitor.

Never must Jane suspect that Edmund's father would have been one, too, but for a whisker of fate.

He turned to face the man at his heels, wondering if he could mask his words as surely as his face. "Perhaps I have reason to mistrust this person."

"Aye, that's so." Turner's teeth flashed bright in the candle glow. "And perhaps I've reason to resent this one. Perhaps we've known each other for decades."

"Perhaps we have, and we're none too glad to see one another again."

Jane folded her arms and looked from one of them to another, but Edmund hardly noticed. He had Turner in his sights now, a Turner that no one knew by another name; that no one loved and admired. Finally, he could speak the truth.

"But perhaps," said Turner behind his mask, "we must, because we've an old score to settle."

"Perhaps the score ought to have been settled twenty years ago, if someone hadn't been far too lenient." The masks made Edmund reckless, the words slipping out as quickly as though they'd been straining against their bonds for some time. "Perhaps I am *not* so lenient, and my patience is running out."

Turner grinned, as though he found this statement delightful. "Perhaps your patience has nothing to do with the matter, as you have far more to lose than I do."

Slightly, so slightly, he tilted his head toward Jane. His smile grew.

One may smile, and smile, and be a villain. Hamlet had spoken those words when he learned of the treachery of his uncle. The man who had brought about his father's death, then slipped into his mother's bed.

An apt verse. Very apt indeed.

"Perhaps I do not," Edmund countered. "Your secrets are not a matter of life and death to me. But to one who narrowly avoided a sentence of—"

"Perhaps you're forgetting how many reputations depend on yours." Turner's eyes had narrowed, but his damned wide smile remained bright as ever.

Jane had gone still during this exchange, her eyes darting from Edmund to Turner. Then she lifted her chin.

"*Perhaps*"—she laid heavy stress on the word—"the two of you would like me to leave you alone to finish your conversation. The waltz is still going on, if you'd like to take to the floor with one another."

She turned on her heel, but before she could take a step, Turner caught her hand. He bowed over it, his lips touching her short glove with dreadful familiarity. "Dear lass, there's no one for me but you tonight. And if I can't have you?" He straightened up, shrugging elaborately. "Well, there's not much point in staying to play games, is there?"

With a nod to Edmund and another bow to Jane, he twirled his cloak around himself and strode off into the crowd. Quickly as that. Gone.

Edmund should have relaxed. Now that Turner had slipped away. Now, *now*, before Jane grew even more suspicious. But his heart was hammering, and his stomach clenched on acid sharp as a blade. *Not much point in staying to play games*, his old tutor had said. As if his every word wasn't a lie. The game was what Turner lived for, and had for decades.

"I'm sorry about that, Jane." Edmund squeezed his eyes shut, drew up the corners of his mouth. Around the silk of his demi-mask, he hoped it would somehow look like a smile. "Silly of me. Don't know what got into me, arguing with a stranger."

"Please. I am not an idiot. He was no more a stranger to you than I am." She craned her neck, probably trying to locate the red turban in the crowd. "Who is he, Edmund? Are you in some trouble?"

"Bad investments? Angry mistress? Nothing of the sort." Edmund spoke lightly. The dreadful moment was falling further away, and it was easier to force a smile.

"I didn't think you had those types of trouble. But there are many others."

"True."

"And? *Are* you in trouble of a different sort? Edmund—is everything all right?"

Damn. It was so difficult to dodge one's way through a conversation with Jane. She was quick to block his every evasion with another question.

"It's fine," he lied. "I just got caught up in the argument. Couldn't bear to let him have you, whoever he was."

"You're not going to tell me what that was all about." She sighed. "Edmund, that's idiotic. You can trust me with whatever is wrong. I'll always"—she paused—"care for you."

So she said. But he was a man of verse and wispy compliments. He, better than most people on earth, knew how little words could mean.

He realized what Jane's pause had meant; that she had bitten back a warmer word than *care*. But he also knew that no love was safe.

If he told Jane the truth about Turner, she'd piece together the rest in an instant. The old revolution; the treason that could have dragged down the family. The suspicious death of Edmund's father; the questionable parentage of his sisters—once the Pandora's box was opened, there was no end to the poison that would leak from it.

And then Jane would hate him. Not only for who he was, but for tying her to him under false pretenses. Though she had never repeated her declaration of love, her feelings for him were the truest he had to cling to. He could not bear to destroy them.

"Please don't worry about it." He kept his voice cheerful, though his insides wrenched with pain. "Please. I'll take care of you, Jane, and everything will be fine."

So many lies. If he were truly a naval officer, he would be court-martialed. Somehow, made to account for his wrongdoing.

That was Turner's goal, wasn't it? The destruction of trust. Yet Edmund could see no way around it; no way through; he had no idea where to go next.

Again, Jane sighed, and Edmund braced himself for a scathing protest.

Instead, she slid her hand up his forearm, then tucked it in the crook of his elbow. "Let's walk out in the garden. There's a full moon."

The moon hung heavy and low, a silver ball lighting the garden paths. It turned the hedges to gray lace; it threw shadows in every corner.

There was darkness aplenty for those who sought it. It just wasn't in the places Jane had expected.

She led Edmund to a bench beneath a trellis, its vines and blooms long since withered by cold. Sheltered from view and from the chilliest breezes by a wall of sharp-sweet evergreens, they could be alone here. And maybe she could get at the truth.

"Sit, please," she said.

"After you." He dusted the stone bench with his gloved hands.

"Always so polite," she muttered. More loudly, she said, "No—please. You sit. I need to stand for a bit."

He accepted this with a shrug and seated himself, then looked at her expectantly. "What's this about?"

As if he didn't know.

But she wouldn't bother asking him again. Since he had hardly wanted to share smaller, bothersome truths, he would certainly not reveal a larger one. Not through words could she convince him to trust her. Every day, Edmund knit them up like lace, tossed them away like gilt paper. Words were beautiful, but frail.

Jane was neither. She was strong enough to share any burden he might be carrying. And she would show him through action that she wanted him; that though he wouldn't trust her with his secrets, he *could*, because she would again trust him with her body.

She just had to think of the right way to do this. Not since the ball at Alleyneham House had they behaved as man and wife.

Summoning her thoughts, she concocted the perfect wife: confident, passionate, saucy, and sweet. She let this self fall over her like a second costume, a cloak over her tight kirtle and full skirts. It warmed her. When she closed the small distance between herself and Edmund, her walk was slow and sinuous.

"What do you fancy, milord?" Her accent was of the gutter, her voice throaty.

Wenchy, just as he wanted. All part of the game.

No other footfalls sounded this far from the house; there was nothing at this distant corner of the garden but night and sky and the faint scent of evergreen, the only plants that hadn't curled away for the winter. Was it cold outside? She had no idea; she waited, rouge-darkened lips slightly parted, to see whether he would play along. All he need do was stretch out a hand, and she would go to him.

He stretched out a hand.

She paused, just out of reach. "How much, then?"

"How much . . . what?" His eyes were so intent on her that his ears seemed to be running a bit behind.

"How much do you want, and how much will you give?"

He shifted on the stone bench, rearranging the tails of his coat. "Well. Since you're asking—everything."

"And?"

"Everything."

She plucked a sprig of evergreen, held it to her nose, then handed it to him. "You mustn't have much, if you're willing to give it all away." It seemed right to drop her serving-wench voice; to throw a bit of crispness at him.

"I must want a great deal," he answered quietly. "If I offer all I have for it."

He dropped the fragrant needles, now crushed, and reached for her again. This time his hand caught hers, and he tugged her closer until she toppled onto his lap.

"Everything, Jane. I want—" He cut himself off. A shudder ran through his body; his arms encircled her.

"More than you can say," she ventured, and he nodded.

She wanted to know what that was, but she wouldn't ask any more. They both had their secrets: his, some darkness in his family's past. And hers, that she had never succeeded in banishing her feelings as she wished. Maybe that was why she hadn't been able to play a part since her wedding: every day, she inhabited the role of someone who was satisfied with her coolheaded marriage.

"You can have it," she said. "You can have everything, Edmund."

In an instant, Jane was straddling Edmund on the bench, her knees to either side of his legs on the stone, her skirts rucked up.

"Your knees will be cold," he said. Why was he talking? Especially when her hands were doing things that a recently virgin baroness should never have imagined.

"I don't feel a thing," she murmured.

"I can change that." His hands began to do things, too. First they lifted her enough to arrange the broadcloth of his coat beneath her knees. Well. She wouldn't enjoy herself properly if her knees were cold or sore.

But then, onward. She found the fall of his breeches and slipped the buttons free, and he returned the favor by exploring in her bodice. With a thumb, he reached beneath the edge of the fabric and scraped lightly over her skin. His other hand gripped her waist, but when she steadied herself by holding on to his shoulders, he sent that other hand exploring, too. Palming her breasts through the fabric, catching a nipple between the lengths of two fingers and tugging, lightly, until it tightened and she pressed herself into the cradle of his hand.

"More?"

"Yes. More." Her eyes fell closed, and with her breasts in his hands, her naked flesh against his, she was the most erotic sight he could ever have imagined. Abandoned to pleasure, and finding it with him. Moonlight on her skin and in her hair; shadows between them to hide the depths of their desire. Surely there was nothing so sweet, so hot, so right as this woman, and he could not imagine how he could ever have thought her anything but beautiful.

He kissed the curve of her neck, let his fingers play with her nipples until she shivered. The skin was petal-soft, yet intriguingly firm, and he learned along with her what sort of touch she liked. They drifted in a pool of pleasure, letting their bodies wake to it, letting it build.

Jane let out a gasp; her hands cradled his face, their

tongues in a tangle. She rolled her hips against his in unmistakable invitation, and he reached between their bodies to finish loosening his fall, to free himself and slide into her wet heat.

For a long moment, they were still, letting the closeness sink through them. Poised at the brink of sharp, shared pleasure, if only they were ready to dive.

They held each other, sinking and rising slowly at first. But soon it wasn't slow anymore, and then there wasn't even any thought; just heat and evergreen scent and the perfect shape of Jane. The pool of pleasure became wave-lashed and wild, its tide tugging them with greater and greater force until ecstasy washed over them like a gale, leaving them spent and gasping, shuddering in the aftermath.

It had only taken a few minutes. It had been the best few minutes of his life.

A wind Edmund hadn't felt before whispered against his neck and throat, blowing at the perspiration there, pleasantly cool on his skin. Jane's head found the hollow of his shoulder and rested there, as though he were everything solid in the world.

His heart gave a hearty thump of approval.

His heart. Not, for once, his ever-angry stomach. No, his roiling body had calmed in this honey-slow moment, and it was just him and Jane and the brutal joy of togetherness.

Not pleasure in having pleased her. Not pleasure in having won her. Just pleasure in . . . her.

The realization was a shock. The hairs on his arms stood on end under his sleeves. His very scalp tingled, as though a current passed through his body.

His wife—his marriage—had never been intended to

give him pleasure. His marriage was an atonement. And this masquerade—it was for Jane. Not for him. This garden interlude wasn't for him.

How had he let this happen? How had he wound up taking, greedily, when it was past time for him to do the giving?

I must want a great deal, he had told her. He had offered all he had. Yet he'd not had to follow through; he'd given her nothing but a fleeting pleasure and a place to rest her weary head.

How did his good intentions always crumble where she was concerned? How, when she didn't know him, or what he'd done, or why he had married her?

And whose fault was all of that?

His. Always and only his.

At last, Jane thought, they were married.

The wedding ceremony at Xavier House had put the ring on her finger and given her the Church of England's blessing. How many times she had given Edmund her body, she couldn't say.

But this was the first time she had given him her heart and he hadn't handed it back with a polite apology. This time, it had felt . . . real. As real as the weight of his arms at the small of her back, or the hard curve of his shoulder beneath her cheek.

She must be cautious, though. She couldn't let him know she'd noticed anything different; not until he was ready to admit it.

She sat up.

"If you thank me," she said, "I will have to murder you. Or charge you a guinea."

There: the smile she loved. In moonlight, it looked even brighter than during the day. "A guinea? Nonsense. I think you're worth much more."

Am I worth ten thousand pounds? Are you glad you married me? But not the promise of ten thousand more would have coaxed those words from her lips right now. She'd won a smile from him, but what now? Anything she said might be wrong.

Instead, she clambered down from the bench, from his lap. Her hips felt stiff; her knees ached. Her fingers and toes were cold.

It was absolutely the loveliest feeling ever.

She shook out her skirts and seated herself next to him on the bench. He made as though to button the fall of his breeches. Before she could think, she grasped his wrist and halted him. "Not yet."

"Oh," he replied. Which apparently meant, *Very well, do as you wish*, because that was what she began to do, and he didn't stop her. This was their wedding night, after all, and she was a bride exploring the body of the man she loved. She stood, knowing the ingrained dance of manners would bring him to his feet, too. Face-to-face, the bench their altar, the fragrant evergreens their witnesses, she vowed: *with this ring I thee wed, with my body I thee worship*. A bride didn't say those words, only a groom. But surely no one could ever have felt them more deeply than she did.

As though it was their first time, she grazed her hand up and down his torso, then coaxed free a waistcoat button, then another. Touched and stroked, her hand sliding under the linen of his shirt and tracing the contours of muscled abdomen. A fingertip in his navel, then up, roving around the curve of his ribs, grasping the hard lines of his back and pulling him closer, closer.

She wanted to press him down on the bench and climb atop him again. But that was asking too much: she couldn't expect him to overlook such eagerness, or to misinterpret such a hunger for him.

Yet he was the one who had said he wanted everything— and that he would pay any price for it.

Downward, she skimmed her palm over his body. A hard rib cage; a hard sheet of muscle across his belly. *Aha*. Yes, that was getting hard again, too.

She had an idea. "We could do something else." She hated that she didn't know the right word for what she was going to suggest. "I could use my mouth on your . . ."

Edmund sucked in a deep, sharp breath. "Oh." His hips jerked back, away from her fingertips.

She tugged him toward her again, until that hot length rested against her belly. "Let us try it." Her free hand skimmed down, finding the shaft, the tightening sac, and she began to sink to her knees.

In an instant, he had caught her hand. Tugged her to her feet. Backed away. "No, Jane." He shuddered, evidently fighting some internal battle. "No, Jane. No. There's no purpose to it. We married to make an heir."

Such a short sentence to change everything.

Not *with my body I thee worship*. No: the six words he had spoken instead were as sobering as a dash of icy water.

We married to make an heir.

He didn't want her mouth on him; he didn't want to abandon himself to pleasure. He only wanted the use of her body, as they'd agreed before marriage.

As quickly as he had spoken those six words, she

realized again and anew, she was his happenstance. She wanted him to trust her, but their marriage had been born in a lie: the woman she'd pretended to be at Sheringbrook's card table, and the money she had lost. Why *should* he trust her with his secrets or his heart? He knew her as the sort of woman who would take rubies, who would sneak and lie, all to make the gamble greater.

Yet she had to ask. "Wouldn't you like it?" She knew he would.

He knew it, too. "It doesn't matter whether I would like it or not."

"Does it matter," she said, "whether I would like it?"

He took an eternity to slip his waistcoat buttons back through their holes. It was like putting on armor, and she knew that even if he answered her, the words would be meaningless. His wall had already gone back up, and it was too strong for Jane. He had worked on it for a long time and had built it well.

"Come inside with me," he finally said. "You must be cold. Put your mask back on, and let's return to the masquerade. You enjoyed the masquerade, did you not?"

Oh, Edmund, Edmund. There were masks aplenty on display tonight, no matter what one wore.

Somehow, she managed to don one that smiled. A baroness in a serving wench's costume was a far less ridiculous combination than plain, stupid Jane Tindall, hoping for her husband's trust.

Chapter 16

Concerning the Baroness's Location

In the morning, Edmund pounded down the stairs, the sound an odd counterpoint to the lightness of his mood. He and Jane had turned a corner the night before. *He* had turned a corner.

When she had offered to give him more, more, more, he had managed the strength to tell her no. He had refused to take something from her.

At last, he'd done right by her. He could face her across the breakfast table this morning with head held high. Hell, he might even manage to eat beef.

The breakfast parlor was empty, though. The salvers gleamed; the room beckoned bright. But no wife sat at the table, destroying a boiled egg or guzzling cups of chocolate.

Edmund backed out again, wondering. Maybe she had arisen early? Breakfasted without him? The idea was a little disappointing.

He located Pye, his butler. "Where is Lady Kirkpatrick this morning? Did she already breakfast?" A thought occurred to him. "Or has she not yet arisen?" He'd certainly done his best to wear her out the previous night. A smile played on his lips; the memory of their garden interlude fogged his brain.

It took Edmund a few seconds to realize that Pye had not replied. That, in fact, Pye was looking distinctly uncomfortable.

The night-dark garden vanished from Edmund's mind; the morning-cold entrance hall replaced it. Pye never looked discomfited. Pye never showed any emotion except mild disdain.

"Is something amiss, Pye?"

"It's Lady Kirkpatrick." Pye pursed his lips, and Edmund's stomach wrenched. "She's gone, my lord."

"Gone." Edmund blinked. "As in—gone out for the day?"

"No, my lord. She's—"

Fear flooded Edmund's body. "Taken," he whispered. God help him; no, God help Turner. If the man had snatched Jane from this very house, there would be hell to pay.

"No, my lord. Not taken." For some reason, Pye looked more apprehensive than ever.

"What on earth has happened?"

"Lady Kirkpatrick has gone, my lord. Early this morning, she departed with a trunk and her lady's maid. I am given to understand she does not plan to return."

"You mean this morning?"

The butler coughed. Shuffled his feet. These small fidgets showed that something had gone terribly wrong. "What, Pye?"

"She said she will not come back, my lord. Not ever." The butler's eyes looked hollow in his thin face.

"Is that what she thinks?" Edmund's mouth made a grim line. "Lady Kirkpatrick is mistaken."

If she had taken a trunk with her, there was only one place in London she was likely to go. And as soon as he could ready himself, he'd go after her. For her own good; for her safety.

She never wanted to let him do right by her, did she? But he was just as determined as she was.

When her cousin, Lord Xavier, thundered down the stairs of his town house to meet her in the entry hall, Jane expected him to look suspicious. She *hadn't* expected him to look worried.

"Is there something wrong, Jane? The butler told me you said this was urgent. And this isn't a normal hour for calling."

He was still straightening his cravat, still smoothing his hair. Jane felt a pang of guilt at rousting him so early and causing his day to begin with an apoplexy.

"Why should I call at a normal hour, Xavier? I wasn't aware you considered me normal." When her maid tried to sidle away and become invisible behind a delicate side table, Jane caught the younger woman's arm. Together they made a wall in front of Jane's trunk; she wanted to calm Xavier down before he caught sight of it.

Xavier raised an eyebrow. "If you can still manage a sharp tongue, should I presume that no great disaster has befallen? You do appear to have all your limbs—wait. A trunk. You brought a trunk with you?" He tugged at his cravat, raising his chin. "What's going on here, Jane?"

Damn. He was using his Earl Voice.

She folded her arms, using her Baroness Voice. "Nothing. Well. I brought a trunk with me. One of your footmen was kind enough to drag it inside."

"I don't give a damn how the trunk got here, Jane. Explain yourself. Has something happened to Kirkpatrick?"

Earl Voice outranked Baroness Voice. Baroness Voice gave up. "No, he's fine. I assume," Jane muttered. "Look. Xavier. Is it—could I talk to Louisa?"

He unbent a tiny bit. "Is this a . . . woman sort of thing?"

"Yes. Yes, it is. I need to speak with her alone."

Xavier nodded, and with a quiet word to his butler, asked that the countess be summoned to meet her caller in the morning room.

Relief unpinned Jane's knees, and she stepped back so her trunk braced her ankles and calves. "Thank you, Xavier."

Her older cousin looked down at her, his expression wavering between sternness and worry. "Jane. Just— look, are you all right?"

"I am in perfect health."

Judging from the close way Xavier studied her, his gray eyes hadn't overlooked the fact that she hadn't *exactly* answered him.

"You haven't killed anyone, have you?" His light tone sounded forced. "Or—embezzled, or committed some act of—"

"Nothing at all out of the ordinary has happened." She held his gaze. "That's the perfect truth."

He released her hand and waved her up the stairs. "Fine, then. Don't tell me a thing."

Jane instructed her maid to have some refreshment in the kitchen, then began marching up the stairs. She had almost reached the landing when Xavier called her name again. Turning, she saw him looking up at her, perplexed. "Look. Whatever you say—I just want you to be all right. You *are* all right?"

"I'm quite well," she said. "And so is Kirkpatrick."

Xavier shook his head, but he let her go then. Up to the morning room, papered in sunny pinstripes and piled up with books. Jane settled herself in a welcoming wing chair near the fireplace and let the low flames work at her chill. Not that they could touch its deepest parts.

Last night had proven to her that she couldn't continue in her marriage. She couldn't subsist on friendship; couldn't fit neatly inside the boundaries of Edmund's life. A wife with whom he shared no true intimacy. A baroness with no knowledge of his estate.

He simply hadn't made room in his life for a wife, no matter who that wife was. It certainly didn't matter that it was Jane.

So he wanted to be alone, to clutch his secrets close? She would give him what he wanted. Wasn't that what a good wife would do?

From this moment forward, though, she wouldn't worry about being a good wife anymore. She'd had no more success with this gamble than with her last attempt to write her future in Sheringbrook's card room.

The door opened, and quiet footsteps crossed the room. "I've rung for tea and biscuits," came Louisa's voice. The tall countess settled herself in a chair facing Jane's, regarding her friend with some curiosity. "My sister Julia is convinced that any difficult situation is made better with biscuits."

"Why should you think this is a difficult situation?" Indeed it was. Difficult even to begin.

Louisa ticked on her fingers. "The early hour, plus the fact that you brought a trunk. And Alex said your maid looked terrified." She leaned forward, studying Jane closely. "Are you in trouble? Only say what you need, and we'll help you."

"I'm not in trouble," Jane said. "I just need a place to stay. For a while."

Louisa leaned back again. The countess moved with unconscious dignity; bleak envy bled through Jane. Never would she be tall and elegant in grass-green; never would she fascinate her husband as Louisa fascinated Xavier. But then, Louisa knew everything. All Jane knew was that she wanted to escape.

"Considering the number of confidences we've shared," Louisa said quietly, "I hope you feel you can tell me anything. But if you feel you can't, I won't press you. You're welcome to stay here as long as you need to."

Jane started to thank her, but Louisa lifted a hand.

"There's just one problem, which is that Xavier and I are returning to the country for Christmas."

"Oh." Jane hadn't thought she could feel more lonely, especially with a friend facing her. A footman entered with a tea tray. Once he departed, Jane asked, "How long will you be gone?"

"Until after Twelfth Night. Alex wants to make provision for his tenants this year. Something beyond having his steward pass out gifts."

"What's wrong with that?"

"Nothing in itself. A gift of something one needs— like beef—is always welcome. But it doesn't necessarily make one feel one *matters*. Especially if all the gifts are the same."

Bonnets, bonnets, for everyone. "I know what you mean," Jane said drily.

"Oh, good. I was afraid I wasn't explaining it well." The countess turned a becoming shade of pink. "There are a few sentimental reasons for spending Christmas in the country, too. Clifton Hall is where we truly got acquainted, after all."

"You're going to do unspeakable things in the library, aren't you?" Jane grimaced. "No. Don't answer me."

"I wouldn't dream of it." Louisa grinned. "Answering you, that is. But you are welcome to come with us if you would prefer not to remain in town."

The sugar bowl took on great fascination for the countess; she began stirring at the sweetness and letting it fall from the spoon. "However. If—not to speak of anyone in particular—one would rather stay in London to be near the person one loves, then one would be welcome to stay in this house."

"When I sort that sentence out," Jane muttered, "I will let you know what one decides."

"I have faith that one will figure it out." Louisa smiled.

Jane considered the invitation to join her friend in the country; it did appeal, greatly. Yet if she went along to Xavier's country seat in Surrey, she would be the unwanted extra. At best, a pest, just as she'd been for years. At worst—forgotten, as Xavier and Louisa darted around their estate being nauseatingly happy.

"I'll stay here at Xavier House while you're gone," she decided. "At least in London, I can enjoy a bit of scandal."

"Enjoy?" Louisa looked doubtful. "Do you think you would enjoy it? I found it rather dreadful, myself, when everyone talked about me."

"Well. You don't *like* having people talk about you."

"I wouldn't mind them gossiping about me if the subject was my charm and brilliance."

"Hmph." Jane folded her arms. "What I'm saying is that you've never experienced what it's like to be forgotten entirely."

"But I have, Jane." Louisa crumbled a bit of biscuit and watched the dust fall to her saucer. "I *was* forgotten. Too shy to make an impression during my debut Season." She gave a wry laugh. "As you say, anything seemed better than that—to go to London, and have the city be affected not at all by my presence. And so I jumped into an engagement of convenience."

Oh. Jane hadn't recalled that Louisa had once been engaged, then jilted. "Well, someone had to propose to you in the first place for you to become engaged. So you couldn't have been *completely* forgotten."

Jane knew she sounded petulant, and there was no reason for it. Why should she feel so hurt when she was the one who had decided to leave? Edmund should be the one whose heart had been bared and wounded.

But she'd never found a way to reach his heart at all.

There. That was why she was hurt.

"I'm sorry," she said to her friend. "I shouldn't have argued with you. I know you understand."

"I think I do." Louisa set her saucer down. "But you and I are very different people, and the rules of society are different for unmarried ladies such as I was then and for the married baroness that you are now. The sort of tittle-tattle that bothered me might not shake you at all. Or you might be shaken by something else instead."

Jane waved a hand. "Society will soon forget about my disaster of a marriage. But if I'm lucky, this will be the making of me. Everyone will know my name, and no one will overlook me anymore."

Louisa fixed Jane with her dark eyes. "Whose notice do you truly want?"

Jane gritted her teeth. "If one's presence doesn't matter to the people one cares for most," she managed, "then one takes the attention one can get."

"Your use of the indefinite pronoun is most mysterious." Louisa poured out more tea that neither of them seemed very interested in drinking. "I cannot imagine to whom you refer. However, if it makes any difference at all"—she set the teapot down with a clunk—"you matter to me and your cousin. Very much."

Jane turned her head away. Perhaps she could use more tea after all, for her throat felt closed and choked. "It makes a little difference."

A soft sigh broke the long silence that followed. "But it's not the same, is it? The love of family and friends. It's just not the same."

Jane shook her head, still looking carefully away. She would not permit herself any tears. Fixing her gaze on a painting of Clifton Hall—Xavier's country house— under a golden summer sun, she said, "My marriage feels like . . . a house with no furniture in it." She swallowed. "It's enough to keep me safe. But it doesn't feel like *mine*. It's my marriage, but I don't belong in it."

She stared at Clifton Hall without blinking, until her eyes blurred. Had she ever felt at home? Not in Mytchett. Not with Xavier. The only time she'd ever felt she belonged somewhere was when she set a Chinese vase on a drawing-room table.

A hand pressed hers lightly, then lifted. Jane turned to see that Louisa had returned to her chair after the little gesture and was now shifting the tea things around into shapes. The saucers at the points of a diamond. A triangle with a tail. Then she stacked them up. "You have a home here for as long as you want it."

Louisa was wrong, though: this still wasn't Jane's home.

But it didn't have Edmund, tearing up her peace of mind. Wounding her with good intentions; with careful politeness and not a bit of trust.

It didn't have Edmund, and for now that was all Jane wanted.

Chapter 17

Concerning the Circumstances of the Baroness's Departure

"I cannot believe it," Xavier said again that evening. "You shouted at Jane. It's absolutely marvelous."

In the upstairs coffee room of White's, the earl sat in a leather wing chair before a marble fireplace. Edmund, facing him from an identical chair, balanced a brandy snifter in his fingertips. Difficult to believe that he had introduced Jane to brandy only a few days before. Or that she'd left his home this morning.

"I regret my loss of temper," he said to his old friend.

"I don't." Xavier chuckled, then drained his own snifter. "I've wanted to shout at Jane her whole life. And she certainly deserved it today."

"I thought so," Edmund granted. "Though a bout of shouting in a friend's morning room is not in keeping with the way a man ought to treat his wife."

"You were welcome to call. If you hadn't, I wouldn't

have entirely believed Jane when she swore she hadn't accidentally murdered you and stuffed you in a wardrobe."

"What a remarkably specific scene you describe."

Xavier set down his snifter with a clunk on a small side table. "Well, a wife oughtn't to walk out on her husband without so much as a good-bye or a word of explanation. Even for Jane, it's very odd behavior. It's not as though you've treated her ill."

"No," Edmund said doubtfully. "I didn't think so."

Xavier raised his quizzing glass to one eye. "I beg your pardon. Did *she* think so?" His voice had gone sharp.

"She communicated—with some verbal force—that she didn't intend to return to my house because ours wasn't a real marriage."

Xavier let the quizzing glass fall. "I probably don't want to ask for an explanation of that comment."

"Don't bother. I asked, and I got nowhere." Brandy burned down his throat as he took a long swallow. It gnawed at his stomach for an instant, then spread in a blessed enervating warmth through his limbs. He shut his eyes and let his head fall back. "I tried to be kind to her. All the time. But she didn't seem to like that."

"Jane is rather unaccountable. I believe she'd rather be insulted than given a false compliment. Lady Xavier is much the same way." Xavier gave a small cough. "Though a sincere compliment is much to be preferred over other options."

"I tried that. Believe me. I don't think she cares much for compliments, though. Or gifts. Nothing that's easy to give."

Xavier extended his boots toward the hearth. "No, very true. But if you want her back—ah, *do* you want her back?"

"Of course I do."

"Then you'll have to figure out what she does want. And you'll have to decide if you can give it."

Edmund already knew the answer. Jane wanted the truth from him.

Xavier picked up his snifter again, regarded its dregs with some disappointment, and added, "As her cousin, I ought to make some sort of threat. Something like, if you fail to make her happy, I'll disembowel you, or take away all your books of poetry. But since no one on earth has ever been able to make Jane do what she doesn't wish or stop doing something she *does* want to do, I can't see why I should hold you to a higher standard."

"Because I'm her husband. I'm responsible for her."

Xavier shook his head. "Better you than I, dear fellow. Better you than I."

Edmund set down his own snifter on a small piecrust table at the side of his chair. The fire jumped and snapped, eager and well fed in the hearth, and he wondered if he could stay here all night. Being out in company felt entirely different, knowing that an empty house waited at home for one. It was how he'd spent all the years of his adulthood, but now that he'd chosen and lost a wife, solitude felt like a step backward.

Well. That was why he wasn't in solitude now. He was surrounded by men of leisure, men thoroughly convinced of their own worth. Billiard balls clacked; brandy snifters and coffee cups clinked. Cigar smoke drifted through the air, lazy as fog, pleasantly acrid to his nose.

"Lord Kirkpatrick. What a pleasure."

Edmund squinted up at the speaker of this unexpected greeting. Lord Sheringbrook—gambler, card cheat, and erstwhile host to Jane's ruinous game of *vingt-et-un*—smiled down at him. The viscount was tall, and dressed as always in beautifully tailored clothes. His dark hair was slicked back to reveal a pronounced widow's peak.

"Sheringbrook," Edmund muttered by way of greeting. Bare courtesy was necessary: the viscount outranked him, and accusing the man of dishonesty would surely result in a duel.

Besides, Edmund was not entirely sure that Xavier knew Jane's entire dowry had gone to line Sheringbrook's pockets. Or, more likely, gone to pay off the most violent and demanding of his creditors.

"Lost your lady wife, did you?" Sheringbrook smiled. "Talk's gone all over the town."

"She's paying a visit to her cousin's household." Edmund nodded toward Xavier, who gave the viscount a lazy wave.

"Nonsense. Not with all her worldly goods." Sheringbrook tapped his chin with a long forefinger. "Tell me, has she been skinned again, Kirkpatrick? Did you boot her from the house, or did she flee you of her own accord?"

Oh, Lord. Did they have to do this now? Edmund reached for his snifter and, without lifting it, twisted its stem. The amber liquid within began to slosh back and forth.

"Ordinarily, Sheringbrook," he said coolly, keeping his eyes fixed on the brandy, "I would be delighted to accept your judgment of the situation, since you are an expert on skinning those with whom you ought not to be gambling. But in this case, you don't know damn-all about the matter. Women go to visit their friends sometimes, and—"

"Pax, Kirkpatrick," Xavier said mildly. "Sheringbrook doesn't know anything about women. Leave him be."

"You're right," Edmund replied. "I shouldn't have spoken to him like a sensible being."

Sheringbrook choked. "I could call you out for that."

Edmund feigned surprise. "Why, what on earth for? I merely said you didn't know why my wife had chosen to visit a close friend of hers who happens to be married to her cousin."

He smiled, welcoming the chance to slip venom into his honeyed words, to hurt the man who had taken away Jane's choices and who seemed now to want to hurt her again. "But there's the reason, since you're so concerned about her well-being. For which I thank you, by the way. I know you have long been interested in Lady Kirkpatrick's behavior. What an *ace* you are."

Sheringbrook narrowed his eyes, but Edmund turned away. Enough. Enough discussion of aces and cards and what Jane had done to drive herself into Edmund's arms. He certainly had not been able to keep her there.

Enough about that, too.

"You can't keep it a secret," Sheringbrook said coldly.

Edmund heard his footsteps moving away across the plush carpet; not until the sound of footfalls vanished did he look back at Xavier. "Sorry about that. It seems Jane is making both our lives significantly less peaceful today."

"It's not the first such day." Xavier's brows knit. "Look—Kirkpatrick, you needn't worry about Sheringbrook. It's only a matter of time before his membership here is dropped. He's in money trouble again, and worse than ever."

"If rumor's to be believed. He's always managed to skate by before."

"Not this time. If, as you say, rumor's to be believed. His mother's heirloom pearls were stolen, and though he couldn't have done the theft himself—"

"His *what*?" Edmund wondered if his ears had simply given up on the day and ceased to operate correctly. "What has happened to Lady Sheringbrook's pearls?"

In a few sentences, Xavier sketched out the recent theft and Sheringbrook's alibi. "To no one's surprise, he was at a card table. Still, he probably had something to do with it. Rumor has it he's turning to shady dealings to meet his urgent debts."

Edmund would have laughed, if he hadn't felt a little ill. So the ten thousand pounds was gone, was it? Jane had pinned a future on it; years, even decades. Sheringbrook had thrown it away in a matter of weeks.

"Speaking of rumor." Xavier paused. "Sheringbrook's right, though I hate to say it. Talk about Jane leaving your home is—well, it's likely to spread quickly. There's no reason for Jane to be staying under our roof when we're only a few streets away from you. It would be different if she or Louisa were increasing, but . . ." Xavier shrugged. "My mother and Lady Xavier's mother both died in childbed. I'm not eager for my wife to take the same risk."

Edmund said a quick prayer of thanks for the stout good health of Jane's mother. "I don't mind what people say about me. Many people think I'm a bit of a nodcock because I like poetry and giving compliments and making women smile."

"Nothing wrong with that." Xavier looked as though he were struggling not to smile.

"I know." Edmund gave his snifter one more spin; brandy sloshed over the lip. "But that only makes it funnier—to some—that my wife has left me."

The earl went sober at once. "It's not funny at all."

"I hope Jane isn't the subject of mockery," Edmund said. "That's all I hope. She's very dignified."

"Jane? Dignified?" Xavier spluttered again.

"Well, yes." Edmund frowned, thinking. "In a sort of prickly way. She wants nothing but the truth. No secrets. She wants to do everything correctly. She gives and takes no quarter."

"I hadn't thought of it like that. You're right." Xavier gave Edmund an odd look. "I'll try to send her back to you."

"You needn't bother." Edmund motioned for a waiter to refill his friend's snifter. "Nothing will change her mind except her heart. And vice versa."

He would never bar his door to his wife—but why should she ever come back through it? He obviously possessed nothing she wanted anymore. Certainly not her heart.

Edmund returned home a few hours later, more sober than he wished. His first effort to retrieve his wife from Xavier House had failed. There would be a second, even a third, if the situation required. He would not give up on her.

But he had no notion what form the second attempt should take. His best tool was words, and words had failed. Sweet words, pleading words, words of anger. Jane was immune to all of them.

He ought to shove her into a trunk and kidnap her. That seemed like the sort of adventure she'd like.

The smile that crossed his features was bleak.

He moved through the quiet drawing room, where the servants had let the fire dwindle to coals. He lit a taper

in a candlestick; the small flame caught the gloss of
Jane's Chinese vase, seated atop a table that seemed far
too small to keep it steady. Yet steady it remained, though
servants bustled by innumerable times per day to clean
the carpet or build up the fire. The vase wouldn't dare
disobey Jane by letting itself be damaged.

Edmund stepped closer to it; close enough for the candlelight to catch the gilded back of one of the dragon-
shaped handles.

He should send the vase to her at Xavier House.

He'd be damned before he'd send the vase to her at
Xavier House.

He sighed, rubbing his free hand across eyes gone
gritty from fatigue. His old feeling of guilt felt tender as
a bruise. *Dobhránta* again. He'd been stupid without
knowing how. He hadn't tried hard enough, or he'd tried
too hard, or . . .

No. This time something pressed back.

He had tried his best with Jane. His best made other
women happy. It didn't work with Jane: she'd left.

In his old, sad bundle of guilt, he was the one who'd
done wrong. Long ago, he had escaped a situation grown
so rotten that he could no longer breathe its air. And now
Jane had done the same to him, leaving his house, and—

This wasn't guilt he felt; it was anger. Because what
he'd done to her had been *nothing* like what had happened
to him.

If being treated with respect and placed in comfortable
circumstances was so terrible that she had to escape him,
then damn her. There was no pleasing such a woman.

Edmund, I love you.

A wedding-night memory of her quiet voice—half a

sob of passion—rang in his ears, cutting through the clamor of resentment.

I love you. She had said it once, and never again. He hadn't wanted her to say it again. He hadn't even wanted her to feel it because it made his guilt all the worse.

And he knew: that was why she'd left. Because she knew she would never get back as much feeling as she gave, and being faced with the evidence of that—day after day, through endless breakfasts and teatimes and *not right nows*—was, eventually, intolerable.

And in that sense, they were not so very different after all.

His anger vanished, and he poked at the space where it had been, to see what had replaced it. Not guilt; nothing so heavy and familiar as that. This pierced like a rapier, sleek and pointed in its agony.

It was regret.

I love you. She had only said it once. Now he wished he hadn't been so vehement in his reaction. He wished he had known how to help that feeling grow in her. He wished he had said it back, even.

But Jane was immune to words. And Edmund tried not to lie, except out of politeness.

Would it be a lie to say he loved her? He didn't know. He didn't know how to separate love from protectiveness, or respect from desire. That didn't make the feelings false, though, did it? It just meant . . . he wanted her to be all right.

Impatient with himself, he turned and left the drawing room without another glance at the vase. He padded up the stairs, candlestick in hand, to ready himself for bed. All too aware that only one day before, he had made the journey with Jane.

Three weeks before Christmas, and he'd misplaced his wife. The wife who he'd hoped would gift his family with a future—a family that wasn't even his, a future that had lost all its urgency. So Turner had come back; what did it matter now? Edmund had chased Jane away all on his own.

The loss was harder to bear than he had expected. Regret again. But for what? The past he had dwelled on? The future he had laid aside? Or a dream he had never dared to let himself possess?

I love you, she'd said. But only because she didn't really know him.

Yet now, with the quiet of the house like a glowering master, he thought: she had left him, and maybe that meant she knew him best of all.

Chapter 18

Concerning Ice

Scandal didn't wear as well as Jane had expected it to.

If it could be thought of as clothing, she had always imagined scandal as a red silk gown or a pair of gilded slippers—or for a man, a snowy cravat tied in a style entirely new. Something that set one apart, that made even the most beautiful and fascinating people seem more so.

She first suspected she was wrong the day after she left her husband's home in Berkeley Square. She borrowed Xavier's carriage for the quick hop to Grosvenor Square, looking forward to a call upon Lady Audrina Bradleigh. Her new friend—unwillingly draped in jewels, ear attuned to all the latest news—would provide much-needed distraction from the tumult of her own thoughts.

Yes, she had hoped Edmund would come for her, but with heart in hand. Instead, he had brought a finite store of cheerful kindness and a list of reasons why she ought to come home with him. As though "ought to" mattered to Jane Tindall.

Jane Kirkpatrick. Whoever the devil she was.

She had taken pleasure in tapping Edmund's good cheer; letting it run out, wasted, against the insoluble surface of her own stubbornness, until he lost his temper with her. But it was a blank sort of pleasure, less like joy than like the satisfaction of defeating an opponent.

When had Edmund become her opponent?

Jane shook her head, then rapped at the door of Alleyneham House again.

A butler opened the door to Jane, admitted her to the mansion's entrance hall, and took her card into the drawing room.

"We are not at home to callers," rang the voice of Audrina's mother, Lady Alleyneham, even as the Duchess of Penlowe shoved past Jane and marched into the house.

That in itself meant nothing. Duchesses were rather prone to doing whatever they wanted.

But then Mrs. Protheroe—a bawdy, widowed cit who arrived in a crested carriage Jane was fairly certain belonged to the spendthrift Marquess of Lockwood—was also admitted into the house.

"I don't understand," Jane began. "Has there been some mistake with my card? I—"

"Pardon me, madam." The butler cut her off. Before Jane could muster a protest, he caught her by the arm and ushered her over the threshold. With no more of a nod than he'd have given to an underservant, he shut the door in her face.

Jane blinked at the glossy wood and brass for an inordinate length of time.

What had happened? Was it because of Edmund? No, surely not. He would never publicly abuse her. And as far as the world knew, if they knew anything about her departure at all, she was simply staying with her cousin. There was nothing wrong with staying with one's cousin.

Was there?

No, likely Lady Alleyneham was miffed at Jane for some other reason. Her ladyship was a stickler for rank, and she might disapprove of Jane's friendship with Bellamy. Or maybe she hadn't forgiven Jane for botching the curtsy at their ball a few weeks earlier.

Yes. That must be it.

Odd how it could come as a relief, the conclusion that one had snubbed and offended a socially powerful countess.

The next time Jane came upon Lady Alleyneham, she would crumple at the countess's feet. Her curtsy would be a positive debasement. The countess might even find the whole affair amusing.

For now, the door to Alleyneham House was closed to her. All Jane could do was lift her chin and make her way back down the mansion's wide stone steps.

"Where to, my lady?" Xavier's coachman touched his cap to her. Pretending dutifully that he hadn't seen what had just passed.

Jane cast about for some instruction. "Gunter's." She didn't want to return to Xavier House yet, and at the popular sweet shop, she might meet someone she knew. Someone with whom she could talk about the weather, or discuss ideas for Christmas gifts, all while slurping up a peppermint ice.

The carriage arrived at Gunter's after a short drive. Though it was the custom on fine days for waiters to serve ladies in their carriages, the chilly weather had chased the shop's customers indoors. All the better for a comfortable chat. Jane took her coachman's hand and hopped to the pavement, feeling more hopeful.

But when she entered the crisp, chattery little shop, it went silent.

Every person within it looked at Jane, still framed within the doorway, then looked away. Spoons ceased clattering against glass dishes. Tongues stopped their wagging about . . . whatever. It was as though the inhabitants of the shop were ostriches, and their heads had just decisively been buried in the sand.

The scent of sugar and mint stung Jane's nose; her stomach gave a queasy flip. She had not botched curtsies to *all* these people. Which meant she had botched something else.

She wished for Edmund's comforting presence at her side; for his cheerful greeting. The light teasing that would coax smiles from every one of the faces . . . well, she presumed the women in the shop had faces. All she saw was the back of bonnet after bonnet.

"Excuse me," she called to a waiter, determined to brazen her way through the situation. "Might I . . ."

"She *might* do anything," sniffed an unfamiliar voice. "A woman cast out by a doting husband such as Lord Kirkpatrick *might* do any number of ungodly things."

"She might. And then she might find out what others would *not* do. And *not* tolerate." A different voice that time.

Jane's stomach followed its horrid flip with a heavy flop. She couldn't even tell from behind which bonnet the voices were issuing. Did it matter? It could be anyone.

And that meant it was probably everyone.

It would be ridiculous to protest her innocence to the back of a bonnet. But she couldn't keep silent.

She tried to recall the Baroness Walling's porcelain face and gracious smile, then reconstruct the expression on her own features. The mask felt as though she'd donned it askew; it pinched at the corners of her mouth and made her eyes water.

"A woman *might* have reasons for doing something that the world knows not of," Jane said, hoping she sounded calm. Best to end her statement there. It wouldn't be fair to blame Edmund; it wasn't as though he'd beaten her. He was everything kind. Why, he had even ventured after her and tried to persuade her—first sweetly, then forcefully—into coming home.

No, she had said. He wanted his wife back so he could keep her safe and sound. Like a bonnet to be rescued, or a book to be bought. Jane was just another good deed to tick off his list.

"Disgraceful," spoke up another voice. "Admitting it openly like that. The cheek!"

"Is scandal any better if it's kept a secret?" Jane asked the room as a whole.

She didn't know. Society thought so, though. Likely many of the women sitting here, spooning up ices and consuming tarts, inhabited the same houses as their husbands, but lived wholly separate lives. Was suffering in silence better than leaving?

Could it be called suffering if those women never loved their husbands to begin with?

She wondered if she had made a terrible blunder.

The bonnets remained facing resolutely away, though chatter broke out again. Chatter in which Kirkpatrick's name figured prominently. Kirkpatrick, and the women he ought to have married who might have been worthy of him.

Jane's hands gripped the handle of her reticule. She wanted to shake these women, shout at them. *But he's just a man. He's not as perfect as you think. And I am not so terrible.*

She couldn't open her mouth again. If she relaxed her jaw the slightest bit, she'd do something for which she would never forgive herself. Cry, probably.

With jaw clamped shut, then, she pushed back through the door. The explosion of talk behind her was as sudden and loud as a rifle shot.

Well. She wasn't forgotten by society anymore, was she? The thought brought a grim smile to her face.

As her cousin's carriage brought her back to Xavier House, silent and shaded, she realized that she'd been wrong about the feel of scandal. It was nothing so light and bright as red silk; nothing so bracing as starched linen.

Being draped in scandal wasn't even like wearing a sodden pelisse, suffocating and heavy, or a fussy, choking organdy such as those Jane's mother used to choose for her.

In truth, it made her feel naked.

By the time she returned to Xavier House, Jane realized two dreadful things.

First: that the only attention she wanted was from the person she'd left.

Second: that, if her guess was right, the only doors that weren't closed to her were the one she now entered, and the one through which she had left her husband.

Jane had always cared what people thought. She also cared that they didn't think of her at all. But now—

now she was an ingrate and a scandal, her indiscretion unknown but assumed. Kirkpatrick must have thrown her out for some reason, for who would leave lovely, kind, handsome, wonderful Lord Kirkpatrick?

A woman sick of his polite indifference, that was who.

Before her marriage, she'd been so good at playing a part. But the effort of being Lady Kirkpatrick, serene and cosseted and utterly useless, not even permitted to love— well, that had sapped her. She had no energy now for other roles.

"Tea, please," she requested from a servant as she settled herself in Louisa's morning room. The countess was out paying calls, Xavier was trapped in Parliament, and Jane was alone in this sunny room, now gone gray in the weak afternoon light.

A maid entered to light a lamp, then a branch of candles, from the low fire in the hearth. Holding up her hands before the tiny flames, Jane heard a footman enter with a tray. It was a relief to feel something so normal as hungry.

"My lady," whispered the maid as the footman set down the tray. "You've a caller. I just saw him speaking with the butler."

"Kirkpatrick?" Senseless for her heart to leap in that fashion, when she'd sent him away so decisively the day before.

"Can't say, I'm sure, my lady. He's ever so handsome, though." The young woman ducked her head, then both servants bowed from the room.

Kirkpatrick.

Triumph rose inside her body like a small sun, warming her from the inside out. What did words matter? Only action would prove how he felt. And if he kept coming back for her, maybe he cared that she had left. Enough to ignore her angry words. Enough to be able to tell that they *were* angry, even when spoken with determined calm.

She arranged herself gracefully in one of Louisa's tapestry-covered chairs. Ankles crossed, hand over hand. At the last instant, she decided to be caught in the act of pouring out tea; unconcern would suit her better than expectation.

To her lack of surprise, someone scratched at the door a moment later. Jane swooped for the teapot and set out the cups. When she bade the servant enter, he announced her caller.

"A Mr. Bellamy to see you, my lady."

Jane's hand wobbled; tea sloshed into a saucer. "Mr. Bellamy? Are you certain?"

"Indeed, my lady. Shall I show him in?"

"Yes. Yes, you may. Thank you." She set down the teapot, and in the servant's absence, allowed herself five seconds to feel desolate.

Foolish Jane. If one chased a man away, one shouldn't be surprised when he stayed away.

By the time Bellamy entered the morning room, her hand hardly trembled on the spoon. "What a pleasant surprise," she said. "May I offer you some tea? I'm just in from a few calls myself and wanted to warm up."

"No need, no need. I never get cold." He seated himself with a smile, looking like a Christmas portrait from her parents' generation: a coat of red velvet, with hair in a queue and snowy lace at his throat and wrists.

Jane took a sip of her own tea. She usually preferred it sweeter, but the burnt-sugar smell in Gunter's had put her off for the moment. "Living in India as you did for so long? I'd have expected the English cold would get into your bones."

"Now, now, Lady Kirkpatrick. You wouldn't be trying to make an old man of me, would you?" He winked, settling back in the chair Louisa usually occupied.

"Not at all." She sipped her tea in silence, feeling too bruised for easy conversation. Still wounded from the social cuts she'd received earlier, and wary of this man, always so pleasant, whom Edmund liked so little.

A suspicion crossed her mind; just a flash. The figure at Lord Weatherwax's ball had been the right height. But no, the voice had been wrong. A brogue, where Bellamy's accent was flat.

But a voice could be changed. So easily, Jane had become a serving wench for a short time.

"Mr. Bellamy," she spoke up. "What sort of accent do the English have who live in India?"

"Just like this, my lady." He beamed at her. "After twenty years away, I couldn't help but pick it up, could I?"

"But now that you're back in England, you're not around that way of speaking anymore. How did you speak before?"

He tilted his head. "Why, I can't rightly say. I've been all over the world. I speak however I need to speak, I suppose."

"That's a gift." As Jane stirred her unsweetened tea, her hand was steady.

But she wondered.

"Speaking of gifts," he said jovially, "I may be leaving London soon. Had to track you down, didn't I? I couldn't go without telling you good-bye and giving you a little present. Tut, tut, Lady Kay; you're a hard woman to find."

"Nonsense," she said in a colorless voice. "All London knows where I am."

He took a small parcel from an inside pocket of his velvet coat. "It's a bit early for Christmas, I know, but I couldn't wait."

"How kind of you." Gifts. Damn gifts. Even as she undid the parcel, Jane wanted to throw whatever it was into the chamber pot.

Oh. No, she didn't, after all: a glossy black figurine fell into her hand. A carved column, three inches high, capped with a pierced crown, all atop what looked like a galleried vase.

"It's beautiful," she murmured. "A chess piece?"

"A queen."

She turned it in her hand. "Where is it from?"

"France. This is how they like to carve their pieces there. Elegant, isn't it?"

"Very." Without possessing a face—or any human attributes at all—this little figure seemed regal. It had traveled across the Channel, only to rest in Jane's hand. "What is it made of? This isn't wood."

"It's bone. The black pieces are stained. I've the rest of the set at my lodging, if you care to play?"

"I don't know how." She clutched the bone-sculpted piece tight in her hand; once it had been part of a living creature. "I wish I knew how."

"The game is easy enough to learn. I can bring the set another time, if you wish."

Something about the way he said *the game*—yes, she wondered.

She handed the piece back to him. "You must keep the black queen with her friends until it's time for our game, Mr. Bellamy. I couldn't be so cruel as to separate her."

"Ah, but she's a queen, my lady. The most powerful piece of all. She'll do fine on her own. She can move any direction, as far as she wishes."

"It's the king that wins the game, though, isn't it?"

"Very true." He reached for her hand, but instead of taking the chess piece, he folded her fingers over it. "Very true. If the king is lost, so is the game. I see you know a little of chess after all."

"A very little. Only a bit about how to win." She held the queen tightly, liking the way its time-smoothed contours pressed into her fist. Delicate and strong at once. Perhaps a woman had created the game of chess, to grant so much power to the queen.

Bellamy took his leave soon afterward, though promising to return soon with his full chess set "so we can have a proper game of it."

Jane smiled and accepted his kiss on her hand. She drank her tea quickly after he left, wishing she could feel warm again.

The game, the game. There was a game being played, if Jane was not mistaken, and somehow she was a part of it.

That was a bit of an adventure. But it felt just as dreadful as being draped in scandal. Bellamy might think the queen was fine on her own, but Jane was no queen, graceful and strong. She was barely a baroness. And she was lonely, and tired, and hurt.

And there was only one person she wanted to be with.

Edmund had, no doubt, been embarrassed by her behavior. His pride might be wounded, or he might be resentful. She had stolen her own dowry from him, then left him with neither wife nor money nor heir.

When she thought of it like that, he'd had reason to

lose his good humor with her the day before. And she shouldn't have been quite so forceful when she said she'd never return to his house again.

But he wasn't just her abandoned husband. He was also Lord Kirkpatrick, who had never failed to help a woman in need—whether a stranger whose favorite hat had been wind-whipped away, or an old friend who had lost ten thousand pounds.

How desperately she wanted to see a friendly face. Just for a while. A very short while, until she remembered how to be strong again.

Surely he would not turn her away now.

Chapter 19

Concerning Toast

Late that night, Edmund arrived home from the House of Lords. Hungry and bone-weary, he piled his cloak, hat, and gloves into Pye's waiting hands. "Have some bread sent round to the drawing room, would you? I'll make a bit of toast before I turn in."

Instead of the usual "yes, my lord," Pye's mouth simply opened and closed several times. Anxiety gnawed Edmund's insides, but he tried for levity. "You look a bit ghastly, Pye. What has happened? Surely my wife cannot have left me again."

"No, my lord. Your wife"—the butler gulped—"is decorating the drawing room."

Edmund's walking stick clattered to the floor. He wasn't sure which of them had dropped it. "The devil, you say."

Pounding up the stairs, he wasn't sure what sight would greet his eyes. Jane, penitent, hanging wallpaper and begging to be received under his roof again? Jane, saucy as a serving wench, shoving the furniture about?

Actually, it was neither. Jane, oblivious, was standing

on a sofa to hang a sprig of holly atop a painting. This was apparently not her first athletic feat, since every painting in the room was trimmed with holly, and a garland swooped across the front of the mantel.

Edmund cleared his throat loudly. Jane peeked over her shoulder. "Oh, hullo, Edmund. I thought you'd be home ages ago."

She hopped down, still holding a sprig of holly in one hand. Her simple blue gown was dusty, and her straight hair was falling from its pins.

"Yes. Well." His throat felt uncommonly dry. "The Lord Chancellor wasn't particularly concerned with being concise. Devil of a long day. But Parliament won't be in session over the weekend, so I'll have a little time to recover."

She blinked up at him. He blinked down at her. "You win, Jane. I'll ask: what are you doing here? Are you— back?"

"Only for a visit. I thought you needed a bit of holiday cheer around. Doesn't it look nice?" She gestured widely at the drawing room.

"You came back because you thought we needed holly shoved up onto our paintings."

"*Your* paintings," she muttered. "I shouldn't have come."

She made as though to brush by him, but luckily, a servant knocked at the door just then. Edmund accepted the platter of bread and toasting fork he had requested, then dragged a footstool close to the hearth and settled himself.

All the while, his mind outraced his body, wondering how to treat his unexpected guest who should never have been a guest at all. He had to tread carefully, as one would when trying to lay a snare for a fox.

Well. A vixen, to be more accurate.

He speared a piece of bread on the long fork, then extended it over the flames. "Do you want some toast, Jane? I don't see a tea tray in here. If you've been waiting a while, you must be hungry."

Not looking away from the bread, which was turning a lovely brown at the corners, he sensed her drawing a bit closer. "I didn't mean to stay so long."

"Oh, well. As I said, I didn't mean to be gone so long. Glad we bumped into one another."

She was silent for rather a long time. "Yes."

Pulling the fork from the fire, he examined his handiwork. "Needs a bit more toasting on the one side, doesn't it? Would you ring for tea?"

He hid a smile as Jane sighed and trudged over to the bell rope. But she located a few manners for the servant who answered the summons, requesting tea for the pair of them. She then came to stand by Edmund's footstool. "There. Your bidding has been done."

"Would you like some toast?" he asked mildly. "Sometimes I get grumpy when I haven't eaten for a long time."

"You are horrid. Shove over." She grabbed the toast—perfectly browned, if he said so himself—from the extended fork, then wedged herself onto the footstool next to him.

He began the process of toasting all over again as Jane crunched away. He mustn't forget that this closeness was only temporary; some odd impulse of hers to bedeck the room with holly and pine-sharp garland, then take herself away again. Because the scent of warm bread, fresh and slightly sweet, and the soapy-clean scent of

Jane at his side were making him ache in a new and dreadful way: not in his stomach, but his heart.

"You make very good toast," Jane said gruffly.

"Thank you. You do very nice things with holly."

She snorted. "I knew it was stupid. I just had a rather bad day. It seems I've caused a scandal by leaving you."

"You always wanted a scandal," he commented. "Should I offer congratulations?"

Her shoulders shifted. "No. It's—well. It's not so nice. So I wanted to come put a few homey things around you, since I knew you wouldn't have anyone with you at Christmas."

"Ah, you can twist the knife a bit harder than that."

He sensed her grow still. "I'm sorry, Edmund. I felt like I should do something to help."

"I see. You thought I wouldn't miss you if you tossed a few Christmassy gewgaws about?"

Her toast fell to the hearth. "You miss me?"

Bending, he picked it up and tossed it into the fire. "You can have this next piece. It's almost done."

Jane put a hand on Edmund's arm. "You miss me?"

It was so difficult to look at her face. Somehow, though this conversation had begun with her off balance, he had ceded her all the power.

And all the toast.

The thought brought a wry smile to his face. In the firelight, her hazel eyes looked gold; her hair, a ruddy flame. "How could I not miss you, Jane?"

She frowned. "That's not an answer."

"What would you consider an answer?" Impatience grew in him, the pressures of the day clamping like a vise on his temples. "It's always a test with you, Jane, and I never know how to pass it. If I say I'm glad to see you,

you think I'm lying. If I say that I'm annoyed by the very sight of you, I feel like the worst sort of villain. Maybe they're both true at once, though. Maybe I don't know what to make of you, and I never have. But overall, I'd much rather you stay than go. Is that a satisfactory answer for you?"

She studied him with those liquid-gold eyes for a long moment. "The toast is burning."

Edmund cursed, knocking the smoking piece of bread into the coals.

"The next piece should be for you," she said. "You haven't eaten yet."

"Such wifeliness."

"You've no idea," she replied. "When the tea comes, I'm going to make your cup."

"As I take it black, that's not much of a struggle."

"Nevertheless." A servant entered with the tea tray then, and Jane clattered the cups around with great industry before bringing one to Edmund. Tea had slopped over the brim of the cup and filled the saucer.

"Hold it for me," he said. "I'm going to get this next piece of toast right, or starve trying."

Again, she seated herself next to him. Her fingers wrapped tightly around the cup; the saucer balanced on her thighs.

Edmund fixed his eyes determinedly on the toasting fork. The bread. The coals. "Why, Jane? Why are you back today?"

"I told you. I had a bad day and wanted to end it by doing something nice. That's what you do, isn't it?"

"It's hardly nice for me to get a glimpse of my wife, then have her run off again. Am I to expect this sort of torment every time you take a whim into your head?"

"It's torment to see me?"

His vision blurred as his eyes watched the flames dance. "A little, yes. And a little wonderful, too. I already told you that. But you have this habit of not believing anything I say unless it's horrid."

"I believe you."

He almost dropped the toasting fork.

"Oh, let me finish the toast." She reached for the fork; the movement set the saucer atop her thighs to rocking. Tea dripped onto her gown.

"Damn," they both said at once, then smiled.

"Here," Edmund said. "I'll give you a cup for a fork. We sound like footmen laying a table, don't we?" He handed her the nearly done toast on its fork and took the teacup from her hand.

He took a sip, realizing as the hot liquid soothed his throat just how thirsty he'd become. In silence they sat, until Jane handed him the finished toast.

He took it, but instead of thanking her, he blurted, "I thought you might be coming back. For good, I mean. Because you left so many of your things here."

"Like what?" She looked puzzled.

He tilted his head toward the small table on which her Chinese vase sat. "That vase you like so much, for one. Or your horse, stabled out in the mews, eating her head off."

"You bought that vase. It's yours. And the horse, too. Besides, I don't know how to ride."

He choked on a too-large gulp of tea. "You don't?"

"I wanted you to teach me, but you never—"

"Never what? Never read your mind? Never knew what you didn't tell me?"

"I shouldn't have come." She made to rise, but he caught her arm.

"No, Jane. We're going to—what was your phrase? *Discuss it.* You seem to be angry at me about any number of things. I am uncovering new reasons all the time. Like an archaeologist, aren't I? That sounds like the exotic sort of thing you would enjoy."

She set down the toasting fork on the marble hearth, then tucked loose strands of hair behind her ears. "You also bought the atlas. You forgot to mention that."

Edmund was sorely tempted to slosh more tea onto her gown. "It was a *gift*."

"Just because you buy someone a gift doesn't mean she wants or needs it."

"But you did want it."

Jane made a rude noise.

"That is not a response," Edmund replied, stung. "Though if you want to look at the matter that way, then I bought *you* as well. Yet you've removed yourself from my household readily enough."

He wondered if she would fly into a rage at this; he almost hoped she would. But she only sighed. "I know. You own me, and I can never forget it."

Once again, he found himself wrong-footed in this conversation. "No, it's not so, Jane. There's payment, and then there are gifts. Everything I've bought for you is a gift, and that means it's yours, and the cost doesn't matter anymore."

"It matters to me." She jabbed at the coals with the delicate tines of the toasting fork. "It's just another way for me to be in your debt."

A startled laugh burst from Edmund's throat. "*You* in *my* debt?"

"Ten thousand pounds' worth, and that's before we

married and you started buying me other things. That's also assuming you don't charge me interest."

He sprang to his feet, shoving the unwanted teacup onto the mantel and staring down at her. Lord, what terrible pride she had. "You insult me," he said through gritted teeth, "by turning our lives together into a ledger. I am not keeping account."

"I didn't mean to imply that. Only that *I* was keeping account. Otherwise how am I ever to know I've squared my debt to you?"

"What on earth are you talking about?" He pressed a hand to his temple. A nice change, to have a headache instead of the gnawing pain in his stomach. "You left this house because you think you're in debt to me? Are you going to move back when you've paid me, then? Because that makes just as much sense. And while you're here, I *must* know how you intend to work off ten thousand pounds. Because any way I can think of . . ."

"What? Finish your sentence." Now she had stood, too, and was facing him with set jaw across the footstool on which they'd been seated. "What do you think?"

He pulled in a deep breath. "I think," he said in a measured tone, "that you are capable of doing anything you set your hand to, even if that means earning ten thousand pounds. But I cannot think of a way you could do that without placing yourself in danger. And that, my dear, is something I would regret very much indeed."

She seemed to wilt at these words. "Oh. You're being kind again. I can never fight with you when you're kind."

"Then we should never fight at all, because I'm always kind." He tried not to sound bitter.

"Not like that. Not with—oh, compliments and praise.

I mean *really* kind, like . . ." She looked away. "Like I matter to you."

He knew instinctively that an *"Of course you do"* would seem pat in the way she disliked. So instead he returned a question. "What makes you feel you don't?"

Her jaw jutted out. "Considering how you reacted when I told you *one tiny thing* on our wedding night—"

"That you loved me?" He gave a harsh laugh. "That's hardly a small revelation. Surely I can be forgiven for reacting badly."

When she continued to glare at him, he realized the truth. "I can't be, can I? You've never forgiven me for turning away from you."

"Have you forgiven me for saying it?"

"Love isn't something to be forgiven, Jane. It's to be . . ." He fumbled for the right word, then grimaced. "I don't know. I don't know anything about love."

"That was made quite clear to me." She sank, boneless, onto a chair. "Edmund. I left you because I could tell you would never love me. More than that: because I could tell you didn't even *want* me to love you. I thought at first it was a problem with me. That you had a disgust of me for some reason."

He snapped upright. "Nothing of the sort."

"No," she agreed. "Now I realize that. The problem is in you, Edmund. You've left your heart behind somewhere long ago, but you've never gone back to get it. You look for little pieces of it in everyone you meet. You make everyone love you, just a little. But what do you feel in return? Nothing, because you're always looking for what's next."

He felt dull, the blank of a man who has suffered a

dreadful beating and knows the pain will crash upon him any second. "My dear Jane. You describe a terrible person."

"No. Not *your* Jane. I know our marriage license makes me yours in the eyes of the law, but I don't think you've ever seen me as yours. And as for you thinking I described a terrible person—well, maybe that's why you've never laid claim to me."

He made a strange sound in his throat, and her cheeks went red. "I'm not talking about physically. I mean—I don't know how to say it. United in some profound way. If real intimacy was no more than the physical act, you'd have been married a long time ago."

Oh, he felt the blows now; every one of them, bruising his heart, his skin, pummeling him inside and out. Everything she said was a mirror held up to the worst of himself.

No. Not quite the worst. Yet it was bad enough.

He rather thought he ought to sit down.

He made a production of finding a chair; near hers, but not too near. And all the while she kept raining words on him. "I didn't mean to describe someone terrible, Edmund. Just someone lonely. Like me. Someone who wants love, but doesn't know how to get it. I didn't understand that when I left. But now I do. And that's why I come back to visit. But that's also why I can never come back to stay."

At last, she seemed to be out of things to say. She blew a strand of hair out of her face. Crossed and uncrossed her ankles. "Aren't you going to say anything?"

"Why? You're talking, so I'm listening."

"Manners," she muttered. "You carry them too far. I admit, I've never been in this situation before, but my guess is when one's spouse is ranting about the state of one's marriage, one ought to do more than just—"

"Oh, stop, Jane. You'll do yourself an injury if you try to finish that sentence."

Her mouth fell open. She looked at him as though he'd poked her with the toasting fork.

"Don't look so shocked. You said that sentence to me once before. I thought it was funny. I remembered it." He tapped an ear with his index finger. "I *listened*, Jane. That doesn't mean I'm just waiting for you to stop talking. It means I'm letting you finish, to be sure you've said everything you want to. It means I want to think about what you've said instead of flying into a rage at some misunderstanding. But if it will make you feel more valued, I can interrupt you every once in a while. I can rant at you a little and jump to conclusions and belittle your thoughts. I can speak to you sharply. I aim—I have always aimed—to please."

He said all this calmly. Summoning words of his own felt like putting ice on the bruises Jane had inflicted.

"But why? Why do you aim to please?" Her brows yanked into a *V*.

"Because I think it's the right thing to do. Who would not think so?"

"Most people."

He shrugged this off. "Then I don't care about how most people behave. I care about what I think is right. And I care about why you left. And I care about you."

Her gaze skittered away. "But you don't trust me."

A flash of red caught his eye; the berries on the last branch of holly. It lay on the floor between their chairs. She must have let it fall when he'd burned the toast. Or when the tea tray arrived. It didn't matter.

He bent to pick it up, letting the waxy leaves needle his fingertips. "I'd no idea you thought that, Jane. Of *course*

I trust you. You're fearsome, but that only means you make a much better ally than you do a foe."

She narrowed her eyes. "I'm not sure if you're complimenting me or insulting me."

"A compliment, I assure you." He seated himself again, turning the holly in his hand. "I don't trust *me*, Jane. That's the difficulty. And as long as you've any regard for me, I can't bear to tell you anything that might cause you to stop."

"So you *don't* trust me. Not enough to decide how I feel about you."

"Is that all you want from me? I could tell you how to feel. Then I could be like you, laying down the law without knowing of what I speak."

Again, Jane's mouth fell open. Edmund felt a sort of barren triumph in having shaken up her impressions of him. *Yes, my dear; the dog has a bark* and *a bite. Did you think he was entirely tame?*

"I've listened to you, Jane, and I freely admit that you are right about a great many things. I haven't trusted you as I should. But here's a question for you: are you glad you married me? Or do you regret it?"

His stomach wrenched; bile rose into his throat, and he pressed his fist against his breastbone, willing it back down.

"Your stomach pain?"

"Don't worry about it. Just think of the answer. Or—no, maybe there's no purpose to that. We're just as married in the eyes of the law whether you love it or hate it. I just wondered."

The moment had passed, and he relaxed his fist. The holly leaves had been crushed in his fist; small cuts crisscrossed his palm.

"Are *you* glad or sorry?"

He sat up straighter and shook out his hands. "For myself, glad. For you, sorry."

"For myself," Jane echoed, "both."

"Better than I hoped." He rose to his feet, paced over to look into her Chinese vase, as though it held secrets and answers and all the wisdom of the ages. "It's not enough, is it?"

"That depends on what you mean," she said crisply. "There's enough regard between us not to humiliate either of us in public. But enough to live under your roof again? No. I can't bear it."

"Nor could I."

A startled gulp rushed from her. Instead of apologizing, walking closer to her, he strode farther away. Poking up the fire again, though the coals had already been scattered.

He turned his head; from the corner of his eye, he saw that she had wrapped her arms around herself. Yes, the room had chilled, but nothing in the fireplace would help that.

Edmund stretched out his arms to clutch at the mantel, fingertips holding tight to cold stone. His head half-turned, facing her, he said in a clipped voice, "I know you wish our marriage could be different. You want more from me. Well, I want to give you more, but you don't want what it is I can give. You want some—some fake me. The real Edmund—he's not who you want at all."

He let his hands drop, then straightened up, still facing away. "And, Jane, when I see your hurt and disappointment that I'm not what you want, I don't know which of us I'm more disgusted with."

* * *

Jane clutched her arms around herself tighter, tighter, but there was no way to hold her heart steady, to keep it from being sliced. She swallowed. Waited until she could become the baroness: cool and collected. "We probably ought to have been this frank with one another before we married."

"I don't know if we could have been." Edmund gave a harsh laugh. "I wouldn't even have imagined this conversation. No one has ever put me through such trials as you."

"Is that a compliment or an insult?" How many times had she asked him this question?

He shifted a few objects on the mantel. "It's both, I suppose."

Somehow that answer felt right. Brutal and jagged, it cut through the numbness within her. She chose her next words carefully, unfolding her arms and looking down at her hands. "I think we started off wrong."

"In this conversation?"

"In every way. Me gambling, you trying to protect me. Sheringbrook cheating at cards. Any agreement made in a makeshift hell was sure to be a devil's bargain."

"You think it went wrong as early as that." He was silent so long that she permitted herself to look at him.

He had steepled his hands, resting his chin on the fingertips. The firelight made angles of his features. He looked older and harsher than she recalled.

Or perhaps she hadn't seen him clearly for a long time. Her girlish love had been for an idol of kindness, but he hadn't known her at all. And what did she know of him? Only his ironclad decency; none of the demons that had forged it.

She could almost laugh at the absurdity. Here they sat

face-to-face before a fire, to all appearances a contented married couple.

But appearances were nothing. And soon enough, she'd go back to Xavier House, and she and Edmund would both be alone.

How long would it be before he took a lover? Her mind shied from the idea, but she made herself think of it. It was inevitable. Why . . . just look at him.

She looked, and looked, and looked. Oh, that clean jaw. That strong-boned face, lightly freckled; those shoulders, broad and fit. She knew every inch of his body; she knew nothing of what went on inside his heart.

Eventually he looked back at her. "I won't apologize again, Jane," he said quietly. "Not for marrying you. I think we did each other some good."

Her throat caught. "You covered my debt at a desperate time. That was very kind of you."

He made an impatient gesture. "Kind, kind. I won't be thought of as kind. It was selfishness, Jane."

For a moment, she could only stare. "How so?"

"I needed a wife. I knew you wouldn't be able to turn down my suit—well, proposal—if you were indebted to me."

Her fingers clutched at the muslin of her gown, rumpling and creasing it. "I would have taken you on any terms. Any at all."

"Then, yes. But now?"

With an effort of will, she shoved back tears. This kind, bright, beautiful man—how could he be so stupid? She left him, yet she couldn't stay away. She hung holly and evergreen in his drawing room. What the devil did he *think* she felt for him?

She knew the answer: he didn't trust in or want her

love for him. He never had, and there was no reason to think he ever would.

So she mustered some dignity. "Things are different now."

If she hadn't known every line of his body, every flicker of his expression, she would probably have missed the tiny ways in which he collapsed. Shoulders sank, mouth tightened; such small movements that anyone else would have missed them.

Jane wished she had missed them, too. He was disappointed, somehow. In her, or in himself? There was no way to know. Edmund, of all men she'd met, turned his feelings inward and let himself be eaten away. Yet he kept the outside braced and strong. Already, he managed a smile for her.

"Why do you crave notoriety so?"

"Not 'do,'" she murmured. "'Did.'"

His smile went flat. "Whatever tense you prefer."

"The tense makes a great deal of difference. I wanted to be noticed in some way because I never had been before. I was always just Xavier's little country cousin. I knew no one would ever take note of me for my beauty or brains. Being outrageous . . ." She trailed off, her throat catching. "It's all I've got."

"Friendship? A husband? A mare, a maid, a modiste? Were these all to be thrown away for the sake of a scandal?"

"Not for the *sake* of one. The scandal was only an unintentional result."

"Ah. So you threw it away for nothing." He said this calmly, as though working out her preference on something commonplace like the disposal of used tea leaves. How and why should one dispose of a marriage?

And if she no longer wished to be outrageous, what did she have left? A bunch of old loves and desires, ill-fitting and ready to be packed away. Nothing to don in their place, except the longing for escape.

But the only person left to get away from was herself.

"I'm sorry," she said. "I did what I thought was right."

"And now?"

"I still think it's right," she said, for lack of anything better to say.

"Ah." He moved to the L-shaped sideboard and poured out a snifter of brandy. He held it high, letting the light turn it to liquid gold.

Another man might have made a mocking toast to her, said something cutting or bitter.

Not Edmund. He was good to everyone, even the wife who had turned him into an object of gossip. He simply looked at the brandy for a moment, then handed the snifter to Jane. "I'm glad you came, Jane. It was time we talked about these things."

"Past time," she agreed.

For tonight, they had said enough. So she stood, and he followed her to the door. They made their way through the corridors in silence; not even their footfalls sounded on the carpets. Their weave worn thin with time, these antiques were faded history. Jane was but a moment in the life of this house.

When they reached the spiraling tiles of the home's entrance, Jane remembered entering it on her wedding day. She'd taken her gloves off. Edmund had carried her upstairs and made her . . . no, he hadn't made her his. At least, what they had done in that bedchamber hadn't changed the matter. In one sense, she had always been his; in another, they had never belonged to one another at all.

Her hand reached up, stroked the line of his cheekbone. For a flicker of a second, his eyes closed and he pressed into her touch.

They drew away at the same time. Jane took her gloves from a servant and pulled them on.

"Thank you for calling," he said.

"You're welcome." She hesitated. "I could call again some time."

"Or I could call on you?"

"As though we're a courting couple?" They both considered the absurdity of it. As she picked up her reticule, Jane was first to shake her head. "I'm sure we'll meet again soon."

So she left him. It wasn't until the carriage had rolled away from the house that it occurred to her: she'd forgotten to ask just why he'd needed a wife so desperately.

Or—as her heart gave a little flutter—what good he thought she had done him.

Chapter 20

Concerning Plans and Plots

"Lady Kirkpatrick." The butler trod so silently, Jane hadn't heard him enter the morning room of Xavier House. "A caller wishes to see you."

He presented her with a silver tray, an unnecessary bit of fuss for the lone calling card resting upon it. Such a tray should be heaped with invitations.

Well. Maybe not on a wintry Sunday morning. All the polite world was at church right now, except for Jane. Not that she had ever been particularly polite.

She snapped up the card. "Lady Audrina Bradleigh?" Not the name she hoped for, but it would be good to see her friend again. For Jane, London had shrunk to Xavier House and Edmund's home. A bit more company in either would be welcome. "Please show Lady Audrina in. I'd be delighted to see her. And have tea sent in, too."

The butler bowed and withdrew; a few minutes later, Audrina entered, dark and glowing with cold and color. Her pink-gray cambric gown was trimmed in rich red velvet; Jane made note of the shade. She ought to wear other colors besides green.

Shaking back the long sleeves of her celadon gown, she clasped her friend's hand in greeting. "I'm glad to see you. We're a pair of godless heathens this morning, aren't we?"

"Not so bad as all that. My mother only attends church because she likes to look at everyone's hats."

Exactly why Jane had stayed home. She should have joined Louisa and Xavier, but she just couldn't bear to be looked at today, hat or otherwise. The *ton* went less to lift their hearts in prayer than to lift their eyebrows and whisper to one another.

"I was feeling poorly this morning," Jane excused.

"Me, too. Or so I said. I've a very convincing cough. Mother couldn't wait to get away from me, lest I give her a cold that will make her nose all red." Audrina flung herself onto the morning room's sofa with alarming force. "My mother was dreadful, turning you away when you called. I'm so sorry. I tried to tell her you were calling for me, not her, but she just started giggling nervously and offering cake to all our other visitors. As if I wasn't even talking."

"Ehrm." This was the closest Jane could bring herself to disagreeing with the my-mother-was-dreadful statement, as politeness surely warranted. "Your mother wants the best for you."

"No, she wants the best for herself. Dukes for sons-in-law, and perfectly behaved daughters until that magical moment arrives." Audrina leaned forward, her voice dropping low. "I've got to ask you, Jane. How did you get the courage to leave Lord Kirkpatrick? And how much money do you think a woman needs to . . . escape?"

Jane gave a hollow laugh. "You've no idea how many times I tried to calculate that very thing before I married."

Audrina frowned. "But it's your marriage you're escaping, isn't it? I thought—"

A footman entered with tea things, and both women went silent as the tray was arranged. Once they were left alone again, Jane folded herself onto a chair near Audrina. As she held a warm cup in chilly fingers, she considered.

"I think," she began, "I've always wanted to escape one thing or another. My marriage is only the latest in a string of lives I've left behind."

"Do tell." Audrina abandoned her lazy posture, sitting up rapt. "Have you been a pirate? Or worse, an actress?"

Jane laughed. "That sounds dire, doesn't it? I don't mean I've been anything interesting. Just that I've never been happy where I was."

Her brow puckered; she hadn't realized how long she'd been running.

"What about now?" Audrina asked. "Is it better now that you've left your marriage?"

"I haven't left my marriage. Only my husband."

Audrina looked skeptical.

"It's not the same thing. Though I can't explain how. I just know that *I* don't think it's the same thing."

Audrina still looked skeptical. "If you say so. You're the one who would know."

"I don't know anything." Jane forced a smile. "I'm no better off living in a different house. Escaping *from* something doesn't help if you're still the same unsatisfied pirate or actress at heart. Escaping *to* something might work, but I never had that part figured out. I almost did once, but—well. I didn't have the money, in the end."

"How much money? If one just wanted to go to, say, Scotland. And disappear. How much?"

The avid look on her friend's face was giving Jane an uneasy feeling down her spine. She could imagine a future conversation with Lady Alleyneham: *I may not know how to curtsy to you, but I told your youngest daughter exactly how to run off to Scotland! Happy Christmas!*

"Are you all right? Can I help you with—"

"No. I'm fine." Audrina lifted her chin. "I'm fine. Just wondering about some things."

Jane tried one of Edmund's dodges: answering a completely different question. "You asked me how I had the courage to leave Kirkpatrick. Really, it took no courage at all."

Audrina blinked. "But polite society is so critical of you now, yet you're not caving. That takes bravery."

Jane waved a hand, setting her cooling tea to quivering in its cup. "I didn't think of society's reaction when I decided to leave, so it doesn't count. Honestly, I just cut and run. It would have taken far more bravery for me to make a go of my marriage. To try to earn my husband's trust instead of just assuming I should have everything I wanted, all at once." Her hand shook, and she set the teacup down on a small table at her side. "I didn't mean to say that. I—I hadn't thought of it that way before."

Their marriage had foundered in its first storm, but they hadn't built it very solidly to begin with. Why should they have expected it to sail along smoothly for the long term? Had either of them thought that far ahead? No, marriage had been an escape for them both.

"But you shouldn't stay where you're unhappy. Should you?" Audrina sounded as uncertain as Jane felt.

"Not if you're in danger." Jane squinted into the cool light filtering through the room's tall windows. "I wasn't in danger, though."

No, she had simply been on a hunt for happiness. Only the real article would do: bright and pure. Something Edmund hadn't a prayer of buying for her. "But if I had no idea how to find it myself, why should I expect that he would hand it to me?"

"How to find what?" Audrina asked.

Jane only realized she'd spoken part of her thoughts aloud when her friend replied. "Happiness," she explained. "The best escape."

"It would be, wouldn't it?" Audrina sank against the sofa's back again, a dreamy expression on her face.

For a few moments, the two friends let their thoughts unroll with the ticking of the mantel clock; then the earl's daughter stood. "I'd better return home before the rest of my family gets back from church. Thank you for letting me talk to you, Jane."

"Likewise." Jane stood, shaking her hand in farewell. "Everyone else I've seen lately is a relative or a servant paid by a relative."

"To be fair, your cousin *did* give me five pounds to call on you."

"Ha."

Audrina grinned. "I'll try to call again soon." And then she was gone, leaving Jane behind in the morning room.

The sudden silence seemed heavy and cold, and Jane busied herself with unnecessary tasks as her mind raced. She poured out dregs, stacked up teacups, poked up the fire, and wondered.

Wondered whether Audrina craved escape, with her

questions about courage and money and Scotland. What did she want to escape from—or to?

She wondered the same for herself.

She couldn't have dreamed so long of escape if she hadn't had love to lean on. Her mother. Xavier. More recently, Louisa. They were so much a part of her life that she took them for granted, never doubting that if she left, they would welcome her back. And so there was no danger in thinking of running away. She had never done anything on her own: leaving Edmund for Xavier House, gambling with Sheringbrook wearing Xavier's jewels—always, her plots and schemes depended on others to help her.

But Edmund didn't have that foundation. He had left Cornwall as a boy and never returned. He had no one to rely on; nothing but himself. So he'd built that self up bright and strong, and he'd won Jane's heart without even meaning to.

And for that, she had left him.

Never before had it occurred to her that she blamed Edmund for failing to make her happy. Yet she had told him, more than once, that he wasn't responsible for how she felt. She shouldn't put that burden on him. It didn't belong anywhere except herself.

It was heavy, though; so heavy to admit that she had been wrong. Not wrong in loving, or wanting to be loved, but in giving up. Jane Tindall had never given up on anything; there was no reason for Jane Kirkpatrick to be a poorer creature.

She sank onto the trellis-patterned carpet before the hearth, hands extended to catch the fire's warmth.

Two days ago, she and Edmund had talked frankly at last. They'd lanced wounds. Gotten angry with one another. She couldn't love him anymore for being her white knight, pure of heart. He was selfish and jealous and high-handed; no better inside than other men.

But. She could love him for something different. Better. Real. Because no matter what he felt inside, he chose to give the world his best. Even when it was a matter of determination more than desire, he pieced together goodness after goodness, leaving people the better for being around him.

And because of this, she—selfish and jealous and high-handed herself—had a new world of reasons to love him.

With a world of reasons, though, there was no place to hide from what she wanted. No way to escape her desperate longing for him to return that love.

She pushed herself to her feet. Enough. Enough, now. She must think of what she had that was good. Of the love she possessed. Though she had once thought he took her with nothing, that she was irretrievably in his debt, she brought more to their marriage than she had realized.

To one side of the morning room stood a fine-grained walnut writing table. The black chess queen stood at the corner, watching her fruitless fidgets.

Jane strode to the table, drew a sheet of paper toward her, dipped a quill, and began a letter. "We're playing a different sort of game now," she told the chess queen.

My dear mother, she scrawled. *As Christmas draws near, I am wishing you very happy. I know you prefer not to travel to London, so I shall send Christmas to you. Kirkpatrick and I chose this lace for you . . .*

Writing his name was a tiny, harsh pleasure. And writing to her mother, who would enjoy the rare letter very much, was a pleasure, too. A sweet one, as Jane imagined Mrs. Tindall's ruddy face lighting up, knowing her only child was thinking of her.

Jane continued her letter for a cheerful page, omitting the news of her recent scandal. Ringing for a servant, she asked that the finished letter be bundled with the lace she'd chosen weeks earlier. If sent now, it would reach Mytchett before Christmas.

She wouldn't spend Christmas with her mother, but she loved her homely, contented mother no less for the distance between them, or for their differences. They had each found a world to live in that they liked.

And even though, in the whole of the *beau monde*, only a few people would speak with her, Jane didn't feel as though her life was small anymore after all.

"Your sandwiches, my lord."

"Thank you, Pye." The week's long sessions in the House of Lords had put Edmund behind on his correspondence, and he intended to spend this drizzly Sunday afternoon catching up on the papers that cluttered his desk.

Instead of leaving the study after depositing the tray, Pye remained standing by Edmund's desk. The butler was far too well-mannered to fidget, but the tension of his posture fairly shouted of strain.

Edmund set down the penknife with which he'd been sharpening his blunt quills. "Something you wish to tell me, Pye?"

"I don't wish to speak out of turn, my lord."

Edmund laid down his quill as well and fixed the butler with his full attention. "Please. Speak freely. Is something amiss?"

The butler took a step forward. "Not as such, my lord.

I simply wondered whether we—that is, the household staff and myself—might be expecting Lady Kirkpatrick to return often. If so, we can make appropriate arrangements for her comfort."

"I have no idea." Edmund pinched the bridge of his nose, expecting to ward off a headache at the thought of Jane.

But it didn't come. And the plate of sandwiches looked good. He took one and studied it: thick, indelicate slabs of bread, ham, and cheese. When he bit into it, the salty-smoked flavors seemed like the first food he'd ever eaten. Instead of rebelling with a twist of pain, his stomach growled for more.

"Very good, Pye," he said, once he'd swallowed his massive bite. "My compliments to the cook."

As the butler turned to leave, Edmund added, "Pye, as to your earlier question."

"My lord?"

"I don't know what Lady Kirkpatrick plans, or how often she might return. But I think she'll call again."

The butler's mouth twitched. What a red-letter day this was turning out to be. "Very good, my lord. I shall see to her ladyship's comfort when next she calls. Might we also put up a bit more greenery to mark the holiday?"

"Make it mistletoe," Edmund agreed. "In every doorway, if you please."

No one could refuse a kiss under mistletoe. Why, last year, at Xavier's house party, Jane had almost smothered him with kisses under a berry-covered branch.

He'd thought she was young and eager and wild. He hadn't known she loved him then. If he had, he could have been wiser.

When Pye bowed himself out, Edmund stuffed the rest

of the sandwich into his mouth. So. His butler had almost smiled at the idea of Jane's return. The servants liked her, didn't they?

Hell. *He* liked her, and the house seemed empty now that she was gone. But less so than it had earlier, before she had called.

He didn't know what she was doing with her time now that she was living apart from him. But that not-knowing didn't lead, as Turner had vowed, to not-trusting. He trusted Jane not to betray him in the physical sense.

Turner had failed, as always, to account for human decency. Within her family, Jane had the reputation of being a terror, yet she was good through and through. Loving. Thoughtful. Honest. The opposite of Edmund himself, whom everyone thought of as good and who came from stock as dirty as a pig farmer's trousers.

Which reminded him: his steward in Cornwall, Browning, had sent the requested parcel. It squatted in the chair across Edmund's desk, where he had been ignoring its presence for days. No more.

Dusting his hands off, he rose from his seat and looked down at the paper-wrapped package. Time to learn whether Turner had been telling the truth.

He sliced the string with a penknife, then unfolded the paper to reveal a stack of small leather-bound volumes. His father's date books. He had hoped they were still located in the ancestral home somewhere, and the capable Browning had located them. It looked like he'd sent the former baron's notes from all of the 1790s.

It was distasteful to think of one's own conception, or the conception of one's sisters. How much Edmund would rather pretend that his generation alone was sexual;

that the human race had, until his birth, sprung from flowers or been dropped from the sky.

Unfortunately, he could not. Someone had fathered his sisters. And Edmund turned the pages of the date books to see whether that person could have been the late Lord Kirkpatrick. The baron had kept careful account of his travel; he was often in London for the Season, or with friends in the Home Counties, where the hunting was easy and the land was soft and gentle.

The records showed that the baron had been gone a great deal of time. Oh, it wasn't impossible that he had fathered Catherine and Mary. Babies came in their own time, and he had been at home some time between ten and eight months before the birth of each of Edmund's sisters.

But did they resemble the late lord? Edmund's eyes were like his father's, blue as the sky never was in London. His mother's, too, were light. Turner had dark eyes.

What about Mary and Catherine? He couldn't remember.

He shut the book and looked at its black-leather cover, tooled in a pattern of scrollwork. A great *K* was chased in gilt in the center of the cover. Here was the year 1794 as his father had lived it, so distant in time and memory as to bear no relation to anyone Edmund had known. He had been only four years old. Tutored by the ever-present Turner, already sopping up history and language. Ignorant of, oblivious to, the man's true nature, or his mother's feelings.

Maybe Edmund hadn't wanted to return to Cornwall because he hadn't wanted to see how much his mother missed Turner. Maybe he hadn't wanted to see the sorrow on her face—not for the husband who had died, but for the lover who had left.

Since Jane had left him, Edmund felt he had gotten a taste of that sorrow. She had wanted escape more than she wanted him, despite her profession of love. In the end, he knew, she hadn't loved him enough to stay. Just as he knew his parents had not loved each other, or their children, enough to do right by one another. Their family ties were coarse and brittle, nothing but habit.

Such knowledge destroyed a family—but what did it do to an individual? It had eaten away Edmund's insides; it had robbed him of sleep.

But it had not destroyed him.

He hadn't always been happy. He hadn't always been sensible. But overall, he'd been . . . decent. As a boy, he'd done his best, just as he strove to now. He wanted to do right by everyone, especially those who relied on him. He just didn't always know how.

Jane was certainly proof of that.

He made a stack of the date books and slid the pile to the corner of his desk. For a moment he simply stood, lost in thought.

Then he took a candlestick in hand and made his way up to the attic, where the family portraits were stored.

Chapter 21

Concerning a Portrait

Jane had spent the first weeks of her marriage learning the Berkeley Square house. For all her exploration, though, she'd never ventured to the attic of the building that had so briefly been her home. There had always been enough to occupy her on the floors below.

But Pye had said Edmund was up here. And so, on this chilly Sunday afternoon, she would be, too.

Her heeled slippers clattered on the wooden treads of the stairs. The flight was narrower here than on the ground floor, or the first or second. An upper landing took a rectangular bite from the rear corner of the attic. Along the front of the house, door after door indicated where servants' chambers had been portioned out. At this hour, they were busy about their work or enjoying a half day out, and the space was utterly quiet.

Turning, she faced the back of the house. Two more small chambers had been divided off here. Beyond them, stretching back to the corner of the house, was a chaotic tangle of cast-off furniture, piled draperies, and leaning stacks of paintings.

Jane squeezed past a heavy Georgian corner cupboard, abandoned in place as soon as it had been muscled up the stairs. Light filtered dimly here through small windows, half blocked by the accumulated discards of more than a century of inhabitants. Cold leaked in beneath the rafters.

And to one side stood Edmund. Absolutely silent; perfectly still. His left hand gripped a canvas covering; his right fist was clenched at his side. Pale dust smudged his dark coat, surely unavoidable in this close, cluttered space. Far more unusual was the expression on his face.

If Jane had to put one word to it, it would be *wistful*.

She had never seen Edmund wistful. Not when a dance came to an end. Not when she had departed last night. Not when, those few endless weeks ago, she had admitted she loved him.

Wistfulness meant you wanted something you couldn't have. She'd never been able to figure out what he wanted before.

Unable to resist learning the truth, she sidled past a pair of tea tables, one stacked facedown atop the other. The unsteady affair rocked as Jane brushed past, and a board betrayed her with a squeak.

Edmund whirled at once. He squinted; the light filtering from behind him must be casting Jane into shadow. "Pye? Is something amiss?"

"Why you always mistake me for Pye, I'll never know." Jane edged a step closer, keeping a wary eye on the stacked tables. "It's not as though we resemble each other."

"Jane." His clenched fist relaxed. "I didn't realize you meant to call today."

"I didn't." Was his heart pounding as quickly as hers? "Today we both find ourselves in an unexpected place." With a sweep of her arm, she indicated the storage area.

"You didn't expect to visit?" His other hand released the wadded canvas, letting it fall over the picture that had made him look so wistful.

"I thought I ought to come today."

"Yes." He looked down at the painting. "I did, too."

So focused was he on the painting, she couldn't bring herself to pepper him with questions. Except for one. "May I see it?"

"It's hardly worth looking at." But he pulled at the edge of the canvas drape again, drawing it back from the painted surface. Jane stood at his side.

The portrait was large, more than five feet in height. A family was arrayed in oils amidst a garden cluttered with Roman columns and stonework. The standing figure of a man at the center of the image was almost at her eye level. Though his hair was powdered and pulled back in a queue, his straight nose and brilliant blue eyes proclaimed his relationship to the man at Jane's side.

"He has your eyes," she murmured. "Is this your father?"

"Yes. And my mother and sisters." Edmund's voice was clipped.

Jane ventured a glance at him; his jaw was set, lips pulled tight. And when she looked back at the portrait, she saw the essential difference: that mouth, that chin. His father's was slack, even with the flattering brush of the portraitist to give it strength.

The woman's features held all the decision her husband's lacked. Her chin was lifted, a firm jaw that added to her austere beauty. Like the man's, her hair was powdered in the fashion of the previous generation. Her seated figure was swathed in rich reds, with jewels about her wrists, throat, fingers. Perched on one knee, almost painted in as an afterthought, was a very young child with fair hair, wearing the full-cut gown and ringlets of an infant. Two other children were tucked into the edges of the portrait. A girl with fair hair, about five years of age, and a boy on the left. He was only partially shown, his shoulder and one arm out of the picture. His other hand reached up for his father's shoulder; his face appeared at the level of the weak-chinned man's upper arm. The boy's expression was stern, as though he'd been ordered *be a little man.*

"This was the last portrait done of my family," Edmund said quietly. "In truth, it was the only one done. My parents realized that they'd never managed to get us painted, so the year before my father's death, the three of us children were daubed into the wedding portrait of my parents."

"Why not commission a new one?" Jane wondered. "You look like such handsome children, but there's hardly room for you in this painting."

"There was hardly room for us anywhere." He made as though to release the canvas cover again, but Jane stilled his hand. Warm fingers under hers; the same hand that had been painted, so long ago, clutching his father's shoulder.

"Why do you never see them?"

He scuffed a boot along the floor, looking for all the world like a bull ripping up its pastureland. "I don't wish to return."

"Then why don't they come here?" She knew she was prodding and prying, but what had she to lose?

Her question had silenced him. His shuffling feet went

still; even his breathing seemed shallower. "I'm used to things as they are."

Jane's nostrils flared. She was ready to rip up a pasture herself, or to shake Edmund by his sturdy, broad shoulders until his teeth rattled loose in his head.

But a quiet thought cut through her frustration: *used to things*. He hadn't said he was happy, only that he was accustomed to the present state of affairs. And she knew she hadn't imagined his wistfulness. A wistfulness that had nothing to do with Jane, yet made her feel closer to him all the same, because it revealed something that he wanted.

A family.

"Your sisters." She paused, not wanting to press too hard and shatter the moment. "Did they like their gifts?"

"I'm not sure." He rubbed the edge of the canvas between his thumb and forefinger. "I never hear from them. They used to send me little notes when they were girls, but I never knew what to write them in reply. I eventually just asked them what I could send them, and they told me. Now we simply communicate through my man of business in Cornwall."

"How horrid."

Edmund pulled in a deep breath. "It's best for all of us. They get what they want of me, and I know they are taken care of."

"If you think that giving someone a hat is taking care of her, yes."

Why had she said that? She hadn't come up here to pick a battle with him, but to pick up clues. What made Edmund happy or wistful. Why he never visited his family in Cornwall. What drove him to look at paintings he'd had hidden away long ago, judging from the dust motes shaken free of the canvas, floating in the weak light.

But he didn't fight her. This man, who had inherited his mother's determined jaw and his father's deep eyes, only bowed his head. "It's not. It's nothing of the kind. But it's all I can do."

"Why—is that?" She changed her question to a milder one. *Why don't you go back*, was what she'd wanted to ask. *What happened to all of you?*

"We haven't been a family for a long time. Were we ever? It took a painter to bring us together, and even then, only on canvas."

This time he did let the painting's cover fall over the image. "It's no wonder I made a muck of our marriage, is it? If we learn by example, I've had very little to go on."

"What rubbish. We cannot possibly learn everything by example." She folded her arms against the cold that leaked in around the window frame. "If we did, I'd still be living in a poky little cottage like my mother. Probably *with* my mother. Seeing the same people every day, living my life in the same tiny rounds." She took a deep breath. "Sometimes people don't belong in the family they're born into. And it doesn't mean you're a bad person. Or they are."

"But you *do* belong in your family. With Xavier, I mean. Your cousin. You're so much alike, in your stubbornness and daring."

Yes, she thought so, too. And she knew herself to be lucky now. "One reprobate can always manage to locate another."

He gave her a dutiful smile. "What I mean is, at your cousin's estate, you found a place you felt at home. In that, I envy you."

"Because you never have?"

The silence that followed was like a fine crystal: leaden and fragile. Jane fumbled to fill it, but everything seemed the wrong shape for her mind, her throat, her tongue.

Without a single word, he'd let her know how utterly their marriage had failed to take root. He'd let her know that there had never been anything for it to grow in. He regarded himself as too ignorant, too parched, to nurture any sort of relationship.

"You're wrong," she said. "You are so, so wrong."

"I wish I were." His anger, coming so rarely in quick flashes, would be far better than this. Now he seemed not wistful, but resigned. "Come downstairs, won't you? I think we've both seen enough up here."

"No." Before she could think better of it, she'd drawn closer to him and twitched back the canvas covering over the old portrait. "You're wrong, Edmund. And maybe I was, too. Sometimes people shape us by showing us what we *don't* want to be like. I didn't want a small life. And you don't want to be like this. A fake family, putting on a show in public."

"No, but that's hardly meaningful. Who *would* choose such a thing?"

A harsh laugh broke from Jane's throat. "I've lived among the *ton* for a far shorter time than you, yet I'd guess many people do."

"Not you, though."

She looked at the painted face of the boy, already handsome, already shoved aside. "No, not me. I'm too— what was it? Stubborn and daring?"

"Real disdain is better than a fake love."

It wasn't fake, you idiot. "Well." She made herself smile. "I hardly feel disdain for you."

"But we still have . . . nothing." His brows knit, and he, too, studied the faces. "You once said you loved me, but I didn't know what to do about it. So I lost you."

Still, always, he thought it was his doing when the people around him acted dreadful. What unutterable arrogance; what an unbearable burden. "You're not responsible for the way I feel, Edmund. I've told you that before."

He shook his head, and this time when he covered the painting again, she stepped back and let him have his distance. "I don't understand love. I was a fool to think I could do better than they."

"You're a fool, all right." She slashed the air, an impatient gesture. "I'm going downstairs, and I'll see myself out. I'd say, 'Enjoy your wallowing,' but that would defeat the purpose."

She had already turned away and eased by the face-down table before he spoke.

"Jane. Wait. Stay."

"What do you want?"

"Tell me what you mean," he said. "Tell me why you think I'm a fool."

Slowly, she turned on her heel. The effect would be one of great exasperation, and therefore—she hoped—he would pay more heed to it. An answer one had to drag forth was far better than unsolicited advice.

"Oh, Edmund." Her voice dripped with pity. "There are so many reasons. Where should I begin?"

Humor touched the corner of his mouth. "Stubborn," he muttered.

"You're a fool to think our marriage never had a

hope simply because your parents were unhappy. You're a fool to think you know nothing of love because you weren't raised by a loving family."

He lifted his brows, but before he could interrupt her, she charged ahead. "You know *everything* about love. You're drunk on it. It's your opium. For years, you've lived to make women love you in a thousand tiny ways. Every ball. Every conversation. You couldn't let them rest until you'd squeezed out a bit more love, and returned it, too. You're good to everyone, Edmund, and that doesn't come from an empty heart."

By the time her voice trailed into silence, her own heart was thumping, as if to say *I've had enough. Let me out; let me get away.* For whatever this revelation meant for him, if he took heed of it at all, it could mean only bleakness for her. This man, so full of love, could offer none to his wife.

"That's not love, Jane. None of that. It's more like—" He cut himself off, frowning.

"You already admitted that you didn't know anything about the subject. I won't argue with someone so ill-informed."

Unwelcome tears were beginning to well at the corners of her eyes. "Excuse me," she said, and turned away from him to blunder back through the cast-off furnishings.

Stop it, she told herself. *You're a baroness now. Have a little dignity.*

By the time Edmund caught up to her at the stairs, her face was back under her control. The tears were banished. But as usual, his expression was a mystery. She never could tell if he was angry or hurt. Or whether he was a thousand miles away, not thinking of her at all.

"You," he said, "have a most remarkable ability. You

can say the kindest things and have them sound insulting. And you can also call me a fool, time and time again, and make it sound like a sweet endearment."

He turned his head to the side, and light filtering through the open doorway to the catchall room caught his profile.

All at once—finally—she understood. Because that light caught him in the eye, contracting the pupil she could just barely see.

"You're looking at me," she said. "When you turn your head like that. You can see me. You—you look at things that you don't want people to know you're looking at."

His mouth crimped. Turning his head to face her, he squinted a bit in the slice of light that came through the doorway. "I never could deceive you."

"You deceive everyone." She choked off a laugh. "Xavier thinks you're trying to look like Byron when you snootle around like that."

"Byron—snootle—I—" Failing to emit more than two syllables at once, he settled for shaking his head. "I am a fool, aren't I?"

"Yes. You're a fool." She did her best to make it sound like a sweet endearment, as he'd said. This time she was the one who turned her head away. "I ought to be going now, I think."

"I'll see you out." No argument. But then, it wouldn't be good manners to argue.

In silence, they walked down stairs, more stairs, yet more, until they found themselves in the marble-tiled entrance hall. Jane remembered how gray it had been before she lived here. He'd lived with grayness for so long, he hadn't realized things could be different.

"You know," he said mildly, as she began tugging on her gloves. "You're a fool, too."

Jane's chin jerked. "I most certainly am not."

"Yes. You are." He lifted a hand as though he wanted to touch her, then let it fall again. "If you have so much faith in me, why did you leave?"

A face she knew so well; every plane and contour. Who was the man behind those handsome features, though? What did she know of his heart?

Not enough. Far too much.

"It wasn't you I was trying to protect." The admission was as painful as that first time she'd said she loved him, and he apologized.

"I see." He started to turn his head to the side, then paused. The effect was of a man with a dreadful crick in the neck.

"You can do your sideways-head peek," Jane said. "I won't tell your secret."

He smiled. "No need for such subterfuge. Not right now." He stepped closer to her; so close, she could see the freckle at the corner of his mouth. He smelled like clean linens and citrus; good enough to bathe in, good enough to eat. "May I kiss you good-bye?"

She blinked at him. "What? You want to kiss me?" The question seemed better suited to a couple just coming to know one another, not trusting the depths of their regard. It seemed odd to hear such a request from her husband, who had kissed every part of her body, who had never felt the need to ask before.

Perhaps he had never doubted her answer. Now Jane wasn't even sure if anything made him her husband besides a special license, a signature, and a few witnesses.

And . . . and this question. *Say it again. Please.*

He did. "Well. Yes. That is, there's mistletoe above us. Do you see? But if you think a kiss would—"

"Yes," she interrupted. "Yes. You may kiss me."

His eyes went dark, as though he was ready to loose the emotion he'd been bottling up. He caught her face in his hands, and Jane let out a sigh, ready, melting already.

For a few long seconds, he only looked at her, cradling her face as though astounded by the sight of her. And just when Jane began to feel self-conscious about his scrutiny, he lowered his mouth to hers.

Not a hot tangle of lips; not a sign of frantic lust. It was a light, deliberate brush of his lips over hers. Slow, so slow that every fiber of her body seemed to wake and unfurl toward him. Sweet, so sweet that she felt herself dissolving like sugar. He simply held her, teasing her mouth as though he was learning the feel of it. As though he liked the lesson.

Then he stepped back. His hands traced the curves of her ears, the slope of her jaw, then dropped to his sides. "Thank you."

The first time she had told him she loved him, he thanked her, and it sounded like an apology. It was the beginning of the end for them.

But this thanks—this sounded like gratitude. Like a simple, unexpected joy had caught him unawares.

Jane didn't know what it meant. She didn't trust her own impressions; she'd been too muddled and scrambled and hope-filled and let down even to know her own mind or heart.

"Come back any time you like, Jane," he said quietly. "But only if you intend to stay."

He helped her into her cloak; found her gloves on a side table and drew them onto her hands. Each gesture was so simple, so tender, that her icy resolve cracked into jagged pieces. "Is that a threat, Edmund? Or a promise?"

He traced the line of her cheekbone, then let his hand fall. "It's a promise. With me, it's always a promise."

Chapter 22

Concerning a New Variety of Plans and Plots

Just as Edmund had requested, Jane didn't return for another visit. Why she had chosen to become compliant at last, he had no notion.

He wished he hadn't given her an ultimatum. He meant it as self-preservation, but Jane probably saw it as a challenge. Which of them would give in first?

And did giving in mean staying apart, or finding one another again?

The endless days in the House of Lords kept this question from wearing a groove in his thoughts. Bills were put forth on misdemeanors and seditious meetings, preventing seditious meetings, protests against the prevention of seditious meetings—the unrest and bloodshed at Peterloo had shaken the staid upper crust of society. The two houses of Parliament agreed that they must act, but could not agree how.

Familiar, very familiar, to one touched by the Irish rebellion twenty-one years earlier.

Each day, Edmund returned home so tired that he almost didn't notice the quiet of the house. He entered the drawing room so seldom that he hardly saw the garland across the mantel beginning to droop.

He asked Xavier, when they caught sight of one another in the House of Lords, how Jane fared. All Xavier could say, or would say, was that Jane remained at Xavier House, seemed not to be committing any crimes, and was learning to play chess.

So the pages of Edmund's date book turned, and all of a sudden it was the week before Christmas. As his carriage trundled him through London, spices teased his nose from the open doors of bakeries. Some drivers had added strings of bells to their horses' reins, the jingle a pleasant counterpoint to the city's usual cacophony of wheels clattering over stone, of raised voices and animal bleats and whinnies. Even the weather added cheer; instead of autumn's miserable drizzle, the sky frosted rooftops with snow.

The streets and shops seemed busier than usual as the polite world hunted for gifts. Though Edmund had already arranged for a sensible gift of mutton, grain, and cloth to be distributed to his tenants, Jane's words echoed in his ear.

If you think that giving someone a hat is taking care of her . . .

No, he didn't think so, and he'd said as much. He'd also said he didn't know how to make things different with his family.

So, on this snowy evening, he began with his tenants.

He drafted another letter to Browning, inquiring whether any of the tenants had a particular interest in learning a trade, or reading, or music. Something to show that they weren't all the same; that he cared what they liked.

At the last moment, he lettered a postscript asking what his sisters and mother had thought of their gifts. Then he sealed the letter, franked it, and tried to put it out of his mind.

But his thoughts lingered on Cornwall: stone cottages with gently bowed roofs; tors and rocky hills; sandy shores under a watery sun. He looked out the window of his study, wishing he had a better view than rows of houses. Snow-frosted and bright though they appeared, the city seemed to press on him sometimes.

Without intending to, he had built a life that was small. When had that happened? And why had he never realized it before?

Soon his time would be his own again, though; only two more grueling slogs remained for the House of Lords. After the day's session ended on December 21, the nobles would toss the nation's business to the House of Commons and melt away, freed for a week—though some would leave for the country, not planning to return until spring. Xavier and his countess would dart off to Surrey, leaving Jane behind in Xavier House.

Edmund wondered whether the solitude would lead her to return. But he suspected that nothing—not scandal, not solitude, not a fortune in Spanish gold—would convince her to return before she was ready. If that time ever came.

Pye's knock at the door was a welcome interruption.

"A Mr. Bellamy has called for you, my lord. Do you wish to receive him?"

Not a welcome interruption, after all. Damn Bellamy. Turner. He should have left London by now. "I suppose I must. You may show him in, Pye. And if you've left him alone downstairs, we'd better count the silver before he leaves."

The butler's brows lifted. "I shall see to it myself, my lord."

A few minutes later, Turner bounded through the study doorway.

"You look gleeful," Edmund said. "There's no need for polite inanities, is there? Shut the door and tell me what the devil you're doing in London."

Turner knocked the door shut, then dropped into the chair across from Edmund. "Stealing things."

"Are you being metaphorical or literal?" Edmund shook his head. "What am I thinking? Both, of course. Turn out your pockets."

The older man obliged, still wearing a pestilent grin. "Ah, I could steal trinkets from anyone. From you, boyo, I've stolen something quite special."

"You must mean my wife. No doubt you are aware she no longer lives under my roof. So why are you still in London?"

"The game isn't played out yet."

"It damned well is. You said you wanted to go back to Cornwall once you took away my wife. Well, congratulations, Turner. You've won, though I hardly even needed your help to ruin my marriage. Lady Kirkpatrick has left me, so you can leave, too. Be off with you."

The determined smile flickered. Turner ran a blunt

finger inside the tumble of lace that served him as a cravat. "You'd be content to see me go, would you? And leave Lady Kirkpatrick's name in the mud?"

Edmund's stomach became annoyed by the conversation; he pressed a fist against his breastbone, willing the pain away. "Lady Kirkpatrick's good name cannot be affected by you. And yes, I'd be content to see you go. If you're in such a tearing hurry to go to Cornwall, just leave."

Turner began to blink rather more often. Edmund's stomach settled down as he perceived the best way to pick through this conversation. Turner wanted to play the game? Fine. But Edmund had his own rules.

"I believe you, by the way," Edmund added in a bland tone. "About my sisters being your daughters. They have your eyes. I saw it in a family portrait. That being the case, I'm sure you will treat them well. You must have missed them very much during your lengthy incarceration. Do you think they'll be glad when you tell them they're bastards? Perhaps it will be some comfort to them when you replace the father you all but killed."

"Me? Or you?" Turner growled. "You'd best shut your gob. You don't know a damned thing about what happened."

Edmund shrugged. "If you like. But it was only a few weeks ago that you told me you'd dishonored my parents and that my sisters were illegitimate. I remember that fairly well. Unless you were lying?"

The smile was entirely gone now. "It's the truth, and no denying it."

"Oh, well, that's settled. If you promise you were telling the truth. I've no reason to distrust you."

The look of loathing Turner shot him was enough to

fix a pleasant expression on Edmund's face that was not entirely feigned.

"So. You're here to steal things," Edmund added conversationally. "But not my silver. And it can't be my wife. I'm nearly out of ideas. Care to elucidate?"

"The Xavier rubies."

Edmund's hands clunked onto the top of his desk. "Huh. I didn't expect that."

"Maybe you've heard about a few jewel thefts in Mayfair. I'm not saying I had anything to do with those, mind you."

"Lady Sheringbrook's pearls?" Edmund racked his brain. "That's all I know of. There have been others?"

"Others," Turner confirmed. His oily smile was back. "So says rumor. And Lady Alleyneham, and Lord Debenham, and that Pellington fellow. A flock of pitiful sheep, the *ton* is. A few families are putting up a reward for the capture of the thief. I'm thinking I might take them up on it."

"By turning yourself in? Good God. You stole pearls from an old woman. As though she hasn't enough to be going on with, with spasms in her hands and a son worth less than—"

"Poor woman, yes, with her fine house and her annuity to keep her warm. She's a stingy old bat, not even helping her only child. But there are ways for a man to find the help he needs."

"God," Edmund repeated, scrubbing a hand over his eyes. "You're telling me that you and Sheringbrook are stealing jewels."

"I never said anything of the sort."

"No, you carefully did not." Edmund sighed. "What's this rot about the Xavier jewels, then?"

"Ah, yes. See, that's where you and Lady Kay come into the matter." Turner leaned back in the chair and narrowed his eyes. "The problem is, I think she still loves you. That won't do."

"Why would you possibly think such a thing?" The words came out more like a croak than a question.

"Since she's left you, I see she's lost a bit of her sparkle. Not to say there aren't still ways of giving a gel joy—"

Edmund sprang to his feet.

"—but she's not to my taste. A skinny little plain slip of a girl." Turner raised placating hands. "So touchy, aren't you?"

"Out," said Edmund, advancing around the desk.

"Hear me out, because your family's reputation depends on it."

Edmund missed a step.

"Aha. Thought so." Turner smiled, though his normally smooth expression looked a bit ragged. "Here's what you'll do, then. You'll meet Lady Kay at Xavier House and get her to tell you where those rubies are kept. Seduce her, threaten her, whatever you like. She knows. Sheringbrook says she's worn them before. Once you find out, I'll call on you again, and you'll tell me."

"I'll do nothing of the sort." Footing steady again, Edmund loomed over Turner's chair. "Out."

"I thought you might be *dobh*—er, stubborn about the matter." The words tripped quickly from Turner's tongue. "Which is why I'll tell Lady Kay everything if you don't agree."

"Out." Edmund grabbed Turner's forearm and hauled him from the chair. "Now. And don't touch the silver."

"Think about it," Turner said. "Do you want her to hate you for keeping secrets? Or do you want to pay the smaller price—really, no price at all—for handing over another man's jewels?"

"Why should she believe anything you say? She knows you as Bellamy."

"I have letters from your mam as proof. If I show them to Lady Kay, I needn't tell her I'm Turner, need I? But even if you decide to, I wonder whose lies will bother her more. A recent friend, or the man she married?"

Edmund's hand had gone cold, but he wouldn't relax his grip on Turner's arm. "Out."

Somehow, the man shook free and drew himself up straight. "I'm going. I'll be back tomorrow for you to tell me what you've decided. But one way or another, I'll have those jewels on Christmas Eve. If you won't get me the answer I need, I'll take it from Lady Kay myself."

Revulsion clamped Edmund's hand tight at the collar of Turner's coat. "Out. I won't listen to another word."

"I've said my piece." Again, Turner freed himself, and he opened the study door. "I'll return tomorrow."

"Out." Edmund shoved the door shut behind him, hoping it caught him in the arse.

The sudden quiet roared in his ears; the study's book-lined walls closed in on him. Blackness crept into the edges of his vision, speckled with bright colors. The world twisted and vanished.

Fumbling his way back around his desk, Edmund sank into his chair. He shut his eyes and waited. Waited for hearing and sight to return; for sense to filter through Turner's words.

After a minute, or an hour, Edmund opened his eyes. The dark wood paneling, the neat rows of leather-bound spines on the bookshelves, the warm glow of the lamp and fire were all back in their accustomed place.

The world appeared calm and prosaic, yet one way or another, his life as he'd known it would soon come to an end.

His family estate in Cornwall had more skeletons in its closets than any Gothic novel. For years, Edmund had hidden those dreadful truths from the world. He'd built a life in London, and he had done his best to make it a good one. All the while, he kept his silence, kept up his fortune, found good hands to care for his land. He did this for his mother and sisters, and now for Jane. The women whom the law bound to his protection.

He even left them, or let them leave, to save them pain. Always, he ended up alone.

Only now did it occur to him that their dependence on him surely brought its own kind of pain. Or that he stayed apart, aloof from any deeper emotion, to spare himself, too.

His family knew why. They knew what he was worth. Jane didn't, and that was why she'd been able to fancy herself in love with him.

That was done now, because he could see no way to protect her except by giving her the truth. Turner would thus be disarmed, his greatest weapon placed in Jane's hands. Every scrap of feeling she had for Edmund would be killed, but she herself would be safe.

The idea was not wholly bleak. What might someone

as bloodthirsty and ingenious as Jane do with the knowledge of Turner's identity? His crimes?

Edmund could not imagine. But it was time to find out. Though he had asked Jane not to call on him again for a visit, she had made no such restriction on him.

He rang for his carriage to be brought round.

Chapter 23

Concerning That Long-Ago Winter

The hour was far too late for a caller.

So said Xavier, as he, Louisa, and Jane sat in the Xavier House drawing room. "The house isn't on fire. So who the devil would be hammering on the door at this time of evening?"

Jane had an idea, but she wasn't going to admit it. "It's a Bow Street Runner. To arrest you for tying your cravat in a preposterous way."

"Or to clap you in irons for disrespecting your elders."

Louisa smiled. "You can't think of anyone who might be calling now? Does no one in this room have a wayward spouse?"

"Everyone in this room has a wayward spouse," Jane said. "You two just prefer the term 'strong-willed.'"

"Yes. Well. The proper term can make a great deal of difference." Xavier set aside his quizzing glass and newspaper, then threaded his way through the furniture. Opening the door to the drawing room, he came face-to-face with his butler, whose hand was upraised to knock.

"Ah. Hollis. We theorize that the racket at the door is somehow related to Lady Kirkpatrick. Is this correct?"

"Indeed, my lord."

"Naturally," Xavier sighed. "Since her birth, Lady Kirkpatrick has been the cause of most of the disorder in my life."

"My lord, Lord Kirkpatrick wishes to speak to his wife in private."

"Very well, show him up."

Louisa cleared her throat. "If, that is, Lady Kirkpatrick wishes?"

"Yes." Jane's insides seemed to be practicing a Scotch reel. "Yes, I'll see him."

With a fake-looking yawn and stretch, Louisa stood. "We're remarkably tired, aren't we, Alex? We'll just be headed off upstairs."

"Show Lord Kirkpatrick up," Xavier said to the butler. "I'm not tired in the least, though," he added for Louisa's benefit. "I think I ought to remain in the room during this call. Jane is under my protection."

"No, she's under your *roof.* She's under *Kirkpatrick's* protection. And she's hardly going to have her reputation damaged by a visit from her husband in her cousin's home. Come, we're two people too many for this call."

Louisa gave Jane a quick hug. "Good luck. Ring for a servant to fetch us if need be." Then, grabbing Xavier's arm—ugh, no, a few other parts of his form—she bustled her husband from the drawing room.

And Jane sat.

She had only a few moments to compose herself before Edmund entered, looking like winter itself. He must have come hatless, for his dark hair was beaded with droplets of water where snow had melted; his eyes reflected the frost-blue of his waistcoat, and his coat was dark as the ice of a pond.

His expression, too, was frozen. Jane could not tell what had brought him to her in such a tearing hurry.

"You look horrid," she said. "I mean, cold and worried and—here, come sit by the fire."

Lamplight picked out the gilt on yellow-papered walls; the fire cast a halo onto a wing chair of dark red velvet. With more determination than grace, Jane shoved Edmund into it.

"I wish you'd sit, too," he protested. "I have a lot to tell you."

Jane sat, facing him. Of newborn habit, her fingers found the chess queen in the pocket of her striped sarcenet gown; all hues of green, and unfashionably simple in its cut. "Tell me, then."

"Once I've done, you'll never want to return to me."

"I'll go home with you this very minute if you can say that you love me. I know you won't lie."

He stared at her.

"That's what I thought."

"No, you misunderstand. I didn't realize there was any chance you would return. Ever." His gaze became fixed on something far away. "But before you make such an offer, I owe you the truth about my family. I've never told anyone before. Yet I must trust you." He caught Jane's eye. "I *do* trust you."

Jane forgave him for not professing love right away. She knew he meant to be kind, and she could ignore the nearly-right-but-not-quite things he said when he was kind. Especially when he tossed the word *trust* to her, sweeter and richer than a plum pudding.

"I don't know how to begin, though."

Her insides had abandoned their Scotch reel in favor of a waltz, and she sank, slow, into the promise of understanding. A few coals tumbled in the fireplace, breaking the silence. Then she suggested, "How about with 'once upon a time'?"

"Yes. That will do." He loosened his cravat, then with a strange, tight smile, he began. "Once upon a time, a little over thirty years ago now, an Irish woman married a baron from Cornwall. It was an arranged marriage, and to the home of the husband she'd never met, she brought a manservant named Thomas Turner. He was charming and brilliant, and he soon became the baron's steward and trusted friend. The couple had a son, and when that son grew old enough to behave like a reasonable human, Turner became the son's tutor, too."

"What a versatile fellow."

"Yes, he was." Edmund watched the coals flare and crumble. "He certainly was that. You see, he was also the baroness's lover. Most likely the father of her daughters, born in the years following her son's birth. And he was a thief."

Goose bumps raced down Jane's arms within her sleeves. She slapped a hand over her mouth so she wouldn't say anything. She had to let him speak. Finish. Tell her everything.

His words came faster now, as though a wound had been lanced and was bleeding freely. "In 1798, there was a rebellion in Ireland. Irish Catholics rising up against the English, the old battle. It's been fought many times, but rarely in so bloody a way. It was eventually crushed, the leaders executed, and the movement disbanded. Or so it seemed.

"Turner was a Catholic, and a steadfast Irishman. So

steadfast that he wanted to fund the cause, to revive it in its most militant form. He didn't describe it that way, though. He talked about justice and freedom. Played on the baron's fascination with his chilly Irish wife. The poor baron had never known how to touch his wife's heart— did you say something?"

"No. No, nothing." Jane wished she could feel numb. She wanted to cry for him, but it would be selfish to demand his attention for her tears.

Besides which, she didn't cry. "Go on, please."

"Yes, well, I think he loved his wife, though he didn't understand her. Maybe that was what kept him in thrall to her. Or Turner. They needed my father not at all; their confidence fascinated him."

"But they did need him," said Jane. "At least, they needed his money."

"True. They needed his money very much. And so Turner talked the baron into providing aid for the revolutionaries. Money, jewels, what have you. If the packet had been sent, it would have represented treason."

Jane's insides felt far too heavy for any sort of dance now. She seemed leaden as she listened, as Edmund's story twisted down darker and darker paths.

"The baron was weak and credulous. Besotted with his wife; besotted with the idea of being needed for once. He surely could not have understood what he was doing, because traitors are executed, and their families are stripped of everything. Titles, lands . . ."

"What have you," Jane finished.

With a thin smile, Edmund nodded. "Right. What did Turner care if the baron was found to be a traitor? He could marry the baroness and run off to Ireland with her. And damn-all to the children who bore the baron's name. Or to his servants and tenants, or his distant heirs. Everything would go to the Crown.

"For all Turner's other faults, the son had been tutored well, and by the age of nine, he knew a bit about law. Like many boys, he was fascinated by crimes and gruesome punishments. Also like many boys, he was fond of prying into the business of his elders."

"He sounds delightful," Jane said in a bracing tone.

"He was a dreadful little nuisance. First he realized that his mother and Turner were lovers, and he never trusted his tutor—or his mother, for that matter—again. He had no one left to worship but his father, and he certainly tried to. But not every story has a hero. On the night Turner was to depart for Ireland with the casket of money and jewels, the baron was detained. He ordered his son to take a message to Turner. And the son . . . didn't. He took it to the magistrate instead. He betrayed his own parent."

"A small betrayal to stop a larger one."

"There is nothing small," Edmund murmured, "about a betrayal of one's parent. But the rest can be told quickly. Turner was found with his employer's jewels and taken up for theft. The baron pled for leniency, and instead of being executed, Turner was transported for twenty years. The baron must have burned any incriminating papers. He must have known about his wife's infidelity, too, because he died in a solitary hunting accident that no one looked into too deeply."

"And the son?" Jane's throat closed tight on the words.

"The son never made amends or received them. He inherited a barony from a father who had never again spoken to him after that night." He paused. "When his father died, the family was destroyed. The son blamed himself for this. He soon went off to school and never returned home again."

"And—Turner?"

"After twenty years in Australia, his sentence was done. He stole and cheated his way back to England somehow, vengeance on his mind. He hated the boy—now a man—who had been born of his lover's husband. Who had ruined his dreams of rebellion, or destruction."

Blue eyes gone tawny in the firelight, he gazed at Jane. "You know him as Daniel Bellamy."

For a moment, nothing in the world seemed to make sense. The movement of Edmund's lips seemed foreign, forming words that scrambled in Jane's ears.

"Huh." She stood, took a step toward Edmund, then sank down again, missing the seat of her chair. "Huh. Bellamy."

"Jane. Are you all right?"

She looked up; Edmund loomed over her, his brow creased with concern.

This was enough to snap her world back to normal. Edmund's story was done. He was being kind.

Ridiculous man.

She shoved herself to her feet. "*Me*? I am fine. Just surprised. How are *you*?"

He took her hand. Helping her back into her chair, he rubbed his roughened fingers lightly over hers. "It's not a good story. But I'm glad you know it."

"It's a horrible story." She lifted his hand to her face, pressing her cheek against the warm bumps of his knuckles. "There was only one good thing about it."

"You heard something good in that story?"

"Yes. The hero."

He tugged his hand free. "There's no hero in that story."

"The boy who saved his family's good name, title, and fortune?"

"The boy who betrayed his father and grew up distant from all of his relatives, you mean. A hell of a paragon." He walked his fingers down the swooping wing of Jane's chair, then crouched to sit at her feet. "I didn't know my father would die. But with his wife and most trusted servant betraying him—oh, and his son; let us not forget his son—he had nothing left to live for."

He shrugged, as though the matter of this loss was of no consequence.

But Jane read the rest of his body; he couldn't hide the truth from someone so skilled at lying. The flex of his jaw, the pressure of his fingers; the tightness of the cords of his neck above his loosened cravat. He worked so hard, so terribly hard, to hold himself together. It was a habit of years.

He'd already broken her heart so many times. This time, it broke on its own for him.

"My father wasn't a strong man," Edmund said. "He must have thought escape easier than brazening through one's problems."

"Yes," Jane said faintly. She laced her fingers in his hair; the snow melt had left it gently waving, fine as silk thread. "Yes, it certainly is."

He seemed not to notice she had spoken. Silence held the room; not tightly, but in the hollow of its palm. The tale was done, and now the firelight cradled them, and Jane rested her hand on her husband's head and let the wonder of it all seep through her.

"So long, you've been keeping this a secret. No

wonder you can hardly choke down a meal. This must have been eating you up."

"A lie of omission is still a lie. I'm very sorry I didn't tell you before. I didn't trust that you'd want anything to do with me if you knew the truth." He gave a hollow laugh. "I've demonstrated that I have no loyalty to those to whom I owe the most."

She considered this. "That's one way to think of it. Another way is that your parents put a young boy into a horrible situation. Which, thank God, he could escape. One could also view the matter thus: that that same boy, now grown to a man, has spent years providing security for people who never took the slightest pains to keep him safe."

When she finished speaking, he stood up abruptly. Moved away, into the shadowed corner of the room. "You're wrong."

But he didn't want her to see him. Which meant he couldn't hide what he felt.

Which meant she might have cracked through the stone around his heart at last. Just a little . . . but a crack was enough.

"I understand now," she said. "Why you wanted to marry so quickly. Why you were willing to take a wife with no dowry. You needed someone to support you so you wouldn't have to face Turner alone. And your talk of needing an heir—in case anything happened to you, you wanted to be sure the barony was safe."

"Yes. No? I don't know. It's such a puzzle."

"I've known all the pieces for some time. Now I understand how they fit together." She paused. "I'm so sorry."

"There is nothing for which you need apologize."

"I'm not saying I'm 'sorry for'; I'm only 'sorry that.'

I'm sorry that your family was no kind of a family at all. I'm sorry that you felt so much pain in trying to spare others pain."

She slid to the floor, taking the spot he had abandoned. "I know our marriage hasn't gone as you thought. It hasn't gone as I thought either. I'm sorry for that, too. I don't blame you any more than I blame myself. So I suppose I blame us both to a moderate degree."

Edmund moved back into the golden reach of the lamplight, and she tossed him a smile. He was too polite not to give her one of his own.

"But I'm something more than sorry," she added. "I'm angry, too."

"I thought you would be," he said. "I—"

"Not at you." She rolled over his explanation. "At your father. He left you alone in the world with a man who had already betrayed his family. He made sure Turner had the chance to come back. That's a hell of a good-bye to his son and heir."

Edmund went perfectly still.

"Really, Edmund. If your father had your backbone, he would have taken care of the matter then and there. Made Turner suffer his punishment. A life transport, at the very least."

A bleak smile curved his lips. "I always knew you were bloodthirsty."

"Not as much as your father. He spilled his own blood and made you cover the taint of his sin. Not as much as your mother, either, who mixed her blood with an old lover's who should never have been part of her life."

"You are very critical of people you have never met," he murmured.

"Thanks to your father's own actions, I *can't* meet him.

As for your mother—well, I've met you. I know you. I know you've done your best by her. Did she truly do her best by you, though? And don't," she cut him off, "give me any rubbish about you being the man of the house after your father died. You were only nine years old at the time."

"What's done is done." He sounded grim, but not bitter. "I did the best I could, and so did they. For none of us was it as good as it could have been."

"Surely you don't compare your behavior to theirs."

"No." The shadows under his eyes seemed darker, his eyes old and tired. "No, I compare it to what it should be now. The servants—the tenants—my sisters—they were all innocent. But I have nothing to do with Cornwall, and so I have abandoned them."

"Says the man who sent his relatives expensive hats and a stack of novels for Christmas."

"Ah, well. We've agreed that gifts don't mean anything, do they? They required no sacrifice. Only a bit of time."

"No. *No*. You can't have it both ways. You can't be bad for ignoring them and bad for sending them gifts. In truth, Edmund, I don't think it's bad at all to stay away."

He just looked at her with disbelieving eyes. *Go ahead and try to explain yourself*, his expression said. *This should be entertaining.*

"Well," she began, halting, "there's some self-interest in what I say. I don't wish to return to village life, even though I'd see my mother more often. Do you think less of me for that?"

"Don't. Don't try to make an analogy, Jane. Your mother is cared for, and you've built a life without her—hmm. I mean, you're married now, and your first allegiance is to—oh. That is to say. You've made a home for yourself in London—ah, damn it."

"You see?" She couldn't help but feel a bit smug as he talked himself into a corner. "Either we're both bad, or we're both fine. We're both selfish, or we're both still doing the best we can."

He turned his head away.

"I know you're looking at me from the corner of your eye," she said. "But turn away if you must. My brilliance can be difficult to gaze on directly."

He snorted. "You think you're very clever."

"At the moment, yes." She paused. "But what do you think? Can you hear what I'm saying, as I heard you?"

His lips moved.

"What was that?" she asked.

"I am reminding myself," he said more loudly, "that it is bad manners to swat grown females upon the bottom."

Jane's face went hot. "I suppose that depends on the circumstances."

Edmund choked, and she added swiftly, "But if that's a way for you to say that you know I'm right and you don't want to admit it, that's fine with me. Or not even that. Just—just listen."

His profile was so sharp, she wanted to trace it with a fingertip.

"I've listened," he said. "I have indeed listened. You think of the situation very differently than I do."

"I haven't lived inside it for most of my life, as you have. But maybe because I see it from the outside, I see the shape of things more clearly."

"Maybe," he granted. "But we don't have to talk about it anymore."

"You want to start quoting poetry and scattering compliments about? That's too bad. I won't be distracted tonight." She tried to sound businesslike. "Edmund, Turner's hold over you comes from the secrets he knows. But if the truth about him and your parents came out, what would be the worst thing that could possibly happen?"

"Everyone would know the truth."

"And?"

"And? And what? And my mother would be ostracized. My sisters would never be able to marry. I'd be looked on with scorn."

"It seems to me that most of those things have already happened. Your mother and sisters essentially live in exile. You are well-liked, though, and I can understand why you'd be reluctant for that to change."

"I haven't kept this secret all these years so I could be *liked*."

"Why, then? It won't make a difference in the way your mother and sisters live."

"It would make a difference to you."

"I wasn't part of your life before this autumn." She forced a smile. "So you can't convince me that you've held your tongue for twenty years for my sake."

"You think it was selfish?" He looked as though she'd struck him. "This . . . *thing* . . . that I've taken responsibility for. You call that a selfish act?"

"Not selfish." She considered. "No, not selfish. But not *necessary*. The sins weren't yours."

"But the responsibility is. I hold the title."

"Yes, but that doesn't mean you need be responsible for everything your family has done or ever will do. Every family has black sheep. Let the *ton* baa-baa-baa about them. It needn't affect you."

"But it does," he murmured. "It does. Because I care what happens to them."

She went silent then. There was nothing more to say. He had taken this problem to heart because even after all the pain of his boyhood, his family lived there. He shouldered burdens that weren't his, hoping they would be lifted from others.

It would be admirable, if it weren't so bullheaded.

Actually, Jane could admire the bullheadedness, too.

"There's more to the story," he said. In a moment, he had sketched out Turner's thefts and his lust for the Xavier jewels. "He wants me to talk you into revealing where they're kept. So he can steal them. I'm not fond of the idea."

"Nor I." She thought for a moment. "We shall have to come up with a new one."

Chapter 24

Concerning Tragedie— or Its Opposite

"We?" Edmund seemed more shocked by this short word than by any part of his long revelation.

"Yes, *we*. You and me."

"Why?"

If he hadn't looked so bleak, Jane would have given him the tongue-lashing of his life. "Because we are *married*."

"What does that matter?"

Jane raised her eyes to the ceiling. "Fine, then. Because I am ingenious, and it never hurts to have someone so ingenious on your side. Because you think Bellamy—or ought I to call him Turner?—has an eye for me. Which is due to you, and not me at all."

"Are you disappointed?"

"Of course not," she scoffed. "Though I am disappointed that all his stories about elephants were complete rubbish."

"I've no doubt that they were. If it helps, deception is a lifelong habit with him. You were certainly not the first nor the only one to be fooled by him."

"Sheringbrook a cheat. Turner a liar. Our whole betrothal and marriage has been a series of encounters with shady characters."

"We are a bit shady ourselves." Edmund looked wry. "I've long known it of you. Now you know it of me, too."

"I once thought I was good at reading people. Now I'm not sure."

"Don't begin to doubt yourself now."

"Begin?" A bark of laughter burst from her throat. "I began the night Sheringbrook took ten thousand pounds from me. Everything since then has been a continuation."

"Fine. Don't continue, then."

"How simple for you to say." She shook her head. "But we aren't talking of me. We're talking of how we can help you."

"I wonder if the two might be the same." Edmund seated himself on the arm of her chair, legs braced upon the floor. "You did make a remarkably fine noblewoman at Sheringbrook's house. Aside from your first curtsy in error, you've been a pitch-perfect baroness in public. And I've never seen a more wenchy serving wench than you played at the masquerade."

She looked up at him. "You thought I was wenchy, did you?"

"Extremely." For a moment, their eyes met. That dark night in the garden seemed to spin out slowly, a cobweb of memory tying them together. That quick flame of passion; she had finally, briefly, felt they had a true marriage.

"I'm having an idea," she said.

"I am, too."

"A wenchy idea?"

He laughed. "In a way." He looked at her from the corner of his eye, and his laugh died. She realized that the muscular line of his thigh was almost at the level of her eye. Seated as he was on the arm of the chair, his muscles flexed and tightened. She laid a hand on his leg, feeling the heat of his body through the sleek fabric of his breeches.

"In a way," he repeated. His hand covered hers, trapping it atop the long angle of his leg. "Business first."

"Very sensible."

"I wonder if you would play a part again. For a bit of entrapment."

"A . . . wenchy part?" Her voice sounded thick.

"I was thinking of the sort of wealthy doxy—"

Jane smothered a snort.

"That you pretended to be when you played cards with Sheringbrook." His gaze stroked her up and down. "You were very good at it."

"Thank you," she said primly. "Pure fabrication, since I was neither wealthy nor a doxy."

"I know." He smiled. "You were a lady. You've always been a lady."

Her jaw went slack.

"But what was your idea, Jane? I mustn't volunteer you for something if you've no inclination for it."

She collected her wits. "As a matter of fact, I was thinking that, too. If Turner thinks I think he's Bellamy, and if he doesn't know I know he's Turner, and if he doesn't suspect that I suspect him as being—"

"Please allow me to put a halt to your sentence before my ears break." Edmund stood, releasing her hand, then began to pace. "You are in agreement that, as the wife of

Turner's enemy, you are uniquely poised to carry out a
little scheme?"

"You could put it like that. Yes."

"And you are willing? We shall do our best to make
sure there's no risk to your safety."

"Yes, I'm willing." She hadn't considered that she
might not be safe, but it ought to be no worse than slipping off to a gaming hell on her own. She had probably
been less safe at Sheringbrook's than she would be confronting Turner.

And what made the difference? Edmund. Edmund, not
just there by chance, but by design. Edmund, asking her
to trust in him, yet asking nothing she was unwilling to
give.

"We might need the help of a few others, too," she said.

He nodded. "There are still many details to work out.
But Jane, thank you. Turner and I are locked in a stalemate, and there's no breaking it without you."

"Without whoever happened to be your wife."

"No. Without *you*. Jane." Slowly, he paced the span of
the room. "Jane Tindall, who went to make her fortune by
playing a wealthy doxy—and a spectacular game of
vingt-et-un. Jane, who dared risk that fortune, and who
should have been rewarded. Jane, who is honorable yet
devious. Who is bloodthirsty yet pure of heart. Who can
be a baroness or a serving wench, but is most of all curious and bright."

By the time he was finished speaking, her eyes stung
and she had to tuck her legs up so she made a ball. He
needed her. *Her.* Need was love's cousin. A nearer relation than she had ever expected. "You don't blame me for
leaving you?"

"No more than I blame myself." With a sigh, he laid a

hand on the crown of her head. "Jane, Jane. What are we going to do?"

His voice was tired, as though he'd asked himself the same question so many times that he no longer hoped for a reply.

Until she swallowed the catch in her throat and blinked back the tears in her eyes, she let his hand rest atop her coiled braids. Then she looked up at him; his hand slid to cradle her cheek.

"Here's what we're going to do." She pulled the chess queen from her pocket and held it up. "We're going to work out this plan together. I'll be the wealthiest, wenchiest helpmate you could possibly imagine. And when we're done, you need never worry about Turner again."

And if—when—that was done, what might the new year hold?

She had thrown away something that could have been lovely. But that didn't mean she couldn't retrieve it.

With an ingenious and bloodthirsty plan in place, Edmund almost welcomed the announcement the following evening that "Mr. Bellamy" had called.

"Show him in to my study," he told Pye.

The stage was set. A half-full tumbler of whisky sat atop Edmund's desk, along with several coffee cups, a plate with sandwich ends, and Edmund's cravat, quickly yanked off and crushed into a pile. Before Turner entered, Edmund arranged himself in his chair: haggard, slumped, bitter. The picture of sleeplessness, wifelessness, rootlessness.

In the day since they'd last seen one another, Turner had recovered his oily good cheer. "Well, well, little lordling." He booted the door shut and dropped into the chair opposite Edmund. "You look as though you've had a rough day of it."

Edmund rubbed a hand along his jawline; stubble scratched at his fingertips. "A day in the House of Lords, arguing about who ought to be allowed to attend public meetings, and why, and how. All this after spending half of last night cooling my heels in Xavier House."

"Ah. You were trying to win an audience with your fair lady."

A bitter laugh burst forth. "For a while. But as I waited, and she refused to see me, I realized I'd rather be damned than help you steal again. So home I came."

"You've chosen the—"

"It's not I who'd suffer the most if our family secrets were told," Edmund cut him off. "My mother and Mary and Catherine would bear the brunt of the scandal. So keep that in mind when you're thinking up threats."

He met Turner's gaze. Studying the man closely for the first time since he'd entered the room, Edmund realized that he seemed smaller. Older. The ever-present smile hid crow's-feet and wrinkles, burned into his skin by sunlight and years. The man's hair was threaded with silver, his end-of-day stubble grizzled. Not even a dressmaker shop's worth of lace at his throat and the cuffs of his bottle-green coat could hide the spots of age on his skin.

After all, he was just a man. A man of deep and abiding selfishness, yes, and one who must be stopped. But no longer did Edmund have to do that alone.

First he had to play out this scene, though. He must keep his wits about him.

"As for Lady Kay," Edmund added in a mocking tone, "she has walled herself up tight. She and I are done with one another, Turner. Don't look so surprised. You know I've had a great deal of practice with this sort of thing. Women getting in a rage; me paying their bills and never seeing them."

Turner's smile had gone glassy. "So you've told me before. Your family in Cornwall, I assume you mean."

"Indeed. And I still regard my wife as part of my family, and I won't have you interfering with her." Again, a bitter laugh. "But why need I tell you this? You can try to speak to her or meet with her all you like. Wasn't that your threat? She won't even see you."

"She will. She's been seeing me all along. Nearly every day since she left you."

So smug was the man's expression that it was easy for Edmund to freeze; bluster his disbelief.

"It's true, boyo. Haven't you heard she's been playing chess? Who d'you think's been teaching her?"

The chess queen. Jane had held it up, a talisman of her promise to help him. A sick pang clenched Edmund's stomach, a revulsion that evidently painted itself across his features.

Turner leaned back, satisfied. "Told you the game wasn't played out yet. Next time I call on Lady Kay, I'll get what I want from her. One way or another."

"You disgust me."

"Likewise," Turner said. "Look at you. Look at the way you live. All walled up. Dragging yourself through each day. You might as well be in prison, boyo. You've no idea what to do with your life. You're wasting it."

"Wasting it? By holding my seat in Parliament? By taking care of the family you abandoned?" Many wounds had been opened yesterday; Edmund was still too raw to hide the pain of them. "If you want to see someone who's wasting his freedom, I'll fetch you a looking glass. For twenty years, you've been away from a woman you said you loved. From girls you say are your daughters, now grown up. You act as though you've some sort of moral right to your anger. Blaming me for separating you from them."

"Naturally I blame you. It's your doing that your family—my family—was destroyed, boyo. You know that as well as I."

"I couldn't have caused so much destruction on my own. You and my father laid the fire; all I did was strike the flint. Or declined to stamp out the blaze once started."

He remembered Jane's words: *A small betrayal to avoid a larger one.*

There was nothing small about it. But it had been the lesser wrong, nevertheless.

"If you gave a damn about your lover or daughters," Edmund added, "nothing would have kept you from going to their side as soon as you were able. Instead, you've frittered away months trying to torture me with the thought of you near them." He laughed. "There's no place for you anymore, is there? They're strangers to you now. All you have left is your anger."

He didn't bother looking at Turner. Didn't want to see what the man's face showed. Because the words Edmund had spoken sounded uncomfortably like something he could have said of himself.

"If you know so much about love," Turner said coldly, "why couldn't you keep your lady wife at heel?"

"I don't know anything about love. But neither do you."

The years away had further twisted Turner. Perhaps his mind had dwelled on the wrongs done him, the recompense due him, because the place where his body dwelled was unbearable.

Maybe he had loved Edmund's mother once. Maybe the separation from her—from Mary and Catherine—had been devastating, long ago. But he had waited so long, now he could do nothing but wait; he had let hate grow until it smothered love.

"If you wanted to go to Cornwall," Edmund added, "to act as a father, or a husband, there'd be no danger in it at all. Because you wouldn't hurt them if you loved them, and my feelings about the matter wouldn't signify in the slightest." Sifting through the litter on his desk, he found a coffee cup and tossed back its dregs, brewed and poured not long before Turner's arrival. "You want to play chess? There. I've taken your pawns."

Turner pursed his lips. "Maybe so. But I've still got your queen. Don't be forgetting that."

"No one takes possession of the queen. She's the most powerful piece on the chessboard."

"Without a king in play, though, she's nothing."

Edmund made a noise of disgust. "Enough metaphors. Lady Kirkpatrick is not a chess piece. And much as I am loath to have my family scandal become public, I *am* willing to turn a few Bow Street Runners onto your scent should any more jewels go missing in Mayfair."

He slapped his hands on the desk and stood. "Now. Need I start saying 'out' again fifteen times until you listen and leave? Or will you depart without that sort of tedious repetition?"

"I'm already on my way." Turner rose, the brilliant smile back in place. "Got to prepare a snare for a queen, don't I?"

Edmund glared at the man until the door closed, until he was once again alone.

Then, second by unraveling second, he permitted himself to relax. Rolling his shoulders; rubbing at the crease between his brows. The scene had played out well, he thought; Turner would have been suspicious if Edmund didn't fight back. If he didn't take any action, or threaten any way to stop the man. Instead, he had blended anger and frustration, and Turner had left in a state of uncertain triumph.

Or so Edmund hoped.

He had done all he could; the next move must be Turner's. Then Jane would play. And then, if all went well . . . checkmate.

He sat again and scrawled a few notes: one to Jane, then a few other necessary missives, and had them all dispatched by messenger. In case Turner was watching the house, Edmund instructed that the messenger take care not to be followed while delivering the notes.

Edmund had learned something new about his opponent today: more than he wanted his lover, his daughters, Turner wanted revenge. He wanted Edmund, broken, more than he wanted a family, whole.

Unfortunate, because it meant Turner had nothing to lose. But there was no way he would win, either.

Because Jane had been right about Edmund: he didn't have an empty heart. When he thought himself in danger, his first impulse was to protect not himself, but the women who depended on him. To marry, to father an heir that would secure the barony so his mother and sisters would never be homeless. Not knowing what else to do, he sent them hats and books, but he also gave them much more: every day, they were in his thoughts; every day, he managed his affairs from afar so their lives would run smoothly.

He hadn't thought he loved them. After so many years apart, he didn't even know them. But he certainly loved the idea of a family. And for now, that was enough.

It had been enough to drop him to one knee before a woman who couldn't refuse his proposal. Through great good fortune, she happened to love him at the time. Because if she hadn't loved him, she'd never have become dissatisfied with a marriage of convenience. She would never have left him.

And she would never have led him to think about what he was missing.

There was no sense in wishing his life had played out differently. No sense in it, and yet he ached for what he had never had. Loving parents. Sisters who looked up to him.

A daughter, bold as her mother, or a son and heir with merry hazel eyes.

A wife who knew his every secret and still loved him.

Quite a Christmas wish list, was it not? Too much; far too much to ask.

Time for a distraction. Rising from his desk, he hunted the bookshelves of his study for something to read. Something light and hopeful to help him pass the long, quiet hours of night.

His hand seized upon a slim volume and pulled it out.

The title page smirked at him. *The Tragedie of Hamlet, Prince of Denmark.*

"Excellent," he muttered, turning the page. Melancholy. Depression. Fighting and death. The guards were skulking around the battlements of Elsinore Castle, looking for the ghost of their king, who had been killed when his brother poured poison in his ear—an apt description of gossip if Edmund had ever heard one. "Not exactly what I was looking for."

He flipped another page; then a passage caught his eye. A speech by the guard Marcellus:

Some says, that ever 'gainst that Season comes;
Wherein our Saviour's Birth is celebrated—

It was about Christmas. And during that season,

The Bird of Dawning singeth all night long:
And then (they say) no Spirit dares stir abroad,
The nights are wholesome, then no Planets strike,
No Fairy takes, nor Witch hath power to Charme:
So hallow'd, and so gracious is the time.

Hmm. That was rather nice.

More than nice, actually. Edmund read it again, sub-siding into the chair behind his desk. Marcellus was a minor character in the play. He turned up near its beginning to offer information, but also good cheer. When his countrymen became afraid, Marcellus remained opti-mistic. Christmas, he said, was the time for things to return to their rightful place. Ghosts slept peacefully, and would-be charmers lost their power.

If Christmas was the season for the supernatural to wane, then might the natural go on the wax? With fairies and witches hobbled, could people accomplish miracu-lous feats?

Like reconciliation with one's family, and the past's ghosts laid to rest? Peace in one's heart? Goodwill toward men? The very idea seemed miraculous, after all these years.

He let *The Tragedie* fall shut.

How odd that he should end in a marriage of convenience when his mother had done the same and been so unhappy. But she had already given her heart away. Edmund kept his locked up tight.

Or if Jane was to be believed, he had given it everywhere. But he'd reserved little for her, though she deserved it more than anyone.

Not merely because he was obligated to her, or bound to her by law. No, it was because he realized that Jane would be satisfied with nothing less than the best of him. Not the best bonnets or horses or pastimes. Him.

And so if he could find a way to please her—well.

Well.

That would really be worthwhile.

Chapter 25

Concerning the Queen's Gambit

The days before Christmas fled in a tearing hurry. Edmund's body spent one more day in the House of Lords, but his attention was entirely elsewhere. Scribbling a storm of notes, sent around London in servants' baskets and tucked in with the post. Arranging the pieces on the chessboard, to use an analogy Turner might appreciate.

As the sun began to set on Christmas Eve, Edmund covered himself in an old, battered cloak and hat, then slipped through the back exit of the house. Striding quickly, he cut across the corner of Berkeley Square and joined the throngs of tardy shoppers and servants clutching stacks of parcels and carrying just-plucked geese for tomorrow's dinner, scolding the ever-present urchins whose grubby hands darted into pockets and tugged at reticules. The air smelled of roast meat and carried the tang of cool weather before rain rolls in.

He took a winding route to Xavier House in Hanover Square; it wouldn't do to be seen or followed by Turner at this late stage. The moon was a silver semicircle in the velvet-dark sky; an occasional gas lamp contributed a golden glow. Edmund's feet covered his winding path more quickly than he had expected, and well before the expected hour, he was knocking at the servants' entrance of Xavier House and being admitted by the earl himself.

"When you married Jane," Xavier said without preamble, "my life was supposed to become less complicated. I wanted to be in Surrey by now, you know."

"You are a slave to your own better nature." Edmund shook off his ancient cloak and hat, hanging them on a hook near the door.

"Yes," murmured Xavier. "Or my curiosity. It's been months since I witnessed one of Jane's schemes firsthand."

"I am most grateful that you and Lady Xavier are willing to postpone your travel until Boxing Day."

Xavier waved a hand. "A Christmas dinner can be enjoyed in London just as well as it can in the country. I'll be at Clifton Hall in time to give out the gifts to my servants and tenants, which is likely all they desire." He clapped Edmund on the shoulder. "You and Jane will join us tomorrow for dinner, I hope?"

"Let us see how tonight's events play out."

"As you wish." Xavier shrugged. "Come, I'll show you up to where we'll observe."

They walked through the servants' quarters and up the back staircase, opening the door onto a landing faced by a green door to the servants' quarters and next to it, a closet. "This closet shares a wall with the drawing room," Xavier explained.

"You're going to make us wait in a closet. Really?"

"Yes. Since you don't want to involve the magistrate by confronting Bellamy openly—"

"Not tonight."

"—and this isn't an ancient, crumbling abbey riddled with secret passages, a linen closet is all I have."

Edmund raised a brow.

"I had the table linens taken out." Xavier fiddled with the door handle of the closet. "And a footstool brought in case of need. Does that help?"

"If there's room for three, and a way to peep into the drawing room."

"My dear wife insisted that holes be drilled through the wall, then checked them from the drawing-room side to make sure they're hidden at the edges of pictures. We shall be able to spy upon Jane with no one the wiser."

"And how is Jane?" Edmund swallowed thickly. "Is she all right?"

"Are you joking? My drawing-room wall has been damaged and my Christmas travel plans are upset. I've never seen her so delighted."

"That's good," Edmund said. "So. She's happy. That's good."

"Hmm." Xavier looked thoughtful. "Want to take up your hiding spot now, or wait until the quarry arrives?"

"We can wait," Edmund said. "What about Lady Sheringbrook? Has she arrived yet?"

"She arrived in a hack this afternoon. Louisa and Jane are having tea with her now. Do you want a cup?"

"Yes. Thanks."

Not that he cared about the tea, but he wanted a look at Jane. He didn't disbelieve Xavier, but . . . well, damn it, he didn't need a reason why. He simply wanted to see her.

When the two men entered the drawing room, an odd picture met their eyes. Louisa, garbed in dark-blue velvet, was giving some instruction to a servant. Lady Sheringbrook perched on the edge of a sofa, posture perfect and snowy hair impeccable. Her hands, wracked by tremors, were clasped uselessly in her lap.

Next to her sat Jane, holding a cup of tea. "Would you care for more, my lady?"

"Thank you," said the viscountess. Jane held the cup to the older woman's lips, and she sipped without spilling a drop on her gray silks.

"Ladies," said Xavier. "Lord Kirkpatrick has arrived, as you see, and he is ready to be stuffed into the linen closet."

"Positively eager for it," Edmund agreed, making his bows.

As he straightened up, he caught Jane's eye. She looked magnificent. Her hair was coiled back from her face, which looked dignified and eager and lovely and impish all at once. She was dressed in a silk gown the rich green of holly leaves, with emeralds at her throat, and her eyes shone. There was nothing the slightest bit wenchy about the ensemble, yet she looked irresistible.

Xavier had been right: Jane loved an adventure. It brought out the best in her.

Edmund had never adequately appreciated the best in her before. During their lost weeks of marriage, he hadn't wanted to make demands on her; sharing his bed was already more than he should ask, considering he shared none of his trust.

It was only when he trusted her at last that he realized how much she was willing to give. Brave, forgiving, bloodthirsty Jane.

"I hate to put you in danger," he told Jane. "Xavier and I each have a pistol, and we shall be in the room in an instant if needed."

"Ridiculous," Jane scoffed. "It's only a game of chess."

Louisa finished her instructions, then joined Jane and Lady Sheringbrook. "I thought you were going to play *vingt-et-un*. Isn't that your favorite game on which to lay stakes?"

Jane took a drawn-out sip of tea. "Not for tonight," she said, a bit breathlessly.

Edmund caught her eye. That game of cards—Lord Sheringbrook's cheating, and Jane's loss—had bound them in marriage. Brought them together, split them apart. Led them to this moment, this room.

As he and Jane looked at one another, neither of them seemed to know whether to smile or not.

The butler knocked. "Mr. Bellamy has arrived, my lady."

"Thank you, Hollis," Louisa said. "Places, everyone." With a nod to the servants, Louisa went into action. The tea things were banished; Lady Sheringbrook was helped to her feet. "Jane, set up the chessboard."

Lady Sheringbrook, Xavier, and Edmund crept to the door, footsteps silenced on the carpet. The three of them slipped out of the drawing room and into the linen closet, which was *not* big enough for three, no matter what Xavier insisted. They arranged themselves in darkness and silence. Edmund found that by craning his neck forward and ducking his head between starch-scented shelves—empty of linens, as Xavier had promised—he could catch glimpses of the drawing room through the peepholes. At his side, he guessed Xavier and Lady Sheringbrook were doing the same, the latter with the aid of the footstool.

They were arranged none too soon; Edmund heard a tread on the stairs and a jovial voice on the landing outside the door. "Ah, Lady Xavier. You're looking beautiful tonight."

"You're too kind, Mr. Bellamy." Louisa's voice was all graciousness. "Lady Kirkpatrick awaits your nightly game. Would you like tea sent in?"

"Something a bit stronger, if you've no objection. It's a night for celebration, after all."

"Christmas Eve? Indeed. I'll nose through Xavier's bottles and see what sort of manly beverages he has. Do you prefer port or brandy?"

"Either one." A delicate pause. "His lordship isn't present this evening?"

"No, he's off at White's with Lord Kirkpatrick. He couldn't let his friend see in the holiday alone."

"Yet he left you alone?"

"I'm not alone." Louisa laughed. "I have Lady Kirkpatrick to keep me company whenever I like. Now enjoy your game. I'm for a book, myself."

Nicely played. A part of Edmund would have dearly loved to be sitting before the fire at White's rather than crammed into a closet, head jutting forward like a man in the stocks.

His suspicions seemingly allayed, Turner bade his hostess a pleasant evening, then entered the drawing room. Friendly greetings ensued between Jane and Turner; Edmund clenched his teeth. Then the man came into the range of Edmund's peephole, seating himself facing Jane across a chessboard.

Play began at once, seemingly a familiar routine for the pair. They spoke little and frowned much, moving pieces with deliberation.

Turner was more skilled, judging from the number of Jane's black pieces he collected. Edmund squinted, trying to count them, but the distance was too great or his peephole too small. At least she'd snapped up a few of the man's pawns.

When a servant brought in a bottle of port and some small glasses, there was a pause in the game.

"You're getting good at this, Lady Kay." Turner poured out port with a heavy hand.

"Kirkpatrick." Jane accepted a glass.

"Must you insist on that? Your husband isn't here, dear lady."

She sipped at the port. "Mmm." Another sip. "You're right. There's no need to stand on ceremony, is there? As a matter of fact, you may call me Jane. That's my Christmas gift to you."

Trapped, Edmund could only watch as Turner beamed and clinked glasses with her. It was all a game, he knew. Yet his fists were clenched.

He hadn't realized how difficult it would be to watch, and not just because of the growing crick in his neck and shoulders.

"—don't plan to return to Kirkpatrick, no," he realized Jane was saying. "Though someday I may need to, if I find myself in . . . trouble."

"Trouble? What sort of trouble?"

"Oh. Well." Her flush was beautifully done. "I'm neither wife nor widow, so I ought to live alone always. Without . . ."

"A man," Turner finished.

"Well, yes." A deeper flush. "But forever? I can't imagine doing so forever."

Again, she sipped at her port. "That's good. It's no wonder Xavier tries to keep this just for himself and his friends." She laughed. "I shouldn't be admitting any of this, should I? A respectable woman wouldn't even bring up the idea of straying."

"Now, Jane. It happens all the time." Just for a moment, Turner's hand covered Jane's; Edmund ground his teeth together. "Why, some of the best families have a few bastards."

True. Though Edmund would hardly call his family one of the best.

His neck and shoulders were aching; he wished Jane would pounce. But she was sipping and smiling and toying with one of the white pawns she'd captured. "Bastards; what rot. Birth is an accident. *Action* is what decides a man's worth."

"And what makes a man worthwhile to you?"

"Adventure." She licked her lower lip.

"Ah, well, I shouldn't be using up your evening with chess, then."

"Nonsense. Every chess game is an adventure." She held up a white pawn, squinted at it, then lined it up with its captured brothers. "There is kidnapping; secrecy; strategy. Murder."

"Or suicide," Turner added. "It depends on how good a gambler one is."

"I'm a *very* good gambler."

Closer and closer they leaned across the chessboard. "The queen doesn't always know her power," Turner murmured.

"Some do." Jane sighed and leaned back, her eyes half-closed in a sultry drowse. "Some only wish. I may be a very good gambler, but even I gambled and lost once."

"With Kirkpatrick?"

"In a way." She stretched, giving a little laugh; the emerald on her pendant dived between her breasts.

"It started with Sheringbrook. I see you haven't heard the tale of how Lord Kirkpatrick and I wound up married."

At Edmund's side, Lady Sheringbrook whispered, "This is the worst-played game of chess I've ever seen. Neither of them has a clue what they're doing, do they?"

"I think Lady Kirkpatrick knows exactly what she's doing," Edmund whispered back.

"I think my ears are melting," Xavier groaned.

A muffled grunt told Edmund that Lady Sheringbrook had jabbed Xavier, and they all fell silent again in time to hear Jane recount her long night of gambling at Sheringbrook's, then her sudden, huge loss.

Xavier made a gulping sound, and it occurred to Edmund that until now, the earl had not known into whose pocket Jane's dowry had gone.

Jane then told Turner how Edmund had swooped in to rescue her. It ought to have sounded rather heroic, but Jane described him as a curious bumbler, well-meant but silly. Desperate to catch himself a bride, not caring who.

How much of this was an act, and how much her true feelings?

"I had no choice," she sighed, "but to accept him. So you see, it was never much more than a marriage of convenience. Yet we should never have come to that point. Sheringbrook cheated."

"No!" Turner offered a fair approximation of shock.

She lowered her voice, leaning forward again. "Five aces in the deck. I had to take the loss, or he would have become violent." Her eyes went wider. "A woman alone is all but helpless."

What bollocks. But Turner was eating it up. "I am pleased to tell you, dear Jane, that Lord Sheringbrook has left the card tables behind him for good. He's involved in a new venture now."

"Oh? How do you know?"

Turner laid a finger aside of his nose. "That'd be telling."

"Ah. Secrets." Jane grimaced. "What's his new game?"

"How much do you want me to tell you?" He ran a blunt index finger along Jane's collarbone.

She shivered, wide eyes never leaving his. "What's the price of adventure?"

Turner trailed his index finger down, down, until it caught on the chain of her necklace. "A certain young woman once entranced him with a set of dazzling rubies. As a result, he became interested in jewelry."

Xavier made another sort of strange choking sound. Edmund had a feeling Jane would be receiving an earful later.

"Buying and selling?" Jane asked.

Turner hooked the pendant and lifted the emerald up so it winked in the firelight. "Let us call it . . . collecting."

Now Lady Sheringbrook made a choking sound.

"It was you, wasn't it, Jane? Who wore the rubies?"

She tugged back her necklace. "Once I did. Card games aren't to my taste anymore." Narrowing her eyes, she added, "Tell me more about collecting. Does it take much skill?"

"Not skill, but knowledge. Of where the finest collections are. And then, of how to create a diversion with charm or violence. So the collection can be . . . well . . ."

"Collected," Jane finished. "You intrigue me . . . Daniel."

God, she was marvelous. Everything she said made

her more marvelous, yet pulled her farther away from Edmund.

"Have you a collecting impulse?" Turner asked.

"I have often been told," Jane sighed, "that I've the soul of a pirate."

"The best sort." He drained his port and set down the glass. "Well. What sort of game is to your taste now? Shall we continue chess? Or would you like to talk of collecting?"

"I'm losing the game of chess," Jane pouted.

"Collecting it is, then." Turner smiled. "And in answer to your earlier question, the price of adventure is a collection."

"What do you mean?"

"That set of rubies." Turner's hand, again clutching for Jane's necklace, twisted it around his fingers. "I want them."

"They're not mine to—*give*." Her voice choked out the last word, surprised, as Turner pulled at the chain around her throat.

Edmund flinched, ready to fly to her; Xavier's hand stayed him. "Wait," the earl whispered. "Wait. Just a bit more."

"Jane, Jane," Turner said silkily, "you can't have me think that a tiny matter of rightful ownership matters to you. You took the rubies once; you simply need to take them again."

"I only borrowed them. I don't think borrowing would satisfy a collector, though." Jane kept a sleek smile on her face as she tried, unsuccessfully, to tug free her necklace. "Shall we play some more of our game?"

Once more, then twice, Turner wrapped the necklace around his fingers, pulling Jane forward until they faced each other, nose to nose. "This is the game now," he said, all his good humor vanished. "You'll collect those rubies, or you'll pay the price. You know how gambling works, my *dear* lady, and you've just lost again."

"I don't understand," Jane stalled. "What did I wager?"

Turner's face, contorting, went ruddy. "Yourself, to begin. I'll have those rubies now, you little slut. The only remaining question is whether I shall persuade you with charm"—his fingers, still holding Jane's chain, trailed down her neck—"or violence?" He twisted the necklace again, until the wrought gold cut tightly into Jane's throat.

"That's enough," Edmund muttered. "Xavier, let's go. Pistols out."

In a few seconds, the hidden trio had wrenched themselves free from their awkward hiding place and wrestled open the closet door. Blinking against the lamplight, Edmund careened into the door of the drawing room and flung it open. "Let go of her, Turner. Now."

Startled, Turner leapt to his feet, and Jane took the chance to jump up and dart to the other side of the room.

Edmund tugged his pistol free and pointed it at Turner. He had no idea whether the powder had dribbled out or whether his strained shoulders and arms could even aim properly. No matter. The way he felt, he would happily beat Turner over the head with it.

Xavier came up next to Edmund. "Turner?" he murmured. "Not Bellamy?"

"I'll tell you later."

"It seems there's much to the story I haven't heard." He coughed. "Like the fate of Jane's dowry."

"Later," Edmund barked. "Where's Lady Sheringbrook?"

"Here." Her voice cold and proud, she marched up next to Xavier.

They formed a line facing Turner, whose face was still a mottled red. He had raised his hands and seemed to be struggling to smile. "Now, what's all this? Some sort of mistake. Lady Kirkpatrick and I were merely having a friendly game of—"

"Oh, shut it." Edmund was surprised by how pleasurable it was to say the simple words. "Just shut it, Turner. Three witnesses, plus Lady Kirkpatrick herself, heard your threat. And Lady Sheringbrook reported the theft of her pearls weeks ago. With what we've heard tonight, it won't be difficult to solve that case."

Turner blanched. "You've no proof."

Edmund shook his head. "We've enough. We may not have all the points from *A* to *Z*, but we have—"

"At least every other letter," Jane broke in, rubbing at her neck. "*A* and *C* and *E* and so on."

"She can never be quiet, can she?" Xavier muttered.

Edmund ignored them both; the world was his hand, his pistol, and Turner's dark eyes. "You do have a few choices. You can take your chances before the magistrate. Perhaps at the next assizes, you'll be found innocent. Or perhaps not. As a convicted thief living under a false name, I shouldn't think your chances were very good. Leniency has saved you before, but it won't a second time."

"Or?" Turner's jaw clenched.

"Or you can leave. Go to the Continent. Go to India, finally. Back to Australia, even, if it feels like home. But you must never return to England."

Turner opened his mouth, and Edmund cut him off. "I'm sure you're about to ask what will happen if you do, because that's the sort of rubbish you talk. Well, here's the answer. If any of us sees you, the magistrate shall be notified. What is, for now, a private affair will become public. And at the end of it, a rope awaits you. It's all but certain."

He looked at Turner's eyes, the dark eyes that also belonged to Mary and Catherine. "Don't choose the rope, Turner. For their sakes, don't."

He had never expected this: pleading with the father of his sisters not to embarrass them with their bastardy. Not to make Edmund prosecute him, or pursue his execution. To see the father of his sisters killed, even if Mary and Catherine never knew who the man was.

"Don't choose the rope," Edmund said quietly.

Unblinking, Turner stared back. Then his shoulders sank. "Have you a ship, then?" He spoke in his natural brogue. It had probably been charming once.

"I have," Edmund replied, "and I'll take you there tonight. Xavier, will you tie his hands?"

In a few minutes, it was done: Turner's hands bound, the pistols again stowed, a hackney summoned.

"I think it best," Xavier said, "if we each swear out affidavits of what we've seen and heard, then leave the scaled documents with our solicitors. If any of us meets with an unfortunate accident, the statements shall be opened."

"Excellent plan," agreed Lady Sheringbrook. "Now. What have you done with my pearls, you thief?"

"Handed them over to your son, didn't I?" Turner managed a flicker of his old grin. "Seems every family here's got more than a touch of scandal."

The elderly viscountess seemed to shrink. "Far more. Yes."

Xavier braced her under the elbow. "As far as I am concerned," Xavier said to the room at large, "none of you was ever here, and I passed a quiet Christmas Eve with my wife. But if you would like to join us for Christmas dinner tomorrow, you would all be most welcome. Except for the fellow with his wrists tied."

Jane walked up to Edmund, holding a parcel in her hands. "Here. It's his chess set."

"It's probably stolen."

Jane didn't even look at Turner. "Well, if you can figure out who it belongs to, give it back. Otherwise, let him take it. He's a very good player."

"That he is," Edmund murmured.

With a nod, he took the parcel from Jane, and the whole company trooped downstairs. Edmund and a pair of burly footmen climbed into the hackney along with Turner, and the hired carriage rolled off to the London Docks.

Chapter 26

Concerning a Variety of
Travel Arrangements

Turner's hands remained tied, and he held his silence during the ride to the docks. Edmund took no chances, though: the two beefy footmen sat at attention on the backward-facing seat. One held a pistol, another a knife.

Once they reached their destination, the quartet climbed from the carriage. For the exorbitant price of a crown, the coachman allowed Edmund to borrow his lantern.

The docks at night—even in winter, even on Christmas Eve—bustled and hummed with activity. The engines of trade never halted, and sailors in port would never miss the chance for revelry. Voices of those at work unloading cargo echoed sharp and businesslike, while the drunken shouts of those on leave punctuated the steadier calls. To the city's usual cesspool stench were added the odors of fish and oil, the scents of commerce.

Edmund marched at the head of their party, with the

footmen flanking Turner. Winding their way through stacks of barrels and crates, past warehouses stuffed with luxury goods, they eventually found themselves at the side of a ship: the *Genevieve,* setting sail for the Mediterranean.

"Your passage has been paid," Edmund said over his shoulder as they climbed aboard the ship. "Do you wish to be confined to quarters?"

"Do I have a choice?" Turner spoke for the first time since his hands had been bound.

When Edmund's feet reached the end of the gangplank, the world rocked and shifted beneath them. *Genevieve* bobbed in the gentle lapping of the river water.

"You've always had a choice," Edmund said. "The way you are treated depends on the way you behave."

Turner looked amused for a second; that haughty unflappable expression that showed he thought the whole world *dobhránta* except for himself.

"The captain knows you're not to be trusted, and he can confine you to quarters. Throw you overboard, too. But if you behave, he'll take you to Spain or Italy; I don't care where you end up." Edmund let this sink in for a moment; then he added, "You can start over, Turner. You needn't let your life be in vain, and you needn't have it end."

Turner spat on the ground. "I didn't choose the rope, boyo. But don't ask me to listen to your prosing or I may hang myself." Turner's mouth twisted; a hint of the lean, handsome man the former tutor had been. "All you've got to go home to now is an empty house. Took down a bit of the aristocracy from within, didn't I? Seems I'm a better revolutionary than you ever knew."

One last time, Edmund looked at the man who had formed so much of his life. Turner looked resentful but resigned, his shoulders square and jaw set, graying hair tied back in the old-fashioned queue he favored.

"I suppose I do owe you a debt," Edmund said. "You helped to shape me into the man I am today." He turned away. "Captain, I'm ready to disembark."

The gangplank wobbled beneath his feet, but his steps as he strode away from the ship had never felt more sure. The heels of his boots echoed on wood, then pavement, their thump a counterpoint to the steady beat of his heart. Behind him followed the two footmen.

Faintly, beneath the muddled odors of waste and commerce, he thought he caught the salt scent of the sea. Maybe he was simply imagining it, for he stood at the edge of the sluggish Thames, and the sea was out of sight in the persistent dark.

Still, the new smell filled his lungs, and he pulled in deep breaths and slowed his pace as he drew near the hackney. He hadn't been so close to any sea since his boyhood; he'd gotten used to air filled with smoke and fog and damp. Now, right by the water's edge, the humid air felt different. Chill and bracing rather than heavy and dull; that promise of the sea, stretching away, seemed to scour him of a grime that had blacked him for a long time.

Done. After all this time, it was done. It was time to go home.

Home? Was that Cornwall? The memory of the sea had a powerful pull on him.

Or maybe that pull was simply the relief of being free. Since he'd spent so much of his adult life in the

Berkeley Square house, home ought to be there. But since Jane had left, he'd become more aware than ever that home was nowhere. In truth, it could be anywhere.

Wherever she was.

With one last look at the ship that would carry Turner away, then up at the star-powdered sky, Edmund made his decision. "Back to Xavier House," he instructed the coachman, handing up the lantern, and then he climbed into the carriage.

It was almost Christmas, and there was much he wanted to give.

After the excitement of nearly being strangled, the rest of the evening passed slowly for Jane.

She had returned to Edmund's house with none of her belongings, but with Christmas parcels for Edmund. Best to see how her gifts were received before she returned to him for good and all.

Mistletoe still adorned each doorway. But in the drawing room, the garland was looking rather sad, and the berries on the holly trim had shriveled. With the help of her maid, Hill, the greenery was tugged down and replaced, perfuming the air with its living scent, sharp enough to catch Jane in the back of the throat. She admired the room, then stowed her parcels.

And then she had nothing to do but wait.

She looked about the room, gaze landing on her painted Chinese vase. The glazed porcelain looked different to her now. Once it had held the promise of escape.

Now? It was art. Art she had chosen for her home to make it beautiful.

Eventually she fell into a reverie in a chair by the fire, not noticing Edmund's tread on the stairs until he entered the room. "Jane, thank God. When you weren't at Xavier House, I thought . . ."

Blinking, she sat up straight. "You thought what? That I'd gotten drunk and fallen into the Thames?"

"Uh. No, not that."

"Well, I did use Xavier's carriage to come here. It's not as though no one in the household knew where I was." She sounded like a crab apple, didn't she? She pressed her lips together. "I'm sorry. I didn't realize you'd be looking for me, or that my departure would be a surprise."

"Didn't realize I'd be looking for you?" He strode over, caught her hands, and gave her a hearty kiss on the top of the head. "Jane, it's done. *It's done.* He's on a ship, and soon he'll be gone."

"Do you trust that he'll stay away?"

"I do," he said. "If nothing else, he's good at looking after his own skin. Now he knows he won't be able to do that anymore if he comes back here. None of his so-called love is worth as much to him as his own safety."

"Or he did muster a bit of love in the end by leaving and keeping the secrets. If he truly did father your sisters, it would hurt them to know they're illegitimate. They wouldn't be able to marry well. Your mother would be disgraced. Saving his own skin and being selfless turned out to be the same thing."

Edmund considered. "Maybe so."

"I kept the black chess queen. When Turner opens his set, he'll realize that, and he'll know what it means."

"That you're a thief, too?" His voice was touched with humor.

"He can think that if he likes," she sniffed. "What I mean is, he'll remember the day he took us all on. And he'll remember that he couldn't predict our next move because the queen wasn't working alone."

"Interesting. I like it." He turned his head sideways, looking at her from the corner of his eye. "So you're a queen now?"

"Oh, well. It's the only female piece. I mean, calling myself a bishop would be ridiculous."

"Ridiculous indeed." He looked her up and down. "You were magnificent this evening, Jane. Magnificent. Ah—did you find it a difficult part to play?"

"Some of it was. Some of it wasn't."

"I see." He sighed. "I regret that he touched you. We should have gone in sooner. If we had, you'd never have been in danger and—"

"But I'm fine." He looked as if he was going to protest, and she squeezed his fingers as hard as she could. "I'm fine, Edmund. It all worked out, and everyone is safe."

"We shall have to burn that gown."

"My gown?"

"Well, I hardly mean a gown of mine." He frowned. "It's all rumpled, and Turner pawed it, and—Jane, I'm so sorry."

"I'm *fine*. And I like this gown. Hill will be able to remove the creases."

"There's no need. I'll buy you a new one."

"There's no need," she echoed, "because I like this one. It's one I chose before our wedding."

He tilted his head. "Oh."

"Besides, when I wear it, and when you see it, we

can both remember how brave I was." She smiled. "And how wenchy."

"You were not wenchy. You were a perfect lady." With a final squeeze, he released her hands. "All right, you were a little wenchy. But you said that the part was—"

"Some of it was easy to play, and some difficult," she said primly. "Enough about gowns, though. There's more news yet."

"Oh?"

"Yes, Lord Sheringbrook has left England as well. His mother received the news of it while you were gone with Turner."

"What?" Edmund pulled back. "Are you sure?"

"As sure as anyone with a working set of ears could be. Her butler got the word from Sheringbrook's valet, who was left behind in the flight. Turner was wrong about Sheringbrook leaving the card tables alone. He got himself into debt with some ugly characters and has fled. It seems he's taken his mother's pearls to finance his escape."

Sighing, Edmund sat on the arm of Jane's chair. One arm stretched across the back of the chair to brace his weight; its presence, like half an embrace, made the fine hairs at the back of her neck prickle.

"Poor woman. She did us a great service tonight. How is she?" he asked.

"As well as can be expected. She seemed resigned to the loss of her son and her pearls, since neither was a great surprise to her. Xavier and Louisa offered to let her stay the night, but she said she'd be all right on her own."

"She has her own house, doesn't she?"

"Yes, and an annuity."

"If Sheringbrook has a good steward, his estate could one day recover. It might not even be a bad thing that he's vanished. It will spare his mother a great deal of pain."

"Maybe so. Yet she'll miss him." Jane leaned her head back, letting the strong length of his arm cradle her. "Are we only talking about Sheringbrook, or about you?"

"I don't know." His hand covered her head, teasing free small locks from her rumpled coiffure. "I don't know."

She shut her eyes, the better to savor the ruination of her hair. "Xavier had plenty to say, too, on the subject of gambling and the loss of my dowry."

Edmund laughed. "I thought he might."

"I'm glad he knows. I don't want to keep any more secrets of my own, though I'll hold yours tight." Opening her eyes, she looked up into Edmund's face. Tired and kind and patient and amused; he was so beautiful to her. "And the loss is not so bad as we thought. Lady Sheringbrook is going to sell off her son's possessions to satisfy his creditors, and since he defrauded me"—Edmund made a choking sound, which she ignored—"she will give us some of the money. Even if it's only a few hundred pounds, I'm sure I can turn it into ten thousand as long as I can find a card game with no cheats."

It was impossible to ignore the choking sound this time. "No, Jane. Please don't."

With a forefinger, he traced her features: brows, then nose. His finger lingered on her lips. "I was happy to take you with nothing. Let Lady Sheringbrook give the money to shopkeepers and merchants. I'm well-satisfied with how your gamble paid off."

His finger traced the shape of her lips; she was afraid to speak, lest he pull it away.

"Jane, I told you to return anytime, but only if you were going to stay. Is that what this means, or did you come only to give me the news? Because if you did, it's all right. I won't hold you to that ultimatum. I should never have made it of you, but it was too wrenching to have you return—*oh*. My. Lord."

She had pulled his forefinger between her lips, sucking at the sensitive tip. Catching his fingers in hers, she said, "You were talking too much."

"Huh." He was blinking quite a lot. "If that's what you plan to do when I talk too much, you're not encouraging me to keep silent."

There was no point in pretending she wasn't blushing. "Before I answer, I have some gifts for you."

"Before you answer, I have some gifts for you, too."

"You do?" Disappointment flickered within her.

"It's not a bonnet, for heaven's sake. Don't look so glum." He cut off her protest. "You haven't eaten since tea a few hours ago, have you? We could have a cold supper sent in."

"How is your stomach pain? Would you be able to eat the food?"

He thought about this. "Yes. Yes, I think I could give it a damned good try." He smiled. "I would apologize for my language, except that I think you like it."

"Kind, polite Lord Kirkpatrick forgetting his manners? I am all aflutter."

He opened his mouth as though to reply, then shook his head. "I shall fetch the gifts. Do you mind ordering the supper?"

"I'll do it. Go ahead." Her heart began to thump a little more quickly, but she managed a calm voice as she rang for a servant, made the request, then dived behind the sofa to collect the parcels she had brought in.

Last of all came a roll of brown paper. She wrapped it around herself like a cape, then stood in the doorway of the drawing room.

Under the mistletoe.

Chapter 27

Concerning Proper and Improper Christmas Gifts

If there was one thing Edmund had come to expect from Jane, it was that he would never know what to expect from Jane.

Even so, he was surprised to turn the corner and see her standing in the corridor outside the drawing room, clutching a length of brown paper around her shoulders. "Are you cold? Maybe I really should buy you a new gown."

She rolled her eyes. "It's meant to be a sort of gift. Oh, this was stupid. I knew it." Crumpling the paper in her hands, she let it fall.

"Wait." Edmund dropped the tube he was holding, then strode over to catch her before she could turn away. "Wait. Don't run off. You're standing under mistletoe."

"Yes. That was stupid, too."

"Ordinarily, it's impolite to contradict a lady. But the usual rules don't apply when a kiss is at stake." Edmund searched her face: wide eyes, stubborn chin, lovely mouth. "May I?"

Her lips parted. Since she didn't say no right away, he took that as a yes, and he bent to kiss her. Just a feather-soft whisper, a promise.

With me, Jane, it's always a promise. So he had told her once, and he poured the truth of that into this kiss. Tasting her, sweet and slow as honey. Her mouth opened, lips soft, her tongue a gentle flicker of heat that shot warmth through his whole body.

His hands caught her shoulders, holding her closer. As long as he was kissing her, she couldn't leave; as long as he was kissing her, that was enough.

He was falling, and he loved the fall.

Too soon, she pulled away. "The servants. They'll be here any minute with the tray." Her cheeks had gone a lovely shade of pink.

"They know what mistletoe is for."

"It was only because of the mistletoe that you kissed me?" Her jaw got that stubborn look.

He grinned. "Who do you think had the mistletoe hung all over the house, Jane?"

She was still mulling that over as he picked up his dropped parcel and followed her into the drawing room. And she was right; it was only a minute or two before a servant brought in a tray of sandwiches, a teapot, and cups of mulled wine, sweet-spiced and strong. As the tray and plates were arranged, Edmund pretended to poke up the fire, wondering what the hell had just gotten into him.

Actually, he knew: he had just had his first real kiss.

For the first time in his life, lips had brushed lips without having to close upon secrets; for the first time, he had wrapped a woman in his arms without feeling the need to keep his distance.

When the servant left them alone again, Edmund and Jane settled side by side on the carpet before the wide fireplace.

He stacked up cold chicken and wedges of cheese for each of them, then returned to an intriguing subject. "Jane, tell me more about the gift that required you to be wrapped in paper."

She dropped the bite she was holding. "Huh. Um. It was foolish, as I said."

"If you give me a foolish gift, I'll give you a foolish gift. And no, it won't be a bonnet."

She managed to smile. "Well. It was me. That is—you told me not to return unless I was here to stay." She spread her hands. "Here I am if you want me."

His ears seemed to ring, high and faint. "You're here. To stay. Do you mean it?"

"Yes." She shoved a huge bite of chicken into her mouth.

"That's not a foolish gift. That's the best gift."

She choked. He pounded her on the back. It was really more of a pat or a caress, and it was a good thing she began breathing again because he could only concentrate on one thing: "You're going to stay."

"Yes."

"Why did you think that was foolish?"

She looked away. "If you didn't want me here, I would have felt very stupid indeed. I've always felt a little as if I'm chasing after you, begging you to love me. You gave me an escape tonight by telling me I needn't stay. But I want to have it decided. I want to know what you want of me."

"I want you to stay. I've always wanted you to stay." He touched her chin, that lovely, stubborn chin, and turned her face toward him. "Every time you called here, then went back to Xavier House, I felt I'd lost you all over again. As long as you weren't sure of me, I thought it would be better not to see you and not to be hurt." His hand dropped, fingers clenching. "That's where I was a fool, because not seeing you was its own kind of pain."

She studied him, her eyes flecked with gold from the firelight. "You missed me?"

"I missed you," he repeated. "I love you."

The only sound was the tick of the clock on the mantel; the pop of coals in the fire.

"Nothing to say, Jane? I can hardly credit it." He tried to speak lightly, so she would not know how her silence pressed upon him.

"I trusted you not to lie to me." She folded her legs so she sat in a tight ball. "You're telling the truth? Not just trying to make me feel better?"

"I've never known how to trick you into feeling better, my dear. This is the truth. I love you. Do you want me to say it some more?"

She considered. "Yes."

"I love you, Jane. I think I have for a long time, and I didn't realize it. Like someone who's gotten so cold he's gone numb, and when feeling starts to return, it's such a shock that he mistakes it for pain." His throat went tight. "And then it gets better, and then it's the best thing imaginable."

"Your love is like frostbite?"

"Oh, damn. That's not what I meant. Look, I could

read you a poem. I know just the right one." He narrowed his eyes. "Wait. You're laughing at me."

"A little." She smiled; an eyes-crinkling, cheek-dimpling grin. "Say it some more."

"You can't expect me always to come up with the perfect metaphorical ailment." He laid a hand on her back, rubbing it up and down until her small, folded-up figure began to unfurl. "When I proposed to you, I was relieved to make a marriage of convenience because I didn't want a love match. I came from a ruined family; I had a large hand in ruining it. I blamed myself for my father's death. I knew Turner had come back, but I *didn't* know what he'd do. Above all, I didn't want to destroy anything else."

"Like love."

"Like love," he agreed. "I wanted a sensible marriage, with comfortable distance, so I wouldn't ever hurt my wife."

"You wanted a sensible marriage, yet you married me?" Her voice held a laugh.

"What's not sensible about marrying you? You're bright and well-born, pretty and ingenious."

"Now I know you're just being kind."

"I will never understand," he said unsteadily, "why you persist in thinking of me as the kind one. You are devastatingly kind, my love. You put yourself in danger tonight for me."

"That wasn't the difficult part." She picked up the cup of mulled wine, breathed deeply of its scent, and handed it to Edmund. "The difficult part was pretending as though I didn't want to return to you."

He handed her a cup in return, then clinked glasses with her. "You see? Kind."

"Don't say that sort of thing unless we're alone. My reputation will be absolutely ruined."

Edmund took a sip of the hot drink, letting the wine and spice melt over his tongue. "When you told me you loved me, I felt I'd done you a great wrong. I'd hurt you, just by being myself. By forcing your hand."

"But you didn't know I wanted to say yes. Any time. On any terms."

"You see? I thought of our marriage in too small a way. On its first day, I ruined it."

"I wouldn't say ruined. But giving me the bonnet was a mistake." He would have felt far more chastised had she not scooted closer and leaned against him, resting her head on his shoulder.

"Ah, well. It did look pretty on you. And in my misguided way, I was trying to make amends to you. I knew you didn't want a small life, but I couldn't offer you anything else. Not until I let myself trust you." Her hair softly tickled his jawline as he spoke. "Not until I trusted myself. To be strong enough to face the truth. And then strong enough to share it."

"How do you know you love me now?"

He thought about this. "I just know. Like a man knows when his hand isn't frostbitten anymore."

"That is horrible." She set down her cup, then took his, too. Turning, she straddled him and kissed him squarely on the mouth. "It's so horrible that it must be true. And I love you, too, of course."

He must be a bit fogged from the kiss. Or the end of twenty years' tension. "I am delighted to hear it. Why 'of course'?"

"Why would I ever stop? The better I knew you, the

more there was to love about you. Even the secrets you thought would drive me away—well. I told you who I thought the hero of that story was."

His throat had gone tight. Somehow, he managed to croak, "Not every story has a hero."

"Maybe not. But this one does."

"Kiss me some more," he said.

"Later." She smiled down at him, twining her fingers in his hair. "Before we get extremely distracted—"

"I am quickly reaching that point."

"Tell me, what was your foolish gift?"

He tried to think of something other than her nails whisking over his scalp, her breasts before his eyes, her scent of soap and heat wrapping around him. "Um. Let me think. Oh, I remember. I meant to offer to teach you to ride your horse."

"You did? You will?" She rested her head in the angle of his shoulder, clutching him close. "Thank you. You don't have to."

"I realize that. I'm a baron, not a groom. But I want to because you want me to." She squirmed, and he laid a hand on her back. "Peace, peace. I'm not just trying to please you. *I* am pleased by the fact that you wanted me to teach you. That you wanted me."

"That's just the beginning." She squeezed him tight, then shoved herself to her feet, shaking out her skirts. "I have some presents for you to open."

Quickly, she collected an armful of small packages from a hiding place behind the sofa, then walked back to Edmund and dumped them in his lap.

Bemused, he looked at the litter of paper-wrapped

parcels. "All these are for me? I really should have got you a bonnet."

"I'd have thrown it in the fire."

"You flirt."

She snorted. "Well, it's beside the point, because they're not for you. They're for me. But you get to open them."

Mystified, he did so. The first one was flat, its wrapping gummed closed. When he worked it open, a sheet of letter-paper fluttered free. On it was written in Jane's script: *What makes you happy?*

He held it up, waiting for meaning to waver into existence. "Is this for me to answer?"

"No. Quit trying to take my presents. I told you it was for me. But you need to hear my answer." Hazel eyes, so deep and clear, looked into Edmund's. "Nothing can make me happy except me. But it certainly helps to know that my happiness matters to my husband. He shows me this when he gives me a gift, but most of all, when he gives me his time and trust."

"That seems so simple."

She lifted her brows. "Oh, good. Then you'll have no trouble doing it."

"It doesn't seem like enough to me. It's just . . . me."

"That's all I've ever wanted."

Her words, clean as a new blade, seemed to pry weights free from Edmund. It would take time for him to trust in this: simple truth, love without strings or scandals. His whole life, he had seen love bought, sold, and betrayed, but he'd never seen it freely given. Love without a price on it . . . why, that was priceless.

"You shall have it," he said. "All of me. And I hope you'll give me the same in return."

"Always." She smiled. "That went beautifully. Open some more presents."

"Are they all like that?"

"Cheap excuses to trick you into spending time with me and talking to me, because that is what I want most?" She paused. "Yes. As a matter of fact, one of them reads 'Have Edmund teach you how to ride a horse.'"

Edmund grinned. With such a wife, he could do anything. Even trust his heart. "I shall savor and delight in them all. But let's save them for tomorrow. You must open your gift from me now."

He retrieved the paper tube from its resting place, then seated himself next to Jane again. Her fingers trembled a bit, fumbling the string. Finally, she had the paper wrapping off, and within she unrolled . . .

"*La Sicilia*," she breathed.

Weeks ago, she had looked at this old hand-drawn map of Sicily when they'd visited Hatchards. She hadn't bought it, but he had seen her study it. Had seen her fingers trace it reverently, as though she could feel the contours of the land through the watercolor and ink. Judging from the look of wonder on her face, she had lost none of her fascination with the map.

"You said you didn't want a small life," he explained. "I want to make sure that we don't have one. Together."

Her eyes roved the bright-tinted lines; then, with a smile, she laid the map carefully aside. "I don't think we need to worry about that. When I left, I felt worse than ever, and I realized—that feeling of having a small life isn't a matter of going places, or of having certain things. It's a matter of choice. It's a matter of the heart."

"What's mine is yours," he said. "All yours."

"Likewise." She grinned. "If you're suggesting travel, I would like that very much."

"To Sicily?"

"Someday. But first I thought we could go to Cornwall."

She looked uncertain of how the suggestion would be received. In truth, Edmund had no idea. His first response was a hearty "hell, no," but for Jane's sake, he quelled that and considered.

He'd thought all he had connecting himself to family was legality and duty; but no, he hungered for more. For a real family such as he'd never had. Now that Turner was gone, they could start anew. End the cycle of blame. The purpose of atonement, after all, was to right a wrong. Surely twenty years was long enough for that.

Jane, strong and bright, could be the bridge that brought them all together. "They have a right to know you," he said. "I would like them to know you."

She looked pleased. "I would like that, too."

A soft chime sounded from the clock on the mantel; then eleven more. "It's midnight," Jane said.

"Happy Christmas," Edmund said, and he took her in his arms and kissed her. This was even better than the kiss under the mistletoe; this was sweet and hot and intoxicating, like the mulled wine he tasted on her lips.

Jane broke it off with a gasp. "The gossip about my return to you will be terrible."

"No, it will be *wonderful*. Especially when they remark how besotted I am with you."

She tossed him a wicked smile. "Is that what the gossips will see?"

"Eventually." His lips found her earlobe. "But if you are amenable, I don't think the gossips will see anything of us at all for a while."

"Ah." She shivered. "You want to make an heir, do you?"

"I want a son. Or a bloodthirsty little daughter. Someday." With a flick of his fingers, a button at the back of her bodice came undone. "But most of all, I just want you."

And before the fire on that Christmas morn, without even noticing that they had kicked over the mulled wine, Lord and Lady Kirkpatrick gave each other the gift they most wanted. Each other.